A Jamaican Conspiracy

A Jamaican Conspiracy

A Will and Betsy Black Adventure

David and Nancy Beckwith

ABSOLUTELY AMAZING eBOOKS

ABSOLUTELY AMAZING eBOOKS

Published by Whiz Bang LLC, 926 Truman Avenue, Key West, Florida 33040, USA.

A Jamaican Conspiracy copyright © 2017 by David Beckwith. Electronic compilation/ paperback edition copyright © 2017 by Whiz Bang LLC. Second edition.

All rights reserved. No part of this book may be reproduced, scanned, or transmitted in any form or by any means, electronic or mechanical, including photocopying, recording, or any information storage and retrieval system, without permission in writing from the publisher. Please do not participate in or encourage piracy of copyrighted materials in violation of the author's rights. Purchase only authorized ebook editions.

This is a work of fiction. Names, characters, places, and incidents either are the product of the author's imagination or are used fictitiously, and any resemblance to actual persons, living or dead, businesses, companies, events, or locales is entirely coincidental. While the author has made every effort to provide accurate information at the time of publication, neither the publisher nor the author assumes any responsibility for errors, or for changes that occur after publication. Further, the publisher does not have any control over and does not assume any responsibility for author or third-party websites or their contents. How the ebook displays on a given reader is beyond the publisher's control.

For information contact:
Publisher@AbsolutelyAmazingEbooks.com

ISBN-13: 978-1945772481 (Absolutely Amazing Ebooks)
ISBN-10: 1945772484

A Jamaican Conspiracy

Other Will and Betsy Black Books By David and Nancy Beckwith

A Hurricane Conspiracy

A Calculated Conspiracy

A Narcotic Conspiracy

A Cosmetic Conspiracy

Available from AbsolutelyAmazingEbooks.com

JAMAICAN SINE PAITING

CHAPTER 1

Blue skies smiling at me
Nothing but blue skies do I see

Will Black sang out loud to a feral chicken as he and his wife, Betsy, walked down Duval Street in Key West.

Blue birds singing a song
Nothing but blue skies from now on

Ray Collins, their houseguest from Mobile, Alabama, sang back to him. Ray and Will high-fived. The mother hen and her brood scattered to get out of their way.

A pink-skinned tourist wearing a Brown University T-shirt, plaid shorts, and new buckle-up sandals with white socks gave them a strange look and whispered to his wife, "Uncle Elmer was right. These people in Key West are strange."

"Just look at that perfect sky," Will continued. "You asked me earlier if we have any regrets about moving to the Keys. I'll let you answer that question."

He addressed his comments to their guests who were

staying with them for the weekend. Betsy nodded her agreement.

"It's sure not *old* Mobile," Ray's wife, Sheila, chimed in.

"In a lot of ways that's a plus," Betsy said.

Will Black was an investment broker for RST Securities; his wife, Betsy, was the area president for WB Bank in Key West. Will was a Mississippi Delta native; Betsy was old Mobile. They had met and married during the 1980's in Mobile where they had been friends with Ray and Sheila Collins. Ray and Will had worked together, and the two couples had formed a friendship that lasted to this day despite Will and Betsy's move to Florida. They had even vacationed in Jamaica together. Will had been transferred to Vero Beach as a branch manager for RST. Betsy had carved out her own career in financial services with WB Bank. About the time Will and Betsy's daughter, Lexie, had left for college at the University of Miami, both had been offered opportunities in the Florida Keys by their respective employers; Betsy as the area president in Key West For WB; Will as branch manager in Key West for RST. Life had been good when the Blacks came to Florida and had only gotten better since their move to the Keys. They had maintained their relationship with Ray and Sheila despite the geographic distance between them. Now Will and Betsy had the opportunity to share Duval Street in Key West with their friends.

"In a lot of ways, this place reminds me of the French Quarter in New Orleans," Ray said.

"There's a lot of parallels," Will agreed.

"I wonder what that street vendor is selling," Sheila said.

"Let's find out," Will said.

The vendor had brightly painted irregular globs, most being about the size of a coin.

"May I ask what you're selling?" Ray asked the Duval Street artist.

"Wads of chewing gum, mon," answered the vendor, a dread-locked, thin, thirtyish light-skinned black man. He was wearing a T-shirt that said "By-gum" on the front and "Buy-gum" on the back. He went into his well-rehearsed spiel.

"Jamaican?" Will asked.

"Yah, mon. Reading."

"Boy, is it a small world," Will said. "That was the first place we ever stayed when we originally discovered Jamaica. We rented the Villa Portofino in Reading Heights for a week."

"Yah, mon. I know it well. I used to be the gardener at Karma Bay in Tryall. My cousin Cecil from Anchovy was married to Sally, the cook at Sea View Villa next to Portofino. I've come a long way since then. Now life in the Keys is *Keys irie* since I am without a doubt the greenest eco-artist in Key West," he said proudly. "I've been walking around Key West for several years collecting discarded gum off the sidewalk. I use it as a canvas for my creations. A finished piece of gum-art can take me anywhere from two hours to three days to create. No two pieces are alike. I have proven that even something as lowly as a chewed-up piece of gum can be a work of art."

They examined the Jamaican artist's creations. Each piece was flat and had an irregular shape. There was chewing gum with a happy face, gum with Bob Marley's face, gum with a map of Old Town Key West, one piece that looked like a sunny-side up fried egg. Some pieces had unrecognizable abstract designs. One piece had a housefly painted on it.

Sheila waved her hand over it to shoo the fly, thinking it was real. The group laughed at her.

Will winked at Betsy and said, "We have always

claimed that Jamaicans can make something out of absolutely nothing. Here's proof."

"I've never seen anything like this," Ray said, laughing as he pointed to a piece of chewing gum with Sloppy Joe's building painted on it. He then pointed out a piece with a rooster painted on it.

"You won't see anything like *this* in good old Mobile," Will said, "or even New Orleans for that matter. Welcome to the funky world of Key West where only the abnormal is normal."

"See," Will said, pointing at a sign. "Even the bank in Key West shares a building with Ripley's Believe It Or Not!."

They continued down the sidewalk toward Sloppy Joe's.

At Sloppy Joe's the group was able to get one of the round tables near the side door close to the afternoon's entertainer. C.W. Colt was well into his set when they walked in. He saw them and waved before continuing singing his chicken song.

There's nobody here but us chickens

As if rehearsed, the crowd answered with clucking noises. A waitress promptly took their order.

"What is it in Key West with this chicken business?" Ray asked.

"I'll turn the floor over to my wife, the household historian, to answer that one," Will said, as he took a sip of his beer. "They are one of Key West's great but sometimes controversial traditions, a true love-hate relationship."

"The chickens go back to early Key West," Betsy said. "They were an integral part of everyday life since they were a source of food and eggs. Chickens were also entertainment, since they were used for cock fighting. However, as Key West grew more urban and civilized,

4

cock fighting was outlawed. More grocery stores were opened on the island. As a result, the chicken population grew. They also escaped barnyards, became feral, and began to forage for food throughout the island. The island became divided into two camps - the chicken huggers and the chicken muggers. Some people feel like they add atmosphere to the island. Others think they're a damned unsanitary nuisance."

"I think they're kind of cute," Sheila said.

"Most tourists do," Betsy continued, "but many locals who have had to deal with bird droppings, crowing roosters, and homesteading feathered invaders feel differently. I even heard one story about a lady who forgot to close her doggy door and came home to find a mother hen sitting on her bedroom pillow defending a pile of incubating eggs. When she tried to evict it, the rooster came out from under the bed and pecked her toes."

Everyone laughed.

"Stories like that are what make Key West a city of quirky legends," Will said. "A few weeks ago a naked, crack-binging woman ran amok on Stock Island. She stripped naked and performed lewd acts in the street. The sheriff's department picked her up and had her hospitalized. The next week ... "

Will felt a hand squeezing his shoulder gently from behind. C.W. had finished his set and had come over to say hello.

"Don't let me interrupt," C.W. said. "Finish your story."

Will introduced C.W. to their friends from Mobile before continuing.

" ... the Key West Police Department was called over to White Street. The same woman was once again naked, standing on top of a pickup and yelling in Spanish. She performed a lewd act on herself and jumped into the bed of the pickup. She then lost her balance and fell into the arms of the arresting officer. She was arrested again.

"After her release, she was seen the following week running naked down the street, jumping onto cars near the bus stop. When deputies arrived, residents were out in the street trying to divert traffic while she crawled down Maloney Avenue. As the crowd watched, she crawled up on the hood of a car, rolled over on her back, and spread her legs for the driver to see."

By this time Ray was almost rolling on the floor laughing. Tears streamed down his face; the beer he had been drinking shot out of his nose. Sheila wasn't having much better luck controlling herself.

She blurted out, "You wouldn't even see that in *new* Mobile, not even during Mardi Gras."

Will then added the coupe de gras. "According to *The Citizen*, the woman had no prior arrest record in Monroe County."

C.W. felt compelled to break in at this point.

"Will is telling you a true story. Now I'll give you one. We had a loony case in here the other night," he said.

He instantly had everyone's attention.

"We had a drunken, one-armed, lesbian tourist punch and bite her lover during my performance. By the time the police pepper-sprayed her, her lover had cuts and bruises and a bite mark on one finger. After the officer pepper-sprayed the woman, she kicked him in the groin. He then punched her in the face and held her down until backup could get here."

"I read she hired an attorney to sue the city," Will said.

"Ah, yes, just another dull evening in the Keys," Betsy said. "This place is like no other. Will and I wouldn't consider living any place else."

"Glad to meet you," C.W. said to Ray and Sheila. "I'd love to stay and chat, but I guess I'd better start earning my money again."

He hoisted his glass in a toast. "Three."

He took a swig of Jack Daniels and went back to the bandstand.

"C.W. seems like a really good guy," Sheila said. "I still can't believe the street artist is not only Jamaican but from the only area of Jamaica we've ever stayed in."

"Well, you know what they say about it being a small world," Betsy replied. "My bet is that Mr. Gum fits in well around here."

"Sheila and I have often said," Ray added, "that the week at Portofino was one of the best vacations we have ever had."

"It turned out to be the first of many visits for us," Will said. "We never stayed at that villa again, since one of my clients owned a villa near to Ocho Rios."

"I can still see the drive to Reading," Sheila said.

"So can I," Will said. "Twenty minute drive from Sangster International along the North Coast Highway, left at the traffic light in Reading going towards Anchovy, and presto, there you were."

"The panoramic view of Montego Bay was breathtaking," Ray said.

"Especially at night," Betsy added, "when you could relax in the swimming pool and see the lights of Montego Bay twinkling across the water."

"Remember the night we all decided to go skinny dipping because we thought we had the house to ourselves," Ray said laughing.

"And I also have vivid memories of the next day when the peeping Tom gardener made some remarks letting us know he was there in the shadows."

"It's a good thing we were leaving the next day," Sheila said giggling. "I don't think I could have faced him again."

"And do you recall the day when we were looking for the Town House Restaurant? That was certainly another irie day," Ray said.

"How could I forget that historic 1700's red brick building in the old part of Montego Bay?" Will asked.

"Remember our driver accidentally drove past it on the narrow crowded street? Couldn't park or back up. So a good Samaritan came out and held up traffic so our driver could back the length of most of a block to get back to where there was a parking place," Betsy said.

"And then another good Samaritan, who happened to be a doctor from Mobile, showed us where the restaurant was," Ray responded.

"We certainly made some good memories," Betsy said. "I'll always remember that red snapper topped with cheese, lobster and wine sauce that they cooked in the paper bag."

The group ordered another round and then spent the next hour reminiscing about some of the other good times they had had together in Jamaica.

Ray said, "Do you think C.W. might play *Jamaica Farewell* for us?"

"One way to find out," Will said. "Ask."

> **WOMAN & MANPOWER**
> GENERAL SERVICE
>   (JAMAICA LTD.)
> TEMPORARY AND PERMANENT HELP
> HOUSE PAINTING, CARPENTRY, PLUMBING
> ELECTRICAL WORKS, TOILING, MASONRY
> POLISHING, SIGNS, SECURITY GUARDS
> CALL KIMBERLY upstairs Room 2 phone

CHAPTER 2

Betsy didn't realize it when she made her comment about living forever in the Keys, but she would soon be eating those words. Jamaica was about to come back into their lives. It all would begin with an innocent unsolicited call from WB corporate.

"Ken Scott from Charlotte on line one," Margaret announced.

"Betsy? Ken Scott, how are things in Key West?"

"Going well," Betsy answered.

"So I understand," Scott said. "I got a call from one of your employees, Carson Crown, telling me he had an over-the-top prospect. Something about financing a project on something called Wisteria Island. He made it sound really big. But that's not the reason I'm calling."

Carson Crown was Betsy's most challenging colleague and the WB Bank's resident blowhard. He was always out of the bank on vague missions which seemed to produce little, served on non-profits boards of dubious value, and missed or was tardy to virtually every bank meeting which was often a blessing since he was disruptive when he was present. He had dubious judgment and was constantly elephant hunting at the expense of attaining realistic goals. Will and Betsy never tired of laughing each time they heard Carson's infamous two-syllable word "coldbeer" and his exaggerations about his own well being.

Thank God, Betsy thought. *I'd hate to think my year depended on Carson.*

"I'm going to be in your area Tuesday and need to talk to you," Scott said. "I should be there by late morning. Block out some time, and we'll have lunch."

"May I ask what you wish to discuss?"

"I'll tell you Tuesday," Scott said. "It's a high level matter of some sensitivity that would be best talked about in person. Until then."

He hung up.

"That was a strange call," Betsy said to Margaret. "Ken Scott is coming to Key West on Tuesday to see me, and he wouldn't tell me what it's all about. He did say he had gotten a call from Carson."

"I guess they're coming down here to fire you and replace you with Carson," Margaret said and smiled. "But no, on second thought, they usually fire people on Fridays, and it's only midweek."

"As usual you're about as funny as a one-armed trapeze partner. Now, shut up and get back to work or I'm going to see that you get fired as well," Betsy said. "On second thought, I think I'll just take matters into my own hands and fire you right now."

"You already did," Margaret said, "an hour ago."

"Oh, yeah, I forgot. Well, then just get the hell out of here and get some work done before I have to do it again."

"Yes, mi-lady. Want some coffee? I'm headed that way," said Margaret on her way out.

Tuesday arrived with no further clarification of the purpose of Scott's visit. When Ken Scott entered the office, Betsy told Margaret they were not to be disturbed and closed the door. They exchanged pleasantries.

"My curiosity is killing me," Betsy said. "Why all the mystery about your visit?"

"Because I'm going to offer you the opportunity to further your career and also do a major service for the corporation," Scott said.

"Now I'm really curious."

"I've heard you tell people about you and your husband's extensive vacations to Jamaica," he began.

Betsy nodded her head in agreement.

"Our bank in conjunction with Royal Bank of Commerce in Jamaica has commenced with a very large piece of business there – a piece where you could possibly be of assistance," he said. "Have you read about the Highway 2000 project?"

"Some," Betsy answered. "I have a cursory knowledge about it. Isn't it the upgraded Northern Coastal Highway, A1?"

"You're both right and wrong," Scott said. "Let me give you a synopsis. In 1999 then Prime Minister Patterson initiated the multiyear Millennium Projects Programme to upgrade Jamaica's infrastructure, assist in providing economic opportunities for growth, and create jobs."

"Yes, the plan is to connect Negril to every major town on the north coast and end in Port Antonio with a new modern Highway A1. My husband, Will, and I have said for years that one of the main things holding Jamaica back economically has been lack of investment in the country's infrastructure," Betsy said. "We even had a breakfast meeting with one of Jamaica's behind the scenes power brokers, Earl Levy, the owner of Trident in Port Antonio where he picked our brains on the topic."

"A1 is only a part of the Millennium Projects," Scott continued. "We are not involved in the A1 phase of the plan. It is being funded by the IDB."

"Yes, the Inter-American Development Bank."

"The new highway through Jamaica's interior is the centerpiece of the Millennium Projects," Scott said. "It is a toll road that will connect Jamaica's capital, Kinston, with Montego Bay and Ocho Rios. It will pass through 6 parishes and open the interior of the country for development opportunities in everything from agriculture to information technology and housing. The bank is involved in this."

Betsy started to comment but instead chose just to listen.

"The toll road project is what is known as a BOOT scheme," continued Scott. "That is an acronym standing for Build Own Operate Transfer scheme. The contractor, the Kingston and St. Andrew Corporation, is the concessionaire. It will build the highway, then operate and maintain it as well. It will charge tolls to use the road within a range set by the government. After an agreed upon period the contractor will hand the project over to the Jamaican government at no charge. We are financing this contractor.

"The bank's exposure is massive and requires someone to be our local eyes and ears to make sure things go according to plan. Until now the bank has employed a local representative to perform these duties, but we have begun to suspect of late that this strategy might be flawed. Matters have begun to come to our attention which have made us wonder if this mega-relationship is receiving the thorough ongoing scrutiny and monitoring it both requires and deserves. To be quite candid, we began to wonder if our loan officer has had problems isolating and prioritizing the bank's interests from those of the locals involved. We also feel that certain conflicts of interest resulting from his local ties may have prevented him from doing his job properly. It seems he has not effectively resisted pressures to be overly accommodating at the bank's expense. We therefore have decided it is time for a change and we should bring in someone with no local ties – a person who can clinically and objectively represent the bank."

"I assume I am being considered to be that person," Betsy said. "Have there been specific red-flags?"

"Yes, but since our suspicions are unproven I would prefer not to prejudice you going in. We will let you draw your own conclusions."

"That is probably better. Where will my office be?" asked Betsy.

"Ocho Rios," Scott said. "We have made arrangements to rent you a villa in Discovery Bay should you choose to accept. It is called Sundance.

"I'm going to be candid with you, Betsy. I owe you that. The person you will replace was very well liked by both staff and our customers because he didn't know how to say no. He tried to placate everyone and to avoid conflict and controversy at any cost. Some people might resent the bank's decision to replace him with a person with a firmer hand. Some people might also resent a local man being displaced by a foreign woman. The loan officer doesn't know he is being released. This will be handled shortly before his replacement arrives. Let me assure you, if you choose to accept this assignment, he will be gone before you arrive.

"Since you are one of our most experienced people in commercial lending, have proven management skills, and know the country, you are our number one choice to fill the position. Let me just summarize by saying we think it would be a natural fit."

"I don't know what to say," Betsy said.

"I hope you'll say yes. This will be a temporary assignment. Your job here will be waiting for you when you return. You will be compensated handsomely ... very generously. Deferred comp will be available if you so desire. All your expenses and the expenses of your family including housing and transportation will be covered. If things go like I would expect, this could be the beginning of bigger and better things for you at WB. We think you are *the* person for this job – our number one choice."

"What would be the nature of my duties?" Betsy asked. "Am I just a glorified auditor?"

"No. You will function as a senior loan officer on loan from WB to RBC and answer to both the local RBC president as well as WB corporate in Charlotte. While we want you to function as an officer of the bank and be a part of the local community, your primary responsibility will be to monitor and work with this one very large customer. By functioning as a bank officer you will be in a vantage point to provide us with unbiased local eyes and ears both in and out of the local bank. This will be much more valuable to us than to simply place you in an isolated ivory tower. If I wanted that, I'd just appoint someone to monitor the account from Charlotte."

"So I will have authority, not just be a paper tigress," said Betsy.

"Absolutely."

"I will need to talk to my husband about your proposal. May I get back to you?"

"Of course," Scott said. "I didn't expect an answer today; but, I do want to move promptly. I'd appreciate it if you kept our conversation confidential for the time being."

"Of course! All I know to say now, I guess, is," Betsy said, "are you ready to go to lunch?"

```
WELCOME
   TO
TRAVELLERS
  HAULT
BAR and RESTAURANT
```

CHAPTER 3

After a pleasant luncheon at Sarabeth's on Simonton Street, Ken Scott excused himself and visited with some of the other officers of the bank.

When Betsy returned, Margaret, as usual, pumped her for information. Betsy was evasive.

"I'll let you know as soon as I can talk about it," Betsy told her.

"Well, can you at least tell me if it's good or bad," Margaret badgered.

"I'll just say this, it's not bad," Betsy said.

"Thank God."

As soon as she got a chance, she called Will.

"How'd your meeting go," he asked.

"Certainly discussed the last thing in the world I expected," she answered. "How would you like an extended working vacation in Jamaica?'

"Did we win the lottery?" he asked. "Or did you just hold up the bank? Should I board the dogs so we can go on the lam?"

"I don't think we have to go to the mattress unless there's something you need to tell me about," she said.

"The bank wants me to take a special assignment in Jamaica."

She then explained to Will everything she knew about the proposal, repeating as much of her conversation with Ken Scott as she could remember verbatim.

"I don't know what to say," Will said.

"I didn't either. I told him we'd talk about it tonight."

Will thought about the bank's proposition to Betsy all afternoon. It certainly seemed exciting, and if they could work out all the details, this would be an intriguing opportunity. Will envisioned a possible windfall of income allowing them to dramatically pay down or even pay off their mortgage. They just couldn't let it completely disrupt their lives.

That night they spent the entire evening drawing up a list of pros and cons and questions which needed to be asked. Things like how would Will be able to run his business temporarily from abroad? What would they do about the dogs? Who would watch their house? Their cars? Who would hold things together for Betsy at the bank? Would the New York Stock Exchange consider Will's new location to be an unauthorized branch office? Was it legal for him to do business from Jamaica? Would Will's assistant be able cover for him in an extended absence? Would the bank pay for their expenses to return to Little Torch Key if an emergency arose? They talked to Lexie and got her reaction to the matter. She was excited for them. Before the evening was over, they had filled an entire page of a legal pad with questions and issues that needed to be clarified. They assigned each other every item on the list to research. The more they discussed it, the more each of them got excited about the possibilities. This could be a once in a lifetime adventure.

The bank and RST were both very accommodating to their needs. The compensation carrot the bank put on the end of the stick was almost irresistible. The extra money would leave them debt free.

Betsy said yes. They began to prepare for their departure.

COOL ONE
HEADQUATERS

CHAPTER 4

It took weeks of concentrated effort after the decision to take the assignment in Jamaica was made, but things miraculously came together. RST, while not thrilled that Will would be operating from a third world country, agreed to allow him to conduct his business temporarily from a home office abroad. WB, as they had promised, firmed up Betsy's proverbial offer, a package which was hard to refuse.

The main obstacle the Blacks faced turned out to be what to do about the dogs. Will and Betsy owned a fox terrier named Lucy and a Bichon named Dexter. Under Jamaican law any dog not born and bred in the UK or Ireland was subjected to six months of quarantine before it was allowed to enter Jamaica even though its immunizations were current in the country of origin. This made no sense to Will and Betsy since most American dogs had better medical care than the majority of the people in Jamaica and certainly better than the mongrel dogs they had seen roaming the countryside. The explanation was that foreign dogs are routinely immunized against and have been exposed to diseases that are not in Jamaica, and that the Jamaicans were unwilling to risk that these alien pets might inadvertently infect local animals.

The pet issue almost became a deal breaker. The Blacks were unwilling to be separated from their dogs for six months, especially since for all they knew; their stay in Jamaica could possibly only be that long. The bank used its influence to save the day. Jamaican officials were equally anxious to resolve the issue in light of the big picture of moving the Highway 2000 project along. They did not want to strain their relationship with a major lender if it could be avoided. The Chief Veterinarian for Jamaica's Ministry of Agriculture became involved. He agreed to waive the requirement if Will and Betsy could obtain an international health certificate for the dogs. This turned out to be relatively simple. One problem solved. The next problem was how to transport the dogs to Montego Bay. With no hesitation WB volunteered their bank corporate jet, a Bombardier Challenger 300, to transport the Blacks and their pets.

The night before their departure, Will received a phone call from Terry Cassidy inviting them to come hear him play at Looe Key Tiki Bar. When Will and Betsy arrived, they were mobbed with friends who had converged on the bar to see them off. As they innocently walked in the door, Terry started to play his medley of *Dixie* and *Battle Hymn Of The Republic* in their honor. Well-wishers seemed to be coming out of every corner of the bar. Terry's friend and harmonica player, Ron Baumann, poured Will and Betsy a draft beer.

The group presented Betsy with a new leather briefcase. The leather had been dyed alternately with the Jamaican national colors, black, yellow and green. The colors were not garish, but a rich stain that gradually bled into the next color.

Betsy brushed away a tear and stammered, "We're

really going to miss you guys."

Will added, "I already want to get back, and we're not even gone yet."

Nira Tocco announced, "Your money is no good tonight. We decided give you a Keys farewell. Notice I said farewell not goodbye. We'll be here when you get back to welcome you home."

Will hugged her. "I know you too well. You'll use any excuses for a party. Cheers!"

Betsy's secretary, Margaret, and Will's administrative assistant were there as well.

"Who's going to fire me if you're not here?" Margaret asked Betsy.

"I'll call you once a week and fire you just to keep in practice," Betsy said.

"It won't be the same," Margaret replied.

The celebration was on.

~ ~ ~

Will and Betsy were very impressed with the WB corporate jet. The Bombardier Challenger 300 was a twin-engine super-mid-sized jet capable of traversing transcontinental distances.

The captain gave them an overview of the plane before they took off.

"We're flying two Honeywell HTF7000 turbofan engines. We can carry up to sixteen passengers even though we normally don't have more than eight to ten guests on a trip. This honey of a plane is rated to fly up to 553 miles an hour with a range is 3568 miles. We have a 45,000-foot ceiling and can climb 5,000 feet a minute. She's a real sweetheart," he said.

"This is the lap of luxury," Will said. "What do they call it? A rock-star lifestyle?"

"Yes, they do," Betsy agreed, "just like that time we got to watch the Dolphins play from the bank's sky box."

A Jamaican Conspiracy

"We should have you in Montego Bay in a couple of hours," the captain said. "The weather's great in Jamaica today. Now just sit back, relax, and leave the driving to us."

After clearing customs they were soon in the air. Will and Betsy excitedly looked out the window. The captain came on the radio and informed them that they were approaching Cuba. The captain was true to his word about time in the air. The Challenger touched down smoothly at 10:23 AM in Montego Bay.

The plane taxied up to a new modern-looking building on the eastern end of Sangster International Airport called the IAM Jet Centre.

"This is the VIP way to visit Jamaica," the captain explained. "The facility is only a few years old. It contains dedicated in-house customs and immigration facilities, luxurious lounges, state of the art security, a private meeting room, and high speed Internet. This building has a private road leading into and out of the airport and a dedicated entrance leading to and from the main terminal."

"Talk about the way to fly," Will said.

"This must be how William and Kate travel," Betsy said. "I feel like royalty."

"Has a nice ring to it – Wilson and Betsy – America's royal couple," Will said.

IAM's general manager greeted them as they walked into the clean, modern one-story yellow building. There was even a red carpet on the sidewalk.

"Welcome home to Jamaica," he said warmly and offered them a rum fruit punch. "Your driver will be waiting as soon as you clear customs."

Will and Betsy cleared customs with a minimum of difficulty. Customs officials had been alerted to the situation with the dogs; they were approved to enter the country quickly and efficiently.

After they came through customs, an older black Jamaican man wearing a New York Yankees baseball cap waited for them in the main building after they came through customs. He was tall and thin. He had a small mustache and short salt-and-pepper hair. He walked with a military gait. He was talking to a younger man when he saw them enter the room. He immediately concluded his conversation with "Tekeere of the road" and walked over to meet them, a big grin spreading across his face. His eyes twinkled playfully.

"Mr. and Mrs. Black, I am Mr. Davis. I will be your driver. Welcome to my country. I hope you are having an irie day. I certainly am. It's another perfect day on the island."

He held out his hand to shake hands with them.

"Please Mr. Davis; it's not Mr. and Mrs. Black, but Will and Betsy. We are so glad to meet you," Will said.

"Then please call me Henry," he said, grinning sincerely all the time. "Let me load your luggage into the back of my van. Ah, I see you have two dogs. May I ask their names?"

Betsy introduced the dogs. They both took an instant liking to Henry.

Henry turned to the man he had been talking to. "Me a-go now. Check me later, Cecil, and bawl fey o lovely Antie Margaret 'or me **(call your lovely Aunt Margaret for me)** and tell her I asked about her. She a ooman of reespek **(She's a woman of respect)**." The man promised he wouldn't forget.

Within fifteen minutes they were leaving the airport and headed into Montego Bay. The road was a good preview of the driving conditions on the island.

Though Jamaicans, as a rule, are some of the most laid back people on the planet, there is one exception.

A Jamaican Conspiracy

They seem to be transformed into rally drivers when put behind the wheel of a car. Every driver seems to want to be in front just to win the race to nowhere. This has been known to lead to bizarre driving styles and shocking antics, upsetting most neophyte tourists who are simply trying to accustom themselves to cars that drive on the left-hand side of the road. Though the speed limit in most towns is 30 miles per hour and only 50 miles per hour on the open highway, a person feels as if he is traveling much faster on the unpredictable roads. Speed traps and stoppages to check papers are a daily occurrence on the often bad and storm-damaged roads. This leads to further unpredictable driving and evasion tactics by local drivers. A stone in the road may be a driver's only notice of a completely washed away road. Alert drivers must also keep on the lookout for an occasional free goat that might wander out on the road.

An older Nissan seemed to come out of nowhere and was suddenly riding Henry's bumper. As they approached a curve it darted out and passed, narrowly missing an approaching car and just getting back in its lane to avoid a head-on collision. A bumper sticker on its trunk said "Safety is no accident."

"I see that driving in Jamaica hasn't changed since the last time we were here," Betsy said to Will.

Henry overheard her and commented, "Not to worry, my dear. You are as safe as a baby in a womb with Henry driving."

He waved at a man sitting in front of a rustic open-air rum-bar.

"I-ney **(hello)**. Save me a nex rum and wata **(save me a rum and water)**, Mr. Sleeper," he called out the open window.

"Mos def **(most definitely)**, Mr. Davis," the man called back. "Me bes to Rose."

24

"Is there anyone you don't know?" Will asked.

"People treat you the same way you treat them," Henry said. "What is life without lots of friends?"

He laid on his horn and passed a slow-moving car. It didn't seem to matter that they were going up a hill.

Will and Betsy explained to Mr. Davis that they had vacationed in Jamaica many times and were thrilled to have the opportunity to live there. He was genuinely excited for them.

"So, if you're seasoned visitors to Jamaica," Henry asked as he passed another motorist, "I'm going to start calling you my Jam-Merican friends. You know what that is? Part Jamaican and part American." He laughed at his own joke. "I can see we are going to enjoy each other's company." He waved at a woman walking down the road. "Good day, Mrs. Davidson. That a pretty 'at **(hat)** you have on."

"Good day to you as well, Mr. Davis," she said and waved back. "Jah guide **(May God be with you)**."

Henry aggressively darted out again and passed a slow-moving truck.

"Would you like a Ting?" Henry asked, referring to a local grapefruit based drink.

They agreed it sounded refreshing, so Henry pulled over in front of an open-fronted little shack. The owner recognized him and greeted him warmly. The man also sold meat patties. Will insisted that the sodas and patties were his treat.

The road was two-lanes, narrow and winding. Henry seemed to know by heart where each pothole was and drove around them. Will and Betsy soon started to see familiar landmarks as they headed east. They passed Rose Hall, the home of the legendary white witch, as Henry headed for Falmouth. They soon saw the signposted turnoff for the tiny community of Little River.

It was market day so Falmouth was swarming with locals. A1 then dipped inland away from the sea until they reached Duncan's. Henry pointed out that Harry Belafonte had once lived here in relative poverty. After Duncan's came Rio Bueno, the fishing village that was the setting for the movie *A High Wind In Jamaica*. Henry pointed out to them that some people thought Rio Bueno was where Columbus actually first set foot in Jamaica. After that was Columbus Park, and finally they had arrived at their destination, Discovery Bay.

Will and Betsy were excited to see the wide flask-shaped bay come into view. Within minutes they were passing the Kaiser Jamaica Bauxite Company, where years before the Jamaican Olympic bobsled team, eulogized in the movie *Cool Runnings*, had trained. There were large bauxite freighters flying Russian flags came into view.

"We're almost to the villa," Henry announced as he took a left off A1 Highway by an old worn looking shopping center and headed up a steep hill. The pot-holed asphalt road wound around. Henry had to downshift the car to climb it. They passed everything from mansions to unfinished abandoned properties. Locals walked languidly down the hill. In a few minutes he stopped outside a stonewalled, iron-gated villa. The gate was closed and locked. A brick driveway led to the house. It had taken them a little over an hour to drive from the Montego Bay airport.

Henry smiled and turned around, "Welcome to your new home, Sundance."

> HOUSE FOR RENT

> SQUATERS
> NOTISE
> NO TRISPAS
> ING

CHAPTER 5

Henry honked his car horn to announce their arrival. Through the gate Will and Betsy saw an expansive front yard. A modern house appearing to be one-story was in the background. The house had a large open front porch that ran at least half the length of the front elevation. The porch was flanked by simple smooth white non-tapered wooden columns. Five long sweeping brick steps matching the brick on the driveway led up to the porch. To one side of the main house was a carport and a smaller building used as living quarters for the houseboy. Will and Betsy could not tell from the front, but the house was actually a split level structure that had been set on a lot in which the backyard ran steeply down the mountain from the level front yard.

The entire perimeter of the property was surrounded by a five-foot wall made out of natural native stone on three sides. The back wall was made out of concrete blocks and had a gate leading to an undeveloped lot. An unscreened swimming pool had been built in the side yard to the right of the back veranda. They could see an open double front door from the gate.

Two excited large black Rottweilers rushed the gate barking loudly.

Betsy looked at Will and said, "My God, either of those two huge creatures could eat our dogs like a Milk-Bone."

Will nodded in agreement.

A youthful black man came out the front door. He picked up two limestone rocks and threw them one at a time across the yard like a baseball. The dogs happily chased them. He used this opportunity to approach the gate. Henry, waiting patiently, stood in front of his van.

"Mr. Davis, we have been expecting you."

The young man unlocked the gate and then opened it. About that time the dogs returned with the stones. Each of them crushed the rocks in their mouths with their massive jaws. Will and Betsy now were even less sure whether they should exit the safe confines of the van.

Henry reassured them. "Gina and Samantha won't hurt you unless they know you're not supposed to be here. They're just big playful puppies."

"Who eat rocks," Betsy said and winced.

"Of course, my dear, that's why we call them Rockweilers," he said and laughed at his own joke.

"How do they know I'm a guest?" Will asked. "They didn't ask to see my ID."

"Trust me," Henry said. "They know."

Will and Betsy reluctantly got out of Henry's van. Gina and Samantha rushed up and started to alternately lick and sniff them eagerly.

"See, I told you," Henry said.

"Gina ... Sam ... enough," the young black man said as he pulled the dogs down.

"My name is E.J.," he said to the Blacks. "Welcome home to Sundance where each day is more irie then the last. I will be your live-in houseboy and gardener." He grinned and held out his hand.

Will and Betsy gave him a good look for the first time. E.J. was about six feet tall and very slender. His hair was neatly trimmed and medium length. He wore casual slacks and a short-sleeved white polyester dress shirt, open at the collar. He looked clean-cut and seemed to have no tattoos or other distinguishing marks. Will guessed that at best E.J. was barely out of his teens. He came across as being sincere, non-threatening, and well meaning but naive.

"We have two dogs of our own," Betsy stammered. "Will Sam and Gina hurt them?"

"It will not be a problem," E.J. assured them.

Will and Betsy looked up the driveway and saw standing on the porch a neat, full-figured, middle-aged black woman in a domestic's uniform. She was straightening her uniform and hair. Her broad grin made them instantly feel at ease and welcome.

Will and Betsy walked up the driveway, the dogs leading the way jumping and playing. Henry stayed behind to drive the van into the compound so E.J. could close the gate again.

Betsy said in a low voice to Will, "I think I'm going to like this place."

They climbed the steps. A bright smile was on Leva's face. "Mr. and Mrs. Black, I'm Mrs. Carter, Welcome to Sundance."

"Please call us Will and Betsy," Will responded as he held out his hand to her.

"Then please call me Leva."

A Jamaican Conspiracy

"Good morning, Mrs. Carter," Henry called out.

"And a good morning to you, Mr. Davis," she called back. "I hope all is well."

She turned to Will and Betsy. "Please come into your new home."

Henry and E.J. began to unpack the car. Will and Betsy got Lucy and Dexter out of their pet carriers. Gina and Sam sniffed them. Lucy and Dexter shrank back from the huge dogs initially but then began to sniff them back. Within a couple of minutes the critical familiarization ritual seemed to have been completed.

"See, I told you," E.J. said. "Sam and Gina are just overgrown puppies who want to be friends."

"Unless you're a trespasser," Henry said. "Then may Jah be with you."

Leva began to show them around the house. To the left of the front door was a large modern kitchen. Straight ahead was an enormous great room arranged around a conversation area of comfortable-looking couches backed by six folding French doors which led to an open L-shaped back veranda. The doors were open allowing the ocean breeze to waft through the house. The centerpiece of this veranda was a round dining room table that appeared to seat eight diners comfortably. A bar was set at one end. In the background was a full panoramic view of a seemingly endless Caribbean. Looking over the wooden rail they could appreciate just how steep the lot really was. Parts seemed to almost be a precipitous drop. Down a set of stairs from the porch were a brick patio and a long rectangular marcite-plastered swimming pool. Bougainvilleas were growing up much of the wall. The pool was half out of the ground because of the steep elevation of the lot. The ocean view from the pool was as magnificent as the view had been from the porch. In the other direction they could see Villa Brawta, the villa next door.

"Brawta is an interesting name for a villa. Is that the owner's name?" Betsy asked.

"No, ma'am," Leva said and smiled. "Brawta is patois for getting something free as a bonus. The land it occupies was originally Sundance property. Our owner divided the lot in two, and sold the excess to a friend at a very reasonable cost, enabling the new owner to build a second home on the property. He said two villas on one lot was a brawta or bonus, you might say almost like building something for free."

"Fascinating," Will said.

Will and Betsy paused to take in the view.

"So this is what we'll be forced to endure every day as we dine," Will said sarcastically.

"On a good day you can almost see Cuba," Leva said. "It's only a little over 200 miles from here."

"We seem to be getting farther from Cuba as we move south, Will," Betsy said. "Key West was only 90 miles away."

"Gee, just when I was getting used to being close to Castro," Will said.

Leva continued to show them the villa. At each end of the porch was a French door that led to a bedroom. Inside each bedroom, large open windows once again gave the occupant a breathtaking view of the Caribbean. Each bedroom had its own private bathroom.

Leva then led them down a flight of stairs to the house level below.

"I couldn't tell from the front of the house that it was split level," Betsy said. "This villa is much larger than it appears."

At the bottom of the stairs they found another bedroom, a large game room with a pool table and another full bathroom with a shower stall. A brick patio

A Jamaican Conspiracy

was outside another set of exterior French doors.

"This villa is much larger than our house in the Keys," Will said. Betsy agreed.

"I think the bank chose our new residence wisely," she said.

"Would you like some rum punch now?" Leva asked, "or would you prefer to wait until you unpack?"

"Why don't we wait until we unpack," Betsy said, "and then we can relax, have a drink, and truly enjoy our new surroundings. I hope you will join us for happy hour."

She then turned to Henry and extended the same invitation.

"And please bring your wife," she added. "We would love to meet her."

"Rose would like that," Henry said. "I forgot to mention that we are almost neighbors. We live just up the hill on Primrose Lane. I will call her now and see if she will be available. Shall we make it 5 o'clock?"

Leva and Betsy agreed the time would be ideal, and the Blacks then spent the rest of the afternoon unpacking, exploring the grounds and resting up from their trip.

Henry and Rose drove through the gate promptly at five. He introduced Rose to Will and Betsy. Rose appeared to be about Henry's age. She was neat, average height, and spoke with an educated accent.

Leva turned on the radio to an oldies station. Music immediately filled the villa. Henry tapped his feet to *Money In My Pocket.*

"Dennis Brown," he announced. "We saw him play that at Sunsplash when it was at Chukka Cove. Isn't that what we all want – money in our pocket and a song in our heart?"

Leva mixed a pitcher of rum punch, and the group retired to the back porch to enjoy the late afternoon ocean view. Will and Betsy invited Leva and E.J. to participate in the impromptu party. E.J., who had gone next door to borrow some ice, soon joined them in progress.

Betsy commented, "And just think we have to look at this view every day."

"Views are considered a sacred right in Jamaica," Rose commented.

"Yes," Henry agreed. "A person can get away with many things in this country, but blocking someone else's view is not one of them. One day soon I will show you a partially finished house up the hill. It is owned by a Canadian. When the house was being built, he was in Canada instead of being here to watch after his own interests. The builder mismeasured where the house was supposed to go on the lot and placed it too far up the hill so that it blocked his neighbor's view. He will never be permitted to finish this house. It has been sitting there now for five years. The only solution will be to tear down what has been built and begin again. The owner claims he does not have the funds to do so."

"Why not pass the expense back to the builder?" Will asked.

"That is not currently an option," Henry said, "since this builder is no longer in business. He is what we call fly-by-night."

"I know the term. The bank occasionally encounters such developers in the U.S. as well," Betsy said.

E.J., having returned with the ice, saw the partially empty rum punch pitcher in the kitchen. Not knowing Leva had already added a generous portion of rum, he poured the remaining part of the rum bottle into the punch himself.

The conversation soon turned to the reason Will and Betsy would be living in Jamaica. Betsy explained, without going into detail, her role in monitoring the Highway 2000 project for her employer, the lending institution for the highway. Will told them he would be conducting his own business from an office he would be setting up in the villa.

E.J's double-strength rum punches began to lubricate the participants and make them increasingly comfortable with each other.

Leva announced she had planned a special Jamaican dinner to welcome her new guests. E.J. would be jerking some chicken in the back yard. She would be cooking side dishes of ackee and salt cod, fried breadfruit and fried bammy. Will and Betsy invited the entire group to join them for their inaugural evening meal. They readily accepted. Leva went into the kitchen and mixed another pitcher of rum punches. Betsy and Rose helped her set the table. Then the group retired to the yard so that E.J. could light the grill and heat the coals so he could jerk the chicken. They arranged some lawn chairs next to the swimming pool and got out a portable table. Leva served some Solomon Gundy and crackers that Rose had prepared and brought over for the occasion.

"Have you ever had any Solomon Gundy?" Rose asked Will and Betsy.

They admitted they hadn't.

"It is a fish pâté," Rose explained. "It can be made with pickled smoked herring, mackerel, shad or any other fish you have available. Today I made mine with sardines. I add some hot peppers and other seasonings. If you like it, I'll gladly share my recipe."

As they ate Solomon Gundy and drank more rum punches, E.J. loaded the grill with a natural irregular charcoal that he got out of a plain brown paper grocery bag. To Will's horror he doused the whole thing with gasoline. No one else seemed to notice. After stopping to lob a rock for Samantha, he then threw in a match. There was a tremendous explosion, followed by a fireball.

Charcoal shot into the air. Betsy leaped up and bumped Rose, upsetting the platter of Solomon Gundy she was holding, causing her to throw it up in the air. E.J. lost his balance and tumbled backwards into the pool. Henry yelled "Jesus" and jumped in after him.

Suddenly they heard a terrified shriek from the other side of the fence. Will and Betsy rushed to the fence to see a pale nude white man and woman clamoring from their hot tub. They appeared to be a young yuppie couple. Charcoal sizzled as it rained down into the hot tub almost overriding a moody jazz rendition of *Send In The Clowns* coming from the couple's I-Pod speakers. The dark-haired, pony-tailed clean-shaven man was still clinging to an opened bottle of red wine. Both were barefoot, and after a few clumsy steps they began limping and hopping after bruising their bare tender feet on the irregular rocks. There was no attempt at discretion since they thought they were alone. There was almost immediately a second blast, and Will and Betsy saw the grate from the grill catapult itself over the fence along with the platter of seasoned, marinated chicken parts that were waiting to be cooked. Will could hear the opening surreal lines of a saxophone on the I-Pod wailing *I'll Be Seeing You* just before the grate clanged down only a few feet from where the bathers had been mellowly unwinding only moments before, silencing the I-Pod forever. The victims shrieked again. The man stepped on the slick chicken parts littering the yard, dropped the wine bottle, and slid tumbling into the sticky bougainvillea bushes next to their villa taking his companion with him. Will and Betsy could not see their faces, only two pale asses disappearing into the thorny bushes. The man screamed, "Mother fuc ... " only to be interrupted by his companion howling, "PETER!!"

"What do you want me to do, Miriam?"

A Jamaican Conspiracy

"I don't know, but if you were a man you'd do something," she bellowed back.

Leva screamed, "My God, those guests just arrived today from England. Cora, Villa Brawta's housekeeper, told me her guests are first-timers to Jamaica."

"And probably last-timers," Betsy said, stifling a giggle. "They may never leave the mother country again after this."

"Chalk up one for the colonies. I hope they're not honeymooners," Will said.

"A little adversity should make them stronger. I think they've had an irie first day in paradise redefined for them," Betsy retorted.

"Into a shitty day in Valhalla?" Will added.

Henry had joined them and chimed in at this point. "As I said earlier, I think we're going to get along just fine."

A sheepish soaked E.J., no worse for wear, emerged from Sundance's pool. He had singed eyelashes and hair. Solomon Gundy was hanging from both.

Within minutes a police siren was heard at the gate. The burly cop demanded to know what had happened. When he was told, the officer went next door to check on the shell-shocked renters. He came back shaking his head, trying to suppress a grin, and reported that other than some scratches and bruises in embarrassing places everyone seemed to be OK.

"I guess this means the grill is out tonight," Leva said, "and the jerked chicken as well. Do you mind if we just have bammies and ackee tonight? I'll make some garlic bread to go with them."

"At home this would be what we would call a pizza or Chinese takee-outee night," Will said. "Do you think we should invite our new neighbors?"

"Only if you want to become a grisly homicide victim," Betsy said and then added, "It's certainly not a Solomon Gundy evening." She looked at E.J. and grinned at Rose.

Rose smiled and agreed. E.J. just looked sheepish.

> NOTICE
> NO FORM OF PERSON SHOULD NOT FINE THEM-SELF OVER THIS WORK-SHOP, UNLESS PERMISSION IS GIVEN
>
> **BY ORDER** W. DEAVER

CHAPTER 6

Will and Betsy sat at the round glass-topped dining room table on the veranda waiting for Leva to finish preparing breakfast. An instrumental version of *Do Lord* was playing on the radio. Leva sang the lyrics as she worked. For as far as their eyes could see was a spectacular view of the Caribbean showcasing a cerulean blue sky melting into sun-drenched emerald waters. The morning sky had a fresh golden glow. There wasn't a cloud in sight. This entire spectacle was framed by lush palm trees.

"What a way to start a day," Will said. "There's something about this scene that makes you feel young and glad to be alive." He poured some coffee and went back to reading the local morning newspaper, *The Gleaner*. Betsy was catching up on her bank e-mails on her laptop.

Will giggled to himself and called out to her, "I feel like I'm back in the Keys. Here's a story in the paper about some ganja-toting local cowboy who has been charged

A Jamaican Conspiracy

with carrying a concealed weapon and possession of drug paraphernalia. You won't believe what his name is."

Betsy shrugged.

"Zopittybop-Bop-Bop."

"You're right. You're making me homesick," Betsy said. "You'll never guess what happened at my bank in Key West yesterday. We had a customer urinate in a drive-through bank tube and then drive off."

"Now that's what I call making a memorable deposit, but it was sure a pisser for the teller," Will said. "At least it didn't require a currency transaction report."

"This certainly combines pissed off and pissed on," Betsy said. "I haven't told you the best part yet. This idiot was identified because he left a pre-printed deposit slip in the tube as well."

"I'm glad I didn't have to decipher that soggy saga," Will said.

Leva brought their breakfast to the table. She had cut local fruits into a fruit cocktail. She also had scrambled eggs, fried bacon and made homemade biscuits. It all smelled heavenly.

"Looking forward to your first day on your new assignment?" Will asked.

"Yes, I am," Betsy said, "though sitting here looking at this glorious view and eating this gourmet repast makes it seem like it should be a lazy Sunday brunch we are enjoying instead of a business morning breakfast."

"Oh, I'm sure you'll get in the swing of things in nothing flat," said Will. "After about an hour in your new office, this view will be the farthest thing in the world from your mind. Don't forget to call me and give me your direct phone number in case I need you. I'm going to try to get some of my systems set up around here. It's going to seem strange working from home."

They heard a honk out in the driveway.

"Henry's here," Leva called out.

"Good morning, good morning," Henry said with a smile as he came in the house. "I-ney (hello), Miss Leva. Ya do good dis irie **(delightful)** day?" he said in patois.

"Boonoonoonous **(wonderful)**, Mr. Davis," Leva answered.

Patois began with slaves creating a new language from the many African dialects and combining that with inflections of Spanish, English, and French. To many Jamaicans, patois is the mother tongue. Despite this, most Jamaicans, though they are fluent in spoken patois, cannot write the language. The poet Mutabaruka wittily wrote, "The language we talk, we cannot write, and the language we write, we cannot talk." Patois has not changed much over the years and is a corner of life Jamaicans can call their own, the rights to an impulsive and sometimes confrontational language.

"There's some coffee left," Will said. "Would you like a cup?"

"That sounds wonderful," Henry said. "Don't mind if I do. Then we can head for Ochi."

After a quick cup of coffee and some lighthearted banter, Henry and Betsy set out. As the van headed down the hill, Henry saw the housekeeper from Villa Brawta, the villa next door to Sundance walking down to the shopping center.

Henry leaned out and said, "Morning, Miss Cora. Would you like a lift?"

He stopped, and Cora climbed in. Henry introduced her to Betsy.

"Have your guests recovered from the charcoal incident?" Henry asked.

"Naa **(no)**," Cora said in patois. "She be bex ever since **(She's been vexed ever since)**. That ooman facety an' bumboclot **(that woman is bad tempered**

and the queen of curse words). She husband try romp wid 'er after **(Her husband tried to be romantic afterwards)**. Di man dem beg fa jooks **(The man begged for sex)**. She box 'im face and kick 'im buddy **(She slapped his face and kicked him in his genitals)**. She den yell a' mi' **(Then she yelled at me)**. She den blame it all on dat time of month. Mi see no evidence dat true. Mi do see a bokkle **(bottle)** of Valium by her bed, tho."

"Was she hurt?" Betsy asked.

"She body aright. Only she head bad **(Her body's ok; her head's bad)**. Tween you an' mi, mi tink she English white nyega **(Between you and me, I think she's white trash)**."

They all laughed and promised not to repeat Cora's statements. Henry let her off at the shopping center, and they continued to Ocho Rios.

"I guess we won't be making an effort to get to know those people," Betsy said.

"Sounds like you're not missing anything," Henry said.

Soon Highway A3 had taken them into the tranquil village of Runaway Bay. Runaway Bay, virtually a one-street town, that attracted those escapist vacationers who wanted to get as far away from Ocho Rios's cruise ship passengers as possible. The origin of the name is a matter of conjecture. Ocho Rios's name either came from the legend that it was the Spaniard's departure point from Jamaica after their defeat by the British in 1655, or from the saga saying that African slaves making their getaway to Cuba used it as their point of debarkation. As they were passing Dunn's River Falls headed into Ocho Rios. Henry honked and yelled at his friend, artist Michael Clarke, who was standing out in front of his humble studio. Mr. Clarke waved back.

The impact of Ocho Rios is immediate and affirmative without being assertive or aggressive. Ocho Rios seems to be a happy place, secure in itself. It has not been burdened with being the capital of a parish, like St. Ann's Bay, seven miles to the west. Ocho Rios is neither a commercial nor an industrial center, though Reynolds Jamaica Mines is only twelve miles away at Lyford. With a wide, deep channel ideal for cruise ships, this is a large resort town, but not one dominated by hotels. They are strung out along forty miles of coast from the Jamaica Hilton in the west to Orascabessa, twenty miles to the east. The visual impact of the luxury development Shaw Park Corniche, said by many to be the finest of its kind in Jamaica, or of the hotels and expensive villas that line the coast, is diminished by the fact that they all fit into the landscape. Hotel grounds are not so manicured as to appear artificial. The buildings simply comfortably belong; Jamaicans belong here as well.

Henry took a left onto Main Street, and Betsy got her first glimpse of what would be her home away from home in coming months. National Commercial Bank Jamaica Ltd., known as NCB, was a clean, modern, white stucco building with a glass-door main entrance on the rear side of a covered breezeway. The full-length glass windows flanking the door were covered with vertical blinds. The front door and each window were framed by stucco arches that lined the front of the breezeway. A blue awning covered an ATM machine on the far left. Raised concrete planters were on the sidewalk with a head-high, neatly trimmed hedge of pink hibiscus shrubs. In tall yellow and blue capitol letters, NCB NATIONAL COMMERCIAL BANK was prominently displayed along the top of the building. The sign could be seen from anywhere on the block. Henry found a place to park his van, and they entered the building.

The bright spacious chamber inside was backed by ten modern-looking teller windows. Decorative blue roll-up belts on retractable belt cassettes connected portable chrome stanchions so the bank could queue customers waiting for an available teller. Behind the teller windows was a long brightly colored acrylic mural that stretched the length of the room depicting tropical Jamaican scenes. Linear fluorescent lighting was recessed into the ceiling behind a checkerboard drop ceiling accented in chrome. The lobby contained various chrome-edged kiosks, a customer service desk, and racks of sales material. It reminded Betsy very much of a bank in the United States.

Betsy and Henry walked up to the customer service desk, and Betsy introduced herself.

"We have been expecting you," the lady said warmly. "I'll let Mr. Smith know you're here."

Warren Smith, the bank president, took Betsy back to his office. Henry paid his respects, agreed on a time to pick Betsy up, and then departed. Betsy and Mr. Smith spent some time getting acquainted. Smith then called a short informal gathering of some of his available senior officers to introduce her, and then he led Betsy past rows of cubicles to her office. The office was spacious but not elaborate, furnished with a simple but modern desk and a comfortable looking executive chair. Two chrome customer chairs faced the desk. The credenza had some local woodcarvings. Brightly colored paintings depicting close-ups of tropical plants were on the walls. A filing cabinet was in one corner. There was a floral sofa along one wall. The office was not elegant but more than sufficient for Betsy's needs. He introduced Betsy to her new secretary, Letha Wardlow. Letha apologized that Betsy's new administrative assistant, Bob Blackmon, was not there to welcome her as well. She said Bob was out of the bank on business but would be in later.

Betsy had never been good at guessing a person's age, but she estimated that Letha was in her early to mid thirties. She was a dark-skinned woman of average build. She dressed neatly and spoke clearly. She seemed somewhat reserved. Mr. Smith left them to get to know each other. He told Betsy he would return at noon to take her to lunch.

When he had gone, Betsy made light conversation with Letha, trying not to come across as an inquisitor, but at the same time, trying to learn more about her new assistant. Letha responded to each question but did not elaborate after the question was answered. She seemed slightly uncomfortable. After a few minutes, Betsy realized she was not making much headway in learning what made her new secretary tick. Letha's curiosity about Betsy or her mission with the bank appeared minimal. Betsy had Letha give her an overview of the bank's records and then dismissed her so she could try to gain an understanding of the bank's computer system.

About an hour later, Letha poked her head in the door and asked Betsy if she could get her a cup of coffee. Betsy gratefully accepted. When Letha returned with the coffee, she also brought Betsy a banana leaf with some small triangular pastries.

"These are to welcome you to the bank," Letha said.

"Well, thank you," Betsy said. "These look scrumptious. What are they? Did you make them?"

"They are plantain tarts," Letha replied. "Cooking is a hobby of mine. I made them just for you."

She then told Betsy how the tarts were made. She seemed much more at ease talking about food than she had when Betsy attempted to discuss business. Betsy tasted one. It was absolutely delicious.

The morning seemed to fly by. Betsy was so engrossed that she didn't realize that lunchtime had

A Jamaican Conspiracy

arrived until Smith came back in the door for their luncheon appointment. He told her he was taking her to a local landmark restaurant, The Ruins.

Lunch was a relaxed easy affair. Mr. Smith told Betsy some of the history of NCB. The bank's genesis traced back to 1837, when the predecessor, Colonial Bank of London opened its Harbour Street Kingston doors. The bank had been owned by Barclays DCO since 1977. He told Betsy that NCB was a full service bank offering corporate and institutional banking services, private banking, wealth management and insurance. He said he had begun his career with NCB shortly after leaving school and hoped to spend his entire working career with the bank.

When Betsy returned from lunch, she asked about Bob Blackmon. Letha said he was still out on calls. Betsy asked Letha to let her know when Bob arrived. Blackmon finally arrived about three o'clock. Betsy's door was partially closed, but she could still clearly hear him talking loudly to Letha in perfect English as Letha passed along Betsy's request. Then in a lower voice, assuming he could talk in patois confidentially, he said, "Wh'appen **(what's happening)** pretty seccatery! So wha new brand bakra lak **(so what's the brand new white slave-master like)**?"

Letha responded, "De wizzy wizzy say upful **(The whisper is encouraging)**. Now g'long wi' ju."

Letha came in and asked Betsy if she had time to meet Blackmon. Before Betsy could respond, her door opened and a large, middle-aged black Jamaican dressed in a royal blue long-sleeved shirt, polyester necktie, and black trousers barged into her office. Blackmon was a big man in every regard, tall and pear-shaped. He was grinning from ear to ear as he extended a meaty paw.

"Mrs. Black, Big-Boy Banker Bob Blackmon, at your

service. It is certainly a pleasure as well as a privilege to meet you. I'm positive we will soon become fast friends. I can already tell you are a people person like I am."

As he held out his big meaty hand for Betsy to shake, Betsy noted it was a pencil-pusher's hand, soft and uncallused.

"I would invite you in," Betsy said, "but I guess you're already in. How are you today?"

"If I was doing any better, vitamins would be taking me," Blackmon said.

Betsy gulped and mouthed *Oh shit! This sounds familiar. Carson Crown all over again.*

Blackmon was too self-absorbed to notice her reaction. Without being invited, Blackmon plopped down on the sofa. He stretched out like he owned it. The sofa creaked in resistance.

"Sorry I was not able to attend your introductory meeting this morning, but I had important bank business followed by a luncheon with some highly influential people. If not for these critical conferences, I would have personally welcomed you with a taste of Jamaica at noon today that you would not soon forget. However, the downside for us mega-bankers who have to maximize the hours in each day is that production comes first, pleasure second," Blackmon said. "There's a top producers' Jamaican saying, 'Mi come yah fi drink milk, me no come yah fi count cow **(I am straight-forward and deliver what I promise instead of just talking about it).**'"

Déjà vu CC in Key West, thought Betsy. *Only now it's BB instead. I'm not sure how you say it in patois, but if we were in Havana, I'd just scream 'Aye, yi, yi, yi, yi!'*

"I hope your endeavors were successful," Betsy asked. "May I ask the nature of these conferences?"

"I am the bank's representative on the organizing committee for Reggae Sumfest. It is a highly prestigious appointment," Blackmon said boldly. "Today we were choosing which rum distillery is going to be our major sponsor this year. And of course you can't make an intelligent decision unless you become familiar with the products they offer."

He winked knowingly at Betsy.

Betsy thought to herself, *At WB we used to send our most disposable officers to fulfill community service obligations of this nature. I wonder if they do the same in Jamaica.*

"That was an all-day affair?' Betsy asked.

"It is if you're going to do it correctly, and *we do believe* in doing it correctly. We had a sampling party. You know, sometimes it takes more than one sample to arrive at the right decision." He winked at her again.

"I see," was all that Betsy said. She did not want to get off on the wrong foot on her first day by voicing her true thoughts. "Tell me a little about yourself, Mr. Blackmon."

"Now let's get this straight right now. I am not Mr. Blackmon. He was my grandfather. My friends call me either 'BB' or 'The B-Mon', Ocho Rios' baddest **(greatest)** super-banker from Bull Bay. Call me what you want to; just don't forget to call me for dinner."

He laughed at his own joke and slapped his knee as if he had come up with an original witticism. Betsy winced and accidentally broke the lead on the pencil she was holding.

"My motto is '2B or not 2B' After all, you have a bad reputation to maintain if your middle name is Bogle."

Betsy looked at him quizzically not understanding either reference.

"I am a direct descendent of Paul Bogle, Jamaica's national hero of the Maroon wars."

Betsy still looked puzzled.

"Ah, I see I need to give you a quick history lesson.

David and Nancy Beckwith

Paul Bogle was *the* hero of the battle of Bloody Bay in St. Thomas, a turning point in the Jamaican civil rights struggle. In 1865 a Maroon was imprisoned for trespassing on an abandoned plantation. Bogle led protestors into Morant Bay and broke the man out of prison. The British militia killed some of the protestors. A riot ensued, and Bogle's men took over the town. The British slaughtered Bogle's men in retaliation and hung him. He became a national hero. There is a statue in his honor outside the Morant Bay courthouse."

In his excitement he inadvertently lapsed into patois. "Mi birfrite make me a big bout yah in Jamaica, but still mi nah topanoris **(My birthright makes me a VIP in Jamaica but still I'm not snooty)**. Evahbody mi fren'. Pure bank waan mi **(Everyone's my friend and many banks would love to hire me)**. Mi will be you most trusted advisor. As we say in Jamaica, 'Wi gwaan hab a bashment time!' **(We're going to have a great time)**."

Betsy almost bit her tongue as she said, "I'm sure you'll be an asset to my staff."

"See you inna di lights **(see you tomorrow)**," BB said "Now mi must mek haste **(I better get back to work)**."

With that he was up and gone.

What have I gotten myself into? Betsy asked silently after Blackmon had left.

She heard BB mention to Letha on his way out, "Mi tink dat went well. This shud be peece o cake. She putty in mi hans **(That went well. She's a piece of cake who will be putty in my hands)**. Mi link ju up layta **(see you later)**." Betsy then could hear BB's booming voice all the way down the hall. He poked his head in each person's office as he worked his way back to his own office.

Betsy spent the remaining part of the afternoon familiarizing herself with her new assignment. She was so

47

A Jamaican Conspiracy

engrossed that she again forgot the time and didn't realize the workday was ending until Henry arrived.

"Ready?" he asked.

"Oh sure! Give me a moment," Betsy said and began to gather her belongings. She got her briefcase out of the closet. It was not hers. The briefcase was well-worn and plain brown, not multi-colored. When she opened it, she found it was filled with newspapers.

"Letha," she called out. "My briefcase has gotten switched with someone else's. Do you know who this one belongs to?"

"No, Mrs. Black," Letha answered. "I just assumed it was yours."

"Then someone has been in my office," Betsy said.

"No, ma'am," Letha said, beginning to look guilty and concerned. "I have seen no one here."

"The only time I wasn't here was while I was at lunch," Betsy stated. "Are you sure no one came in here in my absence."

"No, ma'am, I have seen no one," Letha repeated, looking down.

"Walk around the bank with me while we look for it," Betsy ordered. "Is Mr. Smith in?"

"No, ma'am. He has left for the day."

The briefcase was nowhere to be found.

"Well, it's a good thing nothing of tremendous value was in it, though its disappearance will cause me some inconvenience," Betsy said disgustedly. "I guess I've learned my first lesson at NCB. When you're not in your office, you keep your door locked."

She gave Letha a disgusted look.

About that time BB strolled in. Letha asked him if he had seen the briefcase.

"Maybe the bank duppies got it," BB said and winked.

Letha winced and shrugged. BB laughed at her and

then noticed Betsy taking in the verbal exchange.

"Some of my people are so backward and superstitious – just downright country," BB bragged to Betsy. "Personally I don't believe in duppies or Obeah men. Those are old fashioned concepts used to manipulate and to control the unsophisticated masses."

"I'm ready to leave, Henry. I will see you in the morning, Letha. Goodnight, Bob."

On the way home, Henry asked Betsy about the missing briefcase. Betsy told him that Ken Scott from WB in Charlotte had warned her that her reception might not be fantastic, since her predecessor had shown unauthorized favoritism on occasion, and that this would not be the case going forward.

"But I never expected it to manifest itself with someone stealing my belongings right out of my office on my very first day and then blaming it on duppies," Betsy said.

"It's possible you are running into some passive/aggressive resentment since you replaced a popular Jamaican," Henry said. "I'm sure this will pass as they get to know you and you get to know them."

"I hope you're right but it sure makes me wonder what the next shoe to drop is going to be," Betsy said.

"Just remember, 'no cup no broke, no coffee no dash away', Henry said.

"Which means?"

"Even when disaster strikes, all may not be lost," said Henry. "Just keep to the straight and narrow, and things will work out."

> NOTICE
> TRUSPOUS WILL
> BE PRUSSICUD BY
> MANAGER

CHAPTER 7

Will stood at the verandah rail taking in the lush tropical paradise surrounding him. A slight breeze wafted over the rail. Leva was in the kitchen humming a gospel song as Betsy watched her prepare breakfast and asked her about Jamaican breakfast traditions.

Leva patiently explained, "On Sundays Jamaican breakfasts are like a dinner meal in many households. The wide variety of foods offered are such that you become satisfied the moment you sit down to eat. Also during the week many of the same foods served for breakfast are the same as those served for dinner. Jamaicans do not find this unusual because they are accustomed to eating what is available. Another important determinant of breakfast foods is the distance you are from an urban area. People in urban areas will have a tendency to eat foods that are convenient to prepare and easily obtained at the local grocery store. Rural folks, on the other hand, will use foods grown in fields close to their homes. So, as you can see, breakfast

51

A Jamaican Conspiracy

habits are often based simply on geography, leading to urban breakfasts and rural breakfasts."

"Feel free to serve us either type of Jamaican breakfast. We are not afraid to be experimental," Betsy said, "and that porridge you are cooking smells delicious. Will and I don't expect special treatment. Just treat us like family."

"Then you would not object to ackee, or bammy or breadfruit? " Leva asked.

"Sounds good to me," Betsy said.

"How about liver, fried plantains, sweet potato pudding, fried dumplings, salt fish or sardines?"

"I don't know if I'm ready for the salt fish or sardines for breakfast yet," Betsy replied.

Leva only smiled and said, "Breakfast is ready."

"What is that?" Will asked after she brought it to the table.

"Cornmeal porridge," Leva answered. "I boiled cornmeal with milk, sugar, cinnamon, and vanilla."

Just as Will and Betsy began to eat, the phone in the kitchen rang, and Leva answered it. At first she just listened.

"Ju jesta (You've got to be kidding)," they heard her say. "De beast dint **(The cops didn't!)**! Dat 'gainst de **(That violates the)** Kindah Treaty. Dat be chaka-chaka **(That sucks.)**. Wi' gwin hab trouble fi sure **(This is going to cause trouble for sure)**."

"What's going on?" Betsy called out. "I hope nothing is wrong at home."

"No ma'am," Leva replied. "Just some local gossip. Nothing of concern to you."

They could hear her talking in a low voice to E.J., but nothing more was said. Will continued to read his *Gleaner*. Betsy drank a second cup of coffee while E.J. began to clear the table.

They heard a car horn and knew Henry had arrived.

"Good morning, all. I smell cornmeal porridge," Henry said.

"Have some," Leva offered. "Plenty remains, and it won't reheat well."

"If we were both single and I were 20 years younger, I'd marry you," Henry replied gaily. Leva blushed at the compliment.

Henry lowered his voice, "Hab ju hear turrble su-su bout wha beast do to Maroon Rasta, Chiken **(Have you heard the terrible gossip about what the police did to the Maroon Rasta, Chicken)**?"

Leva nodded and shook her head. "Mi hear Chiken bleedy **(I heard Chicken was bleeding)**. It so a fuckery **(It's so unfair)**. So unnecessary afore bashment **(before the dance)**. Mi hear dey cut im dreads **(I heard they trimmed his dreadlocks)**."

Will took note of the little he could understand but tried to lighten the mood. He laughed and said, "Listen to this, folks. This must be my week for name stories. Listen to this."

A police officer in Negril saw a man standing in the middle of the road obstructing traffic. When he was approached by the officer, the man began to walk. The officer caught up with him and asked him what his name was. He said his name was Winston Churchill and that he was born August 6, 1892.

Henry snickered and said "August 6th is Jamaican Independence Day," Will continued.

After being warned of an arrest he said he was the Commissioner of Police and began talking into his hand saying "I need backup, send me backup." Once in custody he said he was Commander Chief 492, a secret operative for Scotland Yard. After he arrived at the courthouse, a deputy recognized him from a previous arrest and booked him under his real name – JOHN DOE.

Everyone was laughing as Betsy entered the room and told Henry she was ready to depart for work.

Will rose to kiss her goodbye and said, "I certainly hope this day goes smoother than yesterday."

"I plan to have a discussion with Mr. Smith this morning about my missing briefcase," Betsy said. "It's really sad that you can't trust something to be safe in your own office. Let's hope it all turns out to be a big misunderstanding. Have a good day, darling."

After Betsy and Henry had departed, Will heard Leva and E.J. talking to each other once again. E.J. looked especially distraught.

"I don't want to pry," he said, "but has something terrible happened?"

Leva and E.J. looked at each other, trying to decide how to answer Will's question.

"There is a report that a young Rasta has been beaten by the police," E.J. finally said.

Letha gave him a look that said he shouldn't continue. E.J. continued anyway.

"The Rasta was cultivating about four acres of ganja in the cockpit country," E.J. said. "It was well known, not a secret."

He hesitated and lapsed into patois as he got more excited. "But dis is not why beast **(police)** haul 'im out to the road and crack 'im skull with the butt of they shotguns. Dey then bound 'im hands, tied a rope around 'im neck, and led 'im like a captured animal back to dey car. Dey did dis in front of 'im whole village. No, de reason dey do these tings is dat de village was going to have a street dance dis weekend. A dance last year got rowdy. Dis Rasta is de deejay scheduled to operate de diesel generator and de sound system for dis weekend's dance. Beast **(police)** wanted to send a message to the town that say 'Better behave youself.' It also say 'Wi in charge' **(We're in charge)**. When people objected to de Rasta's rough treatment, beast **(the cops)** tell dem that Rasta youths are often troublesome. Dat dis one maybe stole something. Dey say you never know with Rastas. You just never know."

"I hope he wasn't a friend of yours."

"We know who his is," E.J. said without elaborating.

"Why did you say it was against a treaty?" Will asked Leva.

"The Kindah Treaty," Leva said.

Will looked puzzled. "Kindah?"

"In the old days the Maroons were escaped slaves living in the cockpit country," Leva explained. "They were determined to remain free. They waged war on the British for over 80 years in the 1600's and the 1700's. The British could not defeat the Maroon warriors but finally were able to get their leader, Cudjoe, to sign a blood treaty. The signing was under a giant mango tree called the Kindah Tree. The tree is still alive today. This treaty gave the Maroons their freedom and land to farm. It also gave them the right to make their own laws. They do not have to pay taxes. They punish their own criminals. Jamaican police have no jurisdiction over them. That's why I say what the police did to that boy violated the treaty."

"Once before, the British violated the treaty, and there was a second Maroon war," Leva said.

"That is fascinating," Will said. "The treaty almost makes the Maroons a nation within a nation. I don't mean to be nosy, but I thought you said the police sheared the boy's hair."

"They scalped 'im," E.J. said in a hushed voice.

"What?" Will said.

"Yes, dey scalped 'im like an Indian," E.J. said in a

A Jamaican Conspiracy

repugnant tone. "Dey shear off 'is dreadlocks with scissors. Dey brought scissors with dem special to shame 'im. No Rastaman no deal wi no dreads **(A Rasta is humiliated without his dreadlocks)**."

He shook his head and lapsed further into patois. "I-man who know I-self cyna deal with no deaders **(Without his dreadlocks he has no self-esteem)**." He began to mumble almost to himself a disjointed dialogue about Jah **(God)** lives in every man, and no man, who knows dat, can fear death. Will quickly lost the thread of the jumbled points the noticeably upset E.J. was trying to make.

"And you know this person?" Will asked.

Leva and E.J. looked at each other for an extended moment.

E.J. finally replied, "We have met, mon. 'Im country boy. It just terrible ting police do, dat all. Rasta canna walk free. Dey still under bondage."

"So unnecessary, so unnecessary. There may be trouble ahead," Leva sighed and said as she put the dirty dishes in the sink.

```
┌─────────────────────────────────────┐
│      WHEATLE'S VARIETY STORE        │
│   & ELECTRICAL SHOE REPAIRS SERVICE │
│           PHONE 973-6100            │
│      RED STRIPE AND DRAGON STOUT    │
│              AVAILABLE              │
└─────────────────────────────────────┘
```

CHAPTER 8

"Here's an interesting story in *The Gleaner*. Hollywood ought to remake *Mr. Smith Goes To Washington* except this time it should be called *Mr. Smith Goes to Jail*," Will announced as Henry and Betsy drank their morning beverages as they prepared to leave for Ocho Rios.

"What in the world are you talking about?" Betsy asked.

"A Jamaican Ponzi scheme. One David Smith, a Jamaican citizen, who now lives on Grand Cayman. Authorities are attempting to extradite him. He's being accused of wire fraud, money laundering, and conspiracy to launder money," Will said.

"How did he supposedly do that?' Henry asked as he sipped his tea.

"By ostensibly defrauding 6,000 investors out of roughly $220 million. Mostly Floridians with a fund called Olint. Promised investors 10% a month with a foreign currency trading system he claimed he perfected. You know the old saying about if something seems too good to be true ... ," Will said.

A Jamaican Conspiracy

"And that there are no free lunches," Betsy said. "My grandmother used to say 'Never give a devil a ride; he'll want to drive'."

"In Jamaica we say 'What sweet nanny goat a go run him belly'," Henry said.

"Which means," Betsy asked.

"It means 'the things that seem good to you now, can hurt you later', Henry said.

"Yes, they can," Betsy said. "I almost forgot to mention that today the bank is sponsoring a seminar on fraud. Detective Carl Berry of the Organised Unit of the Jamaican Constabulary Force will talk about consumer fraud and Jerry Smith, the assistant to Jamaica's Contractor General, will speak about government corruption."

"Surely Jerry Smith's not related to the David Smith, the felon," Will said. "Or Warren Smith, the president of NCB in Ocho Rios. The last name must be a coincidence."

"With a common name like Smith, you never know," Henry said. "That may be where Jerry Smith learned his politricks **(dirty politics)**."

"The article did say that David Smith was a major contributor to the Jamaica Labour Party," Will said.

~ ~ ~

Betsy arrived at her office before nine. Letha was deep in thought on her computer. Betsy almost felt guilty as she took a list of documents out to Letha's desk for Letha to locate in the bank's files until she noticed that what had Letha mesmerized was combing Google, looking at recipes.

"Would you have these documents on my desk when I get out of this seminar?" Betsy asked.

"We're having a fundraiser at the church," an oblivious Letha said. "I'm supposed to cook something special for them to sell. Do you think I should do pineapple upside-down cake or make some mango chutney?"

"I'm sure you'll make the right decision. Please have those documents on my desk when I get back."

"No problem, ma'am."

Betsy's seminar started promptly at 10 a.m. The first segment was conducted by Detective Carl Berry. He showed the employees a fake credit card that had been presented at NCB and then seized by police. He told them that corporate earnings lost to fraud had been J$665 million for the first half of the current year alone, which, bad as it sounded, was an improvement over the previous year's figure of over J$3 billion. He boasted that 75% of their cases had been "cleared up." When asked to define "cleared up," he admitted that it meant cases closed and that many cases had not been prosecuted.

Betsy asked Berry to define where the problem was most widely manifested. He became vague and said only that those affected were "right across the board, from shopkeepers to large companies." He encouraged them to educate their merchant customers on how to become more vigilant and make credit card users prove their card's legitimacy by demanding picture IDs and paying more attention to card security features.

The next speaker was Jerry Smith from the Contractor General's (OCG) office. The talk was not the instructional one Betsy expected to hear. What she heard instead was a political speech defending and justifying OCG shortcomings. Smith alluded to the failure of the state to entrench in the Jamaican constitution buffers to protect the OCG from political interference, the constitution's failure to give the OCG the power to halt a government contracting process that was exhibiting signs of corruption or irregularity, and its failure to increase the sanctions for criminal offenses.

"I filed a formal written report with a joint select committee of Parliament," he reported, "detailing that of the roughly 40 criminal referrals sent by our office to the director of public prosecutions (DPP) over the preceding three years, not one has been brought to court. Over the last eleven years we have referred over 18,000 cases to the DPP. They only acted upon 512 of these matters."

He continued to rail about how the OCG had not fallen short of the mark, the state had. He went on to describe the three anti-corruption offenses specified in Jamaican law and the penalties offenders were subject to.

"Sanctions have remained for the last 28 years at the inexplicable low level. A fine cannot exceed J$5,000, and imprisonment for a conviction cannot exceed 12 months. One thousand Jamaican dollars at current rates of exchange is equivalent to less than US$12. This is roughly the price of four loaves of bread in Jamaica. Obviously, this has made a total mockery the administration's commitment to genuinely and seriously fighting corruption.

"Should the Jamaican State fail to act accordingly, we will all be doomed; it is an incontrovertible fact that a criminal will always proceed with his criminal conduct if the risk-benefit analysis of the situation always suggests to him that it will be beneficial for him to do so.

"Grave harm is being caused, and will continue to be caused, to Jamaica by the failure of successive administrations to act decisively, proactively and aggressively to do what is right by Jamaica, versus doing that which is right by the measuring stick of political expedience.

"My door is open to those who can help my efforts."

When he finished his speech, Betsy made a beeline to the front to meet Smith. She briefly explained her role with the bank and requested an appointment. He seemed genuinely interested in pursuing the conversation, gave her his card and told her to call his secretary to set up a time.

"Your mission and mine are parallel. We can be an asset to each other," he said.

Just as she started to answer, Betsy heard a familiar voice.

"Sir, I am Bob Blackmon, national treasure Paul Bogle's direct descendant, but most importantly, a weighty person in my own right and indispensable resource to NCB's management team because of my understanding and mastery of the subtle nuances of St. Ann Parish's power structure, and how to make it work to one's advantage," BB blustered without taking a breath, shaking Smith's hand, pumping his arm like he would shake it out of its socket.

Blackmon was so wrapped up in himself and his own agenda that he was totally oblivious to the fact that his barging in was interrupting Betsy's conversation. She might as well as been an invisible duppy. Betsy opened her mouth to speak, but Blackmon continued his boast before she could utter her first word.

"Marvelous speech, sir! Marvelous speech! You hit the nails right on the head. Our president and your uncle, Warren Smith, has been detained and cannot accompany you to lunch, so I will be his stand-in. I welcome the opportunity to give you the benefits of some of my ideas on the issues you raised today and to introduce you to other parallel concepts."

"I did not realize he had intended to take me to lunch," Jerry Smith said.

"This may be your lucky day. As I am sure a man of your position and stature knows, the value of fresh input cannot be calculated in dollars. I remember what my blessed grandma used to say. 'The stone de builder refuse will be de head corner stone **(Ideas we spurn we eventually embrace)**."

As Betsy was still digesting what had just occurred, Blackmon put his arm around Smith's shoulders and led him toward the nearest door, leaving her to seethe.

Weighty! Indispensable resource! Subtle! I'd like to subtly weight you down and drop you down a well.

When Betsy returned to her office, the documents she had asked Letha to pull from the files were not on her desk. Letha was again on her computer looking at recipes. Despite her foul humor, Betsy held her tongue and politely asked Letha about them.

"It has been an especially busy morning since you have been gone. I'm on my lunch hour right now," Letha replied. "I'll get them for you this afternoon. What would you think if I made pickled calabash or maybe my secret recipe for pickled pepper sauce for the church social?"

"I'm sure either would be fine," Betsy said. "Please locate those documents for me as soon as possible."

"No problem, ma'am. I'll take care of it as soon as lunch is over."

Betsy tried on multiple occasions that afternoon to call Jerry Smith's secretary. All she got was an answering machine.

BB strolled back in the bank about mid afternoon, picking his teeth contentedly. Betsy invited him into her office.

"Do you realize that I was having an important conversation with Jerry Smith, and you interrupted?"

"I am so sorry. I really am. I had no idea. I guess I just have trouble containing my enthusiasm sometimes."

"You will enhance your value to the bank if you learn to both control your emotions and actions and become more aware of what is going on around you."

"I definitely will take your suggestions under

advisement. Thank you for the sound advice. It is always welcome coming from a senior executive of your long standing."

Now I'm senior!

As soon as Blackmon left, Betsy asked Letha for the files again.

"Soon come," Letha said. "I do have to locate them first. You know, our filing system is rather antiquated. What would you think if I fixed some stewed cashews for the church social?"

Betsy seethed again. This was definitely turning into a two-martini day.

She gritted her teeth and said, "Just get them." Betsy restrained herself from ending the sentence with "damned files."

Her blood pressure rose again when she overheard Letha whisper to another secretary, "Mi boss fas become de white witch of Rose Hall **(My boss is fast becoming the white witch of Rose Hall)**."

At day's end Letha was still trying to locate the missing files.

Soon come! The following morning when Betsy arrived, an incomplete stack of files was finally on her desk along with some coconut macaroons.

Betsy opened the file for the Kingston and St. Andrew Corporation, identified as simply KSAC in most places. In examining the file she encountered a carbon copy of a memo written by Jerry Smith to his superior Dr. Damien Rosser, Contractor General of the OCG.

My staff is instigating a preliminary investigation into an NCC registration application for a subcontractor representing the Kinston and St. Andrew Corporation Road Division. As you are aware, KSAC is a primary contractor for the Highway 2000 project. We will also be conducting a routine examination of the 114 contracts thus far awarded to KSAC for any procurement procedural irregularities. The majority of these contracts involve gully and drain cleaning.

We will advise your office if our investigation uncovers facts needing a more in depth analysis.

This really made Betsy want to talk to Jerry Smith again, but he continued to be elusive. Over the next week she never got through to him, but no one at the OCG seemed to consider it a priority to return her left messages.

Did I misread Smith's enthusiasm at the bank seminar? ... Do I not understand Jamaican protocol? ... He obviously wanted to keep the bank informed about KSAC ... He could have kept the investigation private within the OCG ... Or are there other factors at work that I am unaware of ... Or is my assignment in Jamaica destined to teach me a new level of patience ... Soon come?

```
            JUANITA'S

   BEAUTY       BAIL         BRIDAL
   SALON      BONDING       BOUTIQUE


  MAKE UP   *24 HR SERVICE  WEDDING EQUIPMENT
    SPA      876 973-9717    *TUXEDO RENTAL
  COLOGNE                    *FORMAL DRESSES
 HEALTH SUPPLIES           FLORAL ARRANGEMENTS
```

CHAPTER 9

The alleged police brutality atrocity described by Leva and E.J. bothered Will and made him want to know more. He was aware of the fragile and tenuous relationship the Rastas enjoyed with much of the general population. Even though Jamaica was where the Rastafarian religion had begun, Rastas were often not made welcome there. Instead, they were often made to feel like second-class citizens and denied equal treatment in terms of hiring, in the jobs open to them, and the fact that their religion has never been legally recognized. This lack of recognition prohibited them from performing legal marriages, and their houses of worship did not have the same tax-status as those of other religions. Rastas claim that they are both wrongly blamed for much of Jamaica's crime rate and looked down upon for their use of marijuana, a practice they say brings them closer to God.

Most are not employed in Jamaica's formal sector.

A fact that rankles many Rastas is that Jamaica frequently uses their image and faith as a tourist attraction. While their Rasta image may not be welcome, that same image is a huge moneymaker for the entire country. It is almost like Jamaica wants to have them around without actually having to have them around.

Will arose early before breakfast and went on Google to see if he could find a more detailed report of the beating incident. There was absolutely nothing on the Internet concerning the affair. He read his copy of *The Gleaner* to see if they had covered it. Once again – nothing. He had looked for several days and had finally begun to wonder if the episode had actually occurred at all or if it was merely unreliable gossip. He also had begun to wonder if the whole thing was possibly being simply covered up.

Leva prepared a combination American and Jamaican breakfast for them that morning - pancakes, bacon, and fried plantains. Before they were finished, Henry arrived to take Betsy into Ocho Rios. After they left, Will and Leva discussed the Rastafarian dilemma as she washed dishes.

"I'm not a Rasta, but the way they are treated is not right," Leva said. "Rastas are treated differently because of religion. You wouldn't deny a Muslim a job because they follow Islam. There would be uproar. Just because the passive Rastas don't blow something up because matters don't go their way, doesn't mean Rastas should be taken for granted and treated differently from any other religion. Most people think Rastas just smoke ganja, have dreadlocks, and wear Rasta colors. Because of this, people think they don't deserve the same respect as other religions. Every religion has a different view. Just because Rastas believe in something different and are free thinkers, the mainstream makes jokes out of them. I think Jamaica should have equal rights for all religions, not just the main ones."

NOTICE
**A THIEF LIFE IS SHORT
WHEN THIS PLACE IS
CLOSE AT NIGHT PLEASE LEAVE
THE SPOT DON'T DISTRUVE ME
SAVE YOUR SELF FROM EMBRESSMEN
ITS A WARNING   J. TUMEY**

CHAPTER 10

Within days of getting settled into her new job Betsy received an unexpected invitation from Merle Dunster, the Parish Councillor of St. Ann Parrish. He offered to take her with him to attend the upcoming ceremony honoring the 40th anniversary of rafting on the Martha Brae River in Trelawny Parish. Betsy asked him if Jerry Smith would be in attendance. Dunster responded, "Most certainly. He is one of the dignitaries who has committed to be present for the historic event."

"That sounds wonderful," Betsy said. "I spoke to him briefly at a bank seminar, and I have been trying to set up an appointment with him ever since to discuss some matters."

"Maybe this will be your opportunity. Wear comfortable clothing that you don't mind getting wet - Jamaica casual chic," Dunster said. "We'll be riding in a raft procession. We'll take my car to the event."

"Sounds like fun," Betsy said. "Too bad my husband can't join me for the festivities."

A Jamaican Conspiracy

Jamaican river rafts are approximately thirty feet in length and constructed from bamboo. The rafts were originally used to ferry bananas to the coast. Local legend says that Errol Flynn washed up in Jamaica on his yacht during a storm. He saw the rafts and thought it would be a kick to raft the Rio Grande River near Port Antonio. He added seats and trained the locals to pole, gondola style for his film-star friends along the jungle-fringed river. Soon a tourist industry was born. Because of the popularity of rafting on the Rio Grande, a shorter but similar trip was designed on the Martha Brae River near Falmouth.

As he had promised, Dunster was in Betsy's office promptly at ten on Tuesday to take her to the Martha Brae ceremony. Betsy wore a tropical shirt, shorts and flip-flops.

"Perfect attire for the occasion," Dunster said.

They were soon in Dunster's black Lexus LX450 SUV on Highway A1 headed west around the semi-circular bay towards Discovery Bay. The trip to the Martha Brae River would be approximately forty miles. The garrulous Dunster was eager to talk about the area. He explained that Ocho Rios meant eight rivers and explained how this part of the coast was blessed with streams and waterfalls. He darted in and around traffic in typical Jamaican fashion, seemingly oblivious to it, as he related to Betsy fact after fact about the local region. They passed the post office and the market and then the Reynolds Bauxite Pier on their way towards Dunn's River Falls.

Dunster was proud of the fact that Jamaicans call St. Ann the Garden Parish. He told her no other parish could make that claim. He then informed her that most Jamaicans are mostly descended from the Akan-Ashanti people of Ghana and the Ibo people of Nigeria. This is where the long tradition of woodcarving originated. He explained that there was a confusing profusion of work of uneven quality but that her discerning eye would soon be able to distinguish quality art from inferior art. They saw a profusion of wayside stalls that lined the road and little shops that sold Jamaican patties, curried goat, jerk pork and chicken, and sweet potato pone.

Dunster informed Betsy about St. Ann's two favorite sons, their "Black Moses", Marcus Garvey, and reggae superstar, Bob Marley, whose music had taken the world by storm.

"Marley is Jamaica's Elvis Presley," he said. He then proudly told Betsy about Garvey's belief in the capacity of the black man to create and achieve on his own terms. Both Garvey and Marley were poor St. Ann boys who had started out with nothing more than God-given natural gifts.

He stopped briefly and bought them gizadas and a Ting from a bony elderly woman who seemed as finely chiseled as an old pimento tree. He explained to Betsy that gizadas were flour shells filled with sweetened grated coconut. Betsy told the woman they were delicious and mentioned how much she was enjoying St. Ann Parish.

The woman replied quietly, "Pretty, pretty for true. Thank Massa God. I live here when I was a little child and I never get tired of this. You know, I have no money, but all this beauty belong to me, to me and Massa God. Pretty for true."

They thanked the old woman and Dunster was soon tailgating a bus, honking his horn as he waited for his opportunity to dart out and pass it. Betsy read a roadside safety sign that said "Undertakers love overtakers" as they zipped by it. Betsy just held on and said nothing.

They arrived at the small village of Falmouth, and turned to go the three miles to the Martha Brae River, soon arriving in the embarkation area known as "Rafter's

Village." It encompassed six acres of beautifully manicured lawns situated on a natural horseshoe island. Betsy and Will had visited the Martha Brae before. She could see a familiar recreational area which included picnic grounds, a bar, souvenir shops, a swimming pool, and modern restrooms.

By the time they arrived, the village was already buzzing as people waited for the ceremonies to begin. Betsy noticed a limo in the parking lot and wondered who had been transported to the festivities in such a regal manner. A makeshift stage had been set up with chairs. It was already full of dignitaries, some already sitting, waiting to begin. Some were visiting with other notables.

A mento band with former Jolly Boys member Donald Davidson was performing. Betsy smiled as she heard a modern song she recognized, Amy Winehouse's *Rebab*. Davidson was a white-bearded elderly black man who had dressed for the festive occasion in traditional Jamaican garb. Palm fronds were tied from his waist. Over his bright yellow collared shirt he wore a necklace made from sea oak leaves and ackee. A headdress of flowers surrounded his shaggy hair. An open ten-dollar bill was tucked under his acoustic guitar strings on the headstock by the tuners.

Dunster led Betsy over to Assistant Contractor General Smith. They briefly made small talk, and then Smith apologized for being so difficult to contact. He quietly reiterated his intentions to follow up with her further as soon as possible to discuss the concerns he had expressed in a memo about the Highway 2000 project. As Smith was about to comment further, he was distracted by someone else vying for his attention. Betsy immediately recognized the loud familiar voice.

"Councillor Smith, banker Bob Blackmon ... It is great to see you once again. A spectacular day for a commemoration if I do say so myself. If the occasion were any more spectacular, I just don't think my system could stand the stimulation. Yes indeed, things are fine as frog's hair."

Betsy winced. *The son of a bitch is doing it to me again.* Blackmon began to rattle incessantly about one inane matter after another, so wrapped up in what he had to say, he was completely oblivious to Betsy's presence behind Smith.

As Betsy started to open her mouth, Blackmon turned away suddenly, shaking the hand of another nearby person as he grabbed Smith's elbow and turned him away from Betsy, "Let me introduce you to Jerry Smith, sure to be the next Contractor General of the Office of Contractor General. He is a future leader and man of destiny."

Betsy again started to speak only to be bushwhacked by the unmindful, self-absorbed Blackmon.

"Did you see that football game yesterday?" Blackmon blustered to a stranger. "I'll remember that goalie's save at the end for the rest of my life. My Mongooses have never played better ... a definite day for a coldbeer or two, a *Redstripe* preferably." He gave the person he was addressing a booming chortle followed by a knuckle tap.

Déjà fucking vu. Betsy surrendered for the moment. *My time will come. Surely BB won't be present every time I see this guy.* She turned and noticed a distinguished lanky, bald, black man in an expensive suit. Other dignitaries seemed especially deferential to him.

"That's Sir Kenneth O. Hall," Dunster whispered to her. "He's the Governor-General of Jamaica. He represents Queen Elizabeth in Jamaica."

He then briefly explained to Betsy that although an independent member of the British Commonwealth of

A Jamaican Conspiracy

Nations, the British monarch was still the official chief of state. The queen's power was exercised by the governor-general whom she appointed on the recommendation of the prime minister. The governor-general then performed ceremonial duties, made appointments to public office, assented to bills before they could become law, wielded the prerogative of judicial pardons, and summoned and adjourned parliament. In most matters, the governor-general acted only on the advice of the prime minister.

The ceremony began with the playing of the Jamaican national anthem, followed by a brief prayer. The councillor of Trelawny then introduced the guest of honor, Sir Kenneth O. Hall. He talked of the wonderful tradition of Jamaican river rafting. He mentioned a partial list of celebrities who had rafted the Martha Brae – Chuck Norris, Dionne Warwick, Patrick Ewing, Kenny Rodgers, and Johnny Cash. He described the natural phenomenon of the Luminous Lagoon of Glistening Waters where the river meets the Caribbean, home to the world-famous rare glowing microbes.

Sir Kenneth then recounted the familiar legend of Martha Brae.

"The legend tells of Martha Brae, an old Arawak witch, who lived on the bank of the River Matibereon," he said. "Having heard tales of the Arawak gold, Spanish treasure hunters captured the witch to lead them to the treasure. Pretending to comply, she led them into a cave and then suddenly disappeared. Frightened, the Spaniards ran out of the cave, but the river engulfed them. The witch then changed the course of the river forever."

The governor-general's comments were greeted with muted, polite applause. Jamaicans never tired of hearing stories about how their ancestors had bested the British and Spanish.

After the ceremony, guests were escorted from the concrete pier to 85 waiting bamboo rafts. The captains then took their guests on the three-mile journey down the river. Dunster and Betsy were among the last people to be boarded on a raft. Captain Oscar, their captain, was an affable shorthaired Rastafarian who wore an old red, yellow and green tie-dyed T-shirt and a knit cap. He was a weathered dark-skinned, middle-aged Jamaican. He was barefoot, smoking a cigar. His toothy grin was infectious. He immediately struck up a conversation with Dunster, mistakenly assuming Betsy and Dunster to be a couple.

"I-ney, Praise Jah **(Welcome, praise the lord)**," he said. "Mi Cap'n Oscar **(I'm Captain Oscar)**."

Betsy smiled and said hello.

"Is ju and ju ooman ready areddi, bredda **(Are you and your woman ready to depart?)**?" said Captain Oscar, grinning knowingly at Dunster. He held up his closed hand to greet Dunster fist to fist.

"Fi no me ooman **(She's not my woman)**," Dunster said quietly. "Fi no wid mi **(We don't live together.)**."

"Mi pologies **(My apologies)**," said Captain Oscar. "Respeck **(Respect)**."

"Fi come from foreign **(She's a foreigner.)**," Dunster said.

Captain Oscar looked embarrassed at his error.

He said quickly, "Ju jus cease and sekkle **(You just stop and relax)**. Cap'n Oscar tek care ju. Ju see sumting ju want, mi take mashait and cut it fo ju. **(Captain Oscar will take care of you. If you see something you want, I'll take my machete and cut it for you.)**"

With that misunderstanding cleared up, Captain Oscar began to pole them down the river. There was a procession of rafts around them as they wound their way

A Jamaican Conspiracy

down the scenic river. Betsy could hear each captain regal his VIP guests with idle chatter.

They caught up with Assistant Contractor General Smith's raft when it stopped to buy a Red Stripe beer from a young higgler on the bank. Smith's raft had gotten ahead of them again when another young higgler swam out to Betsy's raft to attempt to sell her a miniature duplicate of the bamboo raft she was on. Captain Oscar offered to carve commemorative calabash gourds as a souvenir of the occasion. He showed them one he had started.

Betsy and Merle Dunster saw Tarzan's swing ahead of them. Tarzan's swing is a rope that rafters use to swing from the bank over the water before releasing themselves for a refreshing plunge in the cool eight-foot waters of the Martha Brae. Jerry Smith's raft had stopped at Tarzan's swing and the riders began taking turns plunging into the water.

Smith's turn to try his luck on the rope arrived. As he swung out on the rope, Betsy heard the single sharp loud crack of a rifle. Assistant Contractor General Smith dropped from the rope like a stone into the water. The water immediately turned crimson around him as if he had been devoured instead by a gator or barracuda. He floated to the surface with no movement, face down. He was dead before he ever hit the water. People on his raft and in the water screamed. His captain dove into the water for safety. The birds on the bank became completely silent except for the swooshing of wings. There was no second shot. Captain Oscar immediately poled Dunster and Betsy into the nearest bank and told them excitedly to take cover. They quickly scrambled to get ashore.

Within minutes the rafters were surrounded by security officers. One asked Betsy the direction the shot had come from. She pointed to the bank across from them. Policemen swarmed that bank. There was no sign of the gunman. He had vanished. He might as well have been a duppy evaporating into thin air like Casper the ghost. The only sign of his presence was the dead man floating in the water with the bullet in his head. The only evidence that remained was Betsy's missing multi-colored briefcase. It was floating in the shallow water as a gruesome reminder of the murder. Betsy would probably never know exactly what Jerry Smith had had on his mind.

For once the blustering Blackmon was right, Betsy thought. *Jerry Smith had most definitely been a man of destiny.*

> DEPOSE
>
> HERE NOT ON THE STREET
> HELP KEEP YOUR TOWN
> CLEAN

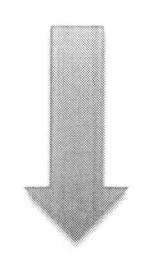

CHAPTER 11

"That's my stolen briefcase," Betsy screamed to the young policeman nearest her.

The policeman gave a puzzled look.

"That briefcase belongs to me," Betsy repeated. "It was stolen."

The young cop looked unsure as to what to do next.

Dunster spoke up. "My name is Merle Dunster, Councillor for St. Ann Parish. May I speak to your superior?"

The officer-in-charge came over. He recognized Dunster immediately and acted eager to listen. Betsy explained how her briefcase had been stolen from National Commercial Bank in Ocho Rios. Betsy told him the multi-colored leather briefcase had been presented to her by her friends from the lower Keys as a going-away present before she and Will left for Jamaica. She asked if she might be allowed to open it and prove her assertion. The officer assented.

When Betsy snapped the locks open on the briefcase, she saw immediately that the identification card in the briefcase was still in its plastic covered pocket. Instead of her belongings, however, a carved mahogany skull eerily stared back at her. The skull was about four and a half inches long and two and-a-half-inches wide and two and a half inches high. It had been carved from a single piece of wood. It was highly polished, and the wood had a dark rich mahogany stain. It seemed anatomically correct. The skull had elongated indentions at the side temples and deep indentions underneath the jaw at the base of the skull. She could easily hold it with one hand. There was a triangle symbol and slight ledge at the base of its triangular nose cavity. Its vacant highly-polished eyes pierced hers. The mandibles were tightly clenched and the rows of perfect teeth almost seemed to grin malevolently at her. While the skull was beautiful and well carved, at the same time, it was a creepy repugnant symbol of death.

Betsy picked the skull up and examined it. The only blemish in the otherwise perfect carving was a hole in the skull. When she looked closer, she could see a bullet in the hole. She was so surprised by this, she dropped the skull. It rolled back into her briefcase settling upright and gave her another evil, almost knowing glare.

A shaken Dunster picked the skull up, examined it, handed it quickly to the cop, shuddered, and incoherently mumbled something to himself that sounded like "that could have been me." He began to sweat profusely.

Betsy asked him to repeat what he had said. He replied that it was nothing important.

Dunster mumbled "Coke" and sat on a nearby bench.

"I think he wants a Coke," Betsy told Captain Oscar and gave the young policeman some money to buy one at the concession stand.

"Do you think this is some dark religious symbol?"

"Possibly," said the cop.

"May I ask where Assistant Contractor General Smith

was shot?" she asked the cop.

"He was killed with a perfect head shot. Whoever the murderer is, he's a good marksman," the cop replied. "The bullet entered Smith's skull very close to where the bullet is in this carving. We would like to keep both your case and its contents for the time being. We will return them to you forthwith."

Betsy excused herself and called Will on her cell phone.

"We've had a death here at the Martha Brae," she began.

"I've been to seminars like that," Will said jokingly. "Who died — the speaker or the audience? You know Georgie Jessel used to say that the human brain starts working the moment a person is born and never stops until he stands up to speak in public, and you know what Mark Twain said ... "

"No, silly, I'm deadly serious. This is *no* joke," Betsy said. She then gave Will a brief description of what had just occurred. He became concerned and offered to drive to the Martha Brae. She told him she was mostly unnerved, and his coming was unnecessary since she was fine. She told him that as soon as they were dismissed, she and Dunster would leave the Martha Brae and return to the bank. She promised to check in with him when they got back.

It wasn't long until they were dismissed. Despite her efforts to put the incident out of her mind, Betsy continued to visualize Smith's body, surrounded by a pink haze of seeping blood, floating in the river.

And how had my new briefcase gotten there? And why? Why the creepy mahogany skull with a bullet through its wooden brain? What was the message being sent? What had Smith wanted to tell me?

Dunster drove more carefully than usual on the

return trip. A truck backfired. Betsy jumped nervously. A car had a flat. She encouraged Dunster to keep going. She realized she must be more upset than she thought. Dunster was silent for the whole return trip as well. No more Chatty Cathy tales about Jamaica's culture and history. He seemed preoccupied with the events which had just occurred. She decided that Dunster must have been more than a passing acquaintance of Smith's.

When they arrived at the bank, Dunster immediately went into President Smith's office and briefed him on the day's events behind closed doors. President Smith seemed also to be visibly shaken and unduly upset when he and Dunster emerged again. Smith told his secretary to cancel his appointments, hold his phone calls, and then retreated into his office for the rest of the day. Betsy wondered if he weren't overreacting.

Everyone in the bank was already gossiping about Smith's killing. As promised, Betsy called Will to tell him that they had now safely returned to the bank.

"I know I sound like a broken record, and I know Smith is a common name," Will asked, "but do you think President Smith was unduly upset because he might be some relation to Jerry Smith."

"He sure didn't say anything about it," Betsy said.

As Letha was trying to pick Betsy's brain about what she had seen at the Martha Brae, Betsy's phone rang. She answered it, thinking it was Will calling back. The voice on the other end was obviously Jamaican however.

"I am called Cudjoe," the caller began. "Today's event was only a warning."

"A warning of what?" a shocked Betsy asked.

"Of what happens to people who involve themselves uninvited into other people's affairs. If forced to, my colleagues and I are capable of making future statements in equally creative ways."

"I don't understand."

"There is nothing to understand. Your job is simply to allow the road project to advance unimpeded by unwarranted complications. That is our only demand, but unlike our ancestors, we will not negotiate. You do not want us as your enemy."

"Why are you calling me? I am a foreigner who has only been in Jamaica for a short time and is simply trying to do her job." Betsy said. "I am not political."

"I will repeat myself. You have a job, and I have a mission. Your job is to allow a project for the good of the Jamaican people to proceed with as little controversy as possible. My mission is to make sure that this happens. The party in power for the last eighteen years has significantly aggravated our fiscal difficulties and left the problems of injustice and inequality largely undisturbed as it has focused solely on winning elections and feathering its own nest. Those days are now over."

"If I don't do my job, the bank will simply bring in someone else who will," Betsy said.

"We will deal with that if the need arises," Cudjoe said. "In the meantime, we are dealing with you, and you have a moral responsibility to the people of Jamaica."

With no warning, the phone went dead. Betsy just sat and stared at her dead receiver.

What have I gotten myself into the middle of?

Dunster walked back in Betsy's office. Deep in thought, she didn't notice him at first but finally glanced up at him.

"What is wrong?" he asked. "You look upset."

Betsy relayed her strange conversation with Cudjoe.

"Ah!" he said. "Now I understand. It is as I suspected. Smith's killing was politically motivated. Not surprising, not surprising. We have many radical factions in Jamaica."

A Jamaican Conspiracy

"Like?"

"Oh, possibly the National Democratic Movement or the New Nation Coalition."

"Wonderful," Betsy said and shook her head. "With me being the monkey in the middle."

At that moment Henry poked his head in the door.

"Ready to go home?" he asked innocently. "Did you enjoy your adventure on the Martha Brae?"

"I'll tell you about it on the way home," Betsy said. Henry looked puzzled.

"Please call Leva and tell her this is definitely a two-martini day."

Fare deal shop

CHAPTER 12

By the time Henry picked Betsy up to take her home, the word of Jerry Smith's death had circulated all over the island. Betsy filled Henry in on what she knew on the way back to Sundance.

When Betsy and Henry arrived, Leva had a pitcher of mango daiquiris made from Sundance's yard mangos mixed for them. As usual she had sent E.J. to the store for ice. Henry's wife, Rose, had brought some goodies by the house. Betsy repeated the day's events in more detail for Will's benefit as they enjoyed a refreshing cocktail. They insisted Henry and Rose stay and join them. Rose had brought a platter of a Jamaican treat called stamp-and-go, prepared using her mother's family recipe. She explained how she had soaked the codfish in water overnight and then poured boiling water over it before adding flour, onions and her mother's secret proportions of various peppers and spices. It was then rolled into hush puppy-shaped patties and fried. Leva agreed that this stamp-and-go was indeed delicious and tried to get Rose to be more specific. Rose was polite but just evasive enough to protect her family secret.

Will was curious and asked where the colorful name stamp-and-go came from.

Henry laughed and replied, "It may be colorful to you,

A Jamaican Conspiracy

but it's very logical to us. Jamaicans love to snack on it during bus trips around the island. These treats are sold from roadside stands. A bus rider can jump down onto the dirt road, then buy and swallow one of these patties, stamp the dust off his feet, and then hop back aboard before the bus pulls away. I like mine with a tomato-scotch bonnet sauce like the one Rose made today."

"Dunster thinks Smith's assassination was politically motivated," Betsy said.

"The Jamaican political scene is not for the faint at heart," Henry said. "Let me give you some insight."

"Please do," Betsy said.

"Post-independence Jamaican politics has largely been a struggle between two parties – the People's National Party, which we call the PNP, and the Jamaica Labour Party, known as the JLP. There are a number of minor parties, but the PNP and the JLP are the only ones with a significant presence.

"The PNP is a social-democratic party closely affiliated with the National Worker's Union. The PNP's leader is Prime Minister P.J. Pettis, whose political philosophy blends free-market economics with a large dose of government largess. They have been the ruling party in recent years. In 2002 they won their fourth consecutive election, making them the first party to accomplish this feat since the introduction of universal suffrage in 1944.

"Despite its name, the JLP is our conservative party with ties to the Bustamante Industrial Trade Union. Its leader is ex-prime minister Edward Seaga. He is an autocratic, cynical, bullying self-promoter instrumental in the creation of murder-ridden one party enclaves which we Jamaicans call garrisons. He is commonly accused of fostering the cocaine trade for political ends. He has also been indicted on charges of massive tax fraud."

"Wowee," Betsy commented. "It sounds like Jamaicans are caught between the devil and the deep blue sea."

"Sure does. You certainly know a lot about Jamaican politics," Will commented. "The way you describe both parties, I'm not sure which of the two evils is worse."

"We Jamaicans are a very political people," Rose replied. "In fact, we're sometimes too political.

"The one thing the PNP and the JLP have in common is a flair for corruption and pandering. That is what we Jamaicans call politricks. Graft is a way of life in Jamaican politics, cronyism is entrenched in the system, and the government's so-called social and economic support programs are a gravy train for contractors who have political connections. Leading officials are usually political appointees eager to cash in for themselves before the next change of government."

"And now Will and I are pawns in the middle of this den of tropical iniquity," Betsy said. "Wonderful! I'm beginning to appreciate Dunster's comments. I think I need another drink."

"You're going to make a drinking man out of me yet," Will said as he poured.

"This is no laughing matter. There may be a faction trying to create unrest to pressure the governor into calling a national election," Henry said.

"You must be careful, dear ones," Rose said. "Election time can be an especially explosive affair, though things have calmed down since the late '70's and early '80's when hundreds of Jamaicans lost their lives in partisan killings in garrison constituencies. These constituencies are zones where political parties maintain control through thuggery.

"Violent retribution and intimidation are still

A Jamaican Conspiracy

common. During the heady '70's, individual politicians developed strangleholds over low-income areas in Kingston by pandering to the neighborhood dons. These gang leaders would deliver blocks of votes in exchange for government contracts and other largess such as jobs and housing. Political discipline was and still is sometimes enforced with Armalites and M16 rifles."

"You're being pretty rough on them, Henry. The way you describe Jamaican politics reminds me somewhat of the Daley machine in Chicago," Will said.

"Or Huey P. Long in Louisiana," Betsy said. "Is there a significance to the name Cudjoe? To us, it's just one of the Florida Keys."

"Captain Cudjoe is one of our most important national heroes," E.J. said as he poured everyone a fresh round of drinks. "He and his sister, Nanny, were the two greatest Maroon leaders who ever lived. They forced the British to sign the Kindah Treaty."

"That's the second time I've heard the term Kindah Treaty mentioned," Betsy said.

"In the 1700's, the main leader of the runaway slaves who called themselves Maroons was a short, stout, illiterate, shoeless, underdressed man everyone called Captain Cudjoe. Despite his shortcomings and limited resources, he had endless energy and the motivation to remain a free man. He was also a very skillful tactical field commander and remarkable leader. Using sniper and ambush tactics, he and his men fought the British successfully for over fifty years. The British finally decided Cudjoe could not be defeated so they grudgingly negotiated the Kindah Treaty with him. That treaty is in effect and governs the Maroons to this day," Henry said.

He then told Betsy essentially the same facts about the Maroons Leva had told Will a few days earlier.

"So someone is using Cudjoe's name for some

nefarious purpose?" Betsy said.

"That appears to be the case," Henry said.

Suddenly with no warning, there was a crash out front. Gina and Samantha began barking ferociously. Lucy and Dexter streaked out the open front door and joined them, yapping loudly as they ran. E.J., grabbing a butcher knife as he ran, rushed out the front door to see why the dogs were barking. The rest of the party immediately joined them. The stone fish finials on top of the wall on each side of the gate were in smashed pieces on the ground. Gina leaped up the wall trying to get to the objects that had replaced them. Atop the wall, where until minutes ago the decorative fish had been mounted, two life-size transparent skulls now glowed in the dark in a ghostly manner. Each was luminescent and put off a bizarre white gleam as it radiated light. The eye sockets glowed. The teeth smiled ominously and seemed to be mocking them evil-mindedly.

Other than the two glass skulls, there was no sign of an intruder. Gina and Lucy were almost out of control. E.J. grabbed Gina while Will grabbed Lucy. Henry and Will walked closer. Their nocturnal prankster had left no additional hint as to his purpose.

"A duppy's been here," E.J. gasped. "I know he has."

"Duppy, my ass!" Will said disgustedly. "Those skulls are man-made. They're glass vodka bottles shaped like crystal skulls. I've seen them before. Our Keys neighbors, Mike and Kim Schulte, gave us one like that out of their bar. They were not placed there by a duppy. They were put there by someone with a sick sense of humor."

"Why are they glowing?" Betsy asked.

"They've got some kind of liquid in them. We can get it analyzed. Get them down, E.J.," Will said.

"Not me," E.J. exclaimed. "I'm going to have a hard enough time sleeping as it is."

A Jamaican Conspiracy

"If someone is trying to send us a signal and scare the crap out of us, it sure worked on you," said Will.

"Me too. More and more, I'm beginning to appreciate Dunster's concerns," Betsy said.

"And those concerns could be justified. Yes, they could be justified," Henry said.

At that moment, a white Toyota Chaser, with a cracked windshield, drove away into the dark.

"Do you think that possibly could have been Cudjoe?" Betsy asked.

Will shrugged and said, "I don't think it was our guardian angel."

"I agree," Betsy said. "Google says guardian angels aren't driving dinged white Toyota Chasers this year."

Henry just smiled.

> **THIS WEEK ONLY**
> **THIS STORE OFFERS**
> **50% OFF**
> **OR HALF PRICE**
> **WHICHEVER IS LESS**

CHAPTER 13

The following morning when Henry came to pick up Betsy, Leva quietly summoned him into the kitchen for a brief discussion. Will and Betsy could barely overhear them talking.

"Wa'ppon **(What's happening)**, Miss Leva," Henry said.

"Mi worry all de eveling Miss Betsy bout to getta a card played on she inna dutty politricks **(I worried all night about Miss Betsy getting dragged into dirty politics)**," Leva said.

"Dat wud be a fuckery **(That would certainly be an injustice)**," Henry said.

"So wha yu gwin do bout dat? Don yu le dem play a card on she **(Don't let them do her dirty)**," Leva scolded.

"Jesum piece, mi don no fo sure. Mi no wan su-su bout dat **(Christ, we don't know for sure. I don't want to just spread gossip about the incident)**,"

A Jamaican Conspiracy

Henry replied.

"Well, sum'ady got do sumpin **(Well, somebody has to do something)**," Leva said.

"Mebe mi need kyarri dem to Cuzzin Winter. 'Im a don gorgon. 'Im no wha need do **(Maybe I'll carry them to Cousin Winter. He is a very well respected person. He'll know what needs to be done)**," said Henry.

"Yu got nuttin to lass **(You've got nothing to lose)**."

"More time **(I'll talk to you later)**," Henry said.

"Aright **(OK)**. Galang wich yu **(Get along)**. God spare life **(we'll talk tomorrow)**."

~ ~ ~

Henry was unusually quiet and seemed preoccupied on the trip into Ocho Rios. A familiar higgler, the vegetable lady, held out her arm and hand, letting her wrist flop limply, Jamaican's traditional way of thumbing a ride. Henry didn't even slow down, seeming not to notice her.

Leva was quiet that day as well, refraining from singing her usual gospel songs. Will put on the stereo the Bellamy Brothers' *If I Said You Had A Beautiful Body Would You Hold It Against Me*, a song that normally made her smile. This song normally put her in a good mood, but she seemed to barely notice. Will surrendered and turned his attention to his office affairs.

He heard Leva complaining to E.J. about some maintenance issues at the villa. Before lunch he again overheard a phone conversation between Leva and another housekeeper about the many things in Sundance Villa that needed attention and her frustration over her failure to communicate these deficiencies to the villa's absentee owner who now lived abroad. The atmosphere seemed unusually strained, so different from the previous night before the intrusion of the glass skulls when everyone had been laughing, drinking mango daiquiris and eating stamp-and-go. How quickly the atmosphere had changed.

Henry's mood was still tentative when he picked up Betsy that afternoon. Betsy began to wonder if she had inadvertently done something to offend him. She was finally forthright with him as they approached the gate of the villa.

Henry reluctantly pulled up a stool to the kitchen island counter, and Leva made him and the Blacks some tea. She also put out some coconut macaroons she had made that day.

After a cookie and part of a cup of tea, he finally began to tentatively open up.

"I apologize if I have not seemed like myself today," he said to them. "We have all become very fond of and respect you. You are not American guests any longer but our Jam-Merican friends. We are afraid that there are political factions you do not understand who will likely cause you danger. We don't want to see that happen."

"We won't hesitate to involve the police if we're in danger," Betsy said.

"Don't put too much stock in the police," Henry said. "The average policeman is exemplary. They can be civil, courteous, and dedicated to upholding the law. Yet the force is sometimes beset with corruption, especially when politics are involved. Some branches of the police even have a reputation for execution style killings and other criminal misconduct."

"We heard a rumor of a Rasta who was humiliated and injured recently," Will said, "but I've found nothing in the news to confirm the incident."

"I'm not surprised. What happens and what is reported can sometimes be two different matters. Besides, in Jamaica, Rastas are a special situation," Henry said, "but what happens to Rastas can happen to everyday people as well."

Leva nodded in agreement.

"Your job, Miss Betsy, cannot help but involve you in high-level politics where the stakes are extremely high," Henry continued. "While members of Parliament are immune from arrest and protected against lawsuits arising from their duties, an official may lose his position or be forced to resign as a result of losing his seat in Parliament or the confidence of the prime minister. Also, any minister's success depends on more than his individual ability. They depend on both his power and prestige. There is a Jamaican saying, 'The higher the monkey climbs, the more him expose.' People will go to any lengths to protect themselves. You are going to find many conflicts of interest with you being caught as the monkey in the middle. Your job is not an enviable one."

"I appreciate your concerns for our welfare. I assume this conversation is leading to something other than a simple warning," Betsy said. "My job is what it is. I was sent here to protect my employer's interests."

"Yes, it is. I would like to introduce you to my cousin Colonel Ferron Winter," Henry said. "He is the Maroon Chief in Accompong Town. He is a wise and highly respected man. He can be a worthwhile ally or a dreaded adversary. *If* he will meet with you and deems you worthy of his council, he will be a valuable ally going forward. Colonel Winter is somewhat reclusive and makes it a point to stay out of Jamaica's limelight, but since he is family, I think I can convince him to have an initial meeting with you. If nothing else comes of it, the meeting will be a valuable learning experience and history lesson."

"Where is this Accompong?" Will asked.

"It is a village in the hills of St. Elizabeth Parish. It is one of two areas originally settled by runaway slaves because it was isolated enough to be safe from both the Spanish and the British. The village was named for Cudjoe and Nanny's brother, Accompong. Assuming Colonel Winter agrees to meet you, I, of course, must drive you there and introduce you. He would never meet with an outsider otherwise."

Will looked at Betsy. "What do we have to lose?"

"Excellent," Henry said. "I will get back to you as soon as possible. You will find Colonel Winter to be a warm and honorable man. I feel certain he will feel the same way about you. I would also like for him to examine the woodcarving found in your briefcase at the Martha Brae, Betsy. Would you attempt to recover it from the police?"

Betsy said she would try.

"So, I bid you a good evening until I see you in the morning," Henry said.

Leva walked Henry to the door. Will and Betsy could hear them talking.

"'Ow mi do **(How did I do?)**?" Henry asked.

"Yu mashit up **(You were a huge success)**," Leva replied. "Yu tole trut bout beast **(You told them the truth about the police)**."

"Everting will cook and curry wif Col. Winter **(It will be taken care of with Col. Winter)**," Henry said.

"Mi hope. Tekeere of the road **(I hope so. Be careful)**," Leva answered.

"'A new broom sweep clean, but an old broom know ever' corner.' Little more **(See you later)**," Henry said and climbed into his van to go home.

> PLEASE NO PISSING
> IT'S
> UNHEALTHY

CHAPTER 14

As he drank a cup of high-mountain coffee and waited for Leva to prepare breakfast, Will brought up the *Key West Citizen* on his laptop using his electronic subscription. Betsy finished putting on her makeup and joined him, pouring herself a cup as well.

"I can tell very little difference between the Baronhall Estate high-mountain coffee Leva buys and the Blue Mountain coffee that sells for twice as much," she said.

"Neither can I," Will agreed. "They are both delightfully delicious. Just think, we always have gourmet coffee available right off any grocery store shelf. Coffee fanatics elsewhere would give their eye teeth to be able to readily buy either one."

"Yeah, just like we get fresh gourmet orange and grapefruit juice on the Treasure Coast," Betsy said. "Sometimes we take our little luxuries for granted. You know, we truly have had a good life together wherever we have lived."

Will nodded his head. "Yes, we have, but mostly because we have each other."

Will glanced at his laptop and giggled. "Listen to this.

A Jamaican Conspiracy

You're not going to believe this Keys story."

Man Scams To Cook His Own Meal

Police say a Stock Island man took the Denny's restaurant chain slogan "America's diner is always open" too far, marching into the Key West Duval Street location announcing he was the new boss and then cooking himself dinner. According to Key West police, Sonny Summerland, a resident of Stock Island, walked into Denny's on Tuesday dressed in a maroon tie and black trench coat, carrying a briefcase. He strode into the manager's office, told her he was the new general manager, and then fixed himself a burger, fries, and a soda before police arrived. "This is why you don't dine and dash, kiddies," Summerland yelled out to diners as officers took him away, police said in a release. Police found a stun gun in a hip holster under his coat and crack pipes in his briefcase.

"I love Jamaica dearly," Betsy said, "but I still miss the Lower Keys."

"Same," Will said. "Don't fret. We'll be back soon."

"Now don't forget," Betsy said as Leva served them breakfast, "we're invited to Sean and Tuppance McIver's house tonight for a dinner party. They said it begins at seven."

"That's really nice of them to host this party to give us a chance to meet the people in the neighborhood," Will said. "Reminds me of when we first moved to Vero Beach. Jim and Nancy Large had a similar function to welcome us into the Castaway Cove family."

"Speaking of reminding, I was telling President Smith at NCB about the McIver's kind gesture. He launched into an amusing discourse on the concept of time."

"Time?"

"Yes, time. According to Smith, there *is* no time in Jamaica. He used this illustration. When guests are invited to arrive at seven or eight, they might not arrive until ten or eleven. Many locals don't even own a wristwatch, and most cannot tell you exact dates. He said he even once had a guest arrive the following evening, wondering if he was late. Another example he says is Jamaican television where broadcasting programs at approximate times with ten to fifteen minute delays is considered normal. As Jamaicans are fond of saying, 'Soon come.' It is not uncommon for a Jamaican to wait for days or even weeks to pass between 'soon come' and an actual event. According to Smith, when a Jamaican is waiting for someone who will 'soon come', it is wise to find a shady spot, then stretch out and be patient. Things left to do until tomorrow will become less important and will often never get done at all. In retrospect, we will find these things often didn't need doing at all."

"I guess that sounds like timely advice," Will said and smiled.

"I guess in Jamaica time waits for all men," Betsy retaliated.

"I guess it's safe to say that the old saying, 'Don't count every hour in the day, make every hour count' was not written by a Jamaican."

"Smith said Jamaica will soon teach me patience and faith as well as the delightful ability to relax and enjoy life while waiting. One day will move quietly into the next day, and then into weeks, without any apparent passage of time."

A Jamaican Conspiracy

"That way of thinking makes Keys-time seem break-neck by comparison. Having spent much of our lives at a hectic pace, we just may have a wee bit of adjustment ahead of us."

Just as they finished breakfast, they heard the familiar horn on Henry's van as he honked for E.J. to open the gate. After a few pleasantries, Henry and Betsy were off for the bank.

~ ~ ~

That evening Will and Betsy walked, fashionably 15 minutes late, over to the McIver's villa. It seemed like a polite time to arrive, but no one was there when they arrived except their hosts, Sean and Tuppance. They were immediately served cold rum drinks and the conversation began to flow easily as they sipped the evening's first cocktail. No other guests arrived for almost an hour, giving the Blacks a chance to become better acquainted with their hosts and to relax a bit. The verandah glowed pleasantly in the waning sunset light.

After a while, people began to drift in. Some walked down the street from neighboring houses. Those who did not live within easy walking distance arrived by car. The Blacks were introduced to people from all walks of life. They met expatriate British and Americans, Orientals, African Jamaicans, and Indians. There were businessmen, artists, doctors, teachers, and government workers. Everyone seemed to want to "hug-up" on Tuppance. Rum began to loosen people's tongues, including Will's and Betsy's.

Will found himself engaged in conversation with a Scotsman and an American expatriate. Will told them about how the stone fish finials by Sundance's gate had been destroyed by a vandal and then replaced by the glowing glass skull vodka bottles.

The Scotsman suggested a local tradesman who could

replace the finials with new ones. He offered to send the man over to Sundance to evaluate the job at hand. Will also told him that Sundance had other issues that were causing dissatisfaction with the house staff and how he was supporting Leva's attempts to convince the villa's owner to authorize the expenditure of the funds necessary to bring it up to snuff.

The American, who up to this point had been quietly listening, then offered his own advice.

"Before you begin renovating the villa," he said, "you must take the time to understand the Jamaican tradesman temperament. Otherwise, you will find yourself going insane. 'Soon come' is not just an expression. It is a national mindset.

"Let me describe a typical Jamaican work week on a day by day basis. Monday is spent recovering from the previous weekend and contemplating life's challenges. Tuesday is dominated by preparations for Wednesday which is the nationally accepted workday. On Wednesday you will see your tradesman hard at work noodling, inspecting, and then ciphering on his hands. Palms are Jamaica's legal pads. He will write entire columns of numbers on the palms of his hands which will be of little use because these numbers will soon be obliterated. This will cause him to write additional numbers on his hands. This may save paper but crucial information like phone numbers, names and other facts will inevitably soon be lost. Much conversation and urging will ensue about the proper positioning of things, leading to endless discussions about the ever-rising cost of building materials. A paid helper will then be sent to search for the essential missing components needed to complete the job. Hours will pass and the helper will finally return empty-handed telling both the contractor and customer that the vital pieces 'soon come.' By then the workday will be finished.

"Wednesday evening is spent with rum and friends celebrating another hard week's labors. Thursday is then spent preparing for the upcoming weekend. On Friday the party begins. Saturday is reserved for music and dancing. Protocol forbids them to think of tools and toil on a Saturday since it is a time to party and celebrate life. Sunday's pace becomes more mellow. It is the time to think of going to the beach or engaging in romance. The day culminates in a small Sunday night party. Monday requires resting and recovering from the weekend and once again sorting out life's issues. No problem, mon. There is plenty of time to prepare on Tuesday because Wednesday 'soon come.'"

The Scotsman agreed. "Bravo! I couldn't have stated it better myself."

At that moment Will heard a bell chime as Tuppance summoned her guests to their first course, bowls of steaming, delicious, golden pumpkin soup glistening in a sea of chicken broth. More rum was served, and conversations continued unabated. As tongues continued to loosen, politics became an increasingly popular and often heated topic of discussion.

A second bell summoned the guests to a huge table straining to hold a veritable Jamaican feast. There was roasted jerk chicken, red peas and rice, and boiled chocho next to a huge bowl of garlic-laden callaloo. This was next to a platter of fried fish. A plate of pickled scotch bonnet peppers had been prepared to kick a guest's taste buds up a notch. The enormous salad seemed to contain every known vegetable. This was beside a thin-cut string beans seasoned with butter and nutmeg. There were yams. Oxtail floated in a dark rich gravy. There was potato salad, beef that had been roasted in thyme, and fried plantains. Finally there were mounds of jerk pork ribs that had been barbequed over pimento wood and then doused with a hot pepper sauce. All the while, more rum was made available. Tuppance made a short speech welcoming Will and Betsy to the neighborhood, and then everyone dug in. Partiers made short work of first helpings, and second helpings were soon disappearing. Just when everyone swore he could not eat another bite, Tuppance unveiled fried bananas aflame with rum.

"I've never seen this much food, even at Thanksgiving," Betsy said as they walked home under the clear dark Jamaican sky. The stars were so bright they looked like they were holes in the floor of heaven. The Blacks paused to look at a very distinct big dipper.

"What'cha thinking about?" Will said.

"You, and about something I read a long time ago," Betsy said. "If people sat outside and looked at the stars every night, they'd probably live a lot differently."

"My grandmother used to tell me about the starving children in China," Will said. "They certainly wouldn't be starving in Jamaica."

"I may not eat again for a week," Betsy said.

"I'll remind you of that when Leva starts cooking breakfast tomorrow morning," Will said.

"If you do, I'll tell her to load your eggs with scotch bonnets and salt cod," Betsy said.

What a welcome to their new Jamaican neighborhood! Will and Betsy walked home feeling rum-high and truly blessed.

"I sure hope Henry runs late tomorrow morning," Betsy said.

"Morning 'soon come'," Will said and hugged her

> MR RUDOLPH ROBERTS SAYS
> TAKE UP MY YOAK
> MY BIRDING IS LIGHT
> GOD SAYS.

CHAPTER 15

Henry came by to pick up Betsy just as she and Will were finishing one of Leva's delectable breakfasts. This morning's surprise was ackee and bacon sandwiches on her homemade hard dough bread with some boiled green bananas on the side.

"I'm really getting spoiled on gourmand breakfasts," Will commented. "When we get back to the States, it's going to be hard going back to a simple bowl of raisin bran or a couple of slices of toast. Do you think we could smuggle Leva into the country?"

"That's the only way you're going to get these elaborate breakfasts unless you cook them yourself," Betsy said. "I cook breakfast only on weekends, and not always then."

"But you have so many other wonderful attributes that make up for this shortcoming," Will said.

"I have good news," Henry announced when he arrived. "Colonel Winter has agreed to meet with you. I tentatively set it up for this Saturday. Shall I confirm the date with him?"

Will and Betsy looked at each other, shrugged, and said, "Sure, why not?"

"I will pick you up early on Saturday, but only if the weather is good," Henry said. "It is a three and a half hour drive. Some of the roads are pretty bad, so I don't want to take the van to Accompong Town if it has been raining. Since the Maroons refuse to pay taxes, the Jamaican government devotes very little in the way of resources to maintain roads primarily used by them. Do you mind if Rose accompanies us?"

"I think that would be lovely," Betsy said. "We look forward to sharing this adventure with both of you."

~ ~ ~

Will and Betsy heard the familiar honk at the front gate early Saturday morning. E.J. ran out and opened the gate for Henry and Rose to enter. They dropped Leva off at Columbus Plaza shopping center at the bottom of Primrose Hill before getting on Highway B3 headed for Brown's Town. Will rode shotgun with Henry while Rose and Betsy took the middle seat. Rose brought a picnic lunch. Since it was market day, they stopped briefly in Brown's Town so Rose could buy some fresh produce before getting on A1 to Jackson Town. At Jackson Town, Henry changed highways once again to B6, and they were off to Appleton and Maggotty.

The last thirty minutes of the trip was challenging. The beaten and pitted back road was as lousy as the view was fabulous. An American car probably would have rattled itself to death on this bumpy road, but Henry's van, a true Jamaican vehicle, had yet to meet a pothole it couldn't handle. As they bounced and jostled slowly towards Accompong amidst the sudden slopes and jagged limestone face of the Cockpit country, Will commented that he was now starting to appreciate how hard it must have been for the British to penetrate Maroon territory in the 1700's since there was no road at all.

They knew they had arrived when they saw an open gate with a blue and white sign saying "Welcome to Accompong." Henry commented, that until recent years, the streets of Accompong had been closed to visitors.

"Not more than thirty years ago, these gates were shut to outsiders. Now they have been permanently opened," Henry said. "Permission had to be granted by the Colonel before a visitor could enter. The Colonel still governs this peaceful community, but in recent years, he has opened Accompong to tourism."

"How many people live here?' Will asked.

"Somewhere between two and three thousand," Rose answered.

"Nowadays, there's often little to differentiate Maroons from any other Jamaicans," Henry said. "Rasta influence and television have taken their toll. They even now have a police station."

"They never had a police station?" Betsy asked incredulously.

"They didn't need one. They have been virtually crime free," Henry said. "The people of Accompong are law-abiding and trustworthy. Their secret name for themselves means 'Mighty Friend', and, indeed, a Maroon is the best friend a person can have. In fact, Maroons have the longest life expectancies in Jamaica. It is not uncommon for them to live to be over 100."

Henry advised them not to rush their business with Colonel Winter. "Be patient. Let him take the lead," Henry said. "If you are in doubt, watch me for signs of the proper protocol."

What they saw as they entered Accompong was a small, self-sufficient, rural farming community. It was laid out around one main road running up a hill. Neatly trimmed gardens of native plants and trees surrounded

A Jamaican Conspiracy

small concrete homes with tin roofs. A small provisions store at a three-way intersection near the center of town, a church, and a local gathering place called Flashy's Place lined the steep, winding mountain road. Henry gave a quick friendly wave to some locals and received an immediate likewise response.

He stopped at Flashy's Place, and the group exited the van, stretching from the long ride. A domino game was in progress on a rickety table with a precarious lean. It was loosely nailed to a tree and had rough planks for seats. Flashy's was a cross between a bar and a corner shop. The hut could not have been more than five meters square but still seemed quite a social hub.

"Mr. Davis," said a local with a gold-toothed smile as he limped over to the van. "What brings you up our way?"

Henry inquired about the limp. Flashy smiled and said it was from a recent motorbike "mashup."

A group of men watching an old television turned to see who Flashy was talking to.

"Flashy, I want you to meet my Jam-Merican friends, Will and Betsy Black, and my wife, Rose," Henry said. He then introduced each in turn.

"I have brought my friends to Accompong to meet with the Colonel," Henry continued.

"Dowdie," Flashy called out in English-like creole to a bearded twentyish young man with a bulbous tam barely containing his Rastafarian dreadlocks, "Fetch the Colonel." The young man nodded and left immediately.

Flashy flicked open cans of Red Stripe to welcome each of his new friends. Will and Betsy looked around. The shelves were sparsely stacked with more beer and tinned vegetables.

Someone turned off the television and put a nickel in an old jukebox. The small room was filled with familiar sounds of Al Green and then an Otis Redding song. This was followed by John Holt singing a reggae version of *Mr. Big Stuff*.

"He only put five cents in the machine," Will observed. "How many songs will it play for that small amount of money?"

"Three of course," Flashy said.

"Of course," Will agreed. "I should have known. Mr. Davis tells me Accompong is crime free."

"There hasn't been a crime here for over 250 years," Flashy said as he drank his beer.

"Now, Flashy, you're exaggerating," Henry said.

"Well, I am being slightly economical with the truth," Flashy admitted. "There was a robbery here several years ago, but we don't normally count it since it was committed by an outsider."

Before *Mr. Big Stuff* ended, Dowdie returned. He was accompanied by a dark-skinned, older, slender but muscular balding man who walked with the erect military-like gait of a person accustomed to being in charge. Will guessed him to be about Henry's age.

"That must be the Colonel," Will whispered to Betsy. "I wonder if they played *Mr. Big Stuff* as a tribute."

"What did you expect, *God Save The Queen*?" Betsy whispered back.

"For some reason I was thinking about *Big Bad John*," Will whispered.

The new arrival smiled when he saw Henry and Rose and vigorously shook Henry's hand. Henry made the introductions.

Will's first impression of Colonel Winter was that of a big fish in a small pond who, despite Jamaica's penchant for greed and graft, had remained simple and true to his roots. He did not appear to be well-heeled by American standards. His Jamaican English was precise and well mannered, and he carefully avoided the use of patois. A short, sudden brief command brought Flashy scooting out with a bottle of Wray and Nephew rum. A large wooden spool of the type used for heavy-duty cable or wire was rolled out, turned on its side to be used as a makeshift table. An assortment of mismatched chairs soon surrounded the spool. Flashy put the bottle of rum, an ashtray, and an odd assortment of glasses on the makeshift table and poured a shot of liquor into each. Rose offered to share the picnic luncheon she had prepared for the trip. The Colonel agreed this was an excellent idea.

At first saying nothing, Colonel Winter sipped his rum slowly, savoring his food. Henry was also silent and patiently waited for the Colonel to break the ice. Will and Betsy followed Henry's cue. After a few sips and a few bites of jerk pork and a piece of his festival, the Colonel smiled and began with a few pleasantries. He informed them that the Maroons were the first to jerk meat because it was a low-smoke way of curing their food. This was important when they did not want to reveal their campsite locations to the British. He spoke enthusiastically about the village's upcoming celebration of the heroic Captain Cudjoe's birthday and invited Will and Betsy to participate. He told them of his goal of familiarizing the world with the real Maroon people. He articulately described his people as being a nation within a nation and spoke of how in 1739 his ancestors had signed a peace treaty still in force today with the British that gave them semi-sovereignty over this area. He described the Kindah Treaty as a sacred charter. He boasted that Cudjoe never lost a battle to the British army. He proudly chronicled the details of the 1738 battle of Accompong in which Cudjoe routed the British army and slaughtered every soldier except one. This was the last battle ever on Accompong soil. He told them how, as an elected official, he ran Accompong with the assistance of a 32-man council and how the treaty allowed the Jamaican government to intervene and interfere in the case of a capital crime.

Will asked The Colonel if there was any truth to the recent talk of police violating the treaty by unfairly rousting a Maroon Rastafarian.

The Colonel became subtly defensive and evasive.

"There are things that my position does not give me the luxury of discussing," he said quietly.

"I was merely wondering if this infraction really occurred, or if it might merely be local gossip," Will said. "There was no news coverage of the event."

At this point, Colonel Winter changed the subject and asked to see the mahogany skull found in Betsy's briefcase at the Martha Brae. Will took the hint and did not bring the police brutality case up again. Winter picked the skull carving up and slowly turned it, rubbing and examining it from every side. When he was finished, he put it back down, still not commenting on it. He then asked Betsy to recount her conversation with the person calling himself Cudjoe. Will described the glass skull vodka bottles found on Sundance's wall. Colonel Winter only listened. He asked about the nature of Betsy's duties in Jamaica. When The Colonel felt that he had the information he needed, he suggested that he would welcome the opportunity to now give them a tour of Accompong and the surrounding area. Will and Betsy readily accepted.

Henry remarked to Will out of Colonel Winter's earshot that the tour invitation was a positive sign.

"It is a special honor to be given a tour by the Colonel personally," he said. "This is a matter he normally delegates to a subordinate."

Colonel Winter procured a half pint of Wray and

A Jamaican Conspiracy

Nephew from Flashy, pocketing it, and then led his visitors on a short stroll to one of the town's two main sights, the town museum. All the while he continued talking about his town.

"Farming simply is not viable anymore," he said. "We must focus on tourism. Our rich history lends itself to low-maintenance, culture-hungry tourists looking to take daytrips off the beaten track. We must capitalize on that strength."

At the museum he had the curator demonstrate how to blow an abeng, the Maroon war horn. Abengs are made from a cow horn with the tip cut off. This was how Maroons communicated with each other during their wars with the British. Blowing through a square hole cut into the concave side of the abeng produced a sound that could be heard for miles and could only be decoded by those who knew how. Next they saw a demonstration on how to play a traditional Maroon Gumbay drum.

From the museum Winter walked them through the commons, past a small craft and herbs shop, and then a burial site. He led them to the Kindah Grove, all the while telling them more about his people. He lamented the fact that even though most Maroons still honored and respected both the Heritage Treaty and Maroon customs, a small minority of male youths were now desirous of change and pushed for the Accompong Maroons to forfeit the privileges and customs granted by the treaty and totally immerse themselves into the tax-paying Jamaican population.

"Such a suggestion will always be defeated by well-thinking Maroons, for it will dash to naught what past Maroons warriors risked their lives so desperately and arduously to obtain. Modern Maroons must still remain united in spite of our minor differences and occasional setbacks. All Maroon villages must remain unified and respect their vow to never serve the British Monarchy or the Jamaican government though we will always honor our pledge to pay due respect to both," Colonel Winter said.

He expressed his fears of the long-term effects a recently opened Accompong Internet café was beginning to have on the Maroon way of life and candidly discussed steps he had taken to reduce commercialism during the annual Maroon Festival. He had banned the selling of non-traditional and imported wares during the festival.

"Some of our young people forget that the celebration's purpose is to commemorate the birthday of Captain Cudjoe," he said. "People should not come here to buy imported clothes and shoes. They should be here to journey through our history and customs."

Within the Kindah Grove, Will and Betsy saw a small area of grassland and jutting limestone rocks that surrounded the sacred Kindah Tree, a fruitful mango tree firmly rooted in Maroon myth and ethno-history. It was here that the two rebel Maroon tribes forged their alliance. It is here that Cudjoe signed the Kindah Peace Treaty that insured the freedom of the former slaves. "Many of my people call it the 'Blood Treaty' because it was signed in blood by the Maroons and the Englishmen as well."

"It is here that the Maroons assemble each January to celebrate and honor their ancestors. The Kindah Tree's sign "We are family" symbolizes the common kinship of this Creole community with their hard-earned common land. Beyond the Kindah Tree, Colonel Winter showed them the reputed final resting place of Captain Cudjoe and his brothers and lieutenants. Most graves were marked with cairns and boulders, were overgrown by bush and brush, and only weeded preceding the annual January Maroon Festival.

"I will take you to the Peace Cave. It is only a short walk," The Colonel announced and led them towards a third burial area that was once the headquarters for Captain Cudjoe's military camp.

"Our greatest challenge to our autonomy which we are now facing," he said, "came with Jamaica's political independence in 1962. The country's new constitution did not address the question of the political and legal status of the Maroon communities in the post-independence Jamaica. Although we have a good relationship with the Jamaican government, we want to be recognized in the Jamaican constitution. I want the Jamaican government to fly the Maroon flag beside the Jamaican flag. I have also called upon the United Nations for recognition. After all, we are a sovereign nation."

The short walk described by the Colonel turned out to be about forty-five minutes. The group followed him unguardedly into the bush using a path they could not see. They were soon out of sight of the smoke curling from kitchen fires in the village. Here and there they would occasionally break out of the dense forest and cross over a hand-tilled area. Before long, the land began to look the same in all directions. The high ridges of the cockpits seemed to flow out towards the horizon as they circled one deep basin after another. It seemed to them that the land was pathless. Finally they spotted two huge limestone boulders. They had to be careful and watch their feet closely to avoid slipping off the trail and sliding or falling into an overgrown pit that went straight down for several hundred feet to a swampy bottom. They suddenly realized that they had lost sight of the Colonel and nervously scrambled between the boulders only to see another deep pit. It wasn't as deep as the first pit but was just as vertical.

They became disoriented and began to be unsure

about the reliability of their senses and to question everything. They even wondered if the amiable Colonel had possibly lured them into some sort of gigantic trap for some nefarious reason known only to him, and if he had abandoned them, would they would ever be able to find their way out of this remote morass.

After what seemed like an eternity, they heard the Colonel's voice coming from a place very close by. It was almost surreal and sounded ritualistic. The Colonel sounded like he was no more than three feet away, but he was invisible to them.

"Colonel, where are you?" Will cried out uneasily.

"I'm in the Peace Cave," came an echoing reply. The voice seemed to come from the huge boulder on Will's left. Was the rock itself speaking to them?

They scrambled to the other side of the rock. Near the back, where the room-sized boulder seemed to protrude from the ridge, they saw a narrow wedge of darkness about two feet high. Will crawled over to it and called out that it appeared to be a cave-way entry. The Colonel's voice was coming from inside. He took a chance and squeezed partially through the opening.

The massive boulder was hollow. Once Will had entered, he stood in a rock-walled chamber. Mottled light flowed into the cavern from five or six finger sized openings in the wall and ceiling. These openings had not been noticeable from the outside. The Colonel stood waiting for him. Will told everyone else it was safe to enter the cave. Within minutes all were safely inside. The damp, cold interior reminded them of an ancient rustic stone church. On the walls were paintings and other marks. The crude artwork was mostly stick figures of people and animals. There was also writing unlike any that Will and Betsy had ever seen. The Colonel said that these were Arawak Indian pictures and messages.

He then told them how the Maroons would hide out in the cave and then at their leisure kill the British one by one. He motioned for Betsy to come near to him. He showed her two peepholes. From the outside they were higher than a man's head, but from the inside, were on eye-level and aimed slightly down. She peered into one of the holes and had a panoramic view of the area outside. She then looked out the other hole and had a panoramic view of the remaining countryside. The Colonel showed her how a man could fire a rifle or musket through these holes and kill the person on the other side with the victim's companions never knowing from where the bullet had been fired. The terrified troops would then more than likely flee back to where they had come.

"This is why we called it the Peace Cave," Colonel Winter explained. "Because we never gave it up until we knew peace would follow. I hope we never have to use caves like this again, but then, one never knows. Armageddon may yet come."

He related how Cudjoe and his lieutenants had walked back from this cave to meet with the British colonel and sign the Kindah Peace Treaty.

"Before we leave," The Colonel said, "we must honor our Maroon ancestors who fought and died for our people."

He withdrew the half-pint of rum from his pocket. On each wall of the cave, they took turns spraying rum from their mouths across the drawings and marks. He then lit a small fire from available kindling, burned the remaining rum, and doused the fire. Afterward before departing, he gathered some sticks of wood and stacked them neatly in the cave for the next visitor. Winter told them on the walk back to Accompong that a rum bottle was placed at the cave and replenished annually as an offering to Cudjoe's duppy who lives inside the cave.

When the party had safely returned to Accompong, The Colonel bade them all farewell and thanked them for coming. Just before they departed, he told them that he found the use of Cudjoe's name to be an upsetting sacrilege that would necessitate his involvement and that he would initiate the appropriate action.

The Colonel and Henry embraced. He gave Rose a big hug and told her he hoped to see her again soon.

Henry's parting words to the Colonel were simple, "Tanks, mi cousin. Mi no yu no fuhget **(I will not forget your kindness)**. Jah guide **(May God bless you)**."

```
┌─────────────────────────┐
│   AUTO GREACEING        │
│   DONE HEARE            │
└─────────────────────────┘
```

CHAPTER 16

"Do you realize that this Saturday you will have been the current mistress of Sundance for one month?" Leva said pleasantly to Betsy. "It has been the most pleasant month E.J. and I can remember."

"Thank you, Leva. That was a sweet thing to say," Betsy said. "Y'all have become just like family to us as well. It seems that destiny smiled upon Will and me when he brought us here. It seems like we've been living at Sundance forever."

Leva brought some of her homemade fruit cocktail to the table and poured Will and Betsy some freshly brewed high-mountain coffee.

"I've got a grand idea," Betsy announced. "Why don't we celebrate our anniversary this Saturday night? Just the four of us. I'll take over your kitchen and cook you and E.J. a meal for a change. Not Jamaican cuisine, but a feast we would serve company back in Florida. It would be fun for us to serve you for a change."

"Sounds like a great idea," Will said. "I'll be in charge of the bar and the music."

Leva's eyes twinkled and seemed to get misty. She

117

agreed that it would be an evening she and E.J. would remember and treasure forever.

Leva began to sing merrily as she finished cooking breakfast. There was an extra bounce in her step. The song she chose, *Jesus Is Standing By,* almost remarkably enough sounded like the tune of Ben E. King's smash rhythm and blues hit, *I'll Be There.*

Will watched Leva and then smiled at his wife. "You did good," he said and gave her a thumbs-up. "Great idea, my dear."

By Wednesday, Betsy had chosen a menu. She would have seafood gumbo, halved avocado's stuffed with crabmeat, and key lime pie. She would get Henry to drive Leva and her to Brown's Town Saturday morning to buy the ingredients while E.J. and Will got things ready at the villa. Leva was thrilled to be invited to go on the shopping trip.

"We'll just have a girl's morning out," Betsy said.

By Saturday, Betsy was as excited as Leva about their pending field trip to Brown's Town.

As Henry drove, Leva explained that Friday was the prime day each week for the Brown's Town market. Goods were brought in from the surrounding hill villages and family farms. The higglers, loaded with sacks and boxes, would arrive before dawn, jumping off buses. The top of the bus would be buried by huge bags of coconuts and copra that had been tied haphazardly down with a maze of ropes. By the time dawn broke, the higglers were in their stalls awaiting their first customers.

Highway B3 to Brown's Town was an enchanting drive, and Henry's van was up to the steepness of the grade. They traveled high into the hills, winding through jungle-like vegetation. Everywhere Betsy looked, she saw cave-filled limestone cliffs sprouting lush native greenery. One section called Orange Valley was especially breathtaking with long views through pastures down to the Caribbean. A white Toyota Chaser with a dinged windshield discreetly followed at a distance all the way. Betsy was surprised it never passed them since everyone always passes everyone else on Jamaican roads. After all, passing in Jamaica is a national pastime.

As they entered Brown's Town, market day's hubbub of activity was a profound contrast to the long, quiet drive from Discovery Bay. Pushcarts raced by as minibus drivers loudly solicited passengers on the main street. They passed an old stately Anglican church surrounded by pine trees before arriving at the main market, a throwback to a bygone era. A tall English clock-tower building crowned by a zinc roof covered the entire market area. The contrast between the intense sun that burned the pavement and the dark, cool market made Betsy blink when she first walked inside. Flea-market-like stalls were brimming with shoes, clothing, house wares and various what-nots.

Leva explained to Betsy the significance of bargaining and then advised Betsy to leave that function to her. They left Henry watching the van and catching up on the local gossip with some men he knew.

"The higglers hope you will bargain. They would be disappointed if you didn't since it is a social form that allows for more than mere bargain hunting. It encourages conversations and debates. Notice when I first ask a price, I always show shock and disgust at the answer, no matter how low the price is. I will immediately put the item back and walk away muttering loudly about the state of the world. I never even glance back. The higgler would then have the advantage. Next I walk around, look in other stalls and finger that higgler's goods. When I return, the price will have fallen dramatically. That is when I buy. It is traditional and is what they expect."

A Jamaican Conspiracy

Since they were here only for food, Leva and Betsy did not tarry by the clothing booth but crossed the street to the fruit and vegetable market, a much more modest structure built from haphazard patches of rusty zinc and wood. Leaky roofs were patched with whatever unlikely patching material was available. One hole had even been patched with a vintage Playboy magazine opened to the "Playgirl of the Month" page.

Before them, Betsy saw rows of women seated next to multi-colored mountains of fresh pungent fruit, vegetables, and spices. From a tall mound of avocados, Betsy selected three large ripe ones. They passed displays of both Irish potatoes and sweet potatoes. Leva picked out two luscious pineapples, and farther down the same row, a bunch of fat, ripe bananas. They passed a lady chopping sugar cane into bite-sized pieces. There were fresh carrots, callaloo, ackee, and chocho. Betsy smelled fresh thyme, nutmeg, black peppercorns and purple scallions. Leva purchased some of each. She bought some red plum tomatoes and some snowy white Jamaican cabbage. Betsy bought enough key limes to make her key lime pie. They picked out some other fresh citrus together. Betsy was even able to find okra.

This sweet produce smell was soon replaced by the pungent smell of salt-fish. Here Betsy found the shrimp, crabmeat, and fish she would need to make her gumbo. They struggled to take all the sacks back to Henry's van. The aroma of thyme filled the car all the way home.

Betsy noticed Henry peeping more frequently than usual in his rear-view mirror and inquired why.

"I may be imagining it," Henry said, "but that same white Toyota Chaser that was behind us this morning is behind us again."

When they got back to Sundance, Betsy began the pot of gumbo. She steamed and picked the crabs. Then she showed Leva how to make and properly brown a roux and explained its importance to gumbo. She then squeezed the fresh limes for the key lime pie. It felt good to be the teacher instead of the pupil for a change. Leva listened diligently and was careful to only observe and not butt in.

"Too much rata neva dig good ole," she said.

"Which means?" Betsy asked.

"Too many cooks spoil the soup."

Before the festivities began that evening, E.J. excused himself to go freshen up. The next time they saw him, his hair had been slicked back with pomade into a semi-ducktail, and he was wearing a zippered black leather jacket, leather pants, white socks and some scuffed boots that were too large for him. A chain hung out of one of the pockets. His eyes were hidden by aviator sunglasses. He swaggered into the room and began to sing a reggae karaoke-like rendition of *All Shook Up.*

"What the ... ," Will involuntarily uttered. "Where did you get that outfit? That looks ... uh ... uh ... sharp."

"Thank you; thank you very much," E.J. answered in an affected baritone voice.

Leva laughed and said, "I guess it's time you learned what E.J. stands for – Elvis Jessie."

"I think I need to pour us each a daiquiri before we hear the rest of this," Will said.

"Good idea. I may need a double for this," Betsy said. "After all, it *is* five o'clock somewhere."

"Bob Marley dreads wouldn't have surprised me," Will said, "but Elvis? You weren't even born while he was alive. I'd think you'd identify more with Michael Jackson."

"My last name is Aarons. I was born in St. Ann on the tenth anniversary of Elvis's death," E.J. began. "The Obeah man told my mother that this was a sign that I would grow up to be a king. So she named me Elvis Jessie."

"The Obeah man was almost right," Leva said

121

jokingly. "Kingtoo, you definitely are the push-broom king of Sundance."

"Did you call E.J. Kingtoo?" Betsy asked.

"Everyone in Jamaica has at least two names. They have their given name, but then they have their 'pet' name," E.J. explained. "My pet name is Kingtoo. A pet name is usually given to a person by their friends or loved ones. It doesn't have to reflect truth. For instance I have a friend we call Fatty who is 120 pounds soaking wet. Another friend is called Sticky because of the way he eats mangos. You'll soon meet my best friend, Chicken. We call him that because he has a long neck."

"Growing up, our real names were used only by our parents, relatives or teachers – especially when discipline was being administered. Your close friends and arch-enemies always called you by a nickname," Leva said. "If you despised your nickname, you were wise to keep it to yourself. You just answered to it because if other people ever got wind of how you really felt, they would repeat it at every opportunity. When you become a true Jamaican, we'll come up with a pet name for you as well."

"So, what is your pet name, Leva?" Betsy asked.

"Honey-pye," Leva answered and blushed slightly.

"Sounds like Jamaicans are haunted by the ghost of nicknames past," Will said.

"Duppies, not ghosts," Leva said. "Don't forget; you are in Jamaica now. If and when you truly become Jamaican, we will give you a nickname too."

The evening went very well. It was like an evening spent with old friends at home. Leva compared Betsy's seafood gumbo to Jamaican fish tea. She told them how Jamaicans would boil fish heads, strain out the head, and then add chocho, carrots, potato, onions, and green bananas. Of course, it would be seasoned with scotch bonnet peppers.

Will and Betsy were slightly repelled by the thought of eating boiled fish heads but agreed it was probably just an acquired taste.

"Why do you call it fish tea?" Will asked.

"Because it is non-alcoholic," Leva answered. "Any non-alcoholic beverage in Jamaica can be called a tea. People will sometimes strain fish tea and use it for a beverage or maybe even as baby food."

After everyone had two heaping bowls of gumbo, Will told the story of how, as a child, he had once gorged himself on gumbo. When his stomach began to ache, he looked at his mom and said, "Mama, I don't think I like gumbo anymore."

Betsy suggested they go out by the pool to enjoy their key lime pie. The night was dark and starry with almost perfect visibility. The number of stars was impossible to count. It seemed as if the daytime sky had dropped a curtain and then pinned it down with stars. The patterns of the constellations popped out of the sky bright and clear. The horizon approaching the ocean was remote with distant rims on the edge of space.

As they enjoyed an after dinner drink and listened to reggae play in the background, the lights suddenly went out and the dark became almost pitch black. The music stopped. Even the crickets were silent as if waiting to see what would happen next.

"Oh my God, the power's out again. I wonder how long it will be this time," Leva said. "E.J., get the candles and a flashlight."

E.J. ran for the house as he attempted to comply with Leva's order. He located the necessary items and ran back cradling a burning candle. As he approached the pool, E.J. tripped over his own clunky feet. The candle went flying into the swimming pool, extinguishing immediately. The flashlight clunked to the ground and rolled into the dark.

A Jamaican Conspiracy

His pompadour hair fell into his eyes. E.J. attempted to brush it out of the way, in the process coating his hand in pomade. When he tried to retrieve the flashlight, it squirted into a bush next to the pool patio. E.J. awkwardly grabbed for it, tripped over Will's leg, and did a flailing belly-flop back into the dark water.

They looked up. Gina and Samantha were barking wildly at a figure in the dark. The man hesitated as if assessing the situation and then vanished out the back gate. Will helped E.J. out of the pool, and E.J., with all four dogs, slogged behind the intruder, awkwardly hip-hopping across the stony yard. Will and Betsy looked down. One of E.J. motorcycle boots had come off and stared silently at them.

Will looked at it and laughed.

"Does this mean that Elvis has left the building?"

"Chasing a peeping-Tom," Betsy said. "This isn't funny anymore; it's scary."

E.J. came limping back in.

"He drove off in a white Toyota Chaser," he said.

"My Lord! What does this guy want?" Betsy asked.

Leva shrugged and said, "When herrin mauger, him bone slow **(Evil deeds will reveal themselves)**."

"That's no comfort," Betsy answered.

"No worry, Miss Betsy. I'll watch for him," E.J. said. "I won't let him hurt you."

> **LITTLE HOPE
> FLOWERS NURSURY
> PHONE 952 2971**

CHAPTER 17

Betsy had not heard from Councillor Merle Dunster since right after the Martha Brae incident. She was surprised, therefore, when Letha told her he was waiting on line 2.

After exchanging a few pleasantries, Dunster stated the purpose of his call. He wished, on a day mutually agreeable to them all, to invite Betsy and Will to join him for lunch at Evita's in Ocho Rios. Betsy understood why Dunster wished to take her to a business luncheon but wondered why his offer included Will. She told Dunster she'd get back to him. A luncheon was arranged for the following Friday.

Evita's is at the top of a steep hill on Eden Bower Road in Ocho Rios. The hill is so steep that most cars have to drive up it in first gear. The restaurant, which specializes in Northern Italian cuisine, is in an authentic 1860's gingerbread style house with wooden floors and a mahogany bar. From its verandah, diners peering through a canopy of dense tropical foliage have a magnificent birds-eye panoramic view of the Taj Mahal Shopping Center, the cruise ship piers, and much of Ocho Rios. Eva, the owner, calls one wall in the main dining room her "Wall of Fame." It contains autographed pictures of the celebrity diners she has fed over the years. First time diners are inevitably drawn to gawk at pictures of The Rolling Stones, Princess Margaret, Sir Anthony Hopkins, Jimmy Buffett, and the rest of the long list of famous faces. Though they were not considered regulars, Will and Betsy had patronized the restaurant on multiple occasions in the past.

Henry drove them to the restaurant and arranged a time to pick them up again after lunch. Dunster was apparently considered a regular because Eva herself came out to greet them upon their arrival and escorted them to a prime table by the veranda railing. Their waiter suggested snapper fillets sautéed with orange sauce. They all agreed that sounded great. The waiter pointed out that the dish could also be prepared with capers and then baked. Betsy took that option while Will and Merle ordered the original recipe.

The conversation turned to Jerry Smith.

"Investigators have been reluctant to comment on the progress they have made in finding the sniper," Dunster said.

"I'm surprised that there hasn't been more of a public outcry or pressure from the press to solve the case," Will said.

"Jamaicans do not shock easily since they are not strangers to political violence," Dunster said, "The police sometimes wisely find it prudent to simply look the other way on sensitive cases, especially if there might be a possibility of a powerful person being involved."

"Do you mean someone like Dudus Coke?' Will asked. "I've read about him."

Merle Dunster looked very uncomfortable and glanced around him.

"Heavens no," Dunster said quickly, "and you would not want to be quoted as making that accusation. I would also strongly advise you not to voice that sentiment to just anyone since the Shower Posse is probably the largest posse in Jamaica. At last count, my office had reports of 27 posses operating in Jamaica. Large ones like the Spangler Posse, the Dunkirk Boys Posse and the Tel Aviv Posse are very powerful, not only in this country but in others as well. People of Dudus Coke's ilk can be vicious and retaliatory if they feel threatened. Often it is prudent for the authorities to only pay lip-service to investigating controversial situations and hope they simply go away rather than confront powerful people and make permanent enemies."

"You make it sound like these people are running the country," Will said.

"In some ways they are," Dunster continued. "The Shower Posse controls Tivoli Gardens in Kingston and produced one of our prime ministers, Edward Seaga. They have used their deep resources from the narcotics trade to become political power brokers and are insulated not only by their posse but the public at large. They spend large sums of money to benefit the impoverished urban neighborhoods that spawn them. In many cases they enforce order better than the police. Recently a posse almost beat a man who was caught stealing a car in their territory to death. I have seen signs in posse controlled districts saying things like 'After God, then Dudus' or 'Jesus died for us, so we will die for Dudus'."

"You make these dons sound like Robin Hoods," Will said.

A Jamaican Conspiracy

"Or like the Mafia dons in New York's Little Italy," Betsy added.

"There are parallels," Dunster answered. They are poor ghetto-born locals who have broken the cycle of poverty the only way they know how and have become very corrupt and rich. Wanti, wanti, can't get it, getti getti no want it."

"Meaning?" Betsy asked.

"The have-nots covet what the haves take for granted."

Betsy then mentioned to Dunster that it had been brought to her attention that Smith had instigated a possible preliminary OCG investigation of KSAC's Highway 2000 contracts and asked Dunster if he were aware of either an ongoing investigation since Smith's death or any other impending problems. Dunster wanted to know the source of her information. Betsy told him politely that bank policy forbid her to disclose her source to him, but in her position, she was obligated to get to the bottom of the matter to protect the future interests of her employer.

"That could possibly explain Smith's removal though I have no reason to think anything is amiss with the project, However, I feel obligated to caution you that a subsequent inquiry might also put you in harm's way," Dunster said. "It could rile powerful parties and become dangerous since it would be construed as an outsider meddling in local affairs you don't understand."

Betsy asked Dunster if he might possibly make a discreet inquiry into whether the investigation had continued after Smith's death. Instead of giving her a straightforward response, Dunster briefly frowned and then launched into an irrelevant diatribe on Jamaica's positives qualities.

"I do not want this to leave you with a negative attitude about Jamaica. Yes, we have problems and issues from time to time, but Jamaica and its people have evolved into a nation which in many ways is the envy of larger nations who've yet to grow as we have. *Out of many, one people*. That is our national motto. Unlike the United States, we have no hyphens when we describe our nationality. We're simply Jamaicans. Look at how Jamaicans have impacted the world in virtually any field you care to mention – sports, the arts, literature, the media, entertainment, medicine, agriculture and yes, even law."

Will and Betsy agreed that Jamaica had accomplished much for a country its size.

Dunster seemed to feel he had neutralized Betsy's request and redirected the conversation once again.

"You are in the investment business, are you not?" he asked Will.

Will nodded.

"An exciting business that has always fascinated me. Sometimes I regret that this was not my path in life instead of public service, but my country called, and I answered. I am told that there are meaningful rewards to be had from many investments if one shares mutually beneficial information with a fellow professional. As you say in America, 'one hand washes the other.' Jamaica can be a land of opportunity if a person plays his cards right – an investor, with advance knowledge of coming events, can find opportunities to purchase things significantly below the market. Opportunities an outsider rarely ever hears about – all because he has become allies with the right people – people who have an incentive to share their knowledge or guidance. I have a close friend, Neville Hamilton, who I think you might find you have much in common. I can introduce you. He is a very successful and wealthy man. You might be mutually beneficial to each other. I have found our friendship to be rewarding from time to time," he said.

He stopped to let the thought sink in and took a sip of his tea.

Will and Betsy looked at each other in disbelief but said nothing. They remembered that name from the Keys, and it did not bring back warm and fuzzy memories. Will and Betsy had long suspected him to be somehow behind the disappearance of former Monroe County Commissioner, and Reverend LeRoy Cho-Arturo.

"But Mr. Hamilton is a private man who likes to remain at all times under the radar screen," Dunster continued. "It is good for business. He would be reluctant to become involved with someone not equally discreet, and especially would not wish to do business with a person who has attracted undue attention from engaging in an idealistic public crusade."

> NOTICE
> NO LOFTAS. IF YOU DON'T HAVE NO CAUSE. PLEASE DO NOT ENTER THIS PREMISES
> MR. WRIIGHT TIME IS UP
> NOW IS MR. M. FORRESTER'S TIME
> TRESPASSES WILL BE PERSUCETED BY ORDER

CHAPTER 18

Will found Merle Dunster's comments about posses to be perplexing as well as somewhat unnerving, and he wanted to know more. He decided to ask Henry.

"What can you tell me about Dudus Coke?" he asked.

"Coke is a vicious wolf in sheep's clothing," Henry answered. "He is not a man a person wants to have for an adversary. He will pay school fees for children, help single mothers raise their children, promote young entertainers, resolve disputes, and keep the peace in Tivoli Gardens one day. Then he will personally carve up a rival with a chain saw the next. In fact, the torture and dismemberment of rivals and enemies is a common occurrence as are shootouts with law enforcement officials trying to arrest his people."

"Sounds like the Jamaican Godfather," Will said.

"Tell me more."

"As you know, Jamaica was once the world's largest producer of bauxite," Henry began. "However, the decline in world demand for bauxite in the 1960's crippled our economy. As a result, workers migrated from the countryside into the cities, especially to Kingston. They crowded into already crowded neighborhoods. Many were Rastas who believed in ganja as a meditation tool. These new arrivals survived in an urban environment of abject poverty, rampant ganja use, and political corruption. Violent gangs began to be formed based primarily on neighborhood boundaries and political affiliation. Both the JLP and the PNP used these gangs to influence the electoral process. Over 400 people were killed in the election of 1980 alone. Even Bob Marley almost lost his life."

"Really."

"Oh, yeah, really," Henry continued. "In 1976 Prime Minister Michael Manley persuaded Marley to play a free PNP concert to ease tensions between the PNP and the JLP. Two days before the show, assassins invaded Marley's home and seriously wounded both Marley and his wife. He played the concert despite both chest and arm injuries."

"These guys really did play hardball," Will said.

"And still do. If a candidate got elected, he would then reward his supporters in the gang with projects for their neighborhoods as well as basic municipal services."

"I'm starting to understand, the politics of jungle survival. You cross them and you get lead poisoning," Will said.

"Or Hole-otosis," Henry said.

"Where did the name posse come from?"

"The gangs adopted this name because of their fondness for American westerns. To them the word was synonymous with their fondness for violence to enforce their political will and their territorial desire to protect their neighborhoods from intrusion by rival gangs. To this day, violence is important to a posse member, because with it, he can prove his manhood as well as develop a reputation for being aggressive."

"I.E., become an up-and-comer," Will said.

"It was only a matter of time for the posses to branch out and start smuggling ganja. Of course, this led to dealing in harder drugs like cocaine and PCP. Initially this was done because they needed money to buy the automatic and semiautomatic weapons they needed to engage in the perpetual gang war being waged in Kingston. From there it was a short hop to firearms trafficking, money laundering, murder, assault, robbery, kidnapping and fraud."

"Now I know why Mr. Dunster seemed nervous when the subject came up," Will said.

"Stories of posse exploits are legendary. I have been diverted more than once on the highway when posses blocked the road to all vehicular traffic in order to set up a temporary runway for a drug plane. They would use highway emergency flares to outline this makeshift runway. I also remember a tale that on one occasion a U.S. smuggler had flown a load of ganja out of Jamaica, but he made the mistake of paying for it with counterfeit U.S. currency. He later made arrangements for a second load of ganja and flew to Jamaica to pick up this load. As reprisal for being cheated on the first load, the posse set out the runway flares in a crocodile infested swamp lying parallel to the highway. The results of the trip were not what the pilot had envisioned.

"Posses and crime were a primary reason Rose and I moved to London," Henry said. "We did not want our children to be raised and possibly influenced by the outlaws who seemed to be running Jamaica. We returned once our children were grown. We are not alone in our sentiment. I heard on a recent television program that 80% of Jamaica's educated people have migrated to other industrialized nations, citing their number one reason being escaping crime."

"Where did the name Shower Posse come from?" Will asked.

"Because they used to shower their rivals with bullets," Henry answered.

"Is that what you call a holier than thou shower?"

"One of the real growth industries in Jamaica is the security business," Henry continued. "Everything from guard-dog breeding to gated communities and walled compounds like Sundance. The haves have been forced to constantly protect themselves from disillusioned have-nots who have placed their trust in a politics of change and betterment, of promises of jobs and more jobs, and who now view the system as having delivered them nothing in return. Their view of the system is that it is loaded against them. One reason for the popularity of reggae and dancehall is because so many of their songs reflect this pessimistic view of life."

"I never thought about that," Will said. "Did I understand you right that the posses are engaged in government contract work?"

"Very much so," Henry said. "More of our politricks in action. Contracts are regularly awarded to business partners of posse dons. This is a convenient way of creating business enterprises that will filter resources back to the dispossessed. Believe it or not, talk to the unemployed youth found on any street corner and you will find that posse owned businesses like Presidential Click and Incomparable Enterprise are iconic realizations of success to these urban poor. They see these enterprises as one of the few ways for people like them who were born in the ghetto to become 'smaddy' **(somebody)** without becoming a reggae singer."

> PNP LOOSE
>
> JLP WIN

CHAPTER 19

Letha Wardlow brought a short stack of file folders into Betsy's office.

"Here are some of the files you asked for," she said nonchalantly as she chewed on a snack.

"Two weeks ago," Betsy said without looking up. "I hope your job hasn't been too taxing since I don't want to get a reputation for being a bakra **(white slave master)**. I did not know when I asked you to find them that it would be such a monumental task. Were they classified 'for the Lord's eyes only'?"

Letha looked puzzled and then embarrassed, but suddenly she understood Betsy's cryptic "bakra" comment. She blushed as it dawned on her that Betsy understood more patois than she had previously thought.

"They weren't filed where they were supposed to be," Letha said apologetically. "I finally located them under a stack of papers on BB's office sofa."

"BB's mother obviously didn't train him to put things back where he got them?" Betsy asked.

"Well, he *is* such a busy man, always on the go," Letha said quickly, "you know, with all the important meetings and conferences he has to go to and everything."

"And everything," Betsy said sighing. "Why are they grease stained?"

"I guess BB was eating his lunch while he was perusing them."

"Figures. By the way, what are you eating? It smells absolutely divine."

"Totoes," Letha said. "I made some for my Wednesday night prayer meeting. Want one?"

"What are they?"

"Oh, I just mix up a little flour with cinnamon, nutmeg, sugar, and vanilla extract, and when they're baked, I cut them into squares. It is my grandma's recipe," Letha said anxiously.

"Sure, I'll try one, and bring me a cup of coffee while you're at it. I assume that can be done in less than two weeks unless all the coffee cups are in BB's office."

Betsy spent the rest of the morning familiarizing herself with the up-to-now elusive Kingston and St. Andrew Corporation files. By lunch she had made a list of items she wished to clarify.

An inordinate number of the right-of-ways seemed to be owned by a company named Incomparable Enterprises. The name vaguely rang a bell, and she called Will to ask if it meant anything to him.

"Sure," Will replied. "You heard the name from me. It is a company reputedly controlled by the most powerful don in Jamaica, Dudus Coke. Henry told me about it."

"Of course," Betsy said. "The Shower Posse from Tivoli Gardens."

"The same."

Betsy looked at the file with renewed interest. There was nothing in the file stating that a Christopher Coke was associated with it. The president was one John David Grey. She also saw the names Hopeton Boothe and Queisha Hamilton as officers. The name Hopeton Boothe was a well-known name in Jamaica. He was a legendary local boy who had become a multi-millionaire and was often featured in the press with various celebrities. Some thought him to be the wealthiest man in Jamaica.

Hopeton Boothe was a poor kid raised in the slums of Port Antonio. He rose to fame as a producer of many of Jamaica's music stars. He was credited with the popularization of the rock-steady genre of music. He started his own record label, which produced much of the rock-steady music of the '70's and also filmed the first major Jamaican movie to become an international hit. The forward-looking Boothe then became a pioneer again when rock-steady evolved into reggae. Now he owned a resort chain called Swingles that featured all-inclusives throughout the Caribbean. Its target market was young, affluent swingers, and its devotees were worldwide. Boothe was now a polo-playing darling of the jet set who was married to a titled token white wife.

Hopeton Boothe is in bed with the likes of Dudus Coke? Betsy asked herself.

The name Queisha Hamilton also rang a bell with her. *Surely it couldn't be the same Queisha Hamilton that Will and I encountered in Key West during the Blanchard investigation?*

Betsy's memories went back to thoughts about the LeRoy Cho-Arturo, Dub Bootee, and Green Rainbow Ministries. She decided a call to Michael Howell at *The Key West Citizen* was in order to verify her suspicions. She reached Michael on her first phone call.

"Michael, this is Betsy Black with WB Bank. I hope you remember me."

"The banker! Of course I do! This is a pleasant

139

surprise. What can I do for you?"

"Does the name Queisha Hamilton ring any bells with you?"

"Does it ever," Michael said. "It brings to mind both the best and the worst days I've ever had as a Key West newspaper man."

"In what way?"

"She called to give me the biggest story of my career, sent me on the biggest wild-goose chase I've ever been on, almost got me fired, and ultimately led me to the most important exposé of my career."

"Sounds like quite a roller coaster," Betsy said. "Would you mind filling in the details on your experiences with her?"

"Is there the possibility of another story?" Howell asked.

"I can't promise you that," Betsy said, "but if it does turn out to be the case, I won't forget your generous assistance."

"Fair enough."

Howell then repeated his experiences with Queisha.

"Several years ago I was contacted anonymously by Queisha giving me dirt on then County Commissioner LeRoy Cho-Arturo. I was able to identify her through another informant. She sent me on a wild-goose chase to Jamaica, supposedly to get the evidence I would need to do an exposé on the Commissioner. He was running for Florida legislature at the time. All I returned with was a computer disk full of Jamaican dancehall music. My editor was so pissed that I had been duped into squandering newspaper resources and coming up with absolutely nothing in return, that I almost lost my job. For awhile afterwards, I got assigned as punishment every menial story that came into the newsroom. Then ... I don't know what happened ... I guess maybe the thieves had some dissension in the ranks ... I mysteriously got anonymously in the mail the disc I needed to do my series. Cho-Arturo dropped out of the congressional race and disappeared. He's never been seen since. Some people think he may be dead. His pal and rabbi, Ike Blanchard, the drug smuggler, got sent to prison."

"Oh yes, the Blanchard affair. I remember it well," Betsy said.

Betsy's next call was to her friend, Key West Police Chief Walter Wanderley.

"Betsy Black," Walter said. "We sure miss you around here. No one does coffee breaks like you do. How are things in Jamaica?"

"Well, I certainly have my challenges here," Betsy said. "What's happening in Key West?"

"Oh, just the usual screwy wackiness," Walter said. "Last night we had a guy leap through Wendy's drive-through to steal the money out of the register – the one on Roosevelt by Publix. The cashier refused to let him get away. She grabbed him by the shirt until her fellow employees could pin him. They held him down until my man could get there and arrest him.

"And we had a naked man steal one of the fire trucks from the Big Pine fire station. He drove about two miles before he lost control of the fire truck and careened off of U.S. 1. The truck flipped and he was trapped inside. When the rescue workers freed him, he assaulted two sheriff's deputies."

"Sounds like everything's normal," Betsy said and laughed.

"Normal? What's that?" Walter said.

She then told Walter about Jerry Smith's assassination at the Martha Brae, her stolen briefcase, the glass skulls on the villa wall, and the trip to Accompong.

"Please be careful," Walter said. "You're not in

Kansas anymore, Dorothy."

"I realize that, and I'll heed the warning. Now, I need to pick your brain, Walter," Betsy said.

"Pick away. Just leave me enough to do my job."

"Does the name Queisha Hamilton mean anything to you?"

"Sure. She worked for Green Rainbow Ministries. She got picked up several years ago passing funny money at a mall up in Miami-Dade. She convinced the Feds she was a victim not a perp. I haven't heard anything about her in quite a while. I don't think she lives in the Keys anymore," Walter said. "Why do you ask?"

"Her name appears as a corporate officer on paperwork for a customer of the bank down here in Ocho Rios."

"Be doubly careful," Walter said. "I remember now that her uncle Neville Hamilton reputedly leads a group of Jamaican thugs – bad Jamaican thugs."

"One more thing, Walter," Betsy said. "Did the lab give you the results back on that chemical I sent you for analysis?"

"Yes," Walter said. "It was phenyl ester with a fluorescent dye that had been mixed with hydrogen peroxide. That's what light sticks are made from. Where did it come from?"

"That's the liquid that was in the crystal skulls left on top of our wall. Thanks, Walter. I'll stay in touch," Betsy said.

"Betsy, please promise me you won't take any unnecessary chances."

"I won't. I promise."

Betsy then pulled the file on the Kingston and St. Ann Corporation. Now it was time to learn more about the mysterious KSAC and see if she could identify just what Jerry Smith had been concerned about.

There was a summary sheet in the file showing the contracts KSAC had outstanding in relation to Highway 2000.

114 contracts – value $96 million. That certainly makes them a major player. Well worth monitoring.

She looked further through the documents. Some familiar names popped out. John David Grey, Queisha Hamilton, Hopeton Boothe.

So KSAC tracks back to Incomparable Enterprises which tracks back to the niece of questionable Neville Hamilton which tracks back to major crime-boss don Dudus Coke. This is getting incestuous. I can see why Jerry Smith hoisted red flags. And maybe there was more involved than politics. I sure would like to know more. Maybe I should be calling Dr. Damien Rosser at the Office of the Contractor General.

She dialed Dr. Rosser's office. He was in a meeting. She left word. No return call.

The following morning she called Dr. Rosser's office. He was once again in a meeting. He would be given her message. No return call.

She called the following afternoon. Dr. Rosser was in a meeting out of the office. If he returned before the end of the workday, he would probably have time to give her a call. No return call.

She called Merle Dunster the following day. He claimed he had been able to find out nothing about an investigation into KSAC. He would get back to her. No return phone call.

The following Monday she called Dr. Rosser's office. Once again he was not available. She asked to speak to his assistant and explained the nature of her inquiry. She was told that the OSG could not confirm that an investigation was underway, but even if there was, policy prohibited confirming that fact with an outsider.

There seemed to be stonewalling happening, and without some help, she would most likely learn very little.

```
LiTTLE HOPE
FLOWERS NURSURY
PHONE 952 2971
```

CHAPTER 20

"I was talking to a client in Key West yesterday," Will told Betsy as they ate another of Leva's scrumptious breakfasts. "Seems like we missed the social event of the season."

"Oh yeah. What was that?"

"Richard Schmidt over at Pirate Radio in the Keys bought a Cheetos shaped like a seahorse on eBay. Then he auctioned it off at a benefit for Reef Relief. He got $500 for it."

"Another prodigious milestone in Key's history," Betsy said.

"You have such a way with words," Will said. "I've decided, after giving the matter much thought and doing advanced correlation analysis, that we erudite securities brokers will never have the same in-depth command of the language arts as you super-bankers. My studies found it is necessary to have a last name and sir name with the same first letters like 'CC' – Carson Crown, 'BB' – Bob Blackmon or Betsy Black."

She shot him a finger.

"Now, now. No one-syllable words."

"I try not to talk down to people but instead use symbolism within their communications boundaries," Betsy said.

"Touché."

"Back to the world's most expensive Cheetos. What would you do with something like that?" Betsy said.

"Eat it?"

"Very slowly and savor every morsel," Betsy said. "Well, thanks for the memories and days of mental masturbation, but I guess I'd better get ready for another day of 'fun and games with Dick and Jane' in Ocho Rios."

"How are things going?"

"I wish I knew," Betsy said. "I'm having more trouble than I anticipated compiling a meaningful overview of Highway 2000, and no one seems to be in any hurry to return my phone calls and other queries. Other than that everything is going letter-perfect. My gut tells me there's a lot more I need to know beyond what I'm seeing on the surface, and it may not all necessarily be good."

"And maybe you don't want to know," Will said.

"Except I'm being very generously compensated to quickly get my arms around the total picture and then to make intelligent recommendations to the bank's decision makers."

"And then draw the correct conclusions from the facts."

"I think I may have to finish my fact-finding in the field," Betsy said.

"Nothing like seeing things for yourself first-hand. After all, that's why you were sent here. Anyone can sit behind a desk."

They heard Henry's familiar honk at the front gate. E.J. immediately went out to let him in. After Henry exchanged a few pleasantries and Betsy gave Will a goodbye kiss, they left for the Ocho Rios.

Betsy's morning was pretty uneventful until BB came into her office carrying a nondescript cardboard box.

"A courier dropped this off for you," he said. "I happened to be at the front desk, so I snagged it just in case it's something important."

"Thanks, Bob. That was thoughtful of you."

The box was medium sized, about 8 inches square, and was very light - almost like it was empty. Betsy opened it, and there was a sudden pop and a mini-explosion. A fine powder filled the room. Betsy got a face-full and sneezed. She was covered with the powder as was her desk and all the files on it. BB looked like he had been in a doughnut bakery explosion. White powder clung to his dark skin. He unconsciously jerked back and his glasses slipped off his nose. He looked owl-eyed like a person with a sunburn who had been wearing sunglasses too long at the beach. Not only were Betsy's clothes covered, but the sticky oily residue stuck in her hair. The air conditioner distributed the fine powder and the sulfur smell as well throughout the room.

"What the hell," Betsy uttered.

"But a wah di rass **(What the fuck)**," BB let slip and then looked embarrassed.

She examined the box more closely. The box had been rigged with a 9-volt battery, which had been attached by wires to a switch and a tiny motor. Paper clips had been used as an electrical conductor. The powder had been contained in an open toilet paper tube. An empty soda bottle had caused the explosion noise.

Letha ran in and saw them.

"Who would want to pull this prank?" Betsy asked. "Do you think it could be anthrax?"

"Oh, no ma'am. I know what that is. That's hoodoo

A Jamaican Conspiracy

powder," Letha declared.

"What?" Betsy said.

"Hoodoo powder," Letha said. "Somebody want to put a hex on you."

"That man I saw in the lobby must not have been a courier but an Obeah man," BB said shaking his head. "This is not good."

"What did he look like?" Betsy asked.

"He was dressed in a long, red robe, and his head was wrapped in a red cloth," BB said.

"And that didn't seem strange to you?" Betsy asked.

"Well, now that you mention it ... ," BB said.

Betsy sighed. She looked back in the box and saw some dried chicken bones.

"This definitely is not good," Letha said. "Bones means this is black magic. Bones is the King of Death. Someone means you harm."

"I'm getting out of here. Us super-bankers don't need no bad luck," BB announced and ran from the room.

About that time Betsy's phone rang. It was Will.

"You wouldn't believe what just happened to me," he said.

"It can't be any more shocking than what I just went through," she said.

"Someone left a box at the gate with both our names on it," Will continued. "E.J. brought it in to me. When I opened it, it exploded and covered my whole office with powder."

"The exact same thing just happened to me," Betsy said.

"Wha ... ."

"Letha says it is a hoodoo spell from an Obeah man," Betsy said.

"Leva told me the same thing. Mine had chicken bones in the box," Will said.

148

"So did mine. Letha says that bones mean it is black magic."

"So who have we pissed off beyond all belief?" Will said.

"Probably not we, dear, it's most likely me," Betsy said. "I'm the one who has been trying to dig into sensitive business issues. Without knowing it, I must be rattling somebody's cage."

"So you're to blame. There is a lot of money involved in the Highway 2000 project. So who do you think is the hoodoo?" Will said, trying to lighten her mood. "I guess I should warn you now, if the hoodoo man gets me, I'm going to come back and haunt you."

He started singing Bo Diddley's *Who Do You Love*.
*I walked 47 miles of barbed wire
Used a cobra snake for a neck tie
Got a brand new house on the roadside
Made out of rattlesnake hide
Who do you love. Who do you love. Who do you love ...*

"This is not the time to try to be funny, Hoo-doo Doody," Betsy said. "How-bout I see you tonight. I've got to report this."

"Oh, I'm sure it's just some prankster trying to put the fear of God into you, but since we don't know who we can trust, maybe we ought to keep this to ourselves until we can talk to Henry."

"OK, I'll try, but I'm sure Letha and BB are probably spreading the gossip."

When Henry came to pick up Betsy that afternoon, she told him about the morning incident. He asked if she had saved any of the powder. She showed him the box. He took a sample and told her he was going to have it analyzed. On the way home, they talked about Obeah and Obeah men.

"Obeah has its roots in Africa. It is still widely practiced in Jamaica despite being banned during the late 1700's," Henry said. "Obeah is primarily used to cause harm and is done out of either malice, envy, or what we Jamaicans call 'bad mind.' The Obeah man is asked or hired to 'put a blow' or 'work' on someone to make them ill, experience due hardship, bad luck, become mentally ill, or, in extreme cases, die."

"Sounds like a witch doctor," Betsy said.

"Precisely! There are a number of people on the island who practice this activity. There is the traditional Obeah man, healer men or women, or bush doctors. Some Christian-based shepherds or spiritual mothers use their supernatural powers only to achieve good and will not engage in evil acts. Others use their powers for black-hearted reasons. Obeah men have a very loyal following with the masses. Especially up in the hills, many people have turned to the supernatural out of desperation since there are a number of medical disorders for which there seem to be no adequate treatment or cures."

"So a person's medical problems are instead thought to be a matter of demonic possession," Betsy said.

"If I were to take you into a drug store in downtown Kingston, you could purchase a variety of oils. These oils are sweet-smelling chemicals without any real effect. Some are for success, some to promote healing, some are to tie a person into a relationship, and others are to get rid of someone. They have names – 'compellance' oils, 'tan-there' oils, 'draw-back' oils and 'come-back to me' oils. A pharmacist once told me these oils account for a significant portion of his sales."

When they arrived at Sundance, Henry also asked Will for a sample of the powder that had exploded there. He then promised to get back to them promptly.

"This is definitely a double martini day," Betsy said

after Henry had left.

"I could not agree with you more," Will agreed. "E.J., the bar is now open until further notice."

The evening was uneventful until later that night after Will and Betsy had gone to bed. About midnight Gina began to bark uncontrollably. E.J. switched on the yard lights and stumbled, sleepy and barefooted, out the servant's quarters to see what the problem was. He was trying to pull up his pants as he ran. He stubbed his toe on some limestone rocks. A shadowy hooded figure was spraying graffiti on the front wall.

"Rahtid bumboclot, get yu go **(damned ass-wipe, get out of here)**," he yelled in patois as he slipped on a rock and almost fell.

"To rass, batty 'ousebwoy **(fuck you, faggot houseboy)**" came a shout from the shadows.

E.J. was not to be deterred.

"Nuh ramp wid mi, bloodclaat **(Don't fuck with me, douche-bag)**," he yelled angrily, now limping.

"Gwey **(fuck-off)**," came the answer.

Suddenly E.J., distracted by a spider web he had run into in the dark, tripped over his pants, which were still hanging at half-mast. His belt buckle popped him in the head, drawing blood. He went down cursing and flailing and accidentally rolled down the incline into the intruder.

"Ah wha di ... ?" the intruder uttered as he sprayed E.J. with paint as he jumped back up onto his feet.

The intruder began to point with the paint can and laugh. "Yu face fava shit (you look like shit)."

"Gunkona **(Go fuck yourself)**," E.J. yelled. "Get 'im, Gina."

Gina leaped as E.J. attempted to rise. She knocked the intruder flat again. The intruder's partner, who had been spraying the street-side of the wall, pulled him over the top to safety.

Gina rushed the locked gate only to be red spray-painted by the second intruder.

By this time Will had sprinted down from the main house and was showered with handfuls of pebbles being heaved over the fence. The two nocturnal graffiti artists turned, shot up the hill and quickly disappeared like ghosts into the darkness. A few seconds later a third shadowy figure ran by going in the same direction and disappeared into the black night as well. Will helped E.J. limp back to the house as Gina continued to bark.

"Do you know those two?" Will asked.

"You mean three," Betsy said.

"Never saw any of them before in my whole life," E.J. said.

"Someone definitely doesn't like us," he told Betsy as she stood there in her pajamas.

"As I told you earlier, you have this unnerving effect on people," Will said. "Have you considered Dale Carnegie?"

"Gunkona **(Go fuck yourself)**," Betsy said and smiled.

"You're getting good at patois," Will said as he gave her a thumbs up. "Let's just look at the damage in the morning when we can see better. There's nothing more we can do tonight."

"Good idea," Betsy said. "I don't want to go out there in the dark, and I don't want you to either. There may be more uninvited guests."

At that moment a white Toyota Chaser raced by Sundance heading down Primrose Hill.

> WHEN THE
> LION
> IS SEPLEIG
> DON'T TRY
> WAKE HIM

CHAPTER 21

As soon as it was light, Will, Betsy and the staff went out to examine the mutilation of Sundance's front wall. It was splashed with black hand-painted drawings of owls and wild cats, along with strange part-human, part-animal creatures. The largest of these appeared to represent an occultist's sphere of influence. They could not decide what creature it represented. On the other side were pentagrams and inverted crosses. These were sprayed with red paint.

Betsy was apprehensive; Will was annoyed; E.J. and Leva were worried. After breakfast Henry arrived.

"What in the world happened here last night?" he asked.

They explained the previous night's vandalism.

"Jesus! These are definitely black magic symbols," Henry said. "It looks like I need to place a stronger sense of urgency on my follow-up promise to yesterday's incidents than I first thought."

Leva said she would call Sundance's owner to get the authority to paint the wall and also repair the previous damage to the finials. Will took pictures of the graffiti with his digital camera and scanned them into the computer for the owner to see. Henry requested copies. Betsy and Henry left shortly thereafter for Ocho Rios. E.J. quietly vanished into his room.

About mid-morning, E.J. let a person Will had never seen before in the gate. From the kitchen, Leva also recognized and greeted the newcomer.

"Glad bro real gald **(Greetings)**, Chicken."

"Hail Heile **(greetings to you as well)**, Kingtoo."

Leva was playing gospel music in the kitchen. Chicken joined her, and soon they were singing a duet of *He's Got The Whole World In His Hands.*

When they finished singing, E.J. brought the visitor into Will's office.

"This is my best friend, Mikey Mo Mullens," E.J. said.

Mikey Mo was a skinny, tall, dark man who had short uneven dreadlocks that made him look like he had been the victim of the mad barber in *Sweeney Todd*. Will thought Mikey Mo looked like a black Ichabod Crane. He had a toothy infectious smile, and his arm was in a sling. His nose was mostly hidden by tape, and there was a cut on his forehead. He appeared to be about E.J.'s age. He was wearing a T-shirt that said Conquering Lion Tribe of Judah. He held out his fist to do a fist-to-fist greeting with Will.

"Raspeck **(Respect)**, Mr. Will," he said.

E.J. told Will that he and Mikey Mo had been friends since childhood.

"He and mi be lak bredda since wi be bwoys **(We've been like brothers since we were boys)**," he said.

He told Will that Mikey Mo hoped to one day be a

reggae sensation, but in the meantime he sold lobsters to the locals and woodcarvings to the tourists.

"So you're an artist?" Will asked.

"No, mon," Mikey Mo said, "but I know the artists who live in the cockpit country. I buy their carvings and resell them on the coast. I grew up with most of the carvers. I can get other things up there from time to time to resell as well. Jah lead me to good stuff. Mi can mek a ting **(I can make arrangements)**."

He air-smoked an imaginary joint and winked knowingly at Will.

E.J. shook his head disapprovingly, "No, mon. 'E no use ganja **(he doesn't use marijuana)**."

"No, I'm more of a rum man myself," Will said and smiled. "Did I hear Leva call you Chicken?"

Mikey Mo looked slightly embarrassed.

"It 'cause he have long skinny neck like chicken," E.J. said and laughed.

"E.J. tells me you got problems," Mikey Mo said. "I see what he talk 'bout. It appears you possibly got duppies **(ghosts)** at this villa."

"I don't think so," Will said. "We just had a little trouble with some hoodlums. I don't think they'll be back. They painted graffiti on the wall and threw a few rocks. I'm sure it was just some teenage vandals."

"Oh, they be back, awright," E.J. said to Mikey Mo "De got big trouble 'til yu get sumbody to get rid of dese duppies. De trow rocks too **(they threw rocks too)**? Duppy lak to trow rocks. When duppy trow rocks, trouble soon come. Yu get they help **(Get them help)**."

"I think we'll be OK," Will said. "Not to change the subject, but what happened to you?"

Chicken and Kingtoo exchanged glances and hesitated before speaking.

"Mi have unfortunate accident," Chicken said. "Mi be

A Jamaican Conspiracy

right as rain soon."

Mikey Mo tried to change the subject.

"Mi get well, but yu face allas look lak shit **(I'll get well, but you'll always look like shit)**," he said affably to Kingtoo and laughed as he playfully elbowed Kingtoo in the ribs.

"Mi run into spider web **(I had an encounter with a spider web)**," E.J. said.

"Dat very bad," Mikey Mo said. "Dat not spider web. Dat was duppy. Mi a-go now. Glad to meet you, Mr. Will. Have irie day, Miss Leva. More time **(See you later)**, Kingtoo."

"Check me later **(Talk to you later)**," E.J. said and escorted Chicken to the gate.

"Yu promise mi you get dem help," E.J. said to Mikey Mo at the gate.

With that Mikey Mo, aka Chicken, nodded and took his leave.

"Nice guy," Will said after Mikey Mo had gone, "but he sure has some hang-ups about duppies. You don't believe in duppies, do you, Leva?"

"Sure do," Leva said. "Duppies are real in Jamaica. They are restless spirits. Good duppies are usually dead loved ones who dream you **(appear in a dream)** to give you good advice or information, but bad duppies can do you harm and have to be set on **(gotten rid of)** by someone like an obeah. Especially if it be a rolling calf or Ol' Hige."

"Yu allas **(always)** gotta be careful if yu go out into countryside at night, 'cause yu really don't want to meet a rolling calf," E.J. said and shook his head. ""E a big, calf-like duppy dat rolls long de road **(He's a big, calf-like duppy who rolls down the road)**. Block yu way and chase yu wif wicked intent **(He'll block your way and chase you)**. 'E have blazing red eyes that gash fire and drags a chain **(He has blazing eyes that shoot fire and drags a chain)**. To escape, yu got to drop objects for it to count, get to a crossroads before it can get there, and den stick a pen knife in de ground **(the only way to escape is to drop objects for it to count, get to a crossroads ahead of it and then stick a pen knife in the ground)**."

"Why do you drop things for it to count?" Will asked.

"Because a duppy can't count past three. If 'e get past three, 'e get confused and have to start all over again," Leva said.

"I see. I guess that's logical. Who's Ol' Hige?" Will asked.

"Ol' Hige be a witch who sheds her skin and flies at night. She look lak an owl. She suck yu breath out while yu sleeping. She lak suck **(likes to suck the)** breath outa babies especially. If yu find her skin, yu put salt and pepper on it. She won't be able to put her skin back on because it burn her too much," E.J. said.

"How do you know when you're around a duppy?" Will asked.

"Because dey have high nasal voice and make you feel lak yu head is growing and yu body feel hot. Yu can make duppy go away by wearing yu clothes inside out or cursing or exposing yu private parts," E.J. said.

"I guess I have a lot to learn," Will said and went back to work.

Early that afternoon Will had another visitor. He was a slightly disheveled older Jamaican. He wore nondescript thrift-store quality clothing.

"Mi name Rupee," he said. "Mi told yu have duppies."

"I think you have the wrong house," was all Will could think to say.

"Chicken send me," he said. "Mi trap duppies."

"You mean like in *Ghostbusters*," Will said.

A Jamaican Conspiracy

Rupee did not understand the analogy and looked puzzled.

"Mi Maroon from Accompong. Only Maroons have gift to catch or remove duppies. Mi have chased away more than 70 duppies over last 30 years. Mi in demand all de way to Spanish Town."

Even though Will didn't believe in ghosts, he was curious to learn more.

"Mi learn duppy catching from Mother Rosie, leader of de Accompong Zion Church. Mi tek over when she lose de gift. De leader before her become jealous because she so good. Rosie si seh doing fine and she did bad mind suh 'e write she name pon parchment paper and bury it inna di back yard. From dat she cyaa do it again. Mi take she place because mi chief blower of the abeng **(I learned to catch duppies from Mother Rosie at the Accompong Zion Church. I became the duppy catcher after she lost her ability to do so when a jealous person wrote her name on parchment and buried it in the backyard. After that, she lost her powers. I was chosen to replace her because I was good at blowing the abeng)**."

"That was terrible," Will said. "I'm so sorry for her."

"Yu problem might not be duppies but fallen angels. Mi find out fo yu," Rupee continued.

"Fallen angels?"

"Yeah, mon. Fallen angels are angel-like beings that can be summoned by one person to kill another. People call dung fallen angel at 10 in de day, 10 at night or at midnight. Once dem come a death y'know unless yu under heavy guard. A nuh everybody can si (see) fallen angel, but if yu cyaa (can) see it yu ago (also) hear it. It mek a rumbling soun' wen it a come, so wen people come to me, dem always a seh duppy a haunt dem. But once dem tell me bout di soun, mi can safely tell dem she a

158

fallen angel. People allas want mi guard dem from di angel dem cause dem kina fraid a di ketching ting cuz dem allas a seh what if dem escape. **(Fallen angels are summoned to kill people. They can only be called at certain times and though they are invisible to most people, they can be identified by the rumbling sound they make which is typically identifiable only to a professional. People call me to protect them since they are afraid of what will happen if they catch one and it escapes.).**"

Will was becoming more curious by the minute.

"So what do you do?"

"Mi use half-pint bokkle with rum in it. Mi drop a dollar coin inside and after reading a Psalm, de fallen angel will have no choice but to enter the bokkle. Mi den cover bokkle and tek it and bury it **(I use a bottle of rum with a dollar in it and then read a Psalm. The fallen angel goes in the bottle to get the coin and then I bury it.).**"

"What if it's a duppy, not a fallen angel?" Will asked.

"Mi no ketch duppy jus suh eno, yu cast or chase dem away **(If you can't catch a duppy you chase them away)**. If yu waan ketch duppy yu affi trap it inna di grave **(If you want to catch the duppy you have to trap it in a grave)**. Mi also use abeng to either attract duppies or cast dem away **(I also use my abeng to attract duppies and then get rid of them).**"

"The abeng?" Will asked incredulously.

"Yeah, mon, di duppy dem love di sound a di abeng eno. Once mi trow some rum inna it and start blow it, dem just follow di soun' of it, an mi just lead dem away where dem neva to return **(Duppies love the sound of an abeng especially when you put some rum in it. They follow the sound, and I then lead them away).**"

A Jamaican Conspiracy

"And what's this going to cost me?" Will asked.

"Mi get ridda duppy or fallen angel for J$90,000," Rupee said.

"Let me get back to you on all this," Will said. "Thanks for coming by."

"Don wait too long. Dis serious business," Rupee said. "I be in touch again."

With that Rupee took his leave.

Wow! What a day this has turned out to be, Will thought. *These two-martini days are coming closer and closer together.*

> COWANS
> DRESS PARLOR
> SPECIALIGE IN
> BRIDES AND BRIDE
>   MAIDS

CHAPTER 22

"Letha, would you ask Bob to come down to my office?" Betsy asked.

"He's not in the bank yet."

"But it's mid morning."

"He had a breakfast meeting," Letha said.

An hour later.

"Letha, is Bob in yet?"

"No ma'am, but I'm sure he'll be here soon. His breakfast meeting must have run over. I'll let him know as soon as he gets here that you need to see him. Soon come."

"Was it a breakfast or brunch meeting?" an exasperated Betsy said sarcastically. "Where'd BB go – a jaunt to Little Palm Island, Florida?"

Letha gave her a puzzled look in return and just shrugged.

"I'll explain some other time. If he arrives, just tell him I need to see him," Betsy said impatiently.

A Jamaican Conspiracy

Shortly before lunch Bob poked his head in the door.

"Hear you're looking for me, bwana," he said. "What can I do you for on this fine day. Yes, a fine day. In fact things are fine as frog's hair." He glanced at his watch. "I've got just a minute or two before my luncheon appointment."

"Lunch?" Betsy said. "You just got here. One more meal and you'll explode."

"Well, you know what the wise Jamaican said – 'mi come yah fi drink milk, me no come yah fi count cow.' **(I'm working here to do business, not just talk about it.)**," BB said. "Now, what can I do for you?"

"I'm becoming extremely familiar with that proverb," Betsy said. "Letha has been trying to locate some KSAC files for me and has been having a hard time finding them. She found some of these files in your office. Do you have other files that pertain to the Highway 2000 project?"

"Yes, as a matter of fact, I do," BB said. "I've been familiarizing myself with them as well."

"May I ask why?"

"I have recently been designated as the coordinator for St. Ann for the Champions in Action festival. Are you acquainted with it?"

"Afraid not. Would I be consuming too much of your precious time if I asked you to fill me in?"

"Each August, Presidential Click, one of Jamaica's premier corporations, sponsors one of the largest music festivals in Jamaica in St. Catherine. The festival proceeds go to children's programs in the inner city neighborhoods in West Kingston and the surrounding area. It is a huge event. International superstar Sting played last year. This year we are scheduled to have Wycliff Jean from Haiti as well as Beenie Man, Buju Banton, Assasin, Ninja Man and other international stars. It's a real feather in the bank's cap that I have been afforded this honor. Super-banker in action is part of Champions in Action. Only fitting."

"So what does that have to do with the Highway 2000 bank files?"

"I wanted to learn more about Presidential Click and its sister companies like Incomparable Enterprises so I can maximize this opportunity to bring in business for NCB."

"*If* the bank wants to initiate those relationships," Betsy said. "You do know that these corporations are supposed to be a front for Dudus Coke and the Shower Posse, don't you?"

"Oh no! The files say the principals are Neville Hamilton, one of the most outstanding and respectable businessmen in Brown's Town as well as Hopeton Boothe. Mr. Boothe is a true Jamaican legend. I could make a career from being his banker alone."

"There you go elephant hunting again," Betsy said. "BB, as a senior officer, may I give you some heart-felt advice? Don't spend all your time hunting elephants. The chance that you'll bring one down with a peashooter is remote. Now where are those files I need? Can you bring them to me when you return from lunch?"

"No, ma'am. I think I accidentally left them at home."

"Get them to me ASAP, please."

"Yes, ma'am."

BB had spun on his heel and left Betsy shaking her head in disbelief. Moments later Letha poked her head in the door.

"I made you some coconut macaroons," she said. "Wouldn't it be something if BB brought Hopeton Boothe into the bank? I think Boothe's so dreamy ... and he's sooo rich. And BB is right about Champions in Action. Spragga Benz deejays it. Last time I went I saw TOK, Elephant Man, Puff Daddy and Bounty Killer."

A Jamaican Conspiracy

"Oh, I'm sure it's a killer of a festival. Whether it would bring in the kind of gorilla bank relationships the bank desires, now, that's another matter."

Back at Sundance later that day, Will, Betsy, and Henry were having a rum and coke on the verandah and enjoying the late afternoon view of the sky and ocean. The sky was the smorgasbord the pastels painters so often depict when they draw tropical skies. The conversation was easy and relaxed.

They heard a car honk at the gate. Gina and Samantha rushed down to see what was going on. Lucy, as usual, ran in the wrong direction.

Will looked at Betsy and said, "Are you expecting anyone?"

"No, are you?"

E.J. opened the gate. A blue Hyundai Kia drove in, and Bob Blackmon stepped out.

"Oh, hi, Bob," Betsy said. "I didn't expect to see you up our way. Would you like to join us for a Cuba libre?"

"I don't mind if I join you. A rum on the rocks, please," BB said. "It's been another exceedingly challenging day. I brought those files you wanted."

"Yes, life at the top can be so daunting. Thanks, but the files could have waited until tomorrow. I didn't plan on working on them tonight," Betsy said.

"Well, I have a breakfast meeting the. I thought I'd bring them to you now. Nice villa," BB said. "Do you own it?"

"No, unfortunately it's being leased," Betsy said. "Want me to show you around?"

She gave BB a quick tour and introduced him to the staff while Will made him a rum on the rocks. BB asked if he could have it with a Red Stripe chaser."

"What in the world happened to the front of your wall?" BB asked after he joined them on the veranda.

"Oh just some vandals, but some superstitious people have suggested maybe we have duppies or fallen angels," Will said in a scoffing tone of voice, "and it just so happens I've got the perfect someone who has offered to take care of the problem for us."

"Duppies?" BB said, giving Will a look of alarm and glancing around nervously. "Fallen angels?"

Will told him about the recent events culminating in the concrete fish finials by the gate being smashed and then replaced with glowing glass skulls. BB's eyes got wide, and he took a long pull on his drink and slugged down some Red Stripe.

"Similar to the mahogany skull found in your briefcase at the Martha Brae?"

Betsy nodded.

Then Will told BB how the graffiti symbols had been scribbled on the front wall both inside and out and how perpetrators in hoodies had thrown rocks at him before disappearing into the dark.

BB's eyes got even wider and polished off his drink.

"Duppies throw rocks when they become upset," he said and shook his head.

"Why are you looking worried?" Betsy said. "I thought you didn't believe in duppies. Let me see if I've got this quote right, 'Personally I don't believe in duppies and Obeah men. Those are old fashioned concepts used to manipulate and control the unsophisticated masses.' Am I quoting correctly or am I having a senior management moment?"

For the first time in his life BB had no response. He quickly excused himself, thanked them for the drink, said he was late for dinner, and climbed into his car to leave. E.J. opened the gate. The Hyundai Kia refused to crank. The battery wouldn't even turn over after a couple of attempts.

165

A Jamaican Conspiracy

"It was running perfectly when I drove in," the now jittery BB said. "Your duppy must have gotten in the engine."

BB was really starting to look rattled. Betsy called Henry. He brought his jumper cables and got the car cranked. A feral cat chose that moment to climb down from the tree in the front yard. All four dogs instantaneously went on frenzied high alert and began barking in unison while chasing it. This rattled BB further, and he backed off the driveway into the tree. He started to pull forward, but the terrified cat leaped through the rolled-down driver's-side window. BB panicked again and rammed the opened gate. The cat screeched and jumped back out the window. BB banged his knee trying to get out of the damaged Kia. The moment the dogs re-spied the cat, Lucy lunged for it. BB tripped on the cat's tail, sending the cat spitting and clawing its way up the back of his shirt as he hit the ground with a thud. Just as BB staggered drunkenly back onto his feet, Gina leaped and knocked BB flat a second time. As he slipped on a loose limestone rock, he came down on the cat again. He began careening clumsily down the incline with the angry cat holding on like a log-flume rider for dear life. The dogs followed. When he was finally able to stop himself, the snarling cat streaked through the iron gate with the dogs only steps behind. E.J. took off after the dogs, his skinny arms flailing over his head.

The mute BB sat up looking dazed and confused. His clothes were in tatters, and he was scratched from head to foot. He had partially ripped the sole off one of his shoes. It flapped like a clown shoe. When he finally tried to stand, his knee gave way, and he sank back to the ground for a third time.

"Are you Ok?" Will said. "Should I fix you another drink?"

Betsy shot Will a dirty look. "I think he's had enough."

BB finally managed to form words and said, "I want to get out of here. This place is haunted."

The Kia was completely dead. Henry offered to tow it down to a mechanic's shop on 1A. BB jumped into Henry's van, refusing to spend one more moment at Sundance. He told Will and Betsy he would call his wife to pick him up at the auto mechanic's shop.

The following morning when Betsy arrived at the bank, her office was covered with tiny black specks. Ants had already found some of them.

"Letha, what is this? Didn't the janitors clean up in here last night? If so, it looks like they delivered instead of took away."

"Yes, ma'am," Letha said. "The janitors were here. That's birdseed. BB put it out early this morning as duppy repellent. He put it all over the bank. He say your house has duppies and fallen angels, and now they after him as well. He say unless he takes immediate action, they will put a hex on him and prevent him from ever being a super-banker again."

> CROOK'S BEAUTY SALON

CHAPTER 23

Leva secured the requested permission from Sundance's owner to hire a contractor to do some repairs at the villa. The owner asked Will to help oversee the work. Leva decided to go with Charlie-Red Conlon, the tradesman who had been recommended to Will at the McIver's dinner party. Since Conlon lived in the hills and didn't have phone service, Leva asked Henry if he would drive to Conlon's house and ask him to come down to Sundance.

The following day, after returning from taking Betsy to work, Henry came by the villa to tell Will he had located Conlon. Will asked his advice on dealing with Jamaican laborers.

Henry took a sip of tea and thought for a second before speaking.

"There is a Jamaican proverb that says 'Dog say 'im won't work, 'im wi sidone an look, for 'im must get a livin **(If a person cannot make a adequate wage, he should simply sit and watch)**.' This and several other

A Jamaican Conspiracy

Jamaican proverbs will give you a clue to the origin of an entrenched, counterproductive work ethic that is the by-product of slavery and its aftermath. If workers feel that reward doesn't measure up to effort, very little energy will be expended."

"Please be more specific," Will said.

"At the core of these proverbs is the underdog's perception that work does not always yield benefits for the laborer. There is another cynical proverb that says 'Bakra's **(white man's)** work never done.' More directly put," Henry paused and took a sip of tea, "since white man's work is never done, there is no point in attempting to do it. This proverb also implies that work is seen as bakra's business, making work the act of working for someone else, thus making wholehearted work a betrayal of the worker's own interest. Therefore, many people rationalize that it simply doesn't make sense to engage in futile activity, work being futile activity.

"This same non-work philosophy has sometimes been adopted by Jamaican government employees, making them an ongoing challenge to deal with. The government is seen as a faceless bakra to which one is not personably accountable. Government's work is never done, so why try. There is even a proverb that says 'government work never done.'"

Will just shook his head.

"Since honest labor is not fairly rewarded, trickery becomes a strategy for survival," Henry continued. "There are two proverbs that make this attitude clear. One says 'Yu never see empty bag 'tan **(stand)** up.' The other says 'Yu never see full bag bend.' In other words, the hungry worker is too empty to stand while the well-fed worker is too full to bend."

"If you're trying to discourage me, you're succeeding," Will said.

170

"No, I'm just giving you the Jamaican perspective," Henry said, "but don't forget you have one great asset who understands the way things are done. I mean Leva, and with all modesty, I do have extensive construction experience myself."

That Monday a short wiry older man and a young helper approached Sundance's gate. He had walked miles from his hill-town home carrying his canvas tool bag. His saw showed outside his heavy bag. He identified himself to E.J. as Charlie-Red Conlon.

He held out a twisted and gnarled hand for Will to shake. Will immediately had a language problem since Charlie-Red only spoke patois, while Will's ability to communicate in this language was still limited. Will showed him the jobs needing to be done – the French doors that did not shut properly, the finials which needed replacing, the graffiti on the walls which needed painting over, and other maintenance items on Leva's list.

Charlie-Red looked at the wall with the graffiti, shook his head and mumbled something Will could not understand about duppies. The assistant just stood there and nodded at whatever Charlie-Red said.

As Will tried to explain each job, Charlie-Red would just look puzzled and say something like "Yes, me Boss," and then E.J. would translate Will's request for him. Will showed him the stone pineapple finials that had been selected to take the place of the destroyed fish finials on the posts by the front gate. Charlie-Red nodded and mumbled his approval since pineapples have long been considered a symbol of hospitality in the Caribbean.

When this was done, Charlie-Red tried to explain in patois to Will that he would return the following day to start on his assigned projects. He then ambled off with his nameless helper back up the hill.

True to his word, Charlie-Red and his companion

arrived at Sundance on Tuesday morning. As he stood and looked at the graffiti covered wall, he said "a lickle lick." Will's blank expression let him know that they were not communicating. Charlie-Red repeated himself, saying "a lickle lick" and held his gnarled thumb to his mouth in a drinking motion. He repeated his request again. "A lickle lick a' licka **(a little lick of liquor)**." Will continued to look puzzled. Finally he said, "Jes a licka lick. De rum, mon, de rum." Will called E.J. out into the yard. E.J. explained to Will that what Charlie-Red was trying to convey was that since the damage to the wall had been caused by duppies, it was imperative that white rum be splashed on it before repairs began to keep the duppies from returning when the job was completed.

Will finally understood. E.J. went up to the house and returned with a six-pack of Red Stripe, a bottle of Wray and Nephew rum, and some ice. Charlie-Red and his assistant's eyes lit up, and the ritual began. He sprinkled rum on the wall and the place on the posts where the finials would be replaced. Toasts were offered to everyone's health and to the success of the project. Will presented Charlie-Red and his nameless assistant with RST baseball caps. It soon became obvious that no work would begin that day. When the rum and the beer were gone, Charlie-Red announced that work would begin on Wednesday and left to trudge back up into the hills with his assistant, proudly wearing their new RST caps.

As he was leaving, Charlie-Red urged Will to consider as an even further duppy deterrence also allowing him to kill a rooster and sprinkle its blood on the wall before the work actually began. E.J. translated the suggestion to Will. Will shook his head, and told E.J. to tell Charlie-Red that this would not be necessary.

Charlie-Red was true to his word. He and his assistant were at Sundance early Wednesday morning to begin replacing the stone finials.

Charlie-Red began by appraising the possible positioning of the pineapples. The first step was to empty his bag and meticulously arrange his tools on the lawn. Most of these tools consisted of an odd hodge-podge of pieces of metal, oddly twisted wires, sticks, and a beat-up triangle. A long discussion then ensued between him and his assistant. They turned the pineapples over and over as they mulled the ideal placement that would best position them for properly welcoming future visitors to Sundance.

He then brought out an ancient, rusty hammer that was almost completely rounded from years of hard use. It was attached to a short splintered tree limb handle. He began to hollow a base in the top of the column. He balanced the stone pineapple on his little sticks. He then stood back, gazed on his progress, and discussed matters in patois with his assistant. Once a consensus was reached, each little stick was adjusted over and over. They would raise the pineapple a little, then lower it a little, and then raise it again until they agreed that it was just right. Then they would remove the sticks and the process would be repeated. Will would walk out from the house periodically to inspect their progress. The pineapple looked perfect to him. Charlie-Red would shake his head, remove the sticks, and begin still another time. By noon, one of the pineapples had been finished. After taking a lunch break, work began on the second finial. Just before Betsy and Henry were due to arrive back from Ocho Rios, Charlie-Red pronounced the second finial perfect. He laid some fresh concrete around the base of both of them, let it set for a few minutes, and then pulled out all the sticks. Will had to admit, the pineapples were perfectly level. Charlie-Red smiled broadly as he was congratulated by his assistant. Then he shook Will's hand. He put his sticks,

A Jamaican Conspiracy

wires, and hammer back into his bag as he and his assistant prepared for the long walk home. Before slowly and silently ambling up the road, he announced to Will that they would return the following day to work on the next project. Within minutes Betsy and Henry drove into the driveway.

Will pointed at Sundance's new pineapples and announced, "This is definitely a two-martini day, and I didn't even do any of the work."

Betsy look puzzled.

Henry just smiled knowingly.

> **JACKSON'S HARDWARE & FURNITURE**
> CAVE VALLEY PO BOX 45, ST. ANN
> **SPECIALIZE IN RADIOS TV.
> STEREOGRAM FRIDGEATORS AND ALL
> TYPE OF BUILDING MATERIAL ETC.
> SAND GRAVAL MARL BLOCKS
> CEMENT STEEL
> (PROMP DELIVERY)**

CHAPTER 24

Betsy closed the final file folder and moved it out of her way. She had now completed her initial forensic audit of the Highway 2000 project. She looked at her legal pad and silently read the notes she had taken and highlighted certain items she wanted to review further. She felt about as prepared as she could be with the documents she had at her disposal. She glanced again at her list of unreturned phone calls relating to the project. Now, instead of relying on the words of others, she needed to roll up her sleeves, get out of her office, and go into the field to observe matters for herself firsthand.

On the way home that afternoon, she asked Henry if he would be available the following day to drive her around. He said, "Of course."

Instead of going directly to the bank the following morning, Henry and Betsy drove on A4 towards Montego Bay to see some road clearing work being done by KSAC.

175

The work had only barely been started. A small idle crew of men was standing around chatting and smoking ganja. She made a record of the number of men present. She asked to see the foreman and was told he had gone into Ocho Rios to pick up needed items. She looked on her records. The name of the general contractor was listed as John David Grey. The laborers spoke only patois. Henry probed them, but they seemed to know very little about Grey. Bank records showed his office to be a St. Ann address off of A3 on Parry Town Road. She instructed Henry to drive her there.

When they arrived at the office of record, they found on an unpaved back road a ramshackle metal building surrounded by a rusty chain-link fence with a padlocked gate. The front door was slightly ajar, and a window was broken. A piece of the rusted metal roof had peeled back at one corner. The only sign on the building said *No Truspis*. The overgrown parking lot was dominated by tall weeds and housed on the back of the lot a derelict Bobcat and some rusty 40-foot containers. No other equipment or materials were stored on the premises. If Betsy had not been told it was an active business, she would have mistaken it for a junkyard.

"This certainly doesn't look like a typical home office," Betsy commented.

"Certainly doesn't look like a company that would be awarded multi-million dollar government contracts," Henry agreed.

"Why would you even bother to lock this place?" Betsy asked. "There doesn't appear to be anything anyone would want to steal."

"Only reason I can think of is to keep squatters out," Henry said.

"I can't think why they'd even want to stay here," Betsy said. "Maybe we've got the wrong address."

Henry drove her back to the bank. The address checked out. She tried the phone number she had been given and dialed it. A man answered the phone in patois. She identified herself and asked for Grey. The man told her he was unavailable and hung up before she could leave a message.

She checked her file and jotted down a pro forma weekly payroll number. She divided this by what she considered to be a fair wage to try to estimate the approximate size of the company's employee count. The workers at the job site numbered only 10% of her hypothetical number.

The following morning she got Henry to take her again to the job site. Nothing had been accomplished since the previous day. Once again she saw a skeleton crew standing around talking to each other. She approached a bulldog looking man who seemed to be in charge. He told her that the job would be completed in the near future, "soon come," and that the project was being delayed by an equipment failure. She once again wrote down the number of workers present.

She called Grey's phone number only to be once again told he was supervising work in the field. She got Henry to take her back to the job site.

Henry and Betsy drove up to the inactive work site and politely asked if anyone had seen Grey.

"Yu agin," the foreman replied rudely. "Wa mek yu continue come back-back **(Why do you continue to come back?)**? Mi tell yu mi no know where Mr. Grey be."

"Wi told him was out in da field," Henry responded politely. "Is dey another work site?"

"If Mr. Grey wan' to talk to yu, he seek yu out. Now, yu tek yu bakra **(white slave master)** an' go - now."

He began advancing towards Henry and Betsy in a threatening manner with a shovel in his hand. The men

A Jamaican Conspiracy

in his crew began following him brandishing their tools as well. Betsy and Henry started backing away. Henry glanced around for a weapon. Betsy stumbled over something behind her and almost lost her balance. Henry caught her before she fell.

They glanced back and saw the "something" was a man holding a machete. He seemed to have materialized out of nowhere. The young man was wiry with sinuous muscles. Betsy guessed him to be in his twenties. He was neither overdressed nor underdressed. If Betsy had run into him on the streets of Ocho Rios, she probably would not have given him a second look.

Betsy gasped involuntarily. She had momentary visions of being caught between two groups of homicidal laborers and being hacked by one while they were beaten to death by the other. The headline *American Banker Found Slain* popped into her brain.

The new arrival stepped around them and with one vicious swing of his machete, cut the shovel handle the foreman was holding in two. The foreman dropped the remnants of the shovel and began to back away. The crew dropped their tools and began to retreat as well.

"Mi' wan' no truble here today," their rescuer calmly said in patois. "Undastan?"

The foreman said nothing but nodded his comprehension. He motioned his crew back with a wave of his huge hand.

The man then turned to Henry and Rose.

"I think it would be better if you left now," he said in flawless English.

He then stood quietly, holding the machete, and watching the work crew while Betsy and Henry got back in the van. Henry began to back away.

Henry slowly drove back to A3 saying nothing. Betsy shuddered as she thought about how close they had both

178

come to being severely hurt or even possibly killed. Henry kept eyeing his rear view mirror. He finally spoke.

"That 1996 white Toyota Chaser with the cracked windshield is behind us," he said.

"Could it be the stranger who just rescued us?" Betsy asked.

"I don't know," Henry said. "I can't tell who's driving."

"Let's hope the driver's our guardian angel," Betsy said.

"We certainly seem to have one somewhere, but why would he continue to following us?" Henry said.

"I get the feeling that his presence there may not have just been a coincidence," Betsy said.

Henry said nothing.

> NOTICE
> PLUMMING
> ANYONE WHO NEED
> TO REPEAR BATH ROOM PIPE
> TOLIET PIPE WASH HAND PIPE
> YOU CAN BE CONTACTED THOMAS AT
> 43 HANOVER ST. OR 34 FRENCH ST.
> SPANISH TOWN

CHAPTER 25

When Henry took Betsy back to the bank, she immediately reported the incident at the KSAC jobsite to the Ocho Rios Constabulary Force (police) office. An investigator was sent. Both Henry and Betsy repeated how they had been threatened and how the man in the white Toyota Chaser had saved them. The cop took notes and then drove them to the job site. Betsy watched for the white Toyota Chaser, but it never reappeared. They did not recognize any of the skeleton crew idling about. When they asked about the bulldog looking foreman, the men just looked puzzled and shook their heads. One man nervously said that until now it had been just another uneventful workday. The others agreed with him and swore that they had never seen either Betsy or Henry before that moment.

"Surely you don't think we both imagined this confrontation," Betsy told the investigator.

"I'm sure something happened, but I'm not sure how to proceed. It's your word against theirs. Let's just leave it like this. Call me if you are threatened again."

Betsy called Will on her cell phone and gave him an overview of the day's events.

"Sweetheart, getting yourself killed is not one of your duties."

"We both agreed I needed to do some field research."

"But not in Potter's Field," Will replied.

"Do you have a better idea?"

"Maybe you should take another witness like BB when you go out," Will said.

"Please," Betsy said. "Anyone but BB."

"Talk to Smith," Will suggested.

"I will. This is another of those double martini days," she said. "Over-proof if you have it."

"Why don't I just tell E.J. to break out a bottle and a straw?" Will asked.

"Works for me."

"After this doozy, maybe we should reread Dale Carnegie when you get here. In the long run, that'll be cheaper than the booze bill."

"Cute, but then you'd be forced to drink alone. This is no laughing matter. I'll fill you in when I get there."

Will had E.J. set up the bar by the pool. Soon he and Betsy were in the water watching the sunset. Betsy began to describe to him that day's incident at the road-building site.

"If not for the intervention of our unnamed friend, you might be a widower," she said with a shudder. "I still don't know where our savior materialized from or why he was there," she said, "but he was certainly no stranger to a machete. Henry was looking for a makeshift weapon, but there was no way he would have bested or even bluffed that whole burly work crew. We'd both be bloody statistics right now."

"What I still don't understand," Will said, "is what

you did to set them off. You just wanted to talk to the general contractor. Someone must have given the foreman instructions to intercept anyone nosing around and make sure they never returned."

"It's not like I was walking in there with a smoking gun, and they had been forewarned," Betsy said.

"Did anyone other than Henry know your plans to make a field visit to the work site?"

"I have mentioned to Dunster on several occasions that I am looking for Grey to clarify some items," Betsy said, "but Dunster's my ally. Also BB and Letha knew I was looking for him, but they're both idiots."

"So you think," said Will. "Things are not always as they seem."

At that moment the phone in the kitchen rang. E.J. answered it.

With a perplexed look on his face, he came down to the pool carrying the cordless handset and handed it to Betsy.

"Hit fo' yu," he stuttered, lapsing into patois as he often did when he was nervous. "'E say 'e name is Cudjoe," he said as he handed Betsy the phone and then remained to listen.

"Hello," Betsy said.

"I had hoped we would never have to talk again, but obviously you didn't take our first conversation as seriously as I hoped you would. You are a very fortunate young lady that an intruder butted in at just the right moment today. We'll make sure that doesn't happen again," said the familiar voice.

"What have I done to anger you?" Betsy said. "I don't even know who you are."

"Your presence in Jamaica angers me. You have been politely warned to mind your own business and stay out of local matters," Cudjoe continued. "I clearly told you

A Jamaican Conspiracy

that you did not want me or my associates as enemies. Are you now starting to understand my meaning?"

"I told you the first time," Betsy said. "I am not trying to cause problems for anyone. I am simply doing my job to the best of my ability."

"Maybe you should consider a different line of work," Cudjoe said. "One that is less stressful, or should I say dangerous. After all, foreigners should not involve themselves in Jamaican affairs."

"That is not my intention, I can assure you. I am only here to protect my employer's interests."

Cudjoe's courteous tone suddenly changed dramatically.

"The trouble with interfering Yankees like you is that you don't understand this country. You come in here and six months later, start telling us how we ought to behave. You think you understand Jamaicans, but you don't. If you continue to meddle, we will make sure you never trouble anyone again," he said with venom in his voice.

"Are you threatening me?" Betsy asked.

"How many ways do I have to say it? Do not make the mistake of becoming our adversary. It is not in your *or* your family's best interest. Your guardian angels will not always be around when you need them. Nor will the police. You are on a rural island, *our* island, and we're never far away. And before you call the Constabulary Force again, just remember we have influence there as well."

The phone went dead and Betsy heard only a dial tone. She handed the phone back to E.J. She was momentarily speechless.

About that time a sea gull flew over and pooped on Betsy's shoulder.

E.J. immediately perked up. "In Jamaica this is a sign of good luck to come. This means everything will be all right."

Will and Betsy both just rolled their eyes.

184

> CarWash ya Every Day, Fenda

CHAPTER 26

The following day at the bank was largely routine and uneventful. BB attended a Reggae Sumfest committee meeting; Letha was preoccupied with choosing a menu for a dinner party she was hosting. About the middle of the afternoon, Will called the bank to check and make sure Betsy's day was going smoothly and that she had received no more threats.

"As Jimmy Buffett so succinctly stated 'Just another shitty day in paradise'," she said. "I guess this will only need to be a one-martini day."

"I don't know if that's good or bad," he quipped. "My taste buds are becoming acclimated to doubles."

Betsy arrived home at a respectable hour and soon they were enjoying each other's company in the pool as Maxi Priest sang *Wild World* in the background. Will began telling her of a windfall his clients had gotten from an unexpected tender offer. He also brought her up to date on some recent happenings in Key West.

"A reality-TV film crew was shooting footage at the Key West Airport Monday for an upcoming episode on the Travel Channel when they found a pair of human fetuses in the luggage of two women returning from Havana," he said. "The fetuses were being delivered to someone in Miami for use in a Santeria-like religious ritual."

"That's disgusting," Betsy said.

"The women said they were given the glass jar by a Santeria priest called a babalawo who asked them to deliver it as a favor. They claim they didn't have an inkling what was in the jar. Somehow it got through Cuban customs."

"How old were the fetuses?" Betsy asked.

"According to the *Citizen*, they were 20 weeks old and had been still born."

"Let's please talk about something more pleasant," Betsy said. "I've been exposed to enough unsettling dilemmas over the last few days."

"Well, on a lighter note, someone we know was in the Key West news today."

Oh, yeah, who's that?" Betsy asked.

"Dave Chavka."

"Good old Deputy Dave," Betsy said. "What's he been up to lately?"

"Well, it seems that he saw a bearded man pull up to a black BMW driven by another bearded man who had been known to deal drugs. The man made an illegal U-turn after his business was concluded. When he saw Deputy Dave, he got out of his car and ran into a Stock Island trailer park leaving a woman passenger in the car who claimed she barely knew him. Dave found some plastic bags of cocaine along with a piece of paper with an address in the trailer park in it. When he knocked on the door, the woman who answered it claimed she was alone, but Dave decided to stay and watch things. Well, a few minutes later an SUV pulled up, and someone wearing a blonde woman's wig ran out of that same trailer and dove headfirst into the car. Before the car could take off, Dave ran over and collared his original suspect."

Will and Betsy both started laughing as they visualized a hairy-legged fleeing bearded man in a blonde wig.

"In some places in the Keys he might not have stood out," Betsy said.

"Like at Winn-Dixie on Big Pine Key. Remember the time a smuggler on the lam was reported by a store employee because he looked disheveled," Will said.

"What made that incident so remarkable was that it's rare that a patron in Big Pine's Winn-Dixie doesn't look disheveled."

They could hear the phone ringing in the kitchen. E.J. answered it and brought the cordless handset down to the pool.

"Hello," Betsy said.

"Just call me Buried Blade," the man said, obviously attempting to disguise his voice.

Oh shit, Betsy thought. *Here we go again. Are Will and I the only ones in this country who don't have a street name?*

"How can I help you, Mr. Blade?" she asked.

"The important thing is what I can do for you," the man said. "I am going to help advance your KSAC investigation."

"Who says I'm doing an investigation?"

"Please just be quiet and listen. There are five containers on the back of John David Grey's Parry Town Road address. I think you would possibly find the contents very incriminating."

The phone went dead, and all Betsy heard was a dial tone.

"Another threat?" Will asked.

"No, just the opposite. Now I have a new informer who calls himself Buried Blade."

Betsy then repeated her conversation with Buried Blade in its entirety.

"Christ! Who the hell could that be? Cudjoe's uncle? You know, Leva's right. We definitely need a street name. I've been giving this a lot of thought. You can be Betsy Boop, and I'll be Buckwheat."

"Buckwheat, you definitely have too much time on your hands. Seriously, I don't have a clue as to who this latest character is or why he is pretending to be helpful. It might be Elvis's duppy for all I know."

"With a name like that, he sounds more like a roots reggae singer. Do you think Buried Blade might drive a dinged white Toyota Chaser?" Will asked.

"The thought crossed my mind. I think this just turned back into a two-martini and double-olive day. How would you like to take a field trip with me tomorrow?"

"Funny you should ask. That's what I told myself when I got out of bed this morning," Will said. "I sure wish my wife would ask me if I could take a field trip and capture a crazed and probably stoned Jamaican criminal. When do we leave?"

Betsy then explained to him what little she knew about KSAC.

When Henry came to pick her up the following morning, Betsy explained to him that she wanted to revisit the Grey Parry Town Road property and that Will would be accompanying them. Henry did not seem overly pleased with the day's agenda but reluctantly agreed to drive them there. He took the precaution of going back by his house and picking up a pistol in case there was more trouble.

When they got to the Grey property nothing seemed to have changed. It still looked like a deserted building, not the office of a major government contractor.

"Let's poke around," Betsy said, "and see if we can learn anything. I didn't go on the property the other day."

"I'll wait out by the road with my pistol and keep a lookout for unexpected company," Henry said.

Will and Betsy climbed over the chain-link fence and walked back to the galvanized building. The door was still ajar so they entered the building and saw they were now in an extremely bare-bones office. There was a beat-up desk with a metal folding chair. Some rusty filing cabinets lined the wall. Will rattled a drawer. A piece of angle iron had been threaded through the drawer handles and locked in place with a large padlock. Will snapped pictures with his phone.

"Some office! No computer, not even a typewriter," Betsy commented.

"Don't forget why we came here. Let's go look at those containers before someone catches us," Will said.

They let themselves out of the building and walked back to the first of the five containers. Will guessed its measurements to be about 40 feet. Each had been securely locked and a piece of security tape had been affixed. Will peeked in a crack in the door. The container appeared to be storing office furniture.

"Looks like expensive new furniture to me. Gorgeous wood. I see some tags on some of it. I'm not sure what Buried Blade wanted you to see, but surely that's not it. I expected to see bales of square grouper or something exciting, not the furniture section of Staples. We're not going to see what else is in there without a bolt cutter ...

189

and that's called breaking and entering."

"I guess I'll have to try to think of some other way to learn what these containers are storing."

"What will be the basis of your inquiry? Other than what your anonymous source has almost told you about them, you have no defensible reason to be suspicious and could possibly be arrested for trespassing on private property. If these containers belonged to me, and a snoop like you insisted on knowing what was in them, I'd tell them to stick their demand where the sun don't shine. These containers seem boringly legal," Will said.

"I sure wish I had a Chief Wanderley over here as a resource," Betsy said.

"So do I. Let's get the hell out of here before we get in trouble. We need to think this matter through."

Henry was waiting for them by the van. He quickly put the van into gear and headed back for A3. He continually looked in his rear-view mirror.

"I know I'm probably letting my imagination run away with me," he said, "but about five cars behind us is the damaged white 1996 Toyota Chaser."

```
BEET
oUT
weLDING
AND
SPRAING
```

CHAPTER 27

On Saturday morning, as he and Rose came over to take Leva to the market, Henry noticed a cardboard box by the gate. He mentioned it to Will after he had parked his van.

"I'll get E.J. to bring it in when he closes the gate," Will said. "It's probably from my office in Key West."

"Your office sends a box with flies all over it?" Henry asked.

E.J. was in his apartment with his friend, Mikey Mo, helping Mikey Mo rehearse for an upcoming gig. Will heard the amusing sounds of a cover version of *Love Me Tender* coming from E.J.'s quarters. As so often is the case with reggae cover versions of American hit songs, the artist had taken liberties with the original song and had changed the lyrics to say "kiss me quick." Will could hear Mikey Mo's deejay patter over the top of the song. He was even more amused when E.J. emerged from his apartment decked out in a white sequined jump suit trailing a cape that looked like it had been cut from old drapery material.

Will couldn't resist poking fun and sang a few lines from *The Wonder Of You*.

"Elvis, would you mind gliding down to the gate and retrieving the package there?" he said, stifling a chuckle. "I think it might be someone's garbage."

E.J. and Mikey Mo headed for the gate together. They returned, trailed by a hoard of black flies, holding a smelly box in front of them.

"That smells horrible," Leva gasped.

"Bwaay ... " Rose said as she fanned her face with her hand.

E.J. set the box down in the driveway and opened the flaps. It contained what appeared to be a reddish-hued dead chicken surrounded by black and white candles and a few Jamaican coins. It had been covered with fish entrails which were emitting the extremely pungent odor. Everyone gagged and tried to turn away.

"Put that thing in the garbage immediately before I get sick, but first tie it up in a garbage bag or the dogs are going to want to get in it," Leva said, waving her broom at the disgusting mess.

E.J. and Mikey Mo went in the kitchen for a garbage bag. Flies circled the chicken carcass.

"Who would want to leave this repulsive creature here?" Betsy asked.

"Someone's sure trying to send a foul message," Rose said.

"Well, they certainly succeeded," Will said. "And what a foul fowl it is."

E.J. and Mikey Mo returned with a plastic bag.

"A bokor," E.J. gasped. "Dead chicken sent by bokor."

"Or someone pretending to be a bokor," Mikey Mo

said to himself in a low voice.

Will and Betsy both looked puzzled.

"A bokor is a voodoo priest who serve the loa **(lord)** with both hands," Mikey Mo explained.

About that time the sedated, but very much alive, chicken awoke with wildly flapping wings. Rancid fish guts spattered all over them. E.J. instinctively grabbed for the bird and missed. When he grabbed, a buzzing fly flew down his throat.

"De bokor mek **(made)** a zombie chicken!" E.J. screamed. "Hit be a zombie! Run!"

E.J. started to retch as he tried to dislodge the live fly from his throat. Mickey Mo shrank back in fear as all four dogs came tearing around the house at once. Lucy smelled the putrid guts and started to roll in them. The terrified chicken flew on top of E.J.'s head and clawed for a foothold on his sunglasses and scalp. E.J. began to spin erratically around in circles, raking and slapping Mikey Mo with his cape on each revolution. Mikey Mo grabbed the cape and tried to blanket it over the panicky chicken in an attempt to corral it once and for all. A now blinded and bleeding E.J. stepped in the box of slick fish guts, sending him careening into Rose who in turn took both Will and Betsy down into the stinky glop. The chicken flew into a tree, still grasping E.J.'s sunglasses. The barking dogs leaped and tried to reach it.

E.J. recovered his balance, threw the cape off his face, and saw for the first time that his prize jumpsuit was covered in grass and dirt stains.

"To rass **(fuck you)**," he shouted angrily at the chicken and grabbed Leva's broom to try to whack it out of the tree.

"Don' yu cus-cus lak dat round mi, 'ousebwoy **(Don't cuss around me, houseboy)**," Leva scolded. "Yu respek a lady **(You respect a lady)**."

A Jamaican Conspiracy

"To rass too **(Fuck you too)**," the hyperventilating E.J. screamed back.

Leva slapped him.

The scared chicken answered by pooping on E.J.'s ruined costume. E.J. swung the broom again.

The swing missed the chicken and instead hit a wasp nest in a nearby tree. A cloud of wasps emerged, and the entire group ran for their lives with hundreds of enraged wasps in pursuit.

Will was the first to recover and began to laugh. Henry soon joined him. When everyone else had caught their breath, Mikey Mo suggested that after taking Rose and Leva to Brown's Town to shop, Henry should try to bring Colonel Winter back to Sundance so they could ask his advice. It was unanimously agreed that this was a sound idea, and Henry, Rose and Leva left almost immediately. Mikey Mo called the Colonel.

Henry returned several hours later with Colonel Winter.

"Thank you so much for coming," Will said as he shook The Colonel's hand.

"Glad to be of service," Colonel Winter said. "It is good to see you both again. I have been somewhat concerned about you two."

Will and Betsy led him over to the box of fish guts, smelling worse than ever. Colonel Winter knelt down and examined it. He poked through the box with a stick and noted both the candles and the coins.

Will then took him into the house and showed him the pictures he had taken of the graffiti that had been left on the wall by the vandals as well as the crystal skull vodka bottles. Betsy told him about the boxes of powder they had received both at the bank and the villa and told him about Walter Wanderley's chemical analysis of the contents of the glass skulls. The Colonel listened politely before divulging he was aware of the boxes' contents since Henry had brought him a sample of each in a Ziploc.

Leva brewed their company some tea and served them at the table on the veranda.

"Someone has gone to a lot of trouble to frighten you," Colonel Winter began, "but the lack of consistency tells me that this someone is underestimating your sophistication in matters of syncretic religions."

The Colonel paused to sip his tea and organize his thoughts.

"Let's individually dissect the incidents which have happened," he said. "One thing immediately apparent to me is the inconsistent symbolism. The person trying to scare you has made no attempt to continuously use one kind of black magic. The symbols were instead chosen for the dramatic effect they would have on a religious neophyte. It is also possible they themselves are ignorant of various religions.

"First, the mahogany skull. Skulls are often used as a prop in voodoo ceremonies. Voodoo originated in Dahomey and evolved in Haiti during the time of slavery. Voodoo has many deities which are known collectively as loa. Each corresponds to a Catholic saint. While most voodoo is positive magic, it also has a dark side with the bokors. Skulls are often used as part of a bokor's rituals. Since yours was carved by a local, I had hoped to be able to identify the carver. So far, my efforts have been unsuccessful."

"Isn't voodoo where the concept of zombies originated?" Betsy asked.

"Yes. Bokors have been known to use a deadening potion containing the poison from a puffer fish. The brew makes the drinker appear to be dead. When the person who is supposed to be dead revives, the bokor reputedly will dominate them by giving them a deliriant drug called

A Jamaican Conspiracy

datura which puts them in a detached, dreamlike state."

"What about the glass skulls?" Will asked. "Are they also a voodoo symbol?"

"No. They are more reminiscent of the pre-Columbian crystal skulls which are often attributed to the Aztec or Maya civilizations. Some members of the New Age movement claim these skulls exhibit paranormal phenomena."

"I'm starting to see what you mean by inconsistent symbolism," Betsy said.

"Now let's discuss the graffiti on your wall," Colonel Winter said. "Pentagrams and inverted crosses are symbols commonly associated with Satanists, once again, a symbolic contradiction."

"Well, so far we have a satanic bokor from Mexico," quipped Will.

"Let's talk about your exploding boxes," the Colonel said. "The powder you received at the bank contained sulfur, chili powder, with a pinch of asafetida. This concoction is known as 'get away powder.' 'Get away powder' is designed to get rid of any person who is bothering you. The one sent to Sundance contained dirt, mistletoe, sulfur, orris and sage. We call that mixture 'lost and away powder' because it is used to get rid of someone who is a nuisance. Both powders are most often obtained from Obeah men."

"We certainly have plenty of Obeah men in Jamaica," Mikey Mo said.

"The chicken you received today is reminiscent of Santería," Winter said. "Santería evolved in Cuba and was originally called Lucumi. It recognizes multiple gods corresponding to Catholic saints, each of which has its own function. The followers of Santería believe in ebbo or sacrifice. Chickens are very commonly used as a sacrifice victim. The only explanation I have as to why your chicken was merely drugged instead of killed as is the usual custom is for the drama it would produce."

He paused to give them all a chance to digest his observations.

"The fact that your anonymous caller has adopted the name Cudjoe is meant to make you or your staff think that the villa has a duppy problem. My guess is the name was chosen more to make your Jamaican associates nervous than it was to scare you since, as foreigners, you would most likely not have a true appreciation of Cudjoe's historical significance in Jamaica. Personally, since Cudjoe is one of the Maroon's most important historically significant figures, I find it quite distressing that someone would choose to use his name in such an abhorrent manner. So to summarize, your tormentor has either accidentally or purposely mixed signs from Satanism, Santería, Voodoo, Aztec, Obeah men, and duppy superstition in an attempt to rattle you."

"So what do you suggest we do?" Betsy asked.

"Nothing at this juncture, except don't let these amateurish attempts frighten you. I guess you simply have no choice but to be very careful and wait for the next shoe to drop. If the perpetrator determines that his efforts to scare you are not accomplishing their purpose, his intimidation efforts may escalate to a more direct and more dangerous level."

"I will be vigilant and protect my Jam-Merican friends," Henry said.

"And I will use whatever resources are at my command to do likewise," Colonel Winter said.

"Thank you for coming all this distance on short notice, Colonel," Will said.

"And bringing with you another two-martini day," Betsy said.

Winter looked puzzled. Leva and Henry knew exactly

what she meant.

~ ~ ~

The next shoe dropped the following Monday when BB came into Betsy's office waving the morning newspaper.

"Have you seen this, boss lady?" he said and handed her the paper.

Officials Say Construction Barn Fire Was Intentional

St. Ann – A construction barn fire was intentionally set on Sunday officials said. The Jamaican Constabulary Force office in Ocho Rios is investigating the fire, which started about 6:45PM on Sunday at 1712 Parry Town Road. The barn, registered to the Kingston and St. Andrew Corporation, was unoccupied at the time of the fire, Officer Matt Joski said. People with information are asked to call the JCF office in Ocho Rios at 876 388-7108 or the Arson Hot Line at 800 362-3004.

THE IS MY SHEPED
 FATHER
THERE FOR I SHALL NOT
WANT
SNOKONES

CHAPTER 28

"Henry," Betsy said, "do we have time for a side-trip on the way home?"

"I guess that depends on what kind of side-trip you have in mind," Henry said. "I don't think we have time to go very far."

"I had Parry Town Road in mind," Betsy said.

"Why would you want to go back there?" Henry asked.

Betsy showed him the newspaper article BB had given her.

"You're the boss," Henry said.

Soon they were on A4 heading for the KSAC's construction barn. As usual Henry passed several people he knew and either honked at them or waved. A respectable matronly looking woman stood on the shoulder of the road holding her arm out horizontally in front of her, letting her wrist loosely flop up and down, Jamaicans' customary way of thumbing a ride.

"Ah! Mrs. Leland," Henry said. "She goes to our church. Do you mind if I give her a lift?"

"Not at all," Betsy said. "As long as she doesn't take

us terribly out of our way."

"She won't," Henry said as he slowed the van. "I'm sure she's going to visit her daughter, Samantha, and her son-in-law, Todd. Todd and Samantha just had their first child – called it Andrew. They live right on our way."

"Mrs. Leland," Henry greeted her. "I-ney **(Good Morning)**. Yu need mi gi yu a lift **(Do you need a ride?)**?"

"I-ney yu, as well," Mrs. Leland replied. "Dat wud be irie, Mr. Davis. 'Ow Mrs. Davis **(That would be wonderful, Mr. Davis. How's Mrs. Davis?)**?"

"Shi is wunnerful. Whey yu go?"

"Mi daughter, Samantha's."

Henry smiled at Betsy. "Told you so."

He then introduced Betsy to Mrs. Leland.

"Yu in Cash Pot?" Mrs. Leland asked Henry.

"No, but mi tink Mrs. Davis is," Henry responded and laughed. "Shi allas try to outsmart the Chineyman."

They continued to make small talk for a few miles until they reached Mrs. Leland's destination.

"Tanks. More time **(See you later)**. Tank God tomorrow is Chewsday **(Tuesday)**," she said as she got out of the car.

"Aright. Taak care," Henry said as they drove away. "'Ave an irie rest of Monday."

"What did she mean by the Cash Pot?" Betsy asked.

Henry explained to her that the Cash Pot was a form of lottery based on a game called Drop Pan that had been brought to Jamaica by Chinese immigrants. Tickets numbered one to thirty-six were sold island-wide. There was a minimum price but no maximum price on each ticket. A number would be randomly drawn by the operators of the lottery, and the holders of that number would then win multiples of whatever price they paid for their ticket.

"Each number has at least one meaning or what we call 'a mark'," Henry went on to explain. "For example, 31 is the lizard mark, 32 is the ripe mark. The participants use these marks along with 'rakes' to help them to decide what number to buy."

"What's a rake?" Betsy asked.

"Oh, guesses, dreams and various other signs."

"And what did you mean about Rose outsmarting the Chineyman?"

Henry laughed and said, "Tradition has it that an anonymous sneaky yellow Chineyman picks the tickets and constantly tries to outsmart the buyers. Part of the challenge is to try to outguess the Chineyman."

Henry turned and they began driving down Parry Town Road. Soon Betsy could smell the scent of the recently doused blaze. The tin building was a blackened forbidding hulk. The razed weeds surrounding it looked like they had been part of a controlled burn.

"Why would someone want to burn this raggedy old place down?" Betsy asked. "Insurance maybe?"

"You said there were securely locked filing cabinets in the building," Henry said. "Maybe their contents were the target of the arsonist."

"Mind if we peek in the window?" Betsy asked.

Henry shrugged.

They peeked in the glassless window. The furniture and filing cabinets had been in the building when it burned. They could see their charred remains. Nothing could have survived the intense heat.

"Notice something missing?" Betsy asked as they walked back to the van.

"What exactly?"

"All five of those huge containers of furniture are gone," Betsy said.

"Strange they weren't still here when the place went

up in flames. They had to be a real challenge to move," Henry said. "Maybe it was a coincidence someone moved them out of harm's way just in time."

"Isn't it," Betsy answered as she snapped some pictures with her cell phone. "I'm not a big believer in coincidences. I'm ready to go home now. I've seen what we came to see."

I sure wish my mystery caller had been more specific about those containers' contents, she thought to herself as they drove away. *My curiosity is growing about them all the time.*

When they arrived at Sundance, Henry excused himself and went home. After he left, Betsy told Will about their visit to Parry Town Road.

"So what's your next move?" Will asked.

"I really don't know."

Will then told her she had just missed seeing Mikey Mo. Betsy rolled her eyes and said in a low voice, "My lucky day."

"Mikey Mo was rehearsing for the big gig. The topic of duppies came up after he played Marley's *Duppy Conqueror*. E. J. then volunteered to share some ways we can protect ourselves from the duppies he feels are haunting Sundance," Will said.

"I think I need a drink before I hear this," Betsy said.

"He had several suggestions to prevent the duppies from molesting us," Will continued. "He first suggested that we persuade our landlord to paint the house a different color to confuse the duppies."

"That would go over with George and Trudy like a Baby Ruth in the swimming pool."

"He also said each time we enter the gate we should turn around three times so the duppy won't follow us in, as well as leave a bowl of salt and water at the front door since duppies don't like either substance."

"Anything else?" Betsy asked.

"Since duppies can't count, he recommended we should leave 10 coffee beans at the entrance of each room," Will said.

"Excuse me while I make myself a double," Betsy said with a sigh.

"When you hear the rest of our conversation, you may want to make that over-proof," Will answered. "I teased E.J. about all his superstitions concerning duppies. He told me Mikey Mo, because of his Maroon lineage, had the gift of recognizing duppies more than most people."

"What did Mikey Mo say," Betsy asked.

"Nothing."

"I never knew Mikey Mo was Maroon," Betsy said.

"Nor did I," Will said. "Do you remember the incident, when we first moved into Sundance, of a Maroon Rasta deejay purportedly being beaten by the cops? He then had his dreads shorn to humiliate him."

"Sure, and then no one was willing to discuss it with us. When you tried to investigate it online, you came up empty."

"And when I brought the incident up to Colonel Winter, he glossed it over.

"Yeah, and discussing it seemed to make him very uncomfortable."

"Also, do you remember the first time we met Mikey Mo not much later, and he had his arm in a sling? If you'll also remember, his nose had been broken, and he had a gash on his forehead."

"Uh huh. He claimed he had been in an accident which he didn't want to talk about. "

"And that accident also trimmed off his dreadlocks?" Will said. "I don't think so. There're too many parallels here for me. What if Mikey Mo was the Maroon Rasta who was undeservedly rousted by the cops?"

"You may be right," Betsy said. "My guess is that maybe the locals did not feel comfortable with spilling their guts on such a sensitive matter with white American outsiders they had only recently met."

"Would you have, if the tables had been turned?" Will asked.

"Probably not."

"And now we know why Mikey Mo has such a good in with so many wood carvers in the hills," Will said.

"Sure," Betsy said, "they are his people."

"By the way," Will said, "Mikey invited us to come to the street dance he's emceeing this Saturday night. It is going to be in the parking lot of Columbus Plaza shopping center here in Discovery Bay. It is being sponsored by the Peoples National Party as a political rally to garner local support for its candidates for the next election. He said E.J. will be there helping him, and we'll be perfectly safe since we'll be their special guests."

"It sounds like fun. I'd like to see both Mikey Mo and the Jamaican political system in action. Did you accept his invitation?"

"Does a grizzly bear shit in the woods? Of course, I did."

"Excellent. Should be a fun evening."

A & P ENTERPRISE
* CHEES   CHIPS *
* SWEETS   CHICKEN/NOODLES *
* CHEWING GUMS *
* BIDCUITS   BOOKS *
* CIGARETTS *
* SOUP   POWDER *
* CURRY   PENCLES   SEASONING   PEPPER *
ETC.
*SCHOOL SUPPLIES

CHAPTER 29

Excitement mounted at Sundance as the week of the PNP Columbus Plaza street dance progressed. Mikey Mo and E.J. were preoccupied with choosing a playlist for the party. This would be Mikey's first outing as a Stone Love selector. Up until now, he had only either spun records or found records for them. Stone Love was the most powerful and most popular sound system in Jamaica. In the early 1970's in uptown Kingston, a selector who had called himself Wee Pow had started Stone Love on a small home component stereo system. It had grown to become a Jamaican institution that played in such large cities as New York and London. In an age where to be a selector or DJ was the goal of many young Jamaican men, to be a Stone Love selector was the ultimate, the apex of one's career.

Mikey Mo diligently practiced belting out hypnotic

chants and sounds in E.J.'s apartment. From his office, Will could hear them each day in the background. He was shocked to hear the toxicity in some of Mikey Mo's lyrics, especially since Mikey Mo would be working a PNP political affair.

De beast fi ded! **(The police must die)**
Pliiz maak mi wod **(Please mark my words)**
Gimi de Tek-9 **(Give me the Tec-9)**
Shuut dem laik bod **(Shoot them like birds)**

Wow, Will thought. *That sure sounds like someone who has had a really bad experience with law enforcement.* He wondered again if Mikey Mo was the Rasta who had been beaten and sheared by the police.

Next he heard a political song about compassionate leadership followed by another alarming song with homophobic lyrics.

Aal batimanfi ded **(All faggots must die)**
Fram yu fok bati den a kappa ahn led **(If you fuck bottom then it is copper and lead)**
No man no fi av a aneda man iina him bed **(No man should have another man in his bed)**

Boy, he thought. *What a repertoire! This is not the good old laid-back smiling Rasta I've seen hanging out at Sundance. This is a frightening guy with some serious anger management problems, and I sure wonder about the underlying reasons.*

Even E.J. commented on the toxicity of some of the selections.

"Yu canna do 'at an' stat wit Stone Love **(you can't do that and hope to keep working for Stone Love)**," he told Mikey, "Dey now clean."

Around Will, Mikey Mo continued to be the happy-go-lucky Rasta Will had been accustomed to. He helped E.J. do his chores each day and was thrilled when he had the opportunity to show off and educate Will on his

206

knowledge of the nuances of and terms used in Jamaican music.

"Yu know what de riddim is?" he asked Will.

He then proceeded to explain to Will that the riddim is a musical instrumental that a host of artists ride. In reggae it is very common for producers to record a riddim and then have hundreds of different artists sing or deejay their own lyrics and melodies over it. He went on to tell Will that it was common for entire albums to be devoted to various artists riding the same riddim.

To demonstrate for Will, Mikey played a riddim track he called the "sleng teng". This, according to him, was the most popular riddim track ever devised and had been used with thousands of songs.

"Fascinating," Will said sincerely.

Will's interest encouraged Mikey Mo to then explain a dubplate. This is what Mikey Mo had been rehearsing in E.J.'s room all week. He explained that "a dubplate" was a one-of-a-kind recording performed over a musical section called "a dubwise" that was heavy on drum, bass, and dub effects. A dubplate was normally created by a dancehall artist or deejay for a sound system like the one he would be using at Columbus Plaza on Saturday night. On his dubplate, Mikey told him he would be voicing brand new renditions of original songs over this canned instrumental. He incorporated adlibs boasting about the specific sound he wished to represent.

"In dub songs de virtual absence of vocals creates de perfect empty canvas providing a way for the listener to meditate on Jah **(God)**," Mikey Mo said.

Saturday finally arrived. E.J. got Leva's permission to leave Sundance early to help Mikey Mo set up his sound system. Henry agreed to drive Will and Betsy down the hill to Columbus Plaza later and told them to call him on his cell phone when they wished to leave. He would gladly return later to pick them up.

Columbus Plaza was the primary shopping center for Discovery Bay. It was behind the Texaco station on Discovery Bay Road and consisted of: a grocery store, a hardware store, a flower shop and wedding center, a laundromat, a furniture store, a real estate office, a patty shop, a pharmacy and other miscellaneous retailers. A lady sold fresh produce, and the inevitable moneychanger was usually present with his bodyguard in the parking lot.

The buildings were old and somewhat shabby as was the uneven asphalt entrance and parking lot, but Columbus Plaza didn't seem faded and seedy that night. The place was festive and electric as people began assembling to delight in the much-anticipated party.

The event organizers gave away green t-shirts with the familiar PNP sunburst imprinted on the front and "Stand Up Jamaica" on the back. The party anthem, *Jamaica Arise*, could be heard coming from the sound system. Rum and Red Stripes were everywhere as well as the ever-present smell of ganja.

Even though the party was in its infant stage, the din, as people visited excitedly with each other, made the affair sound like total chaos. Some people were preparing food. The Blacks saw huge pots of vegetable soup in mess hall sized metal pots. They could smell fish cooking in makeshift outdoor kitchens. Will asked one cook what smelled so good and was told it was fried shark. Wood-burning grills had been set up to jerk pork.

Their attention was drawn to E.J. who was on the bed of a custom diesel British Leyland truck helping Mikey Mo set up. E.J. had on his party duds. He wore black baggy pleated dress pants and a loose patterned sport coat that seemed to almost swallow him. He had on a slightly yellowed polyester white shirt and a thin one-inch necktie with a geometric pattern reminiscent of those popular in America during the Eisenhower years. On his feet were scuffed white buck lace-up shoes. In his lapel was a PNP button. He was setting up two turntables, a mixer, a battery of speakers, plus multiple components of super high-tech electronic and computerized sound equipment. Surrounding him were stacks upon stacks of classic as well as the latest music. Will and Betsy looked at each other and grinned.

"Kingtoo! No blue suede shoes?" Will shouted. "And we mistakenly thought Elvis was dead. Tonight you aren't 'Kingtoo but 'The King'."

E.J. grinned from ear to ear.

Mikey Mo wore a knit hat that reminded Will of a pair of loud argyle socks. The alternating red, yellow and green colors zigzagged crazily on it in an almost argyle-like pattern. Over an oversized black Bob Marley t-shirt, he wore a round pendant that contained a peace symbol with the Jamaican national colors. His pants were the loose, baggy cargo style. Completing his outfit was a pair of partially tied black Converse high-top sneakers.

Stickers with past and present PNP political slogans decorated the truck. *We Put People First, Change Without Chaos, Deliverance Is Near, Stand Up Jamaica, Re-elect Dunster, Elect Neville Hamilton Jr.*

"Chicken!" Will shouted.

"Ya mon, welcome," Mikey Mo shouted back. "Mi glad yu come."

Mikey Mo first played the PNP party anthem, *Jamaica Arise*, and people paused to sing along.

The trumpet has sounded my countrymen all
Awake from your slumber and answer the call

Betsy heard a familiar voice drowning out other ones and looked up towards the truck bed.

The torch has been lighted, the dawn is at hand
Who joins in the fight for his own native land?

A Jamaican Conspiracy

Big Bob Blackmon caterwauled off-key at the top of his lungs. He was wearing a thrift-store looking suit and tie and a porkpie hat.

"Oh my God," Betsy exclaimed. She punched Will in the ribs and pointed at BB.

"'Im seem to turn up lak baad bills **(He seems to turn up like a bad penny)**," Will said in patois and smiled.

"Wha mek yu so speaky-spokey, white buoy **(Why do you want to talk like a foreigner, white boy)**?" Betsy answered to her husband in patois and laughed.

At the song's conclusion, Chicken shouted "PNP to the def **(death)**", and the crowd cheered. The party then began in earnest with Mikey now playing Bob Marley's classic, *Stand Up For Your Rights*.

With Chicken on the mike, an assistant, who he called Rory, spun records. Another assistant, Neco, organized the thousands of vinyl records, flipping through them at a rapid speed to find the next track on his play list. Chicken would tell Rory what to play next; Rory would then tell Neco what to find and give to him. After getting the record, Rory, with an earphone affixed over one ear, a cigarette in his left hand and his right hand on the turntable, spun the record in reverse to get it to exactly the right spot. Suddenly with a lightning touch, he released it. A dancehall tune remixed with a touch of hip-hop blasted from the bank of speakers, and the crowd roared. Chicken shouted "All who respeck yu sistah put yu' han' in the air **(If you respect your sister, put your hands in the air)**," and the beat went on.

Within minutes the parking lot near the British Leyland was elbow-to-elbow with eager dancers. The Blacks were amazed at some of the erotic dance moves they saw. Many women in short shorts and abbreviated tops would bend over so that they were almost touching

210

the floor while their dance partners lewdly pretended to hump them from behind. In some cases both dance partners would end up on the parking lot writhing enthusiastically. Mikey Mo's constant deejay chatter urged the dancers on until many seemed to be in an epileptic frenzy.

Mikey Mo alternated playing popular dance hall tunes with political songs like *PNP Massive On The Move* and *Don't Stop The Progress*.

"If we were on "Bandstand", I would give that song a 10 on beat but only a nine on dance-ability," Will cracked.

"Maybe that's because of *your* dance ability, Dick Clark," Betsy said.

"I wouldn't begin to try to compete with those dancers," Will said.

"Wise decision. These couples make American discos look like revival meetings," Betsy said. "Why don't we sample some of that marvelous food we smelled when we arrived? And I'll even spring for a Red Stripe."

"Don't you mean a *coldbeer*?" Will answered.

They walked over where a vendor was selling beer.

A familiar voice bellowed out, momentarily drowning out everyone around it.

"Your money's no good here, Bank Boss Lady. This one's on me. How 'bout a *icecoldredstripe*?"

They looked up and saw a grinning, sweating BB holding out two beers.

"I told you we'd find a *coldbeer*," Will said.

Betsy decided she was not going to quiz BB about his out-of-place bizarre outfit.

"You *are* saving some energy to boogie with the boogie Bogle of Bull Bay, aren't you?" BB asked.

Betsy blushed and said, "I ... don't think so. You're way out of my league."

"Later then. We got some serious partying to do," BB

A Jamaican Conspiracy

said, "but remember, just put your coldbeer on my tab. Oh, and by the way, this is my date, Queisha Hamilton."

Queisha was dressed in a scanty top and even scantier cut-off jeans.

Will and Betsy briefly told Queisha how glad they were to meet her. Queisha seemed slightly spaced out and barely acknowledged them. Queisha quickly led BB into the crowd.

"Was that an encounter of the third kind?" Will asked Betsy.

"More like an encounter of the turd kind," Betsy responded.

As soon as BB and Queisha left, the vendor held out his hand for some money.

"I thought BB said these were on his tab," Betsy said.

"Wha' tab?" the vendor answered. "Wi don run no tabs."

"What was that you said about getting off easy," Will said.

The next thing she heard was Mikey Mo announcing that they were fortunate to have a special guest performer representing the National Commercial Bank of Jamaica.

"Brudder and sistah, welcome de one, de only ... the Jamaican Blues Brothers ... Jake and Elwood," Mikey shouted.

Betsy looked up again and there was BB and a man she had never seen before on the back of the flatbed. They were both dressed alike.

"Ohmagod," she said and grabbed Will's arm.

"Mi name's Jamaica Jake and dis is mi brudder Elwood," BB said, "and we be glad to be wif yu tonight."

"JJ" aka BB and "Elwood" began to belt out an off-key version of *Bad Boys* as Mikey Mo played a dub track.

Bad boys bad boys
What'cha gonna do, what'cha gonna do
When they come for you

Queisha, barefooted and with a reefer between her

teeth, began dancing wildly by herself next to the truck and every time JJ and Elwood would sing the words "bad boys", she would raise her top and display her ample naked breasts. Then she would lower her top again and bend over backwards until she almost touched the ground and shake her tits at them. Each succeeding time she raised her top, she would tease JJ and Elwood by motioning them to bend over toward her. When they would reach out, she would blow ganja in their faces and then turn, bend over to the front, and shake her ass tauntingly at them. After blowing ganja on JJ and Elwood a few times, Elwood reached over and tried to grab the reefer from Queisha so he could get a good pull on it. Queisha jerked the reefer back, and Elwood accidentally knocked BB's cordless microphone out of his hand. Queisha caught it in mid air and began to rub it like a dildo seductively against her crotch. BB reached out to try to recapture his mike but lost his balance and tumbled out of the back end of the flatbed. When BB hit the ground, his pants tore with a loud *RIIIP!*. The crowd heard a breathless "OOOHH!" in the microphone as Queisha's heel accidentally caught him in the balls. BB stumbled up, bending double and grabbing his wounded crotch, making a moaning sound which got picked up by the microphone, leading to his unintentionally shooting a moon out of his ripped pants with his ample naked ass.

"BB didn't wear underwear tonight," Will shouted as he inadvertently sprayed a mouthful of Red Stripe on his giggling wife.

"Wrong! Look again," Betsy exuberantly shouted and pointed. "He's simply wearing a thong."

"Grr ... oss. TMI," Will yelled back. "There should be a law against some people wearing those things."

Queisha's still-burning reefer went down the seat of BB's ripped out pants, caught on his back-pocket lining,

A Jamaican Conspiracy

and burned the elastic on the thong in two. BB momentarily forgot about his aching privates and began to jump and swat for all he was worth. Queisha also began hippety-hopping since BB had unfortunately stomped on her bare foot.

"Hit's a new dance!" a dreadlocked ganja-smoking man bellowed, as he began jumping and shouting and swatting himself as well. Without thinking, others joined in.

Mikey Mo sensed he was witnessing the possible birth of a new dance craze and quickly cranked up another song. He chose the upbeat dancehall propaganda song *When PNP Comes To Your Town*. He began to rap about the "PNP Stomp."

"If yu believe in PNP, wine **(wind)** yu body," Chicken belted out.

Merle Dunster, with the help of two other men, silently elbowed his way through the crowd and grabbed Queisha by the arm.

"Mi lady," he said quietly but firmly, "yu uncle tinks yu've had 'nough fun fo' one evening **(Your uncle thinks you've had enough fun for one night)**."

She petulantly snatched her arm away from Dunster, in the process catching BB in the Adam's apple. BB made a muffled sound and hit the pavement hard once again. Dunster nodded at one of the men who twisted Queisha's arm and led her away. They stepped right over BB, ignoring his plight.

Dunster shook his head and frowned until he noticed Will and Betsy watching the scene. He immediately broke into a big smile, stepped in front of his henchman to block their view and said, "Mrs. Black, how wonderful to see you. Isn't the weather perfect for a social event? I certainly hope you are enjoying yourself."

Dunster glanced over his shoulder to make sure

Queisha was leaving quietly. She stuck her tongue out at him and shot him a finger. When Dunster was sure she was under control, he turned his back on her and said, as if nothing was wrong, "If you have a moment, I would love to introduce you to our next councilman from St. Ann Parish."

BB was now sitting upright. His eyes were still bulging and slightly crossed as he gasped to catch his breath. Dunster never acknowledged BB as he stepped over him to guide Will and Betsy away from the embarrassing scene to introduce them to a group of people.

"This is the honorable Neville Hamilton," Dunster said. "And this is his son Neville Hamilton Junior. Neville Junior is a PNP candidate for parish councillor."

"Welcome to Jamaica," Neville Hamilton Jr. said graciously. "I hope you are finding Jamaican hospitality to be as gracious as we know it can be."

"Thank you, Mr. Hamilton. I am glad to meet you," said Betsy. "Are you sure we haven't met before. Your voice sounds vaguely familiar."

"All of us Jamaicans sound alike to foreigners," Hamilton said with a chuckle. "May I introduce you to John David Grey?" he then said and introduced them to the pseudo Elwood Blues.

"*The* Mr. Grey with KSAC?" Betsy said. "I have been hoping to meet you. I am WB Bank's liaison on the Highway 2000 project."

"It would be an honor to meet with you during business hours and discuss the project's progress," Grey said. "Call my secretary next week, and she'll set up an appointment."

"I've tried," Betsy said, "on several occasions."

"I'm sorry to hear that," Grey said. "I'll have to speak to her about that."

"I have also unsuccessfully tried to catch you on the job site," Betsy said.

"I so regret hearing that as well," he said. "I again apologize. Currently I have many demands on my time. In our business, when a person gets to work each day, he never knows where he might have to make a management decision to avert a crisis."

He paused and waited for her reply before continuing.

"But Mrs. Black, if I might offer my humble advice, a road building site is a hard-hat area and certainly no place for the uninitiated, and certainly no place for a woman. Someone unfamiliar with the dangers can be injured or even killed on a work site. It can be treacherous even for inspectors. Several years ago here in Jamaica a zealous inspector, after he had been warned of the dangers, was scrutinizing a road-building job site where holes for pilings had been drilled. He accidentally fell into a ten-foot-deep hole and drowned in the ground water before anyone could get him back out. The cause of the accident was never determined."

He shook his head and said, "Tsk, tsk. It was so unnecessary. He should have listened. Now if you'll excuse me ... "

"My condolences about the fire that recently destroyed your Parry Road location," Betsy said.

Grey looked surprised that she knew of the fire. He paused momentarily but then said, "Yes, most unfortunate, but providence was with us. We had moved to our new location shortly before the fire occurred, and we were adequately insured. The records it contained, however, will be difficult to reconstruct."

"Yes, how fortuitous for you," Betsy replied. "As they so often say, timing is everything."

"Now once again, if you'll excuse me ... "

"Maybe we should talk about a less depressing topic.

After all, this is a party," Merle Dunster said. Neville Hamilton Sr. took in the exchange but remained silent.

Mikey Mo began to play the dancehall song, *Highway 2000*.

"Spread love," Mikey shouted into the mike. "Put up yu han' if yu love yu'self."

As soon as Neville Hamilton Jr. heard the opening lines of the song, he said, "Please excuse me as well. Unfortunately this is a work evening for me. They're playing my song. It was such a pleasure to meet you both. Please feel free to call me as well, if I can ever be of assistance."

"Did you just get threatened?" Will asked after they all had left.

"I'm not sure," Betsy said. "What do you think?"

"I think you should take BB up on his dance offer," Will said facetiously.

"The PNP Stomp? I don't think so. I don't think I have the balls for it," Betsy said.

"He doesn't either ... anymore. I think it's time to call Henry to pick us up."

"So we can practice the Stomp on the porch?"

Will just smiled.

217

DO NOT READ UNDER PENALTY OF LAW

CHAPTER 30

As they waited for Henry to pick them up, Will and Betsy could still hear Mikey Mo from the edge of the parking lot. The party kept getting more and more unrestrained and rowdy. Over the din, they could still hear Mikey Mo's DJ prattle loud and clear. *Don't ever be afraid to talk cause life weh yuh live will determine yuh walk.*

"Mikey Mo seems to know his job," Will said.

"Yeah," Betsy answered. "You might say he clucks like a chicken."

Within fifteen minutes Henry picked them up.

"Have a good time?" he asked.

"Great," they both responded.

"So why leave so early?" Henry said and laughed. "This party is just getting started. It won't end until the wee hours of tomorrow."

"Remember, we're only infant partiers compared to Jamaicans," Will said. "We're not party-trained yet."

"You'll never guess who all we met at the street dance,"

Betsy said. She told Henry about BB and Queisha. After Henry stopped laughing, she then told him about John David Grey, Merle Dunster, and Neville Hamilton, Senior and Junior.

"About the only principal player of Kingston and St. Andrew Corporation we did not see there was Dudus Coke," Betsy said.

"And you won't either," Henry replied. "His loyalties are with the Jamaica Labour Party not the People's National Party. After all, the Shower Posse's garrison is Kingston's Tivoli Gardens. Tivoli Gardens produced the JLP's most famous Prime Minister Edward Seaga."

"If he's such a big JLP advocate, why'd he climb in bed with PNP VIP's?" Will asked.

"Greed," Henry replied. "There's a saying that love brings people together. I would say that greed is an equally motivating factor. But this doesn't change his political loyalties. It reminds me somewhat of the two opposing divorce attorneys in the American movie *Divorce American Style* who still played golf with each other on weekends."

"I see your point. I guess politics and business both make strange bedfellows. May I change the subject slightly and recount one of the evening's events which we found a little disturbing?" Will said.

He repeated Grey's story of the nosy inspector who fell headfirst into a concrete piling hole and drowned before anyone could get him out.

"You were a general contractor," Will said. "Have you ever heard of this incident?"

"It's not one I'm familiar with," Henry said.

"Do you think this might have been a subtle warning of some sort?" Will asked.

"Let me just say this," Henry said. "John David Grey works for Neville Hamilton. On the surface, Neville

Hamilton and his colleagues are successful, highly respectable businessmen. This veneer masks a much different reality. Their visible legal enterprises are reportedly merely the tip of a large not-so-upstanding iceberg. Mr. Hamilton is reputed to be as ambitious and ruthless as any don on the island ... as are his associates and backers. I don't know if any incident like this ever occurred, but I am confident it could be made to come to pass if he deemed it necessary."

"That's scary as hell," Will said.

"As for Neville Jr., we used to call him 'Busy-Busy' when he was growing up. He was always a good student, but on the football field had a reputation as a win-at-any-cost player. There was an incident once where Busy-Busy was about to score a winning goal in a crucial game when his shot was blocked. Busy-Busy sprained his ankle and could not play the following week. Within days of this unfortunate game, his nemesis mysteriously broke his own leg.

"Now I understand he is called 'The Nevster.' Neville Senior was a product of the streets, but he made sure 'The Nevster' was properly educated abroad so that he could walk comfortably in circles that would take the family enterprises to new levels. Currently he is the PNP candidate for St. Ann parish councillor. I'm sure Neville plans this as a stepping stone for his son to a higher office and will not tolerate anything or anyone who might interfere with his agenda."

"Now you're definitely alarming me," Betsy said.

"All I'm saying is, be careful," Henry said. "Your job is not worth your life."

~ ~ ~

Will searched the Internet off and on for the rest of the weekend but could find no accounts of an incident similar to the one cited by John David Grey at the street

A Jamaican Conspiracy

party. This comforted him to some extent, but he kept remembering Henry's words. *I am confident it could be made to come to pass if he deemed it necessary.* Henry's final comment also continued to play in his mind. *Your job is not worth your life.* Betsy mused over Henry's comments as well.

When Betsy got to the bank on Monday she asked Letha to send BB to her office.

"He's not here yet, ma'am," Letha said. "He must have had a meeting out of the office."

BB struggled into the bank about mid-morning. He was limping and spoke with a hoarse, raspy voice. He looked so pathetic Betsy almost felt sorry for him despite her intense desire to kick him where he was already hurting. Letha insisted on making him one of her grandmother's home remedies in the bank kitchen. BB swilled the potion and immediately ran to the bathroom to get sick.

BB returned to Betsy's office when he had regained some composure.

"John David Grey told me at the street party that KSAC recently moved to a new office. Do you know anything about this?"

"Yes, ma'am," BB said. "I understand it is quite elaborate. I've heard people say he spent a million and a quarter dollars American for it and that the furnishings ran another three-quarter of a million American or so. Grey approached the bank at one time about financing the building, but I understand it was funded out of pocket."

The telephone rang. Letha said it was for Betsy but could not identify of the caller. Betsy excused the ashen BB who quickly left.

"This is Buried Blade," the caller announced when Betsy picked up phone. "Remember me?" Once again he attempted to disguise his voice.

"Yes, Mr. Blade," Betsy said. "You were the one who called me about the shipping containers on John David Grey's Parry Road property."

"And you found what I told you about?"

"No, Mr. Blade. I did not. The containers seemed to only be used to store some expensive new office furniture. They were removed from the property before fire destroyed the main building. Just what was it that you wanted me to discover? Why don't we quit playing games."

"It is a pity that you were not more tenacious about your follow-up," Buried Blade said.

"Mr. Blade, I am a banker, not a common thief. Breaking and entering is not my occupation."

"I assume you have not been invited to visit KSAC's fully furnished palatial new offices," he said.

"No I have not."

"Well you really should go see them. They have been quite tastefully decorated. No expense was spared," Buried Blade continued. "You should also examine a $780,000 entry on KSAC's billings entitled 'institutional strengthening.' First class furniture has definitely strengthened the impression it makes on its visitors."

"I don't know whether I should say thanks or not," Betsy said. "But would you answer this question, Mr. Blade, just what is your agenda?"

"I'll be in touch again. Good day." The phone went dead.

Betsy did indeed find a line item called "institutional strengthening" but very little to define just what charges came under that category. It seemed to be a catchall classification, a kind of miscellaneous or et cetera. Not only did she see the $780,000 item Buried Blade had called to her attention but a $1.25 million item as well. *An undefined $2 million dollars in expenses is a pretty* *substantial miscellaneous,* she told herself. She spent several hours trying to nail down "institutional strengthening", but by the end of the day, she knew very little more than when she started. How the hell did Buried Blade know about it? And what was his hidden agenda?

Betsy called John David Grey's office.

"I apologize, Mrs. Black. Mr. Grey is not available. May he get back to you?"

The following day.

"I'm sorry, Mrs. Black. You just missed him. I'll give him a message that you called."

The next day.

"Mr. Grey is out of town today, Mrs. Black. I'll ask him to call you when he returns. Is there anything I can do for you?"

The script changed each day, but the results were the same. No John David Grey.

She called Merle Dunster.

"I've been trying unsuccessfully to contact John David Grey about some KSAC business. Do you think you might be of assistance in helping me reach him?"

"Let me see what I can do."

Two days later. Nothing.

She tried Grey's office again.

"May I speak to Mr. Grey's CFO?"

"One moment please."

"Artus Joye."

Mr. Joye. Mrs. Black from WB Bank. Would it be possible for KSAC to provide us with more documentation clarifying the expense items listed as 'institutional strengthening'?"

"Certainly. I need to get Mr. Grey's permission to release the information to you. I'll get back to you as soon as possible."

Once again at the end of that week, nothing.

Within a few days, Will received an unsolicited phone call.

"Mr. Black, Neville Hamilton. We met at the PNP street dance."

"Of course, Mr. Hamilton. What may I do for you?"

"Merle Dunster tells me you are in the investment business.

"Yes, I am," Will said. "Securities."

"I am, in my own humble way, in the same line of work. My investments, however, are not in the world's great corporations but in local real estate opportunities. I attempt to identify profit-making opportunities in the market place and then bring them to sophisticated individuals such as yourself."

Hamilton then proceeded to describe a seaside villa. The price was at rock-bottom levels because of "a very motivated seller". The rental income would provide Will and Betsy an annual cash flow of approximately 25%. Hamilton would structure the deal so that Will and Betsy would have virtually no money out of pocket.

"Why would you offer this investment to me, a virtual stranger?" Will asked.

"Because it is an investment in my future as well as yours. I sense that you and your wife are people I wish to cultivate going forward," Hamilton said. "Just call it an investment in both of our futures."

"I'm flattered, but I think you overestimate our influence," Will replied. "I will mention your offer to my wife when she comes home tonight, but I suspect, considering her business relationship with KSAC, the bank would probably consider the transaction a conflict of interest."

"Mr. Black, foolish idealists don't grow wealthy; realists do," Hamilton said impatiently. "Almost risk-free

225

A Jamaican Conspiracy

opportunities with huge payoffs are rare. We long-time investment professionals learn early in our careers not to let one of these infrequent opportunities pass. Those who do can only be classified as naïve dolts. My intuition tells me you are not such a person. I'll wait to hear from you."

> EATING ROOM
> EATER'S ONLY

CHAPTER 31

Will Black called Neville Hamilton and politely declined the investment opportunity he had been offered. He explained to Hamilton once again that WB Bank considered the investment a conflict of interest. Hamilton seemed disinterested with his explanation and quickly said he had another call coming in. Will thought the affair was over. This did not turn out to be the case. Within days Will and Betsy began to come under fire from previously unexpected fronts.

~ ~ ~

Monday

"Line one," Letha said. "Ken Scott from WB."

"Ken," Betsy said. "Great to hear from you. What do I owe the privilege?"

"How are things going in Jamaica?"

"Very well," Betsy replied. "Nothing yet has happened that I have not been able to handle."

"Betsy, I hope you're right. I'm not going to tactfully beat around the bush and play games," Ken said. "I received an anonymous letter today from someone with the pseudonym of Cudjoe which was cc'ed to the *Jamaica Gleaner* that you are a dishonest predatory banker on the take."

"What?" Betsy said. "That's the craziest thing I've ever heard. Surely, you don't believe it. You know me better than that."

"I certainly like to think so. This Cudjoe accused you of recently using your position at the bank to try to coerce one of the principals of the Kingston and St. Anne Corporation into selling you a Jamaican villa at a give-away price in return for favorable reports on the highway project."

"You have got to be kidding," Betsy gasped. "Just the opposite happened. A principal of KSAC approached Will about selling us a villa at a highly distressed price. We refused to consider his offer ... we considered it a bribe ... and told him that dealing with him would be considered a conflict of interest by the bank."

"That's not the spin Cudjoe is putting on the incident. He is accusing you of being the instigator and KSAC of being the resistant honest party. Since he has sent the letter to the newspaper, I guess you know I'll be forced to formally investigate his charges before we can put the matter to bed."

"Ken, do what you have to do," Betsy said, "but I'm telling you right now you're wasting your time and bank resources on a wild goose chase. I have not and will not ever do anything illegal or unethical. I'm smarter than that."

"I believe you, Betsy," Ken said. "We strongly suspect your predecessor was extended a similar offer and could not resist taking it. That is a matter I did not want to discuss with you when we offered you this opportunity, but you understand the public exposure has put me in an uncomfortable position with the bank attorneys. Please be patient and optimistic. We'll clear this mess up as soon as possible. In the meantime, just keep your head down and do your job being aware that someone is gunning for you."

"Ever think about it this way, Ken? Maybe I'm doing my job too well, and I'm making people nervous. More and more things about this company's way of doing business just don't seem kosher. For example ... and this is something I currently can't prove ... there were about two million dollars of vague almost miscellaneous expenditures which coincidentally approximate what I am being told was spent on a new KSAC building and elaborate furnishings. Their previous building containing most of their records mysteriously burned shortly after my visit. Most likely torched. I might add, the burned building was insured to the hilt."

"For the time being, I am going to proceed on the assumption you are a target because you are a threat to them. I'll do what I can to keep our dogs at bay. Betsy, just don't dump me in the creek. I'll keep you abreast of what I can. I'm truly sorry about these accusations."

"I know the drill, Ken. Thanks for calling and giving me a heads-up."

As Betsy hung up with Ken Scott, she was hit with conflicting emotions. She was perplexed and bewildered. At the same time she was livid and afraid. She wasn't sure which emotions superseded the others. *If these assholes want to play hardball, I'll play it with them.* Henry Davis' words came back to her. *Mr. Hamilton is reputed to be as ambitious and ruthless as any don on the island ... as are his associates and backers.*

Tuesday

Betsy received a puzzling letter concerning Will.
Mrs. Black
I am in love with your husband and he is in love with me. I can offer him a happiness you will never be able to offer. Let him go. Let us be happy. You will find someone else.

Maria
She called Will at Sundance.
"Do you know a Maria," she asked.
"Sure. She was the Puerto Rican in West Side Story. She was one hot babe. Wasn't she played by Natalie Wood?"
"Well, Maria wants your bod."
"But she's dead," Will said. "That's creepy."
Betsy then read Will the letter she had just received.
"Yesterday I get accused of attempting an underhanded real estate investment. Today I get accused of having a Puerto Rican mistress. I guess tomorrow I'll be accused of international espionage. Someone doesn't seem to like me," Will said.
"Or me either. We'll discuss it further when I get home from the office."

~ ~ ~

Wednesday
Will called Betsy at her office.
"You're not going to believe what happened to me this morning."
"Maria paid you a visit."
"I almost wish," Will said. "We just got Henry out of jail."
"What?"
"You heard me right. Henry and I were making a run to the Mo Bay airport to pick up a box from my office when we were pulled over by the cops. They accused Henry of being drunk and took him in on speeding as well as a DUI."
"The only thing he drinks on the road is Ting or water," Betsy said.
"He hadn't even had a Ting," Will said. "He had been sipping on one of those frozen bottled waters that Rose puts up for him. The cops impounded Henry's van. He

then told me to call Colonel Winter. Winter sent some Maroon lawyer down there. I stayed at the jail until the lawyer arrived and the charges were dropped. We're back at Henry and Rose's house now. Rose came down and drove us both back."

"I wonder just what else can go wrong this week," Betsy said.

"You know what they say, if it weren't for bad luck, we'd have no luck at all."

Henry was still steamed as Rose fixed lunch for them all.

"It's a good thing that Maroon lawyer came down and straightened things out. Otherwise we wouldn't all be sitting her right now." Will commented. "How'd you get in so tight with the Maroons anyway?"

"Ferron and I have known each other since we were small children," Henry said. "His nickname was Ferret when he was growing up. You know what a ferret is, don't you? Like a little rat that can slip in and out of anywhere unnoticed. We lived back up in the hills, and he could be virtually invisible when he wanted to be.

"Well, one day when Ferret was nine, he and I were playing and came upon a ganja field by accident. The ganja grower mistook us for government agents and shot at us. He missed me but hit a tree near Ferret. Ferret ended up with a huge splinter in his shoulder. I carried him back to our village on my back. The doctor said I probably saved his life because if I hadn't brought him in when I did, he could have bled to death. He never forgot what I had done for him. When he was made Maroon chief, he made me an honorary Maroon and promised that I would always be protected by them. Since then we have always called each other cousin."

"So that's why Col. Winter agreed to meet Betsy and me. And that's why he was receptive to the plight of complete strangers. Because of his relationship with you."

"That is correct."

"Why haven't you told me this story before now?"

Henry shrugged and said, "Didn't seem to be a reason to."

About that time, the house phone rang. Rose answered it. She silently listened and slowly hung it up.

"Who was that?" Henry asked.

"Cudjoe," Rose answered. "He said you would be wise to drive for someone else."

~ ~ ~

Thursday

Shortly before dinner the phone rang at Sundance. Leva summoned Betsy to the phone.

"Have the last few days reinforced my assertion that you that you do not want to be our adversary?" the voice asked curtly.

"Cudjoe, I presume," Betsy said with a sigh.

"At first we gave you the benefit of the doubt. We thought since you were a person unfamiliar with our way of doing things, you would be a person with whom we could reason. You did not listen. At the Martha Brae, you accidentally saw the demise of someone who underestimated us. That should have gotten your attention. It didn't, and you have continued to try to bumble your way into Jamaican affairs. You and your driver got lucky ... once. Afterwards, we once again gave you the benefit of the doubt and pointed out the error of your ways. We cautioned you that we do have influence with the Constabulary Force. As your driver discovered, this was not an idle boast. Mrs. Black, make no mistake about it, the road project will move ahead on schedule either with or without your blessing. We will not tolerate your complicating straightforward fiscal matters. There is too much at stake. This project is for the greater economic good of Jamaica and will solve many of our problems of justice and inequality. It will be completed on schedule and with a minimum of controversy."

"Just what do you want from me?"

"Let me repeat myself. It will be necessary for you to evaluate the project fairly by established Jamaican monetary and business practices and present it objectively to your employer so that installments will be issued with no delays or controversy. Good night, Mrs. Black."

~ ~ ~

Friday

The last shoe of the week dropped. It began when Leva called out to Will that Charlie-Red Conlon was in the front yard and was asking to speak to him.

When Will went outside, a pacing, sweating Charlie-Red, with his eyes to the ground began to mumble in patois as he picked his twisted, gnarled fingernails.

"Mistah Will, las night mi went out in mi yard afta dark. Mi feel sumthin and hear a sound. As a seh who dat **(Last night after dark I felt something and heard a sound)**, outa da dark dem lick mi wid two stones inna mi back. A duppy say, 'yu stay way far from Sundance' **(As I tried to identify the source, one of the duppies in the dark hit me in the back with two rocks and told me to stay away from Sundance)**."

"You say a duppy threw rocks at you from your dark yard and told you not to work here anymore?" Will asked incredulously. "Did you actually see this duppy?"

"No-one see hit but mi grandbaby," Charlie-Red said, "but mi know from how 'im sound dat hit were a whistling cowboy **(The only person who saw it was my grandchild, but from the sound we knew it was a whistling cowboy)**."

"A whistling cowboy?"

"Yessir," Charlie-Red continued. "'Im go **(It went)** itty-itty-hop, itty-itty-hop."

Will couldn't believe what he was hearing.

"Yessir, whistling cowboy alias ride tree **(three)** foot horse. One foot in front; two foot in back. Hit go itty-itty-hop, itty-itty-hop. Mi run back in the hwose **(house)** cause mi know if hit breathe on mi, mi be dead. Hit trow mi tools at mi and say agin, 'Yu stay way from Sundance, yu unnerstan.' Mi wife vase den jump offa de bureau and break. **(It threw my tools at me and told me to stay away from Sundance and then caused my wife's vase to fall and break.)** So mi hope yu unnerstan why mi canna work fo yu no more."

"What about the jobs you have started here but haven't finished?" Will asked.

Charlie-Red mumbled something to indicate he was sorry.

Mikey Mo, who happened to be visiting E.J. that morning, overheard the exchange and came out to contribute his two cents and try to help.

"If mi rid yu house of duppies, yu go back to work," he asked Charlie-Red. "Mi help yu paint yu house different color. Den mi count ten and write yu name pon parchment paper and bury it inna yu back yard. Den wi have a lickle lick a' licka **(If I rid your house of duppies, will you come back to work? I only need to count to ten, write your name on a piece of paper, and then bury it. Then we'll have a drink of rum to celebrate.)**. Dis mek duppy go way an not come back."

Charlie-Red shook his head and mumbled something again Will couldn't understand. Then he hoisted his heavy canvas tool bag over his shoulder and slowing ambled towards the gate without looking back.

When Betsy came in from work Friday evening, Will

filled her in on the morning's strange encounter.

"Just one more shitty event in one completely shitty week in paradise," Betsy said. "This has definitely been a two martini week."

"What do you want to bet that Charlie-Red's duppy had another name?" Will asked, "and I don't mean just whistling cowboy."

"You mean like a whistling Hamilton, and I don't mean Alexander?"

"Something like that. You're on the right track. I was thinking about calling it the KSAC cowboy. I know I've brought it up before, but maybe we both should reconsider Dale Carnegie. We can probably take it over the internet," said Will sarcastically to lessen the tension.

"It's going to take more than that. This is more of Hamilton's harassment. I'm going to figure out how to put the screws to him," Betsy replied.

"We're in this together. Let's come up with a plan."

"Excellent suggestion. Now just shut up and pour me a drink," Betsy said.

> WATSON'S
> WOODCRAFT
> SPECIALIZED IN
> ANTIQUE TURNING
> AND CURIOUS

CHAPTER 32

The various emotions Betsy felt after talking to Ken Scott gradually became one. Anger, anger, and more anger. Anger gradually became fury. Fury then evolved into resolve. How dare these low-life thugs threaten her job, her integrity, her family! With new resolve, she redoubled her efforts to smoke out just what KSAC was hiding with such a vengeance and to expose them for the scum bags she now knew they were - gangster dons or no gangster dons.

Betsy had to know more about her adversaries. She renewed her efforts to learn about *all* the principals of the Kingston and St. Ann Corporation. The front people were the same names she already knew, Neville Hamilton and John David Grey. One day she finally got the break she was looking for. Letha Wardlow mentioned in passing that Swingles, the all-inclusive resort, had been financed in its early days by the bank. She got BB to locate the old file for her. Besides Hopeton Boothe, the principals were Neville Hamilton Sr. and Jr., Christopher Coke, and Merle Dunster.

Well, well, well, Betsy thought. *My "Judas buddy" Merle Dunster was in bed with hoodlums way back when. I wonder if Neville Hamilton Sr. offered Merle investment opportunities too good to resist just like he did Will and me. The old inner circle appears to be pretty much unchanged. But I don't see John David Grey's name. I wonder if he's just a big nail instead of the hammer.*

On a hunch Betsy began to pull records on Presidential Click and Incomparable Enterprises. The same names including her pal Merle Dunster. She began to think about what she had been told about both companies being a front for Dudus Coke, Don of the Shower Posse Gang.

This is getting more complex all the while, she thought. *If both KSAC and Swingles are a front for organized crime, I wonder if KSAC is their money-laundering arm. Good old Dunster has a vested interest in both. Also I'm beginning to understand Neville Hamilton's incentive for grooming the Nevster for a life in politics.* She thought about the strings the Shower Posse could pull with government contracts with one of their own as an insider.

It was time to take an opening shot across KSAC's bow, and she knew just how to do it. Betsy dictated to Letha Wardlow a confidential internal memo addressed to Ken Scott outlining her suspicions that KSAC was using "ghost employees" to pad their payroll and recommending that KSAC's next draw be withheld until the matter was cleared up.

Letha said nothing as Betsy dictated the memo, but quietly made an additional copy on the printer when she typed it up. She then made a phone call and told the person answering that she had the list of attendees for the "upcoming Kingdom Hall social" that weekend. Her contact thanked her and told her he would get it from her at his earliest convenience. She then put the copy of Betsy's memo in the midst of some church material, sealed it in a large envelope and put it in her desk drawer. The envelope had been picked up before the end of the business day.

The following day Betsy asked Henry to take her to KSAC's road clearing project. She silently took a tally of the number of workers on the site. There were three times as many workers as she had ever seen on previous visits, and they all seemed to be hard at work. This time no one seemed upset at her presence. The foremen simply ignored her and concentrated on the work at hand.

"This is certainly a change," Betsy commented to Henry.

He agreed whole-heartedly.

Before they left, Betsy got Henry to inquire about John David Grey. The foreman politely told Henry that no one had seen Mr. Grey that day.

Two days later she received a call from Ken Scott.

"Tell me about this memo you sent me," he said.

Betsy related to Scott how she had visited KSAC's job site on multiple occasions and had counted the employees present on each of her visits. She also told him the identities of the principals of KSAC she had been able to identify and their respective backgrounds. She told him of their previous business affiliations with each other in Swingles, Presidential Click, and Incomparable Enterprises. She told him of the Cudjoe phone calls and then told him of her failed efforts to contact John David Grey to get his explanation of some of her questions. She also told him, without being specific, that she had other investigations in the works.

When Betsy finished, Scott was momentarily speechless.

"If your findings are accurate, you have validated some suspicions we had when we gave you this assignment. Your predecessor may well have been passively turning a blind eye to irregularities he should have been reporting to us.

"Or possibly receptive to the kind of investment opportunities Will and I found to be a conflict of interest," Betsy added.

"Very possibly. That was one of our suspicions when we gave you this assignment. Now I am becoming increasingly concerned for your safety. Maybe I should reassign you until we better know what we are dealing with," he finally said.

"That's just what they want, carte blanche to run wild again," Betsy said. "Why do you think you got that libelous memo about me being on the take? I refuse to bow down to scum-bag pressure."

"Let me tell you something else," Scott said. "I got a phone call from your Mr. Hamilton inquiring if KSAC's next draw would be on time."

"Did he act like he suspected something was amiss?" Betsy asked.

"I wouldn't say that," Scott said. "The phone call was purportedly routine and polite, but it is funny that the timing coincided with the memo you sent me. It could have just been coincidence."

"As I have said many times before, I'm not a big believer in coincidences," Betsy said. "Let me do some more work from my end."

"Keep me posted, and please, don't forget that these people are obviously amoral and dangerous. If you feel uncomfortable and don't wish to proceed, I can bring someone else into the matter who has a background in handling these matters."

"I hear you, and thanks for your concern, but I'm not going to run or hide from these creeps," Betsy said and hung up. *Maybe it's time that I met the legendary Hopeton Boothe,* Betsy thought as she replayed her conversation with Ken Scott in her mind.

Betsy spent the rest of that day reading everything she could read on Swingles. She had BB bring her everything in the bank that might make her better informed. When she thought she was properly prepared, she told Henry that they were going to pay Swingles a visit. Betsy then called Mr. Boothe for an appointment.

> PLEASE KEEP THIS DOOR CLOSE

CHAPTER 33

Betsy's research proved very educational. Swingles was a chain of vacation resorts operated by SunClubs Ltd., an operating division of Presidential Click Ltd. The resort was built by the government of Jamaica in 1975 for $10 million and opened under the name of Runaway Bay Village. In 1981 it was sold to SunClubs Ltd., and became an all-inclusive tourist complex under the name of Swingles. A few years later Swingles resorts were built in both Negril and Montego Bay. Within a few years, Swingles owned all-inclusives throughout the Caribbean.

The Runaway Bay property was built on 10 acres and contained 230 rooms in a series of three-story buildings. Despite subsequent Swingles being larger (the Negril property encompassed 22 acres and had 300 rooms in two-story buildings), Runaway Bay remained the vacation resort's home office and housed top management.

These adult-only resorts had areas reserved for naturism and nudism. Known for liberal sexual, drug and alcohol attitudes, while public nudity is illegal in Jamaica, these laws were not enforced and were not deemed applicable inside the private resort. After a nude wedding for ten couples on the Runaway Bay property caused protests by the government tourist office and even radio talk show hosts labeled it improper and offensive, a similar all nude ceremony was performed two years later on the Negril property before a larger audience with an even larger group of brides and grooms. On one occasion the resort was used to film nude scenes for a National Lampoon movie. Detractors also charged that Boothe promoted bi-sexual activities at his tropical resorts.

Boothe defended his resorts by pointing out that not all his guests went nude. He said there was a prudish side as well as a nude side to his all-inclusives at the beaches, restaurants and pools, and that every restaurant, except for the nude grill, had dress codes.

Allegations of open sex in the hot tubs at Swingles prompted Hopeton Boothe to deny that he was aware of such activities and to vehemently declare that he was not running a whorehouse. He later sued two vacation companies in a Miami court claiming they made defamatory statements about activities at Swingles. His attorneys sought compensatory damages for false and malicious statements.

Despite his moralistic protestations, Mr. Boothe said in another interview that he felt satisfied with Swingles' image of decadence and debauchery. Boothe's website advertised that "When it's good, it's oh so good, and when it's bad, it's even better and yes, everything you ever heard is true."

Betsy told Will she planned to have Henry drive her to Swingles to meet with Hopeton Boothe. "If you wear your banker uniform to this appointment, you'll stand out like a whore in church," Will teased. "Why don't you wear your naughty banker costume instead? The one you wear at home when Honey-Pye Leva has her day off."

Leva's eyes opened wide, and she grinned.

"Leva, don't you listen to him," Betsy said as she blushed. "And if you'll put a peanut shell and a rubber band on your head, I'll take you as a dick-head," Betsy retorted to Will.

This time, Leva blushed.

"I know you're just being a smart-ass," Betsy continued, "but theme nights are an important part of the Swingles tradition. They have a different costume party every night with themes like 'naughty school reunion', 'pajama party' and 'fetish fantasy'."

"In that case, count me in," Will said.

Leva blushed again.

The following day, Henry drove Betsy to Swingles. The patched and uneven blacktop road became very modern and smooth as they approached the gate. She could see that a solid wall surrounded the entire property. Cameras were mounted at different points along the wall's top. A guard stopped them at the gate. When the guard found Betsy's name on his visitor list, he admitted them with a smile and gave them instructions on how to find Boothe's office.

Betsy and Henry rode down a beautifully landscaped, well-marked road. They passed a volleyball court. Topless players were in the midst of a game. Other topless and bottomless vacationers relaxed on chaise lounges under palm trees and were either reading or simply napping in the fresh salt air. Very few people paid them any mind.

Henry parked the van, and they walked through an open-air informal grill. Both clothed and unclothed people were eating everything from cheeseburgers to jerk chicken and fish. There was a small stand next to the grill where people ate munchies - popcorn, corn chips with cheese sauces and guacamole. Most people seemed to be enjoying a tropical beverage of some sort. The atmosphere was relaxed and languid.

Next they passed a swimming pool. Surprisingly enough, all of the swimmers wore bathing suits. Betsy detected a distinctive aroma of smoke and knew immediately she was not smelling cigarettes.

Henry pointed to a sign that said "Administrative Office." They walked up a colorful tropical porch with two brightly painted rocking chairs to enter the thatched roof building. They were greeted by an attractive Jamaican secretary, who was conservatively dressed and well coifed. She spoke with a precise British accent.

"I am Mrs. Smythe. May I be of assistance?" she asked pleasantly.

Betsy identified herself. Henry offered to wait on one of the rocking chairs on the front porch.

"Please make yourself comfortable, and I will let Mr. Boothe know you have arrived. May I offer you some tea?"

Betsy declined, and the secretary went back to work.

Within minutes, the door to the inner office opened, and a smiling Hopeton Boothe walked out to greet her.

"Mrs. Black, a pleasure. Please come in. Welcome to Swingles," he said warmly.

Betsy had not been sure what to expect. She had never seen a picture of Boothe. He was tall, a thin, mature-looking light-complexioned Jamaican. Boothe looked exotic, and Betsy suspected that he had some oriental blood in his heritage. It was hard to determine his age. Boothe's teeth were white and straight. His black hair was long and styled. The top two buttons on his tropical linen shirt had been unbuttoned and a gold cob doubloon gleamed from a gold mariner chain. A gold Cartier watch flashed from his arm. He wore drawstring linen white pants with the cuffs rolled up and leather flip-flops. He reminded Betsy of a GQ model.

They made pleasant small talk about the resort for the first few minutes. Betsy observed that she was surprised when she and Henry had passed a swimming pool and all of the swimmers had been clothed.

Boothe laughed and said, "We have our prude pool and our party pool. If you would like, we can walk down to our nude pool and spa that are adjacent to our clothing optional beach. We will be having our nude pool party there later today. If you wish to stay and participate, you can go as my guest. You would be a refreshingly welcome addition."

"That would certainly play well back at the bank," Betsy said.

"Well, if you change your mind ... ," Boothe winked and said. "Now, if I can't persuade you to join us, just what may we do for you today?"

Betsy told Boothe that her records indicated that he was a business associate of John Henry Grey's in KSAC, and that she had been having trouble reaching Grey on some bank business. She asked Boothe if he might possibly help her contact Grey. She told him that the only known office she had for Grey was the one on Parry Road which had recently burned.

"Mrs. Black," Boothe said, "I am sorry you are having such difficulty in scheduling a meeting with Mr. Grey, and I sincerely wish I could help you. I understand he is a very busy man. While we at Swingles certainly appreciate the critical importance of having good relations with the bank, I hope you will understand the limitations of a simple innkeeper. My only involvement with the Kingston and St. Andrew Corporation is as a passive investor. My primary concern is to make sure Swingles runs smoothly and that my guests have the most memorable holiday of their lives. That proves to be a demanding 24/7 job. I only meet with my partners in my other ventures a few times a year and get progress reports from time to time. I will see what I can do. My secretary will get back to you, but, in all honesty, I may not have as much influence over Mr. Grey as you do. I hope you understand. I only hope your need to meet with Mr. Grey is nothing that could possibly endanger my own KSAC investment. Now, would you like me to show you around the property or to treat you to a delicious lunch before you depart?"

Betsy politely declined Boothe's courteous offer.

Why does everyone in Jamaica promise to get back to me, but then it never happens? Betsy thought.

Boothe stood up, indicating their meeting had concluded, and they shook hands.

"And if you and your husband ever wish to have a second honeymoon, give me a call and I will arrange an unforgettable weekend for you," Boothe said as they parted.

Betsy said she appreciated the offer.

When Betsy left, Boothe picked up his cell phone and made a call.

"A Mrs. Betsy Black from National Commercial Bank in Ocho Rios just left my office. She was very intent on finding John David. What is this all about?"

The voice on the other end answered. "She's a troublemaker employed by the bank to scrutinize our activities. My inside contact at the bank tells me she suspects that John David is padding the payroll on the highway job, and she is determined to cause problems by exposing him."

"Well, has he been cutting corners?"

"Somewhat. He took a few liberties. No more than usual. We tried to warn him that he was taking a risk, but he didn't listen."

"So what are you going to do about it?"

"I won't go into specifics, but we'll handle things our way," the voice said and hung up.

As they walked back to the van, Henry seemed unusually quiet. When he was sure they were not being observed, he suggested they sit on a bench near the gift shop.

"What's up?" Betsy asked.

"While I was waiting for you, I think I saw someone of interest," he said.

"Who's that?"

"Mrs. John David Grey," he said.

"You know who she is?" Betsy asked.

"I don't know her personally, but I know who she is."

"And you recognized her, and think you saw her here?"

"I wasn't sure until I saw Boothe's secretary head off this woman on the sidewalk as she was walking towards Boothe's office. They spoke briefly. While I couldn't hear what they said, I did hear her call the lady Mrs. Grey. I suspect she was informing her of your visit. Mrs. Grey seemed somewhat flustered after they spoke."

"Where is Mrs. Grey now?"

"Over in the gift shop. Why don't we sit in my van and see what happens next."

It wasn't long before a Honda scooter pulled up. When it did, the woman Henry thought to be Mrs. Grey came out of the gift shop and climbed on behind the driver. The driver was a burly, scowling, younger man. The scooter drove towards the front gate. Henry followed and hoped no one would notice since there were some guests on other scooters between them and their quarry. Henry followed at a safe distance. He had to be especially careful because even when they left the compound, traffic on the blacktop road was light. Betsy called Will on her cell phone to update him on their mission. Will cautioned her to be safe.

The scooter went west on highway A1 to Discovery Bay and then headed inland. They went past sugar cane fields and yam gardens and then up into the mountains through Rising Sun. Betsy and Henry continued to follow

A Jamaican Conspiracy

from a distance. Next they went through Stewart Town. It only took half an hour to reach the crossroads at Stewart Town, but it already felt like they were in a different country. At the crossroads Mrs. Grey made a left turn and briefly headed back towards the coast. The road became very narrow, and they soon saw a sign for the Stewart Town Basic School. The road split around a beautiful old cut-stone church. The sign read Webb Memorial Baptist Church. Henry took the right fork and they passed the Stewart Town Basic School.

"I think I know where they are going," Henry announced.

They passed shanties with cemeteries in the yards on a road that became increasingly rough. Concrete slab headstones or crosses marked the heads of small fenced-in family plots. Betsy noticed homes in various stages of construction. A common practice in Jamaica is for families to start and stop construction as their money came in or ran out. Some families would live in the only completed room in the home and continue to build while living there, sometimes making building projects last for 15 to 20 years.

"They're headed for Dornock River Head," Henry told Betsy.

"What's that?" she asked.

"You'll see."

"Excuse me. I'm going to call Will and tell him where we are in case something goes wrong," Betsy said.

"Good idea."

They paused while Betsy called Will on her cell phone. When he didn't answer, she sent him a text message before they continued downhill and entered a beautiful valley. Recent rain left the road pretty much washed out. Mrs. Grey's driver parked their scooter and walked down a rural road that was not much more than a path. Henry parked and locked the van. He led and Betsy followed. The walk downhill to the river took fifteen minutes. The trail was rough and covered with loose rocks. Two other trails led off this one. Their quarry, with a machete, went straight on the first trail and kept left at the second. Henry and Betsy stayed far enough back to be unobserved and watched from behind giant cotton trees. Soon they came to a cow pasture. They could see the river silently flowing by.

A ramshackle shack sat on the edge of the clearing. The main portion was constructed from concrete blocks and had a rusted corrugated tin roof. There was a single small window with a vertically hinged wooden shutter. One double door on the front was painted a faded green; the other was painted a faded pastel blue. The word *Welcome* had been scrawled on the wall above the doors. There was no porch, only a cracked concrete slab. A crude, rickety, wooden addition had been added to one side. The unpainted building had been patched with whatever had been available. This addition had a pass-through closed with a drop-down wooden shutter. The back of the addition had only a portion of a wall, and Betsy could see what appeared to be a worktable in the open section. She surmised that the building had at one time been a roadhouse since handwritten signs decorated the walls saying *Welcome to Dungu's Place - Fish Tea, Fish, Festival, Natural Juice, and Box Lunch, Everything Lunch Good.* She guessed the addition to be an outdoor kitchen and jerk smoker. The canopy of a huge almond tree hung over the whole building.

Mrs. Grey and her driver walked up to the front door as Betsy and Henry lurked behind a giant cotton tree. John David Grey came out, shook the man's hand, and lightly kissed his wife on the cheek.

Betsy lightly elbowed Henry in the ribs and mouthed,

A Jamaican Conspiracy

"You did good."

She motioned Henry to retreat out of their quarries' earshot.

"Well, we've finally found the elusive Mr. Grey," she said in a low voice. "Now what do we do?"

"Follow him back to town?" Henry asked.

"But he may not be going back to town," Betsy said. "And I don't know about you, but I don't plan to spend the day sitting in the bug-infested weeds to wait on him. Maybe I should just try to have a word with him here where there's no secretary to be a gate-keeper."

"I don't think that would be very smart," Henry said. "Remember these people may very well be connected with Dudus Coke. If that's the case, they are cutthroat hooligans."

"You're right, but do you mind if we just watch for a little while and see what we can learn?"

"You're the boss."

Betsy heard a rustling in the brush behind them. She turned and saw Mrs. Grey's scooter driver glowering at them. He had the machete in his hand. Betsy gasped as a mental image of being hacked to death ran through her mind. The man pushed Henry roughly to the ground. Henry scrambled to recover his glasses.

"Who are yu, duty nyega **(who are you, dirty nigger)** and wa mek here **(and why are you here?)**" the man demanded in a snarling, hateful voice.

Henry tried to stand. Before Betsy could respond, the man swung his machete, barely missing Henry's head. She heard a thud as it hit the cotton tree behind him. The man pointed at the shack with the machete and said one word, "Walk."

The man followed them with the machete menacingly cocked over his head. As they approached the shack, Mrs. Grey came out.

"Maama look a wamifin **(look what I found)**," he said.

"She called back over her shoulder. "John David, cumya hey. Spike fin sum body **(come out here. Zany found some visitors)**."

John David Grey came out and looked them over.

"Well, well, well, Mrs. Black," he said in perfect English. "What would you be doing back here in the Cockpit Country? Get lost on your way to work?"

"Would you believe that I've always wanted to see the back country?" Betsy said.

Grey shook his head.

"You're the one Mrs. Smythe was telling me about at Swingles," his wife said as she began to understand the situation. She pointed at Betsy and said, "You followed me here."

"I've been wanting to talk to you for some time to clarify some items in regard to the Highway 2000 project," Betsy said to Grey. "I've left numerous messages for you."

"As I have tried to explain to you before, I am a very busy man," Grey said. "You need to speak to my accountant."

"I've already tried. I was told the only person who could shed light on matters the bank needs clarification for is you."

"You just don't know how to take a hint, do you," Grey said and shook his head again.

"Fadda, mi get rid of dem, if yu wan mi to **(Pop, I can get rid of them if you want me to)**," Zany said. "Mi shoob dem inna cave, de beast nah evah fin dem **(I'll shove their bodies down a cave, and no one will ever find them)**."

He waved the machete menacingly for effect.

"Mehbe yu leh Zany tek care of dem 'is way. **(Maybe you should let Zany take care of them his way)**,"

253

A Jamaican Conspiracy

Mrs. Grey said to her husband. "Who will know? Neville no kya **(won't mind)**."

Grey looked at his wife hostilely and said, "Yu laba-laba too much, ooman **(You talk too much, woman)**."

He quickly made his decision and nodded his to his son. "Bwoy, mek sure chaka-chaka and put away they cyar. Mi be gwaan wen yu come back **(Boy, Just don't screw it up, and get rid of their vehicle. We'll be gone when you return)**."

He looked at Betsy and said, "You were warned. It's a shame you didn't listen."

Zany motioned them towards the forest, and they began to walk.

Betsy turned towards Grey and said, "You won't get away with this. My husband knows where I am. I called in my location to him on my cell phone."

Grey looked momentarily alarmed but then motioned for his son to continue.

"Yu mek double sure, bwoy, de bodies neva foun **(You had better make doubly sure, boy, that their bodies are never found)**," he said.

As they walked, Betsy was so scared her knees were weak and she felt light-headed. Within minutes, they had left the clearing and were in the dense forest. Henry docilely and silently followed her. All the words of warning came back to her.

Suddenly she heard a thump and looked back. Zany was on the ground out cold. Next to him stood the young wiry stranger who had rescued them the day of their confrontation with the KSAC road construction crew. He was brandishing a three-foot two-inch-thick tree limb. Zany stirred. The man swung the limb again and hit him again. He handled the limb like a baseball bat. Zany did not stir again. She wondered if their rescuer had killed him.

Betsy's mind flashed back to the day the man had cut the construction foreman's shovel handle in two with one slicing blow from his machete.

"Go," he said. "Your van is that way. Get in it and drive back to Ochi. You are not safe here."

They hesitated.

"Now," the man said and pointed in the direction of Henry's van.

As they looked back, the mysterious stranger was still brandishing the tree limb.

Running toward the van, Betsy saw a tussle out of the corner of her eye. Then she heard the sickening thunk of the tree limb again and an "Oomph." She sincerely hoped that their nameless friend was the one doing the thunking.

> BEWRAY OF
> BAD DOG

CHAPTER 34

Betsy and Henry dove into Henry's van. They noticed the white Toyota Chaser parked on the shoulder of the road just up from them. Henry and Betsy drove as fast as they could back into Ocho Rios. Henry impatiently honked his horn at the slow traffic on A1. Neither of them spoke. They tried to regain their composure.

Finally Betsy said, "We almost got killed back there."

"Except for our nameless friend," Henry said. "I told you Grey might be connected to some dangerous people. If our Good Samaritan had not come along, Zany could have dumped our bodies in a nameless cockpit country cave, and we never would have been found."

"I'm going to have Grey arrested for attempted murder," Betsy said. "Let's head for the police station."

Henry cut off A1, went through the roundabout on A3, turned left onto DaCosta Drive, drove east past the clock tower, veered back onto A1, and finally took a left on Evelyn Street. He found a place to park, and they walked into the Constabulary Force office. The office seemed unusually quiet. Instead of the expected hustle and bustle, they saw only a lone desk clerk. Betsy walked up to him.

"I'd like to file a complaint," she said.

"We're taking emergency cases only," the clerk said. "Please bear with me. I'm Assistant Commander Phil Allen. I don't normally work the front desk."

"Jesus, man, emergencies only," Henry said. "This is supposed to be a police station."

"We have the Blue-Flu," Assistant Commander Allen said.

Betsy and Henry looked at each other questioningly.

"We only have a skeleton staff," Allen continued. "The rank and file is having a sick-out. The Police Federation has been demanding a 47% pay increase over the next two years instead of the usual 3% raise stipulated in the Public Sector Memorandum of Understanding. When the government refused to give it to them, the Federation told their members to call in sick. Over half our force did not show up for work today. We don't know how long they will be out."

"So what are you doing?" Betsy asked.

"The ISCF is trying to take up the slack," the assistant commander said, "but they can only do so much."

"The ISCF?" Betsy asked.

"ISCF stands for the Island Special Constabulary Force," Henry explained to her. "They are the reserve force that does menial jobs like directing traffic for the JCF."

"You mean they are rent-a-cops," Betsy said. "Like we use to patrol malls in America."

"Exactly," Henry replied.

"Swell! Just swell!" Betsy said. "We have a dangerous criminal who just tried to kill us, and what do we get - a rent-a-cop."

Assistant Commander Allen looked embarrassed.

"My apologies, madam. It's the best we can do until this strike is over," he said. "The government has been negotiating with the Police Federation for over a year.

Everyone's patience is wearing thin."

"Including mine," Betsy muttered. She then explained to Allen what had happened to them earlier that day up in the cockpit country.

"I would love to investigate your charge," Allen said, "but I'm confined to running this desk until the Blue-flu is over. I hope you understand, but I will let one of our ISCF volunteers try to be of assistance to you."

"Is he an investigator?" Betsy asked.

"Unfortunately no," Allen said. "She's a handler with our canine unit. In fact, she's my wife."

"Then I'm sure she'll do just fine," Betsy said, gritting her teeth.

"Sybil," Phil Allen said. "I have someone here to see you."

He took them back to the cubicle being used by Sybil Allen. Sybil wore blue serge trousers with blue seams down each leg and a white and blue striped short-sleeved shirt. She had three chevrons on her right sleeve to signify that she was a sergeant. She wore a black hat with blue stripes around the top, even though she was indoors. Phil left them and went back to man the front desk.

Henry and Betsy identified themselves and explained once again how they had tracked John David Grey's wife from Swingles to the Dornock River Head. They told her how they had found Grey there, and how his son Zany had almost killed them. Sybil listened excitedly.

"Aren't you going to write any of this down?" Betsy asked.

"Oh, yeah," Sybil Allen said. "I forgot." She giggled. "This is my very first investigation. I'm so excited. I've wanted to share Phil's work with him for so many years."

We're in major trouble, Betsy's eyes signaled to Henry. He silently acknowledged her concerns.

"I think we should return to Dornock River Head,"

A Jamaican Conspiracy

Henry suggested to Sybil.

"I think you're right," she said, "but let me go to the powder room first. I'll be right back."

From the ladies room she dialed her aunt, Letha Wardlow.

"Auntie Letha, Mi just adla call yu **(I just had to call you)**," Sgt. Allen said. "Mi soo excited. Mi bout a go on mi fust crime investigation, and you won't believe who reported the crime – a lady from yu bank, Mrs. Betsy Black. Mi canna talk now. Mi a go **(I'm so excited. I'm about to go on my first crime investigation, and you won't believe who reported the crime – a lady from your bank, Mrs. Betsy Black. I can't talk now. I have to go)**."

"Sybil," Letha said. "Mi excited fo yu. Promise mi yu call mi later tiday or at home tonight and go a tell mi wha 'appens **(I'm excited for you. Promise me you'll call me later today or at home tonight and fill me in on what happens)**."

"Mi will. Mi mek promise **(I will. I promise)**," Sybil said and hung up.

Sybil walked back out to the lobby and said, "I'm ready now."

~ ~ ~

Letha instantly made a phone call to report what she had just learned. Her report was relayed almost immediately, and a harsh conversation ensued.

Caller one: "Did Grey get your permission to try to remove the American bank bitch?"

Caller two: "No. Did you know anything about it?"

Caller one: "Of course not. Do you think I'm that stupid? An investigation with the bank is all we need to bring more unwanted attention to ourselves."

Caller two: "Exactly. It was one thing to try to scare or intimidate her, but I never would have authorized a bonehead move like this. Grey's judgment is certainly becoming questionable."

Caller one: "A loose cannon is something we cannot tolerate."

Caller two: "My contact tells me the bitch has already written one report that is already bringing his labor costs under scrutiny."

Caller one: "And if they investigate that, his other institutional strengthening irregularities will probably be exposed."

Caller two: "That's what I mean. She could open Pandora's Box. Maybe Mr. Grey should be expelled from the organization. After all, there's a lot of money at stake."

Caller one: "Possibly, but that's harsh, though we shouldn't rule it out. Talk to Grey first. Then let's see what happens, and we'll talk again."

Caller two: "I agree. I'll tell my moles at JCF and NCB to be vigilant for signs of increasing pressure. For Grey's sake, I hope things cool down. If they don't, he *is* dispensable."

Caller one: "Agreed. You will keep me informed? And you won't mete out the ultimate punishment without consulting me? I assume Cudjoe is available if his skills are needed in that regard."

Caller two: "Of course. He is dependable."

~ ~ ~

Henry instructed Sgt. Allen how to retrace their steps into the cockpit country. Back to A1. Right onto A3 and southwest to Dornock River Head. They walked down the unpaved path through the forest until they saw the dilapidated shack where Henry and Betsy had cornered the elusive John David Grey. The shack had been evacuated with no sign of life other than the birds singing from the trees.

"I didn't really expect to find anyone home," Henry

commented to Betsy. "If you recall, Grey's last comment to Zany before he led us to the slaughter was 'Mi be gwaan wen yu come back' **(I'll be gone when you get back)**."

The well-meaning but inexperienced Sgt. Sybil Allen didn't know what she was supposed to do next, so they returned to the Constabulary office where Allen could consult her husband about what a seasoned investigator would do next. Henry drove Betsy back to National Commerce Bank; she immediately called Will and gave him a blow-by-blow description of the day's pursuits. He told her to call WB. She promised she would.

The ever-vigilant Letha Wardlow listened in and promptly gave a full account to her contact. Her call was relayed and discussed.

~ ~ ~

"Mr. Grey is out of control," caller one said.

"I tend to agree," caller two responded. "He seems to have had a mental breakdown."

"He sure as hell has had a judgment breakdown."

~ ~ ~

Sgt. Allen's clumsy investigation over the next few days did nothing to locate the slippery Greys; Will and Betsy's anxiety and frustration continued to mount as Grey continued to successfully elude all pursuers.

TOMMYS'
NEW
USED
ANTIQUES

CHAPTER 35

"May I speak to Ken Scott, please?" Betsy said into her phone.

"May I tell Mr. Scott who is calling?" Scott's secretary responded.

"Betsy Black in Jamaica."

"Oh, I apologize, Mrs. Black. I didn't recognize your voice. I'll put you right through."

Scott picked up his phone instantaneously.

"Your ears must have been burning," he said. "I was just thinking about calling you."

"So who's on first, then? You or me?" Betsy asked.

"Ladies first, of course."

Betsy then described in detail how she and Henry Davis tracked John David Grey into the Cockpit Country that morning to try to talk to him about KSAC's accounting irregularities and how they were almost killed.

"I was afraid you might accidentally put yourself in harm's way," Scott gasped. "Did you report the matter to the local police?"

Betsy then told Scott about the fiasco at the Jamaican Constabulary Force office in Ocho Rios and the resulting amateurish investigation.

"I guess I underestimated my adversary. I won't make that mistake again, but now Grey seems to have vanished again," Betsy said, "and the police say until they hear his side of the story, it is my word against his. In other words I'm getting the royal run-around."

"Totally unacceptable response," Scott said with conviction. "I'll get the bank's legal council to put pressure on the local police. The bank will not tolerate someone threatening our employees while they are trying to conduct their jobs. I want all the details immediately including the names of the people you have been dealing with." Betsy gave him her complaint number and promised to e-mail him the rest of the information as soon as she got off the phone.

"Your KSAC memo is going through channels, but the bank has come under sharp pressure from certain Jamaican officials who are threatening legal action for damages if unfounded or frivolous accusations cause Highway 2000 to be delayed or come in over budget."

"How does an outside party even know about my memo? It was confidential," Betsy asked.

"I don't know, but they seem to. I'm trying to get to the bottom of the matter and discover the source of the leak. I guess you realize the problem could easily be on your end."

"I realize that. Do you know who the attorney represents?"

"The threat is originating from the office of a senior official – a Dr. Bedward."

"Wonderful! Just wonderful! Threats from within as well as those from the outside."

"Please contain your frustration," Scott said. "I'm sure in the final analysis the truth will emerge."

"It sure as hell will, if I have anything to do with it.

Now on to new business, Ken. What did you have on your mind today?" Betsy asked.

"I received some compromising pictures of you in this morning's mail," Scott began. "These pictures make it look like you and Will were engaged in a drug orgy of sorts. They appear to have been taken at a street party where you and your husband were possibly using illegal narcotics and maybe even distributing them to other revelers."

"Whaaat!" Betsy said. "You say you got this in today's mail? From whom?"

"Anonymous source. They just arrived here from Jamaica in glossy eight by tens. That's all I know. Have you attended any street parties recently?"

"Yes, as a matter of fact we have," Betsy said, still not believing what she was hearing. "We were invited to a People's National Party fund-raising street dance in Discovery Bay. Our houseboy's best friend was the record spinner. The function was well attended by local dignitaries including the dishonorable John David Grey. In fact, that is where I finally met him face-to-face after repeatedly failing to secure an appointment. Will and I had a good time and did nothing out of line. In fact, we left early when we saw the party turning raucous."

"That's not what these pictures look like," Scott said. "They make it appear that you were in the thick of it not only using marijuana but possibly providing it to other people."

"Ken you know that's not true. The pictures have to be doctored. We both know how easily pictures can be altered on a modern computer."

"Betsy, I believe you," Scott said, "but the woman in human resources who also got a set of these pictures isn't going to be as easy to convince as I am. People in her position tend not to give our people in the field the benefit of the doubt in order to not risk getting blind-sided."

"I know and understand. Their primary responsibility is to be reactive in order to protect the corporation," Betsy said and sighed, "as we all are supposed to do."

"She probably wouldn't have been so dubious had it not been for the previous accusation that you tried to use your bank position for personal gain in a real estate transaction. She has been trained to think where there's smoke there's fire. You'll definitely be hearing more about this. A note attached to the photos said that if the bank could not control and discipline its employees, the news media would be given a copy of the pictures so it could do it for them. Somebody's playing real hardball. I'm sorry I'm the one who had to tell you all this – no, I'm glad I could give you a heads-up. Let me go now. I will call our attorney immediately and see what can be done about your assault. In the meantime, why don't you take a day off and relax. You need to clear your mind."

"Is this a suspension with pay?" Betsy asked.

"Of course not," Scott replied. "This is just some advice from a good friend. You've been through a traumatic experience well beyond the scope of most bankers."

Betsy called Will to tell him about her latest conversation with Ken Scott. Leva answered the phone and told her Will would call her right back. Will dialed her back within minutes.

"Sorry I couldn't take your call," he said. "I was putting out an unexpected fire. Someone sent RST photos that made it look like you and I are dope-heads."

"That's exactly what I was calling you about," Betsy said. "The bank got a set of the pictures as well. Ken Scott suggested I take a day off and regroup while he tries to assess human resources' position and also bring bank pressure on the Jamaican cops."

"Maybe we should," Will said. "We can use the time to think about what our strategy is going to be going forward. I refuse to be taken down and have our careers destroyed by a bunch of third-world thugs – I don't care how well connected they are. Obviously you've really begun to step on sensitive and powerful toes. You're doing what your predecessor never seemed to do. Why don't we follow Scott's suggestion and get with Henry and Rose and take a day to chill out on the beach at Dunn's River?"

"These people just don't know who they're tangling with. I will prevail," Betsy said. "As I have heard Henry say 'Kyarri on wit maga dog, maga dog turn round bite yu' **(If you mess with a mad dog, that dog just might turn around and bite you)**."

"I also heard him say, 'Yu lie wit dawg, yu rise wit fleas' **(If you lie down with a dog, you'll rise with fleas)**."

> BOTTOMLESSPIT
> 65 FEET DEEP

CHAPTER 36

Dunn's River Falls is undoubtedly one of Jamaica's national treasures. The Spanish had called the area "Las Chorreras," which means "the waterfalls" or "the springs." The name was reduced over time to "Ocho Rios" which means eight rivers. The area was named Ocho Rios despite the fact that there were not really eight rivers in the vicinity but only four. In 1657 a battle was fought between the British and the Spanish Expeditionary Force from Cuba for control of the falls. The British prevailed. The property was privately owned until 1972 when it was deeded over to the Jamaican government to use for public leisurely activities.

Dunn's River Falls is an astounding flowing falls that extends more than 600 feet. The falls is frequently featured in tourist advertisements promoting Jamaica. Dunn's River is one of the few rivers in the world that flows directly into the Caribbean. It is also one of the most well liked and most widely photographed travel destinations on the island. James Bond buffs usually instantly recognize it as the site of the well-known scene in *Dr. No* where Ursula Andress walks out on Dunn's River beach in a bikini looking for seashells. The most popular activity for both tourists and locals is climbing up the falls or hanging out in one of the several lagoons or pools along the way, but its devotees also realize it has one of the best beaches in the area.

Betsy decided that maybe Ken Scott and Will were right. Maybe they should take a day off and clear their heads. She called Rose Davis about going to Dunn's River beach the following day. Rose consulted Henry for scheduling conflicts and then called Betsy back saying it sounded like a most enjoyable outing. Rose volunteered to fry some fish and bring other goodies. Betsy said she and Will would provide the liquid refreshments.

Henry picked Will and Betsy up at mid-morning, and they headed east on A3 through Runaway Bay to Dunn's River. By the time they got there, the sun had climbed high from the turquoise Caribbean towards the flawless powder blue sky. As they neared the falls, Henry honked at reclusive artist, Michael Clarke, who was standing in front of his humble art studio. They decided, on a whim, to stop and visit. Mr. Clarke was carving two over-sized mahogany queen conch shells.

"These sure would look good back in the Keys," Will said to Betsy, and then to Henry and Rose he said, "I guess you know that Keys natives are called 'Conchs'."

"Yes, they would. They would make a marvelous conversation piece," Betsy said, "especially since we're going to qualify as 'fresh-water Conchs' ourselves in a few years."

"Ja-Merican Conchs," Henry said. "That makes you a rare breed indeed."

Mr. Clarke, in his usual bashful manner, agreed that he could not think of a place the conch shells belonged more than back in the Keys and promised to reserve both finished carvings for the Blacks.

A few minutes later the group arrived at the falls. Henry parked the van, and they paid their admission fee at the roadside ticket booth. Within minutes they were walking down the worn stone stairs past the observation deck to the white sugary beach. Will and Henry each carried a small ice chest. Betsy and Rose took the beach chairs and the picnic basket.

"This has got to be the Niagara Falls of Jamaica," Will said as he marveled over the silken aquamarine surface of the gin-clear water.

The beach at the base of Dunn's River Falls is one of the best in all of Jamaica. The water is tempered with currents of alternating temperatures from the cold river water and the warm Caribbean Sea. The beach is wide and flat with startlingly white sand and dotted with coconut palms. After only a short stroll, nature-lovers can lose themselves in blossoming tropical foliage of bamboos, ferns, crotons, lilies, orchids, and breadfruit trees.

A full bar and a snack shop was a short walk away. A few exercisers were jogging along the beach. Sun lovers were renewing their tans. The whole picturesque scene was backed by the stunning blue-green waters of the Caribbean.

"This was a great idea," Will said. "I'm glad I thought of it."

Betsy and Rose looked at each other and simultaneously said "Men". They then laughed at their mutual spontaneity and shook their heads playfully as they set up the beach chairs for a day in the sun. Will and Henry became impatient and ran into the water to take a quick dip to escape the tropical heat.

As they were letting the wave gradually wash them back towards the beach, Henry said, "Did you see that tall young Jamaican girl staring at us?"

"Maybe she's just not used to seeing suave debonair Ja-Merican conchs here," Will said, "and I haven't even given her my killer smile yet."

"I don't think that was it," Henry continued. "She looked almost familiar to me – almost like someone I know. I just can't place who or where."

"Maybe she thinks she knows you from somewhere," Will said. "Let's face it, You know half the island, and the other half knows you."

"Maybe we're both right – your animal magnetism and my renown."

"Let's get back to the beach and have a *coldbeer* with the girls," Will said.

"Only if it's *icecold*," Henry said.

They munched on some fish while drinking an ice cold Red Stripe. For the first time in days Betsy was beginning to relax. The four of them decided to play in the surf. Will glanced up at the beach. The girl Henry had pointed out to him was still sitting there alone staring moodily.

"Strange," Will said to Henry, "that a young attractive girl would be here at the beach alone. You'd think she would have brought a companion."

Rose asked who they were talking about, and Henry pointed the girl out.

"It would certainly seem that she would find it more enjoyable to share the day with a friend," Henry agreed, "or that if she chose to come by herself, she would have brought a book or magazine to read. She's just sitting on the beach looking preoccupied."

"Maybe she has personal problems," Rose said.

"Boy, are you two out of touch," Betsy said. "What you're witnessing is called technology withdrawal. Don't you know young people rarely read any more? They play with their computers or cell phones instead. Let's take a dip."

After they finished playing in the surf, the group went back up on the beach to dry off and relax.

272

After soaking up some rays, Betsy observed, "I can't remember the last time you and I climbed the falls."

"It has been awhile," Will agreed. "Remember the time we climbed down the falls instead of up?"

"Sure do. People looked at us like we were nuts," Betsy said.

"Up for a climb?" Will asked.

"I am if you are," Betsy said.

They asked Henry and Rose if they wanted to join them scaling the falls. Both declined but offered to watch all their belongings. Will and Betsy headed for the first rung of the falls. The tall girl made a beeline for the falls as well. Rose excused herself and began to climb the stone stairway to the restrooms. As they pulled themselves up the lower falls, Will noticed that the mysterious Jamaican girl was now above them.

The Jamaican guides instructed groups of novice tourists to join hands in a human daisy-chain at the bottom of the falls. The tourists were soon clambering up the natural terraced stair-steps through the series of cascades and pools. The refreshingly cool water was shaded by the multitudes of tall magnificent tree specimens in the surrounding rain forest. Some parts of the falls seemed more like a man-made theme park than one of nature's wonders. Several small lagoons were interspersed among the vertical sections of the falls. Natural cool plunge pools had been formed in the river rock. Some of the rocks were mossy and slippery. The garrulous guides prattled constantly as they held their charges' hands and carried their cameras, trying to earn the tips they expected at the climb's conclusion.

Will and Betsy always relished the challenge of taking routes up the falls that were different from those taken by the chains of people. This sometimes necessitated their climbing mossy rocks and more difficult inclines than the less challenging established routes chosen by the guides for the daisy-chains.

After scaling one particularly difficult sheer climb adjacent to the stairs, Will looked up and momentarily saw the sullen Jamaican girl above them staring down. Will got a brief uneasy feeling in his gut as he thought for an instant that the girl had a hostile look in her squinting eyes. He was having difficulty hauling Betsy up the last rock as she struggled to get a foothold. The girl retreated down the falls toward them. Will thought momentarily that she wanted to assist him. Just as he pulled Betsy up the last bit of the slippery ten-foot watery precipice, he saw a glint in the sun out of the corner of his eye. He looked up again. The girl had pulled out a meat cleaver. With no warning, she slashed out with it. Will instinctively ducked and almost lost Betsy's hand. Betsy stabilized herself by grabbing a rock protrusion with her other hand. The cleaver slashed in the other direction, this time chipping the boulder.

"Brudda killa. Fyah fi yu **(Brother killer. Burn in hell)**," the girl said viciously.

Will dodged and again almost dropped Betsy. Suddenly they saw a beach towel whiz by, heard a sharp snap, and the girl lost her footing sending her tumbling over the edge, falling the entire ten feet. The girl was so shocked she did not even try to catch herself. She hit the bottom with a dull thud, splashing water, and did not move. Will saw a trickle of red begin to puddle in the water around her head. He looked up. Rose was standing there with a rolled up beach towel in her hand.

Rose smiled at Betsy and said, "We girls have to look out for each other. Hit be she turn to fyah fi she **(It's her turn to burn in hell)**."

Will pulled Betsy to safety and then held Betsy in his arms to comfort her. A shocked guide left his party, scampered over and climbed down to the bottom of the waterfall to see if the fallen girl was hurt. When he turned the girl over, Will could see the would-be murderess had fallen on her own weapon. The weighty cleaver had slashed through her neck all the way to her spinal column. Her spine had also broken from the fall. The neck was grotesquely turned to one side, only held on by the muscles that had not been severed. The girl's eyes stared blankly as the water ran over her dead body. Her artery continued to pool bright red blood which trickled down the falls.

> BOBRAY RAY WALKER
> **MENDING AND RENOVATING**
>
> * ESTB. PRICES *
> *NO IDLERS *
> *NO SMOKING *
> *NO LADIES' PANTS *
> *BY ORDER
> *

CHAPTER 37

"She's definitely dead," Will said to Betsy. "By her own hand. She fell on the cleaver."

"But who is she?" Betsy gasped. "Thank God you were here, Rose. She intended to kill us. But why?"

Rose looked back at Betsy and said matter-of-factly, "I did not like the way she was looking at you. I could tell she was a rude girl. Maybe a thief. That is why I excused myself to go to the ladies room. I wanted to keep an eye on things. I thought she was a up to no good."

Falls climbers began to congregate. They stopped climbing the falls and gawked at the gruesome scene. An emaciated woman began to retch. Her vomit ran down the falls, causing another woman to get sick. As they

A Jamaican Conspiracy

talked to each other in low voices, Will and Betsy could hear a murmur. Shocked vacationers were babbling to anyone who would listen about what they thought they had seen. Will and Betsy heard an American woman chattering.

"See, Wilber, I told you it was dangerous in this drug-infested third-world country. Ethel told me so at the club. I knew we should have gone to Corinth to visit mama this week," she drawled.

Wilber retorted, "Like that busy-body Bible-thumper knows. Ethel's never been mor'n twenty miles from Memphis. Her idea of a dangerous situation is dodging shopping carts at Wal-Mart when they run canned peaches on special. And by the way, when your daddy is on a bender, visiting your mama ain't much better than going to a third-world cesspool."

Will and Betsy grinned at each other.

"Ah'm glad mah dog ain't in that fight," Will said.

"I was just trying to imagine Thanksgiving dinner when that whole clan shows up," Betsy replied.

One of the Dunn's River Falls guides scampered up the stairs to find a security guard.

Will turned to Rose and said quietly, "I wouldn't mention the towel unless the topic comes up. It can only cause complications. If the subject does arise, I wouldn't lie, but I'd only answer the questions asked without elaborating or volunteering problematic information."

Rose nodded in agreement.

"So much for a relaxing day unwinding at the falls and catching the rays," Betsy said.

"Soon Henry is going to wonder where we are," Rose said.

Will spotted a Jamaican boy and called to him. In patois Rose described Henry Davis, told the boy where Henry could be found, and offered him a tip if he brought

278

Henry back. The boy scampered off to earn his tip.

Will looked around and watched the ever-growing throng of rubberneckers. No one seemed be paying the Blacks any undue attention. Will waited for someone to point an accusing finger at them. No one ever did.

"I don't think anyone actually saw what happened," he commented to Rose and Betsy.

"Probably not," Rose said. "Folks here were busy climbing and frolicking in the refreshing water. They were absorbed in their own pleasures."

"Let's see what shoe drops next," Betsy said. "I really don't want to get involved if I can help it, but I'm not going to risk arousing suspicion by leaving the scene until I'm sure it is prudent to do so. We don't need any more false accusations. I'd rather not have one more controversial item to hit the bank at this moment with my name associated with it."

Within a short while, a security guard and a JCF policeman climbed off the stone stairs and examined the lacerated body. By this time Will, Betsy, and Rose had eased onto the stone stairway where they quietly watched the investigation. The policeman seemed to be debating with himself if the body before him was the victim of a crime or if she was a petty criminal who experienced a deserved accident. The cop decided to call the JCF and request a crime scene investigator. The crime scene investigator processed the crime scene and took photographs. The few legitimate witnesses questioned shed little light on the incident. Will and Betsy were not among those questioned. An ambulance arrived, and the law enforcement officers moved the body.

Henry came as they watched events unfold. Will calmly motioned Henry aside and whispered that he would update him on the situation later.

When the ambulance left, they decided it was safe for

them to leave.

"I've seen enough falling for one day," Betsy said.

"I totally agree, dear lady," Henry said.

"Don't we need to retrieve our beach chairs and ice chests?" Will asked.

"I took them to the van before I found you," Henry said.

"Good thinking. So there's nothing to keep us here," Will said. "Let's head for the villa and try to analyze this sordid mess."

"Do you think we should discreetly ask the cops if they have been able to identify the deceased?" Rose asked.

"Not only no, but hell no. I doubt if they'd tell you if they know," Will said. "We've gotten this far without attracting undue attention to ourselves. Let's not risk blowing it now. Surely a death this dramatic at such a prominent public place will be in tomorrow's *Gleaner*."

No one noticed, but the white Toyota Chaser followed Henry's van at a distance on the trip back to Sundance.

As it turned out, Will and Betsy did not have to wait for the girl's death to be reported in *The Gleaner*. Later that day, as they were all sitting around the pool, a phone call came into Sundance, rehashing the day's events. The call was for Betsy.

"This is Buried Blade," the caller began. "The incident at Dunn's River Falls was regrettable, but in retrospect, unavoidable. We are relieved you were not injured. The girl's death was an unintended consequence, but as they say, every action creates a reaction."

"Thank you for your concern, whoever you are," Betsy said. "Reaction to what? I never met this person in my life, though my friend Henry seemed to think she seemed vaguely familiar to him."

"You really don't know who she was, do you?" Buried Blade said. "No, I don't guess you would. Her name is

Zoey Grey."

"Is she related to John David Grey?"

"His daughter."

"Which makes her Zany's sister?"

"Twin," Buried Blade said.

"Ouch! That somewhat explains why she said 'brudda killa. Fyah fi yu' ... But I didn't kill her brother ... I didn't even know for certain he's dead ... *he* was the one who tried to kill me."

There was a silence on the other end of the line.

"Is Zany really dead?" Betsy asked.

"I would rather not comment."

"Will you answer this for me then?" Betsy asked. "Why is John David Grey so paranoid about my inquiries? My queries have been completely routine unless he has something to hide."

"You are drawing unwanted attention to him," Buried Blade said. "Check his contractor's license."

"Why are you helping me?" Betsy asked. "What's in this for you?"

"We have our reasons," Buried Blade said and hung up.

SMOTHER CHICKEN

CHAPTER 38

After the troubling and ambiguous conversation with Buried Blade, Betsy went back through the Kingston and St. Andrew Corporation's file to see what more she could learn about John David Grey's contractor's license. She found that he did have a valid registration as a government works contractor that had been issued by the National Contracts Commission. On the surface everything appeared to be in order. *What in the world was Buried Blade talking about?* She continued to examine the file. Toward the back of the folder, she found a copy of Grey's re-registration application form. *At some point the bank must have requested proof of his continuing compliance for this document to be here. I wonder what I can learn from his application. Looks pretty routine.*

She took the file home that evening and mentioned to Will her inability to spot anything irregular in it.

Will said, "You mind if I take a look at it?"

"Be my guest."

"You're right. Nothing is jumping out at me either," Will said, after perusing the application. "I see the app required him to list his key employees. Do you think these people should be investigated to see if they can shed some light on the enigma?"

Betsy checked a file that showed KSAC's current employees. Not one of the three names appeared – not even one of them.

"That's odd," she told Will. "They may have been key then, but they sure don't appear to be now."

"Maybe you should try to locate them," Will said.

"Fat chance they'd talk to a nosy foreign honky woman. Dey wud tink mi too fass and facety **(They would think I was too inquisitive and fresh)**."

"And besides dat dey tink yu ooman dam lagga head bud **(and besides that they think you women are stupid)**," Will retaliated.

"But as Adam Sandler reminded us in the movie, *Mr. Deeds*, they better never underestimate my sneakiness."

"If I were you, I wouldn't want to trust someone at the bank with this sensitive issue. Maybe Henry could be helpful," Will said. "He's Jamaican, he's smart, he knows construction, and he could talk the bark off a tree."

"Plus he's on our side. If our mysterious friend can call himself Buried Blade, you can just call me 'Sneaky Snake'," Betsy said. "What is going to be his excuse for calling?"

"How about if he impersonates someone who is looking for a contractor for an upcoming job and is trying to find out if KSAC does quality work?"

"Perfect."

Henry listened, grinned, and quickly agreed to be Betsy's co-conspirator.

"Henry Davis, master driver and super-sneaky but budget-priced private investigator," he said with a wink. "Just call me Ochi's 'Spenser for hire'."

The following day he reported to Will and Betsy.

"I'm not sure if my calls yielded information of much value to you," he said. "Each of these people was formerly a laborer in the construction industry. I wouldn't say that any of them are or ever were what you would classify as managerial material. On top of that, not one of them admitted to ever having worked for John David Grey or KSAC. In fact, his name didn't seem to ring a bell with any of them. I think they might be just lackey henchmen and liars as well."

"Henry, you may have uncovered info more important than you think," Betsy said. "It appears that Mr. Grey fabricated a management team on his NCC application, which makes me ask myself why. Surely a company bidding on multi-millions of dollars of government contracts couldn't have been a one man show."

She stopped and thought for a second before she added, "Maybe his true employees couldn't withstand close scrutiny by the Office of the Contractor General."

"Like possibly his employees were connected with some unsavory characters?" Will asked. "Like maybe a posse don?"

"Or possibly they had other undisclosed conflicts of interest," Betsy said.

"There's always the possibility his company was only a shell company from the get-go," Will said.

"If so why the hell would the OCG get involved with a fly-by-night like them to begin with?" Betsy asked.

"Politricks," Henry said.

"I think more research is warranted," Will said. "Henry, Rose is like you – she seems to know everyone. Why don't you get her to ask some of her women friends if they know some scuttlebutt about these people, but please stress with her that she needs to be discreet and that no one should know why she is poking around."

Rose did some ganja gabbing over the next several days and then repeated the gossip.

"Joe Thomas is Merle Dunster's nephew from Fruitful Vale in Portland Parrish. He spent some time in Miami but then returned to Jamaica. The U.S. possibly deported him as an undesirable alien.

"Joe Gerber is from Spanish Town in St. Catherine Parrish and is some unknown relation to Dr. Damien Rosser, the Contractor General of the OCG. My friends told me Gerber has been involved in a long list of petty crimes for most of his adult life; he did time in the general prison in Kingston.

"Robert Fulton from Cave Valley in Cornwall Parrish is the wayward grandson of Dr. Devon Bedward, the Minister of State of the Ministry of Water and Housing. My friend Myrtle says he is a compulsive gambler and the rumor is that he owes money to the Shower Posse. He's also been arrested for wife-beating," Rose said.

"Lovely choice of references," Will commented. "A con, a gambler, and an undesirable alien. What a bunch of lowlifes. If these guys were on KSAC's payroll, maybe Grey was paying off some favors with taxpayer money. Good old OPM – other people's money. Reminds you of how things often get done in America."

"I've heard BB brag about knowing Bedward," Betsy said. "Bedward is number two with the Ministry of Water and Housing which is responsible for awarding contracts for Operation Pride."

"I know his name as well. Bedward's wife was a Smith," Henry said. "Bedward was also formerly an organizer with the National Worker's Union. He had a nasty reputation back then."

"Another Smith? But it is a common name, and most interesting that a degradant ex-con relative of the head of Office of Contractor General was one of Grey's references," Betsy said.

"I hope he's not kin to President Smith at the bank," Will said.

"Rosser's very influential in the People's National Party," Henry said. "He was once a very questionable member of the National Worker's Union."

"What exactly is Operation Pride?" Will asked.

"I sat through a bank meeting on Operation Pride," Betsy said. "Operation Pride is an almost utopian program instituted by former Prime Minister Patterson. The program leaders are attempting to resolve the shelter needs of low-income Jamaicans by establishing new planned settlements as well as improving public health countrywide. Lowering the national unemployment rate is also a goal. The catalyst for the whole process is supposed to be the distribution of government land through the National Housing Trust and the National Housing Development Corporation."

"Grey's references seem to be a most-wanted list of loafers and bums who are blood relatives of some very important power-brokers," Will said. "And to think none of these people admitted they knew Mr. Grey. I wonder what he owed their prominent relatives."

"Definitely raises some red-flags," Betsy said.

The following morning Betsy placed a call to Ken Scott at WB in Charlotte. Letha silently listened.

"Ken, I'm calling to update you on my progress," she said. "I'm convinced there's definitely something rotten in Denmark or, in this case, KSAC."

"Thanks, I need ammo for when someone in human resources calls me and starts to give me pressure," Scott said. "It's just a matter of time until it happens again."

"There were definitely some irregularities on John David Grey's application to the Jamaican National Contracts Commission when he was trying to get KSAC on the OGC's list of approved contractors. Unless you are on that list you cannot bid on government jobs. He listed three key employees with construction experience to show his organization had the depth necessary to perform up to the standards expected of KSAC if it were

A Jamaican Conspiracy

to be awarded a government contract. I had someone contact each of these people, and not one of the three appear to have ever worked for Mr. Grey or KSAC. Coincidentally, they are all related to powerful Jamaican government officials. Without belaboring the specifics on this call, their bios ran up some meaningful red-flags with me."

"Write a full report for me immediately and overnight it," Ken Scott said, "and let me handle things from here. Good job. The old adage says that a good defense is often a good offense."

Betsy hung up the phone and began working on her memorandum for Ken Scott. Letha made notes on Betsy's call and passed on what she had overheard. Letha's contact told her he would make it worth her while to try to secure a copy of the final report. Letha immediately carried Betsy one of her fresh homemade guava cupcakes and a cup of coffee as a mid-morning treat.

Betsy did not hear from Scott for over a week. During that time, she sent him an e-mail requesting an update. Ken answered asking her to be patient and assured her that her memo was being read, digested, and distributed. A few days later, she sent Scott a follow-up. He responded with more or less the same message. Betsy's frustration mounted from the uncertainty.

About the time Betsy's frustration was peaking, Letha buzzed her and said, "Ken Scott on line two." Letha left the door cracked so she could eavesdrop.

"I was starting to feel that I was not being taken seriously," Betsy said.

"Please accept my apologies," Scott began. "We had to dot all our 'i's' and cross all our 't's' before we accused KSAC of being a sham contractor, but the bank's attorneys finally requested that the Office of General Contractor re-examine KSAC's application to be an approved National Contracts Commission vendor. They initially seemed taken aback. They inferred that we were interfering in a Jamaican affair, but finally after more pressure was brought to bear, they agreed to examine the matter. As expected, nothing happened. Then the OCG began to stall and stonewall again. We're debating out next move."

"One of the fishy names is a person named John Gerber, who is somehow related to Dr. Damien Rosser, the Contractor General of the OCG," Betsy said.

"That may explain a lot," Scott said. "I'll be in touch after I read your latest report."

"Let me remind you that I told you awhile back that I suspected KSAC was padding its payroll. I thought only labor was involved, but it may have included the management staff as well."

"I haven't forgotten."

~ ~ ~

Caller one: "I got a call from Rosser."

Caller two: "About what?"

Caller one: "The attorneys at WB Bank in America are inferring that Grey might be a sham contractor who became a government works contractor under false pretenses."

Caller two: "What brought this unwanted attention?"

Caller one: "Mrs. Black. She believes he is padding the payroll with non-existent day-laborers."

Caller two: "Do they have proof on which to base their accusations?"

Caller one: "I don't think so. Rosser has been trying to stonewall. Despite his efforts my informant tipped me that we might have a problem keeping the lid on things. I could not prevent their initial probe, but since then one of my associates has made it clear to each of the three people the bank contacted that they are to either have memory problems when it comes to discussing the company, or they might develop permanent memory problems."

Caller two: "Grey is becoming a problem, isn't he?"

Caller one: "He's a nervous hothead who overreacts to challenges and makes mountains out of molehills."

Caller two: "He can also be penny wise and pound foolish in his use of creative accounting techniques. This tendency can inadvertently jeopardize the big picture."

Caller one: "Botching the confrontation with the bank officer and her driver in the cockpit country was especially foolhardy. If I hadn't had some influence with the Constabulary, the results would have been disastrous."

Caller two: "And the irrational public display by his daughter at the falls was even worse."

Caller one: "Well, both of those young people paid dearly for their lack of judgment. I shall miss them. I attended their Christenings when they were babies. Are you suggesting that we distance ourselves from Grey? You do remember who he is married to, don't you?"

Caller two: "I am very much aware of the internal politics involved. Correct business decisions are not always easy to make. Sometimes one must be objective and take a long-range point of view."

Caller one: "Let me sleep on it. My informant will continue to keep me posted."

Caller two: "Resolving our problem doesn't have to become an explosive situation. Accidents can be made to happen."

Caller one: "Yes, I know."

```
    NOTICE
FURNITURE. AND
CABBNET UPPOLETRY
    MATRESS AND
TAUPAULINING   REPAIR
CALL
CLEVELAND BROOKS.
     AT. HOME
```

CHAPTER 39

"Letha," Betsy said through her open office door, "Please come here."

There was no answer.

I wonder if that girl is in the kitchen again, Betsy thought. "She'd have been much happier as a chef."

She got up and went to look for her secretary. Letha was nowhere to be found. As she went by Letha's desk, she noticed Letha's Rolodex was open to Dr. Damien Rosser's name.

I wonder if I missed a call from Dr. Rosser, she thought. *I have to ask Letha when she gets back.*

A few minutes later Letha returned with a cup of tea and a brownish pastry in a small crunchy tart shell with a pinched crust.

"What's that?" Betsy asked. "Smells divine."

A Jamaican Conspiracy

"A gizzada. We call them a pinch-me-round," Letha replied. "I made them myself."

"What's in it?"

"A sweet spiced coconut filling made with brown sugar. Want one?"

"No thanks," Betsy said. "Did Dr. Rosser call for me?"

"No, ma'am. Why do you ask?"

"Well, I noticed your Rolodex is open to his name."

Letha looked embarrassed and nervously flipped the Rolodex to another name.

"Did you need to call him for something?"

Letha once again looked embarrassed.

"No, ma'am. I barely know the man. Barely recognize him when he came in here."

"Just making sure I didn't need to call him," Betsy said. "You know how I am about seeing that my phone messages are returned in a timely manner."

"You really should try a gizzada," Letha said, trying to change the subject. "I think you would like it. I'll write down my recipe."

The pinch-me-round did smell delicious, so Betsy tried one. Very good. She decided to make copies of Letha's recipe to give to Leva and Rose. When she went to the copier, she noticed some wadded-up paper in the wastebasket leading her to think that there had been either a paper misfeed or that the ink cartridge needed changing. She picked up a piece of the wadded up paper to try to determine the nature of the machine's problem. To her surprise it was a page from her latest memo to Ken Scott. She took the wadded-up piece of paper back to her office.

That's strange, Betsy thought. *This update's hot off the press. I just drafted this yesterday ... and I haven't asked Letha to copy it ... and I certainly haven't shared with anyone else. My office has been invaded again.*

It was upsetting to think that her confidential files and memos were apparently not as private as she thought. *Someone is reading my memos before Scott does.* Since she could not identify the culprit, she decided not to say anything for the time being. For the rest of the day she wondered just who the KSAC mole was and why they were nosing into affairs that didn't concern them ... or maybe they *did* concern them. Was it the bumbling BB? He was obnoxious, but he seemed harmless. Surely President Smith did not use crafty Gestapo type management to monitor the bank's employees ... but after all he was related to the recently assassinated Assistant Contractor General Jerry Smith, and God knows who else. Was it possible that her loyal and affable secretary was loyal to someone other than her? But Letha was only a clerk. What nefarious motive could she possibly have?

Shortly before noon Letha received a call. She immediately lowered her voice and lapsed into patois. Betsy could only hear Letha's end of the conversation.

"Ya, sa **(Yes, sir)**."

"Ya, sa **(Yes, sir)**. Everyting cook and curry **(All is well)**."

"Mi do as yu ax **(I have done as you asked)**."

"Nuh, sa **(No, sir)**."

As Letha talked, she anxiously scrawled on her note pad.

"Mi no who mi fren' an brethren be **(I haven't forgotten who my friends and brethren are, sir)**."

"Mi alas tel di trut, sa **(I always tell the truth, sir)**. Mi no bag-o-wire **(I'm no betrayer)**."

"Shaw Park. Ya, sa."

"Mi lunch at noon **(My lunch is at noon)**. Mi a-go lef soon **(I will be leaving soon)**."

Betsy walked out of her office. Letha inadvertently jumped and tore up the paper she had been scribbling on.

"Mrs. Black, would you mind if I left the bank at lunch?"

"Of course not," Betsy said. "It's your lunch period. Spend it as you wish. There's nothing wrong, is there?"

"No ma'am," Letha said. "That was just my husband. He needs me to pick up some things."

Letha looked at her watch and grabbed a manila folder with some of her papers as well as the outgoing mail.

"I better get this to the mailroom before the postman arrives," she said.

Betsy also grabbed a handful of folders she had been meaning to refile. As they both hurriedly walked down the hall, they heard a familiar blustering voice and a door slamming. BB was backing out of an office with an armful of posters and flyers, mouth running ninety-to-nothing, as usual oblivious to anyone's presence but his own.

"Here's your poster and the concert schedule hot off the press for the Ocho Rios Jazz Festival," they heard BB telling another employee. "They gave them out at our last ORJF committee meeting. The bank is a sponsor so we need to talk it up with customers. Big Show! The Fab 5 will be there and the American blues star, Gatemouth Brown. Backing up, BB stepped on Letha's foot, then stepped on his own untied shoe string and finally got tangled in his own feet. As she tried to avoid BB, Letha bumped Betsy. All three crashed against the wall. An avalanche of papers and mail scattered for at least five feet.

"Mi neva get dis straighten out afor lunch. Mi late areddy **(I'll never get this straightened out before lunch, and I'm already late)**," an agitated Letha said desperately, inadvertently lapsing into patois. "BB, wa dun yu look wha yu go **(why can't you look where you're going?)**?"

"Mi? Yu shoud look wha yu go too. Mi not da invisible mon **(You can watch where you're going too. I'm not the invisible man.)**," BB retorted.

"Just pick up the papers," Betsy said disgustedly. "I'm just glad no one was hurt."

Letha hurriedly scooped up her paperwork and mail and left in a huff. BB stood up and grinned; as usual unfazed by the accident he'd caused. Betsy took her files back to her office to sort them and then put them back in the correct folder and sequence. As she sorted them at her desk, she came across a page concerning KSAC as well as some of BB's flyers.

Funny, she thought. *I didn't have KSAC's file out, and I haven't asked Letha to get it out for me. How the hell did that get in this mess?*

While Letha was out of the bank, Betsy stewed and ate a sandwich at her desk. When she finished, she walked past Letha's desk. She noticed the top blank page of Letha's scratch pad had indentions from Letha's nervous doodling with her ballpoint pen. Betsy ripped off the top page and took it into her office. With a number two pencil, she carefully shaded the blank paper to highlight the indentions. The doodled name "Damien" emerged under a smiley face.

She might not know Dr. Rosser well, Betsy thought, *but apparently when he says 'hi', she says 'how high'. I wonder why she lied to me about it.*

Betsy decided to say nothing but simply be more careful than ever with her confidential papers. She still wasn't sure what was going on, but whatever it was, she sure as hell didn't like it. The relaxed civility of some of her associates at the bank belied something more malevolent beneath the surface, and she was determined to get to the bottom of it.

Betsy's musings were broken by the phone ringing. It was Leva with a list of items she and Henry needed to pick up at L & M Grocery in Runaway Bay so Leva could make a proper feast for Will's birthday party the next evening. Leva promised a lavish feast of both jerk chicken and jerk pork, an assortment of vegetable and fruit dishes, and, of course, a coconut toto cake.

> **WELCOME TO THE BOGLE'S HILLFOOT BOMBULOUNGE**

CHAPTER 40

"Happy birthday, darling," Betsy told her husband at breakfast.

"Thank you, sweetheart. Yes, I'm sure this will prove to be an unforgettable birthday," Will said. "My first birthday celebrated in Jamaica."

"And many more," Betsy sang slightly off key. "Leva has promised she will make it a memorable birthday true to Jamaican practices," Betsy said, "complete with a traditional coconut toto cake."

Leva came back to the porch smiling, humming a familiar gospel tune. "Happy birthday, Mr. Will. Guess who I have on the phone? It's a call from the United States."

"Lexie!" both Will and Betsy said at once. They both rushed to the phone to talk to their daughter.

"What a perfect start to another flawless day in paradise," Will said afterwards. "Just look at that morning sky, and just look at that hummingbird. Mother Nature seems to be even more cheerful and brighter than usual. What could possibly go wrong on a day like today?"

He pulled up his electronic edition of the *Key West Citizen* as he drank his coffee and ate a pinch-me-round Leva had made using Letha's recipe.

"These are truly great," Will complimented her. "Good recipe."

"Every ho ha dem stick a bush," Leva said.

"Meaning?"

"To each his own. But I still think my mother's pinch-me-rounds are far superior," she said as she served a platter. "I'll treat you to some of them some other morning."

Will laughed as he read the paper. "Listen to this."

It's enough to make an honest taxpayer's blood boil. A report by the Treasury Inspector General for Tax Administration reports that recently a single home on Duck Key filed 741 tax returns last year, netting more than $1 million in refunds.

How is this possible?

The Internal Revenue Service didn't think anything was amiss when it received hundreds of tax filings from the same address?

Clearly the IRS lacks the necessary internal controls to prevent this kind of tax fraud.

Will laughed and said, "Well, I'm glad both furtive creativity and ingenuity are still intact in the Keys."

They heard the van's horn and knew Henry had arrived. As Will kissed his wife goodbye, she said, "We'll make this the ultimate birthday celebration. See you tonight, dear."

"I don't see what could possibly derail this day with the karma I feel," Will said. "Even the pre-opening comment is saying the market is going to be good today."

"Ooooo," Leva squealed playfully just before Betsy left. "Hif yu neva had **(If you've never had)** a Jamaican birtday, yu neva lived. Mi canna wait. Ooooo! Yu see."

Henry smiled knowingly at her. Will wondered just what surprises were in store.

Henry and Betsy chatted cheerfully as Henry drove her to Ocho Rios.

"As you know, dear lady," Henry said, "since we Jamaicans are some of the most traditional, religious, and, I might add, superstitious people on this planet, it is only fitting that birthdays be treated as red-letter days and should be celebrated with extraordinary gusto and, of course, lots of food and plenty of rum."

"Leva said she was making a coconut toto cake," Betsy said. "What's in it?"

"Oh, I would have to get the exact recipe from Rose," Henry said, "but suffice it to say it is a vanilla and coconut cake with nutmeg and cinnamon ... and so delicious. In Jamaica we *always* make you a cake for your birthday."

The day went well at the bank. Betsy was starting to agree with Will. Nothing could possibly spoil his splendid birthday. BB didn't even get on her nerves. She mentioned to Letha her excitement at the prospect of the upcoming celebration scheduled for that night at Sundance.

When they returned to Sundance that evening, the gate was open and decorated with helium balloons. More balloons were tied to the porch railing. Mikey Mo had set up a small sound system, and E.J. was in his finest baby-blue sequined Elvis jumpsuit. After the market close, Will had changed into a bathing suit and a tie-dye T-shirt embroidered with a dread-locked Rasta happy-face with the caption "No problem, mon." Rose had arrived early to help Leva with the preparations. E.J. had set up a bar by the pool. Betsy could smell the aroma of jerk slowly cooking on the grill. She and Henry drove in, and E.J. immediately closed and latched the gate behind them.

"You two better hurry and change," Will said as he kissed his wife on the cheek, "or this gala is going to start without you." She and Henry hurried to change clothes and join the festivities.

Mikey Mo had cranked up Ajala's *Soca Reggae Party* on the sound system by the time they came back out. Rose had made tostones al mojo, saltfish fritters, and Jamaican cocktail patties as hors d'oeuvres. Mikey Mo kept the musical party rhythms strongly pulsating with the Baja Men's *Get Ya Party On*. E.J. was dispensing heavy-handed rum drinks liberally while consuming a few himself. He had set up a folding table on the patio so the party victuals could be enjoyed buffet style. Leva brought the coconut toto cake out of the kitchen and placed it as a centerpiece in the middle of the table. Will took Betsy over to admire it.

As they stood there, mesmerized by the tempting cake, the Jamaicans spontaneously doused Will with glasses of rum and water. Before he could recover, they magically produced bags of flour and began to playfully throw clouds of it at him.

"Whaaaa the hell!" Will gasped.

Henry turned to Betsy and said, "I told you this morning we'd make him a cake. I guess I should have phrased it 'make him into a cake'. It is Jamaican tradition."

Everyone began to laugh. Will stood there puzzled.

"It is customary in Jamaica," Rose explained, "to cover the birthday celebrant with flour. The liquid isn't always part of the tradition but it sure helps make the flour stick a little better."

Mikey Mo abruptly stopped the sound system in the middle of the song he was playing. A pregnant pause followed.

In unison the Jamaicans began to sing their traditional birthday song. It was set to the calypso tune of *Matilda:*

> *Hapy birtday*
> *Hapy birtday*
> *Hapy birtday to yu dear Will*
> *Happy birtday*

It was not the happy-birthday song Betsy was familiar with so she just stood there listening during the first verse, but when it was repeated, she fell right into the spirit of the occasion and joined in. Everyone then cheered and kissed Will on his floury cheeks.

Betsy kissed her husband and as she tousled flour from his hair said, "Happy birtday, white boy."

"Mi not a white bwoy," Will said. "Mi a flour chile."

The group laughed. Mikey Mo started to play Toots' *Having A Party* as he toasted Will over the rhythm. Leva began to bring out food. E.J. made another round of rum drinks. Will turned on the water hose and started to wash the flour off of.

With no warning, the front gate banged against the wall with a sharp clang. The power blinked but didn't go out. Two ominous strangers stood there with a battering ram. Everyone scattered except Leva, who was trying not to drop a bowl of hot callaloo. The dogs began to bark and run towards the disturbance. The bent gate hung catawampus on it hinges.

Two BMW 1200GS motorcycles roared through the destroyed gate, stopping long enough for the two men with the battering ram to jump onto the passenger seats of the bikes. They rumbled into the yard. All of the men were wearing police uniforms. Though the uniforms looked official, the men seemed young and tough and reminded Will more of teenage gang members. The driver on the lead cycle stopped and took aim at Betsy with a pistol. A growling Lucy launched herself up the racing Gina's back, over Gina's head, into the arms of the shooter. Lucy's reckless charge completely caught the driver off guard, and he lost his balance and slid to the ground. Will hit the rider behind him with a burst from his water hose. Rose grabbed the pool net pole and jammed it into the spokes on the front wheel of the second bike. The driver flipped over the handlebars and his bike skidded sideways into the pool, almost taking the secondary rider with it. The rider left a bloody streak on the patio as the rough surface ground through his pants and into the flesh of his leg. E.J. grabbed the barbeque grill by the handle and flung its contents towards the rider on bike number one. The man cursed loudly when the hot charcoal and jerk hit him. The cape on E.J.'s sequined Elvis jumpsuit caught on fire, and he began to dance and flap wildly like a bat chasing a mosquito. Will doused E.J. with the hose before the fire could burn him. As the driver of the first motorcycle recovered from his surprise at Lucy's attack, Leva heaved the entire bowl of hot callaloo into his face. He yelped and pulled a knife.

"Bitch boom dogg **(whore)**," he screamed.

"Fyah fi yu **(burn in hell)**," the unintimidated Leva screamed back.

Suddenly from over the wall, a second group of commandos streamed into the yard. The partiers were sandwiched in between the two vicious groups. Betsy knew that she and her friends surely were now toast. Instead of going after the birthday revelers, the second group viciously began to attack the cyclists instead. The first driver went first to his knees under a barrage of blows from a heavy chain and then he fell to the ground. He bled profusely and did not stir again. His passenger was slammed when Mikey Mo heaved his equipment dolly into him, then picked it up again, and banged it with all his strength down into the man's ribcage in a second crushing blow. Betsy could see the man's bent police badge sticking out of his chest, where it had been driven by the force of the blow. Mikey Mo then began to stomp on the would-be killer, leaving his leg limp and mangled. A third commando grabbed the man scalded by the callaloo and snapped his neck. Betsy heard it crack and the man collapsed limply with his head at a grotesque angle, his dead eyes staring vacantly. The final combatant took off, bleeding profusely, sprinting for the gate, with the last of the rescue commandos in heated pursuit.

Before the Blacks and their guests could grasp the enormity of the brief but violent attack, the three remaining vigilante commandos picked up the dead bodies and threw them over the wall before picking up any weapon they saw on the ground. Then without a word, they climbed the fence, jumped, and vanished. Will and Betsy looked around speechlessly at the destruction. Two wrecked BMW 1200GS's were all that remained.

Mikey Mo dialed Colonel Winter on his cell phone. Will mistakenly assumed he was calling the police.

"Is everyone OK?" Will finally croaked to his guests.

"Only mi washing machine know for sure," E.J. said.

Will got a shaky head nod from the rest. The only person who spoke was Henry. "Jesus! Jesus, what just happened?"

Will unsteadily shook his head. "I wish I could tell you."

Will took a keep breath, smiled, and said sheepishly, "Is mayhem also a part of the Jamaican birthday tradition?"

As if on cue, Mikey Mo began to play Jimmy Cliff's *The Harder They Fall*.

This seemed to snap the group out of its stupor.

A Jamaican Conspiracy

Everyone looked at each other and waited for the police to arrive. From the house, they heard the phone ringing. Leva ran up to answer it.

"Henry, this call is for you."

They all went to the house. Will and Betsy could hear him saying, "Hello. Colonel Winter. Yes, sir, everything is all right."

Betsy signaled Henry that she wished to speak to the Colonel.

"Mrs. Black would like to speak to you. Yes, I'll put Mrs. Black on the line. Thank you for your concern."

"Colonel Winter. You're the last person I expected to hear from right now. Do you know who these hoodlums are, and how in the world did you find out about this incident so quickly?" Betsy asked.

Betsy talked to the Colonel briefly and then hung up. She looked shell-shocked.

"Colonel Winter admitted to me that he has been concerned about our welfare for some time and has been having us monitored. Those vigilante commandos who saved our bacon were Maroons he had assigned to make sure we come to no harm during Will's birthday party.

"He said not to call the Constabulary because he's not sure if our home invaders are either impersonating them or if they are really affiliated. He's not sure that the local authorities can be trusted, since some could be in the employ of our enemies."

"Does he think these invaders track back to John David Grey?" Will asked.

"He wouldn't speculate. It might even be Dudus Coke. He would have the money and influence to buy bad cops ... and it certainly matches the kind of vicious tactics the Shower Posse has used in the past."

"I hate to think how far up a creek we'd be without the Maroon sentries," Will said.

"We wouldn't be up a creek. We'd be dead," Betsy said. "The Colonel said his people will dispose of the motorcycles tomorrow. He also said he was aware of the problem we've been having hiring contractors because of the false rumor that Sundance has duppy problems, so his people will replace the gate. He said we should not to worry tonight about security. His men will be on duty. He doesn't think there will be more trouble tonight. He is recommending that his man continue to shadow Henry's van for the foreseeable future."

"There's no doubt who the white knight is; the driver of the surreptitious white Toyota Chaser," Henry said.

After a pause Betsy added, "And I almost forgot, Will, Colonel Winter said for me to wish you a happy birthday."

"I told you this morning nothing could truly go wrong today," Will said, "this came pretty damned close. This has been one helluva Jamaican birthday. Future celebrations will be dull by comparison."

"I won't complain. I think you need to talk to E.J.," Betsy said. "He's sitting over there moping, looking longingly at his ruined Elvis jumpsuit."

"Let's see what we can do for him," Will said.

"Is anyone hungry? If so, I'll see what I can salvage of your birthday dinner?" Leva asked.

"We have a saying in Jamaica," Henry said. "No cup no broke, no coffee no dash away."

"Meaning?" Will asked.

"Even if disaster strikes your home, it's always possible all may not be lost," Henry said. "Let's eat."

> nOITICE
> TRUSPISIS
> WILL BE
> PROSECUT
> ED
> BY ORDER.

CHAPTER 41

Caller one: "I just had a very uncomfortable conversation with our partner from Tivoli Gardens. It seems he lost three good foot soldiers in an unauthorized mercenary operation in Discovery Bay last evening. He was forced to harshly interrogate the remaining participant to identify who ordered this fiasco. He does not like his underlings to show brash initiative on policy matters. It demonstrates a lack of respect for his authority."

Caller two: "I would agree. Tell me more. Keep in mind we are not on a secure line."

Caller one described the raid on Sundance in general terms.

Caller two: "Very poor judgment, and poorly executed as well. Obviously, as I suspected, our associate is emotionally unstable; personal revenge has been placed above the good of the corporation. Do we know the identity of the third party meddlers at the villa?"

Caller one: "No, but I have my suspicions."

Caller two: "Our old adversary from the cockpit country."

Caller one: "Highly likely."

Caller two: "I hate to think that he's involved. Are we going be able to keep a lid on the boondoggle?"

Caller one: I don't know. Surprising enough, my source at the Ocho Rios OCF reports they are officially unaware of the incident, since the villa residents chose not to report it."

Caller two: "That's odd. Apparently they want to keep the lid on the affair as much as we do. I wonder why? What happened to the casualties?"

Caller one: "I don't know."

Caller two: "And we probably never will ... not that it matters now. This is a large island with some very remote locations. Jamaica holds secrets well."

"Caller one: Yes, that fact has served our purposes well from time to time. I had an associate masquerading as a lobster fisherman call on the villa this morning. The grounds have already been put back in order and gate repair is under way. Except for an armed lookout he spotted, a passerby would never know anything unusual was amiss."

Caller two: "Not surprising. Our rural adversary has the resources to do the cleanup quickly and efficiently. I hate to say I told you so, but I did mention to you in a recent conversation that I thought our associate was beginning to exhibit psychotic behavior and could become a loose cannon. You said were going to speak to him."

Caller one: "And I did, but that was before his daughter's tragic accident."

Caller two: "Tragic accident, my ass. She was out of her mind over her twin brother's death, and she did something very stupid. Do you think our associate put her up to it?"

Caller one: "I don't know, but I do think that even if he was not involved, our associate will surely be egged on by his wife to now become involved."

Caller two: "Once again, not surprising. Mother lions are very protective of their cubs."

Caller one: "As well as violently vindictive when something happens to one."

Caller two: "And now something has happened to two of hers in a very short timeframe. Maybe it *is* time we contacted Cudjoe."

Caller one: "As sad as it may seem, I agree. It's a shame – a waste of a valuable resource really. Our associate has served us well in the past. Tell Cudjoe he will receive his customary pay at the job's completion."

Caller two: "Don't harbor regrets, my friend. Remember – 'Sorry for a maga dog, dog turn round bit yu'."

Caller one: Reluctantly, you're right. Will this course of action offend our associate in Tivoli Gardens?"

Caller two: "I will give him a courtesy call before taking action. I don't want him to think we are overstepping our bounds."

Caller one: "I agree. We don't need any additional complications. He can often be sensitive and is not a person we wish to upset. It would also be prudent to inform our associate at Swingles as well and explain the reason for our action. I'd rather he not first read it in the news."

A Jamaican Conspiracy

Caller two: "Good. We each have a mission. I will get a report?"

Caller one: "No. I will not risk reporting unless the matter does not reach a satisfactory conclusion. You will know. Accidents involving prominent citizens are extremely newsworthy and hard to hide."

Caller Two: "I will certainly plan to attend the funeral services. I assume you will as well."

Caller One: "Of course. Proper etiquette demands that we console the widow in her time of grief. Send my best to your wife."

Caller Two: "And my best to yours."

~ ~ ~

Local Contractor Dies In Industrial Accident

A local contractor died in a mishap Monday morning on a jobsite associated with the Highway 2000 project, according to a press release from Ocho Rios JCF spokeswoman, Sybil Allen.

Workers on the scene told Jamaica Constabulary Force investigators that John David Grey of St. Ann Parrish was inspecting a shaft that had recently been drilled for highway support columns when he accidentally fell headfirst into the four-metre-deep water-filled hole.

The JCF inspectors have ruled that the death was an industrial accident.

This incident is the latest in a series of accidents involving the John Grey family. His son, Zany, was recently the subject of an unsuccessful missing persons' manhunt near Dornock River Head. His daughter, Zoey, recently died in a tragic accident on Dunn's River Falls. Mr. Grey is survived by his wife of 25 years, Doreen.

```
LIGHTHOUSE
RESTAURANT
I WILL LIFE UP MINE EYES UNTO THE HILL
FROM WHENCE COMETH HELP, MY HELP
COMETH FROM THE LORD, WITCH
MADE HEAVEN AND EARTH
```

CHAPTER 42

"Have you heard from Letha this morning?" Betsy asked the bank receptionist. "Is she running late again?"

"No, ma'am, she's not running late," the receptionist said. "She won't be in all day. She's taking a personal day."

"Is there anything wrong?" Betsy asked. "She's been either late or left early every day this week."

"Ma'am, she just had some family business to take care of. This is 'nine-night'. She be at the dead-yard today."

"Nine-night at the dead-yard?" Betsy asked. "That's a new one ... Just when I thought I had heard every excuse ever invented."

"Nine-night is a grave affair," the receptionist said. "Maybe you should get Mr. Smith to explain. Here he come right now. I'm sorry. Ma'am, but the switchboard is busy."

"Good morning, Mr. Smith. I understand my secretary will not be in today because it is 'nine-night'," Betsy said politely. "I don't understand what she means."

"Ah, yes, Mrs. Black, I guess you wouldn't. A 'nine-night' is the night before a funeral service – a very serious night to Jamaicans. It happens when a relative or close friend dies. I believe to you Americans, it is somewhat like a wake."

"I am so sorry. She said nothing to me about anyone close to her passing," Betsy said. "Do you know who she lost?"

"I have no idea. She has never shared much about her family at work. The only funeral I am aware of is the Doreen Jane Rosser funeral. I intended to go, but unfortunately I have developed a conflict."

"Is the deceased related to Dr. Damien Rosser?"

"As a matter of fact, she was. His mother, in fact."

"I have dealt with him. Maybe I should go in your place and represent the bank."

"Excellent idea. I will email the particulars to you."

Betsy called Will after receiving the details.

"How'd you like to attend a Jamaican funeral with me tomorrow? A bank customer's mother."

"Sure. That should be an experience," Will responded. "I'll arrange my schedule so I can join you."

On the way home that afternoon, Betsy told Henry of her plans to attend Doreen Jane Rosser's funeral service the following day, showed him Smith's e-mail, and asked him about Jamaican funerary practices.

Henry told Betsy that wakes and funerals are very different in Jamaica than those in the United States or Great Britain. He explained that when a person dies in Jamaica, there is an extended wake that lasts nine days. Since the loved one is no longer suffering in life, this is not a time to mourn but a time to celebrate. At one time, wakes were calm and reserved, but today these gatherings or 'set-ups' are outright parties lasting for the nine-day period. Families will hire D.J.s to set up towers of speakers that are sometimes nearly as tall as the house.

The latest in reggae and dancehall music can be heard from great distances away from the dead-yard. Families will often go into debt to finance an extravagant celebration of the life of a well-liked or well-respected person.

"Sounds like the jazz funerals in New Orleans," Betsy commented.

Henry agreed and continued. He explained that instead of bringing a spiritual bouquet or a sympathy card, guests bring food, rum, and beer for the pending feasts. People will come early each night, stay late, and be dressed in everything from T-shirts and shorts to fine dress clothes. After a few words of condolence, the time is then spent chatting with other mourners, eating, drinking, dancing and, of course, playing dominoes.

"No wonder, Letha had to leave early every afternoon this week," Betsy commented. "She thrives on showing off her cooking for appreciative crowds. I wish she loved banking as much."

Henry explained that the eight nights are just a warm up for the 'nine-night', when all the stops are pulled out. On that night the family prepares the feast of all feasts with a fare typically featuring Jamaican favorites like curried goat, fried fish and bammy, and a generous assortment of other yummy items. There is typically enough food to feed a small army. Many of the people attending 'nine-night' will not be even be known by the family, but are simply people who have been drawn like a magnet by the loud music and mountains of free food.

The belief is that on the 'ninth-night' the spirit of the deceased passes through the party gathering food and saying goodbye before continuing to a resting place. Out of all the nine nights, this night is most revered as the climax of the celebration. Stories and fond memories about the deceased are shared. Prayers are offered.

A Jamaican Conspiracy

Hymns accompanied by drums are sung, and, of course, Dominos are played. A song leader who knows the hymns by heart will 'track' the words by calling out a line for the people to repeat. The food is set up under a tent, but no one is allowed to eat before midnight when the deceased's spirit will pass through the gathering after which the party continues in high gear until daylight.

"When I die, I want to die in Jamaica where death becomes a gastronomic gala that is the commencement of a life phase as joyous as any of life's other major moments," Betsy said.

Henry smiled and continued. Traditionally, on the ninth night of the deceased's death, his bed and mattress are turned up against the wall, to encourage his duppy to leave the house and enter the grave. Henry said that while a person's body is interred in the ground, his duppy will stay in the area for awhile, and sometimes will choose to remain permanently to haunt the living. Persistent duppies will continue to trouble the living until they desperately turn to Obeah men for assistance.

"If the funeral service is anything like the prelims, that should be one heck of a memorable experience," Betsy said.

"I'm sure you won't be disappointed."

"Mi naa jesta **(I'm not kidding)**. Will and mi gwaan hab a bashment time **(Will and I are going to have a great time)**. Did I say that right?"

"Letter perfect, dear lady," Henry said and smiled. "Wi gwaan mek yu a Jamaican areddy **(We will make you a Jamaican yet)**."

~ ~ ~

"Do you know exactly where we are going?" Betsy asked as they drove out of Sundance on the way to Doreen Jane Rosser's funeral service.

"Ah yes, I have been by it many times," Henry said.

"It is a small church. Small is not unusual, since Jamaica has more churches per capita than any country in the world. The church is very beautiful, but without air-conditioning, will probably be quite warm. Did I remember to tell you that embalming is not a common practice in Jamaica? You will see other customs peculiar to Jamaica as well. Do you wish to go to the graveside interment after the church service?"

"Why not?" Will said. "In for a penny, in for a pound." He then asked his wife, "Can you stay away from the bank that long?"

Betsy assured him that she had set aside adequate time to attend both the church and the grave site service, and then asked Henry if grave site services were reserved primarily for immediate family.

Henry assured Betsy that they were not, and all mourners would be welcome.

The church was exactly as Henry had described. There were numerous ceiling fans and wide-open windows that helped cool the late morning service. The people attending were wearing their finest clothes. Men wore suits with jackets and ties while the women dressed in long dresses and traditional fancy hats. Every Jamaican had a small cloth to wipe the perspiration off his brow. Before long, everyone was using a cloth as the number of people gathered quickly heated the church.

As they entered the church, the usher presented Will and Betsy with a program. The program was the most elaborate they had ever seen. It consisted of a glossy picture of the deceased on the front page with a detailed description of the service including all the words to the hymns chosen for the service. The back was a collage of pictures of the deceased and the people she had been close to in life. This program was extremely personal and definitely not something thrown together in the basement of the church.

In the front of the church by the altar was a small quartet consisting of a piano, two guitars, and drums. The service even started somewhat on time, a miracle that did not often occur in Jamaica.

At the beginning of the service the pastor quoted from Ecclesiastes.

"I know that there is nothing better for men than to be happy and do good while they live. That everyone may eat and drink and find satisfaction in all his toil – this is the gift of God."

Will and Betsy took note of those attending. There were some familiar faces. Besides Dr. Rosser and his family, they saw the Hamilton family – Neville Sr., Neville Jr. and Queisha. Sitting with the family was Betsy's secretary, Letha Wardlow. Letha was crying. She sat beside a meaty-looking man who looked familiar, but Betsy could not put a name to the face. Betsy gently elbowed Will and nodded in Letha's direction. She looked in the opposite direction and saw Hopeton Boothe. Merle Dunster was in attendance. In various pews, she saw other faces she thought she should recognize.

The sermon was heated with the pastor throwing out his share of fire and brimstone. A member of the band sang a plaintive touching ballad entitled *Come Home, Come Home, It's Supper Time*. A chorus of young girls sang a catchy resurrection chorus called *No Grace Gonna Hold This Body Down*. After their portion of the service was over, a special collection was taken on behalf of the family. The service was quite long. When Will checked his watch at the conclusion, he noted they had been there almost two hours.

After the lengthy service, the man sitting next to Letha walked her down the aisle to a waiting car and driver, his hand on her arm the entire way. He was dressed in an expensive suit. Betsy guessed it to be custom-made. Two tough looking, fit young men accompanied them – one in front of them and one behind. Betsy was sure they were bodyguards. *Why would my secretary require a bodyguard?* she asked herself.

Will and Betsy's big surprise came as they left the church. Within twenty feet of the door, a vendor was selling cold drinks and ice cream. He was doing a huge business.

From the church, the procession traveled about five miles to the graveside where the final service would be conducted.

"I never would have guessed that this is what has been keeping my secretary preoccupied for the last week. I wonder what her connection is to the Rossers. She told me she barely knew Dr. Rosser. Do you know who that man with Letha was?" Betsy asked after they got in the car.

"Sure do," Henry said. "That was one of the most dangerous men in Jamaica, Dudus Coke."

"*The* Dudus Coke?" Will asked.

"There's only one."

"And he was escorting *my* secretary? You've got to be kidding," Betsy exclaimed incredulously. "I also saw some other faces who I think I have seen in the press. This was *some* big-shot party."

"I told you I didn't think you'd be disappointed, but celebrities were not the reason for my comment," Henry said.

"I'd sure love to know who some of those people are," Betsy said.

"I bet if we had pictures, the Colonel could tell us," Will said. "If they go to the graveside service, I think I could discreetly take pictures with my cell phone. If you see someone you want me to photograph, just nod in their

A Jamaican Conspiracy

direction."

"That's sneaky, but I'm game," Betsy said. "After seeing my secretary in the company of *the* Dudus Coke and seeing celebs like Hopeton Boothe attending, I'm dying to know who some of the other notables are."

"Not an especially good choice of words," Will replied.

They arrived at a small family cemetery. The grave had already been dug. The casket was placed over the hole in a recessed position. Prayers were said and banana leaves were placed on top of the coffin. Hymns and choruses were sung continually. Children were mesmerized by the ritual. Flowers were placed lovingly on the mound. The pastor called for a last look. Each family member, in turn, approached the coffin to say goodbye. In a poignant moment, Dr. Rosser went up to the casket and straightened his mother's collar and touched her shoulder. Letha was the only person who broke down. After she fell to her knees, she was quietly led away by Dudus Coke who placed some money in the casket. Each child of the family was lifted and passed over the coffin while its name was recited. Occasionally, Betsy nodded and Will snapped a picture in the direction of her nod.

After the last person said goodbye to Doreen Jane, the coffin was lowered, a piece of plywood was put over the hole, and wet concrete was shoveled over the grave. The laborers didn't stop until the grave was completely covered.

Henry had warned them that it would not be polite to leave before the service was completed. After the last shovelful of concrete had been tossed, the crowd quietly withdrew and returned to the death yard for more food and drink. There were few tears. Everyone seemed to sense that this was indeed a joyful day. Another saint had gone marching into heaven. Dr. Rosser's mother had had a proper burial.

As they left, Will said to Henry, "Quite a service."

"I didn't think you would be disappointed."

"Why did they pass the children over the coffin?" he asked.

"For the dead not to return and haunt family members, everyone must say goodbye to the corpse, even the children."

"Did you get the pictures, dear?" Betsy asked.

"Sure did, and no one suspected a thing," Will responded. "After I download them, will you get them to the Colonel for identification? While you're at it, why don't you ask him about your secretary as well?"

"Great idea."

"E-mail your requests to me, and let me see what I can do," Henry responded.

~ ~ ~

Later that same day when Henry came back to pick up Betsy, he had some answers.

"That was quick," Betsy commented.

"I forwarded your e-mail to the Colonel, and asked for his assistance."

"He has e-mail?" Betsy asked.

"Maroons may be reclusive and remote, but they do have modern technology."

"I guess there aren't many places left on the planet that the Internet hasn't penetrated," Betsy said.

"That is so, dear lady. That is so," Henry said. "The Colonel complimented you for having a good eye. The people you singled out are wealthy and powerful people. The person in the first photo is Dr. Devon Bedward. Dr. Bedward is the Minister of State of the Ministry of Water and Housing. This makes him second to the Minister of Water and Housing. One of his primary responsibilities is choosing and awarding projects for Operation Pride. Are you familiar with Operation

Pride?"

"Yes, somewhat."

The other person is Anthony Hylton, the Minister of Industry, Investment and Commerce. Both he and Bedward are extremely high up in the People's National Party.

"He seemed somewhat surprised that Dudus Coke, a well known JLP supporter, would risk being seen attending in person. He said he has known for some time that Coke's money was silently backing certain politicians on both sides of the aisle, but until now he could only speculate exactly which ones were in Coke's pocket.

"As far as your secretary goes, The Colonel says Letha Wardlow is Dr. Damien Rosser's illegitimate granddaughter. He says Letha has always had an inferiority complex about being illegitimate and will stop at nothing to prove to her grandfather that she is worthy of being a member of his family. It is known in limited circles that Letha's husband's job at Swingles resulted from Dr. Rosser's friendship with Hopeton Boothe, probably at the suggestion of Coke," Henry said. "One last tidbit. Rosser, Hamilton Sr., Hylton, and Bedward all attended school together at one of St. Ann's oldest schools, Discovery Bay All-Age."

"So, that was quite a gathering. We had top government officials, a music and resort titan, and Jamaica's most notorious gangster. The most shocking news of all was what you found out about Letha. Dr. Rosser has quite a range of friends and relatives, doesn't he?"

"All of whom willing to take valuable time from their busy schedules to pay homage to Rosser's mother. Yes, dear lady, they always say what makes the world go round is not what you know but who you know," Henry said.

"Or who you're kin to," Will said.

"Take this for what it's worth," Henry said. "In Jamaica we say 'show me yu friends, I see who yu are'."

```
THIS IS A HIGHWAY
CENTRE: NO FIGHT. BAD WORDS
ADDLERS KEEP OUT (THINK IT NO WAY
FUNNY)
JUST ONE LOVE
WHO GOD BLESS
NO MAN CURSE
```

CHAPTER 43

Letha returned to the bank the day following the funeral. She put some leftover cake in the employee kitchen. Her mood was subdued as she played catch-up for the days she had been out. As Letha quietly paged through the mound of e-mails that awaited her, Betsy approached her desk.

"I was so sorry to hear that you had a death in the family," Betsy said. "My condolences."

"Yes, ma'am. Thank you."

"I saw you at Mrs. Rosser's funeral service. I was there representing the bank."

Letha looked up - surprised and almost embarrassed. She almost blurted out, "you did?" but caught herself.

"You never told me you were related to the Rossers," Betsy said.

Letha was speechless once again.

"I was under the mistaken impression that you barely knew the man," Betsy continued.

Letha began to fidget with some papers on her desk. She almost spoke, but the phone conveniently rang, and she jumped at the chance to answer it.

Betsy walked back into her office. When she returned Letha was not at her desk.

Ten minutes later Letha came hesitantly into Betsy's office.

"I apologize for not being more forthright," Letha said. "She was my granny. It didn't seem important."

"Maybe not important to you, but after all, the bank does have a major relationship with Dr. Rosser, and I always need to be apprised if there are possible conflicts of interest with employees and customers."

"I know ma'am," Letha said and looked at the floor. "But I've never done nothing wrong, ma'am. I have no conflicts of interest. I hope this won't cost me my job."

"No, Letha, this won't cost you your job, but it is going in your personnel file. I think you've been deceitful, and I'm not sure why. Please be more upfront in the future."

"Yes, ma'am. I will. There's some cake in the kitchen. Do you want me to get you a slice?"

"No thank you, Letha, just go back to work, and once again, my condolences for your grandmother."

"Thank you, ma'am."

Later that afternoon, Betsy repeated the conversation to Will.

"All in all, I didn't learn anything more than what Colonel Winter had already told us," she said.

"I think you were wise not to let her know the full extent of your knowledge. I sure wish you could have asked her about her relationship with Dudus Coke," Will said.

"So do I," Betsy said, "but I never found a way to quite fit the question into the conversation. She was being very guarded and close to the vest."

"One thing is for certain," Will said. "Letha Wardlow definitely requires more scrutiny going forward, especially since we know she owes Rosser a debt of gratitude for her husband's job at Swingles. He could call in that chit anytime."

"That's for sure, if he hasn't already. The fact is Rosser is affiliated with Dudus Coke, and we both know about Dudus Coke's business ethics. Remember what Henry said, 'Show mi yu friends, I see who yu are'," Betsy said.

"Would you be guilty of profiling, my dear? Will asked sarcastically.

"Just wary. Letha's definitely going to be on my radar screen. I just didn't want to alert her to that fact."

"As I said before, a wise managerial decision," Will said.

> CAUTION AIR BREAKS

CHAPTER 44

MINISTER WITH RESPONSIBILITY FOR HOUSING LAUDS OPERATION PRIDE

Hon. Dr. Devon Bedward, Minister of State of the Ministry of Water and Housing, said at a news conference Tuesday that the Programme for Resettlement and Integrated Development Enterprise (Operation Pride) is significantly addressing Jamaica's housing demand issues.

He said that the People's National Party is of the belief that "this progressive concept of ours" will continue to be used as a valuable vehicle to augment the delivery of affordable housing solutions to many needy beneficiaries, particularly low-income earners.

"At the People's National Party, we maintain our belief in this excellent Operation Pride concept, which has seen diverse communities of Jamaicans with differing needs for land and shelter benefit from both greenfield sites and occupied land (i.e. brownfield sites) with infills as well as

> relocation where necessary," he said. "Some of the objectives of the programme include the resolution of the shelter needs of a majority of low income Jamaicans through the establishment of new planned settlements and the upgrading of existing settlements; the improvement of environmental and public health conditions in settlements throughout the country; and the mobilisation of resources in the informal sector towards their own improvement, employment creation and national development."

Will finished reading the article, took a sip of his coffee, and asked Betsy and Henry, "Do you know what in the hell he just said?"

"In America, we call it political double-talk," Betsy said.

"In Jamaica, we say 'A wah di crap yuh chat bout?', Henry said.

"And what does that mean?" Betsy asked.

"It means, 'what the crap are you talking about?', Henry said. "We sometimes substitute other words for 'crap' when we're not in mixed company."

They all laughed.

"Politicos are universally predictable," Will said. "I know Bedward's comments are politically motivated since he's a high ranking PNP official and this is an election year."

"You can be sure about that," Betsy said.

"And you can also be sure that the JLP isn't going to let him get away with anything for long," Henry said.

Henry's prediction turned out to be accurate. Within 24 hours, the Jamaica Labour Party answered and several days of extreme accusations ensued. The JLP spokesperson, Edward Seaga, charged that the People's National Party had established a J$400 million slush fund out of kickbacks from Highway 2000 contractors for its party's candidates to use as campaign funds in the current elections. Seaga said this information had been in the JLP's possession for some time; but, he had not gone public because he had been led to believe that there was a pending audit of Highway 2000's records. He claimed to have submitted his concerns to the Director of Public Prosecutions (DPP) early the previous month but maintained that the DPP did not put much effort or urgency into the matter, saying that Seaga had to check with the police first. Seaga called for a trace to be placed on the missing bank funds to determine whether they had been misappropriated or transferred to personal or political accounts.

Dr. Bedward quickly denied the allegations. He called upon the JLP to turn over any evidence to the DPP to prove the allegations. If the evidence then warranted further attention, he announced he would recommend to the Prime Minister that he establish a Commission of Enquiry to examine the affairs of the Ministry of Water and Housing. Bedward was prepared to let the chips fall where they may.

Seaga retaliated that the Commission of Enquiry would be nothing more than a whitewash and a cover-up. Bedward responded that Jamaica had long become accustomed to Mr. Seaga's "alarmist pronouncements and claims" about corruption and political plots which, invariably, were never supported with credible evidence.

Seaga sent a last shot across the PNP's bow charging that the PNP had established a squad of 1,500 policemen who were being trained to sabotage the JLP's election campaign.

"Henry sure called that one right," Will said to Betsy.

A Jamaican Conspiracy

"Do you think there's any truth to any of these accusations?"

"Who knows," Betsy said, "but you can be sure that since the bank has a major business relationship with some of the parties involved, the bank will be drawn into the controversy."

At mid morning Betsy had a call from Ken Scott at WB.

"Morning, Betsy," Ken said. "I just got a call from the bank's legal department."

"And I bet I know what it was all about," Betsy said. "I've been reading the local press."

Ken told her that attorneys for the Jamaica Labour Party had contacted the bank's legal staff about a possible corruption scandal unfolding in the Jamaican Ministry of Water and Housing that could possibly lead to exposure for the bank as well as public relations troubles. Ken said he needed Betsy to update him on any information that might to pertinent to these matters, instructed her to red-flag the account and any related accounts she considered relevant immediately and told her that the transactions in these accounts would be monitored going forward until the bank was satisfied that the allegations were false. Betsy said she would get to work on his requests immediately.

As soon as Betsy hung up the phone with Scott, she asked Letha to have Bob Blackmon come to her office.

"I will when he gets here," Letha said. "I haven't seen him all morning. He said something about some breakfast meeting."

"But it's ten o'clock now."

"I know, ma'am," Letha said sheepishly. "But you know how BB is; he loves to talk and visit."

"How well I know," Betsy said almost under her breath.

Almost an hour later BB bounced into Betsy office after some brief banter with Letha.

"A merry morning, boss lady," he said, "on another beautiful Ochi day. The kind of day that invigorates and motivates a person to strive for greatness. Can't you feel it?"

"I'm feeling other things since this morning is almost over now," Betsy said, purposely looking at her watch. "Please, Bob, close the door and sit down."

BB nudged the door haphazardly and then stretched out on Betsy's office sofa with his fingers entwined behind his head. Letha moved closer to the slightly ajar door to try to listen.

"I need to talk to you about the Neville Hamilton relationship. You were the account opening officer on his campaign account, and I observed at the Columbus Plaza street party you associate with the family socially."

"Young Hamilton's campaign is going extremely well. He will make a fine councilor representing a fine party. Not surprising since he comes from a fine family."

"Well, if you have been reading the press, you will know that Mr. Seaga is accusing some *fine* candidates from this *fine* party of being a party to a possible appropriation impropriety scheme. The bank is concerned about both exposure and bad press. Do you think the Hamiltons are involved in any questionable activities?" Betsy said.

"Not in the least, ma'am," BB said. "These people are as honest and trustworthy as a tropical day is long. This is all political mud-slinging. Typical JLP election-year smokescreen tactics. They'd do anything to win."

"I hope my caution and paranoia are unnecessary, but I am obligated to remind you anyway that you are a representative of this bank and that your primary duty at all times is to protect the institution, even when there are client friendships involved."

"I know, ma'am. You can always count on me."

"We are red-flagging the Hamilton accounts until the bank is satisfied that no danger exists. We will be scrutinizing the accounts' activity more closely than normal. You are not to disclose this fact to anyone. Do you understand me? No exceptions. There will be no excuses. The price of noncompliance will be dismissal. Also you are to report any pertinent information to me or any information that you even suspect might be relevant. Have I made myself clear? This is not a matter to be taken lightly."

"Yes, ma'am. You can always depend on Big Bob Bogle Blackmon."

"I hope so," Betsy said. "You can go back to work now, or should I say, begin your work day."

"I'll be hard at work all day long," BB said, "from the moment I return from my luncheon meeting."

Betsy just sighed. As usual, BB was oblivious. As he opened the door, Betsy saw a shadow dart quickly across her anteroom moving away from her door. She listened to see if she heard a phone ring or another person's voice. The room was silent except for a chair squeaking as Letha plopped down quickly and then hurriedly pushed her chair up to her desk. No one else was in sight.

I wonder what the hurry to get back to her desk was, Betsy thought. *I didn't hear anything or anyone.*

She walked to her door. Letha was looking away from her, shuffling papers on her desk.

Was that a shamefaced look on her face? Definitely strange. Maybe even guilty?

As it turned out, Betsy didn't have to be concerned about Bob Blackmon's discretion in disclosing the bank's increased monitoring of the Hamilton accounts. Letha took care of that matter instead.

REFRESHMENT PALICE

CHAPTER 45

Betsy and Will sat on the porch at Sundance sipping Appleton rum and eating Jamaican Pickapeppa sauce and cream cheese on Triscuits. It was a recipe that Betsy had introduced to Leva.

"Remember when Ruth McDonnell served Pickapeppa and cream cheese to us for the first time at her house?" Will asked. "Little did we know then that a housewife from Maryland would give us a use for a Jamaican sauce that even Jamaicans didn't already know about."

Betsy agreed, and after eating another cracker, began to recount her day's activities to Will.

"So you think Letha was listening in at the door while you were talking to Blackmon?" Will asked.

"Sure as hell do," Betsy said, "and if that shadow that darted across my door was Letha, she was moving faster than I've ever seen her move. I'm positive it was Letha since she was alone in the anteroom.

"You've always said that if she were a train engine, the caboose would be leading. So now the question

A Jamaican Conspiracy

becomes, why is she being so nosy and paranoid about being seen?"

"Unless she's gathering information for someone else," Betsy said.

"Like possibly Dr. Rosser?"

"A logical candidate," Betsy said. "I wonder what his game is."

"I've got an idea," Will said. "Are you above being devious?"

"I landed you, didn't I," Betsy said and laughed.

"Well, damn. At the time I thought I was the one being devious," Will said as he snapped his fingers.

"That's what girls want guys to think," Betsy said. "Now just what underhanded scheme do you have in mind?"

"Why don't you dictate a fictitious memo to the file," Will said. "It won't actually go anywhere, but she won't know that. We'll put some fictitious info in it, and see if it comes back to you."

"No, I better not," Betsy said. "I might get in trouble for doing that."

"OK, I've got an even better idea," Will said, "but we're going to have to get some help to pull it off."

"I'm all ears, blond and devious one," Betsy said.

"I will call you at the bank on your private line at a prearranged time. You will leave your door open so that Letha can hear the conversation. I will pretend to be a well-meaning informant and will tell you that I have some incriminating information that the bank would be interested in seeing. I'll tell you that I'll leave it for you to pick up at an off-premises site at a certain time. We will arrive early and see who tries to beat us to the punch and pick up the envelope. This will not only confirm if Letha is your snake-in-the-grass, since she is the only other person who will be aware of this situation; but we may find out who her accomplice or employer is. I doubt if she'd risk going to pick it up herself, but whoever she relays my call to will be dying to know more so he can minimize the damage before it gets into your hands."

"Your plan has possibilities, Mr. Holmes," Betsy said, "but I see some problems. Keep in mind, darling. I'm not shooting you down. I'm just being a devil's advocate."

"Fire away, Dr. Watson."

"First of all, where would be a sensible place to pull this ruse?"

"I've given that issue some thought," Will said. "How about Shaw Park Gardens?"

"Oh?"

"Number one, it's close. Number two, there's plenty of places to hide the envelope where it wouldn't be accidentally taken by the wrong person. Three, it would be a good place to set up discreet surveillance," Will said. "Do you remember that old English cannon on display near that big open tent where they show plants and have talks?"

"Sure do."

"I would roll the envelope up and stick it in the barrel."

"OK, good thought. Next question," Betsy said "who will be the lookout. Either one of us would definitely be out-of-place and easily recognized. We can't use Henry either. Everyone at the bank knows him since he brings me to work every day. Who else can we trust?"

"Most people don't know Rose," Will said. "She is trustworthy, and she's intelligent. She would also blend in very well. She can wear a big hat and some sunglasses and be reading a book while she waits."

"That might work," Betsy said, "but what are you going to put in the envelope?"

"Who gives a rat's ass," Will said. "Just something slanderous and gossipy. Our goal is to merely find out who comes to pick up the envelope."

"I've got plenty of propaganda pieces that have come into the bank," Betsy said. Maybe something accusatory from Seaga. There's also reports from the International Foundation for Electoral Systems or the Citizens Action for Free and Fair Elections. I get stuff all the time from a Jimmy Tindigarukayo on empowering Jamaican squatters. He represents something called the International Institute for Environment and Development."

"See, there's plenty of possibilities," Will said. "Pick the most flagrant one, and we'll go with it."

"So if we identify Letha's contact," Betsy said, "what do we do next?"

"I'm still working on that," Will said. "I guess it partially depends on who the person turns out to be."

"What if her contact doesn't show up in person?"

"Then we're no worse off, but you've got the proof you need that Letha's the leak in your organization, and that's she's serving two masters. At that point we'll work on plan B."

"And if this person recognizes Rose?" Betsy asked.

"He'll only suspect why she's there, but then we'll still have his identity. Even if we've lost the element of surprise, we'll still know who we're dealing with. Rose's not going to be in any danger in a public place like Shaw Park Botanical Gardens."

"You know, I think Rose might get a kick out of being a spy," Betsy said.

"Shall we call her Jamie Bond?" Will said. "Or how about Octopussy?"

"I think I'd stick to Jamie," Betsy replied. "Now all we have to do is sell Henry and Jamie Bond on your inventive idea."

"Sometimes I even amaze myself on my ability to

334

think outside the box," Will said.

"Visionary? You wear bifocals," Betsy said and lightly pinched his cheek.

"Only to give me that studious, intelligent look. After all, I am a renowned authority of the financial markets."

"If your goal is to look studious and scholarly, maybe you need to change your glasses, Mr. Magoo."

"You're just jealous because I thought of this plan first," Will said.

"You've just got to get in the last word," Betsy said.

"Every dog has his day. We men don't get to get that privilege very often."

ROOMS FOR RENT NIGHT AND DAY

CHAPTER 46

The Blacks and the Davises sat on the patio at Sundance enjoying the soothing late-afternoon legendary Jamaican sunset. Leva had made them some fish fingers with a tangy dill tartar sauce. E.J. had set up the bar for them. A mellow Reggae radio station played softly in the background. They had invited the Davises to stay for a broiled lobster dinner.

"Have you ever been to Goldeneye, Ian Fleming's house?' Will asked.

"Ah, yes, many times," Henry said. "Tourists often want to see it. Did you know that it is now owned by Chris Blackwell of Island Records?"

"No, I didn't," Will said, "but I'm not surprised. His holdings sometimes appear to be endless."

"Seemingly so," Henry said. "He's owned it since the 1970's. He opened it to the public."

"Fleming certainly made spies seem like real-life supermen," Will said. "Speaking of 007 intrigue, would you two have any desire to participate in some espionage work?"

Henry and Rose looked at each other questioningly. Will then began to outline the suspicions about Letha's ethics and loyalties.

"Letha's presence at the Rosser funeral made me begin to doubt her candor about her past as well as her overall honesty," Betsy said. "I won't go into all the details because I don't want to impugn her character until I have absolute proof; I suspect she is leaking confidential bank information to an outside source. My goal is to find out just who that person is."

Will explained his scheme and the part they hoped Rose would agree to play. Rose said she was willing to participate, if Henry had no objections. Henry unhesitatingly nodded his assent.

"If our plan works, you will never have direct contact with the person who picks up the envelope," Will said. "Will you simply photograph him with your cell phone, and then tell us if you recognize him? If all else fails, give us his description, and we'll try to work with that."

"It may be a her," Rose said.

"That's possible," Will corrected himself.

By the time dinner was served, Rose was getting excited about her upcoming clandestine mission.

"I have a lawn chair I can take, and I know just the perfect straw hat I can wear," she said excitedly, "and, Henry, I'll wear those big sunglasses Aunt Mame gave me for Christmas. They'll be perfect."

"I told you Mrs. Jamie Bond here was the ideal person for this mission," Will said to Betsy as he played air guitar and hummed the James Bond theme.

They all laughed, and Will said, "Betsy will let you know when we have the caper planned."

Will and Betsy decided the opening volley would be a midmorning call from Will on the following Thursday, and then they would spring the trap at Shaw Park on Friday when it was fairly busy.

"I'll call you on your private line at 9:45 AM sharp,"

Will said. "Since it won't go through Letha before you pick up, she'll only hear your end of the conversation. Just make sure your door is open enough for her to hear what's going on, but not so far as to make her suspicious. If she's not at her desk or is occupied so that she can't listen when I call, just say 'you must have a wrong number'. I'll call back five minutes later. Are you up for an academy award winning performance?"

"Is a frog's ass water-tight?"

"I certainly hope so since, if it isn't, he sinks like a stone - just like we might if we screw this up," Will said.

"Don't worry. We won't."

~ ~ ~

Will dialed Betsy's private number at 9:45 sharp. She picked up immediately.

"Betsy Black."

Will began his role-play.

"Who is this?" Betsy inquired and paused for effect. "You say you have some important information for the bank concerning the Highway 2000 project?"

Betsy heard Letha suddenly leave her desk and begin to file papers in the filing cabinet on the wall just outside Betsy's office.

"I'm sorry. I don't believe I caught your name," Betsy said.

Betsy paused again, and glanced at her door. Letha was back at her desk.

"I'm not accustomed to discussing business with people who refuse to give their identity."

Letha got up from her desk once more and began to slowly rummage through another filing cabinet nearer to Betsy's doorway.

"You say you can't afford to be seen giving me this information or to have it traced back to you? You want to leave an envelope for me to pick up? Why should I believe a stranger?"

She glanced towards the door. Letha was listening intently.

"Sir, rudeness does not become you ... Because I'll be sorry if I don't? I see ... OK, let me write this down ... You say you'll leave it in the cannon barrel ... I see. Friday, ... at 11 AM ... I'll be there."

Betsy looked up and pretended to notice Letha for the first time. "Excuse me," she said into the phone and then got up and closed her door. Betsy then wrote "Shaw Park" on her notepad, and circled "cannon near tent pavilion." Then she wrote "11 – Friday." She purposely placed the scratchpad in the middle of her desk where it couldn't be missed.

Betsy hung up the phone and reopened her door. Letha was sitting at her desk, pretending to intently read a file.

Betsy said, "If anyone calls, please take a message, I'm going to the ladies room."

As soon as Betsy was out of sight, Letha picked up the file she was reading and took it into Betsy's office. She noticed Betsy's message, read it quickly, and then returned to her desk.

Betsy called Will from her cell phone. "Well, the curtain has come down on act one, and the seed's been planted. Maybe that seed will germinate and grow. Letha was definitely listening intently to my end of the conversation. I'm sure she fell for it lock, stock and barrel. Now we'll see what happens on Friday."

~ ~ ~

Rose Davis arrived at Shaw Park Botanical Gardens at 10 AM. Henry drove her there and waited for her in the parking lot. She was wearing red and aqua plaid clam diggers and a solid aqua top. She had on her gold snake sandals which buckled on the side of her ankles. She was also wearing a natural raffia straw hat with a wide brim and over-sized squared sunglasses with black plastic frames. Just a lady of leisure having a day in the sun. Henry went in ahead of her and slid the loosely rolled 8X10 brown envelope Will had prepared into the barrel of the cannon by the open-sided pavilion tent. Henry returned to the van, and Rose casually entered the park carrying a webbed aluminum lawn chair. In her over-sized purse, she had a copy of *A Calculated Conspiracy* to read while she waited. She also had her cell phone so she could snap pictures. Rose set up her lawn chair under a palm tree about 15 feet away from the cannon, began to read the book, and waited.

Shaw Park was moderately busy with a mixture of locals and tourists meandering around ogling the exotic tropical plants. A busload of pale elderly tourists with Michigan t-shirts arrived. For a few minutes, there was a throng of people until their guide led the group down the pathway. About thirty minutes after Rose arrived, a man approached the cannon and peered into the barrel. Rose recognized him immediately – Dr. Damien Rosser. She was afraid he might look her way and recognize her, but he seemed to be nervous, in a hurry, and he did not look around him. When Rosser turned to reach into the cannon's barrel to retrieve the envelope, Rose quickly snapped his picture. Rosser grabbed the envelope and beat a hasty exit towards the park entrance. Rose snapped his picture again with the envelope in his hand. Almost as quickly as he had materialized, Dr. Rosser was gone. He never noticed Rose, just as Rose never noticed a man who had driven to the park in a white Toyota Chaser and silently witnessed the entire scene.

Rose waited about fifteen minutes to make sure Dr. Rosser had time to leave the park. She put her book back in her purse, folded her chair, and quickly headed for the

A Jamaican Conspiracy

parking lot. When she got to the van, she was beaming. Henry said nothing as he loaded the chair in the back of the van and drove away.

"Mission accomplished," Rose said. "Everthin' wen fit 'n frock **(Everything went perfectly.)**"

"Did you recognize the person?" Henry asked.

"I sure did. Dr. Rosser," Rose said, "and I got his picture ... twice."

"Well, well, well," Henry said. "So he's Letha Wardlow's secret contact. As they say, all dem a me fambly **(blood is thicker than water)**. I'm not totally surprised."

"Mi uh aso **(Nor am I)**," Rose said as she broke into a big smile. "I can't wait to tell Will and Betsy."

~ ~ ~

"Dr. Damien Rosser," Betsy commented after Rose finished speaking. "I guess I shouldn't be surprised."

"That's the same thing Henry said," Rose replied. "So what are you going to do now?"

"I'm not sure, but at least we know who Letha's confederate is. You both have really been a great help," Will said. "Thank you. We really owe you one. Please, do us one more favor. Promise you won't mention this to anyone."

"No problem, mon," Henry said and smiled. "No one knows but us four."

After Henry and Rose had departed, Betsy asked Will, "So what do you think we should do now?"

"I was serious when I told Rose I really didn't know," Will said. "As I told you before, I don't have a plan B. I was waiting to find out just who we were dealing with before crossing that bridge. Let's sleep on it. Just be sure you don't let Letha know we're on to her treason."

~ ~ ~

When Betsy returned from NCB the following day,

Will said, "I've been thinking about our next course of action all day, and I think I have another brilliant plan. I went so far as to take the initial steps to put it in play today."

"I'm glad you've had a stroke of genius," Betsy said. "I've been wondering all day what we should do next … if anything."

"We've come too far to let this drop now that we are seeing a clear picture for the first time," Will said. "I got my idea from your mysterious 'friend', Buried Blade."

"Who so generously gives me unsolicited information and advice," Betsy said.

"Exactly. Look at this printout off of Google. I found a web site for a company called MIS Defense Products. They make a variety of mobile voice changing devices, which, I might add, they sell at a very reasonable cost."

"Look at this product from MIS. For $24.95 plus shipping and handling I can buy a battery operated keychain voice changer. Let me read you their Internet ad.

This is the smallest voice changer in the world. It measures less than two and a half inches tall and less than one and a half inches wide. Whether you are using your home phone, cell phone or a pay phone, no one will be able to recognize your voice. Simply place it over the phone's mouthpiece, adjust the setting, and speak normally. Extreme settings sound hilarious and are great for practical jokes. Mid-range settings make anyone's voice sound deep and masculine.

Betsy looked puzzled.

"Well, let me explain, my dear. Now that we know that Letha is your leak and that Dr. Rosser is her contact, I think we should find out who else is in their criminal network, and here's how we're going to do it."

Will explained his plan to call Dr. Rosser while disguising his voice. He would try to scare Rosser into overreacting and then see what happened next.

"I'll call him from a phone away from Sundance so his caller ID can't trace the call back to here," Will said.

"And just what do you plan to say to him?"

"I've been giving that some thought too," Will said. "My thoughts began with the principle that there is no honor among thieves. Remember the movie *Charade*."

"Of course, one of my all-time favorite movies," Betsy said. "Cary Grant. Audrey Hepburn. Walter Matthau. It may be the greatest movie than Alfred Hitchcock ever made."

"*Charade* was my inspiration. Everyone in it was always trying to screw over everyone else before those people could screw over them, all the while pretending to be someone they were not," Will said. "Well, my plan is to create some dissention in the ranks of the villains with some figments of my imagination, and then we will see what happens next. Here's how I propose to do it. I'll call Rosser pretending to be an idealistic National Union Worker's sympathizer or PNP member with knowledge that an insider plans to expose political corruption and conflicts of interest of unnamed public figures. I'll tell him I feel obligated to give him a heads-up so that he won't get blindsided by a scandal."

"And who do you propose this rat-fink to be?" Betsy asked.

"How should I know? And even if I don't, who cares. If Rosser asks, I'll tell him I'm afraid to disclose the traitor's name, and I'm also afraid for my own safety if my own identity is ever discovered. As I said, my goal is to create paranoia which will make Rosser and all his compatriots all suspect each other and see where the cards fall from there."

"And if nothing happens?" Betsy asked.

"We're no worse off than we are now, except we're out

less than $35 or so for the voice distortion equipment."

"Sounds like a pretty good risk and reward, even though it's an off-the-wall long shot."

"You got a better idea?"

"No, frankly, I don't," Betsy admitted.

"I was hoping you'd say that since I've already ordered the voice distortion device. I requested express shipping so it should be here in a few days."

"Let's keep this to ourselves," Betsy said. "Don't tell even Henry or Rose. I don't want to take any chances of a leak. There could be repercussions at work."

"I agree. Plus, these people might cut our throats for meddling in their business."

"An unpleasant side effect I'd rather not dwell on."

Little did either one of them know that a man in the white Toyota Chaser was listening to every word of their conversation through a sophisticated remote listening device that had been planted at Sundance.

```
YOUR TYRE RPEIRING
                PLUSING
    CENTRE  PATCHING
              VOLCANIZING
```

CHAPTER 47

Betsy's phone rang at her desk.

"Would you like to dance naked on the beach in the pale moonlight?" Will said in a bass voice, using his new voice distortion device.

"Excuse me, sir, I think you have the wrong number," Betsy said.

"I am not a sir. I'm the hoodoo man who do love your bod," Will said.

Betsy was momentarily taken aback, wondering what kind of crank caller was on the other end of the line. Then she realized it was her sweet but quirky husband.

"Who dat? You aren't a hoodoo man, you're just a hoo-owl," she retaliated. "You either straighten up, or I'll call a voodoo man who can take the hoodoo out of your mojo, Mr. Hoodoo Man."

She heard a snigger and knew she had been correct about the caller's identity. Uh huh – her own hubby. "I take it that your voice distortion equipment shipment has arrived."

"Yes, as a matter of fact, it did," Will said. "How do you like it?"

"Well, I thought I was about to get a hot date. If I hadn't known it was you, I wouldn't have known it was you," she said. "You sound like that actor with the bass voice who does the Allstate commercials."

"You're in good hands with Wilson Black," Will parroted.

"I better be. So now that your toy has arrived, when does your latest plan go into action?"

Will then tested various settings on his new device to try to find the one that was most natural. When they were both satisfied, he told Betsy they would discuss the project further and firm up his talking points that evening over a rum drink. He reminded Betsy to bring Rosser's direct phone number home with her that evening.

Will found where they could purchase a prepaid cell phone. They agreed that Betsy would make the purchase. The following day she took the short stroll down Newlin Street to Main Street, where she walked southwest the short distance to Bag Of Music in the Island Plaza Mall to purchase an inexpensive cell phone. Now they were ready to proceed.

~ ~ ~

Will dialed, and Rosser picked up on the second ring.

"Dr. Rosser, I represent the POP," Will said.

"Never heard of it," Rosser responded. "May I inquire just what it is?"

"Patriotism Over Politics," Will lied. POP only existed in his own mind.

"Still never heard of it."

"You will," Will continued. "We're a politrickster's worst nightmare. Please listen since I'm not going to repeat myself. This will be your only notification. We know about your illegal activities. We also know who your associates are. We have graphic pictures which we will release to the press unless you resign from office immediately. I repeat, this will be your only notification. For the good of Jamaica, we will happily disgrace you and your associates if you force our hand," Will continued to bluff. "Maybe we'll enlighten your banker as well. I don't think you would like Kingston's brickyard prison, and I'm sure the prisoners wouldn't like you."

"You can't talk to me this way," Rosser said.

"Mi mouth a mi market **(I'm free to say what I wish)**," Will said.

"Gwey **(fuck-off)**," Rosser said.

"We'll see who gweys," Will replied. "Have an irie day ... before we POP your bubble. POP goes the weasel, Dr. Weasel."

Rosser slammed the phone in Will's face.

Rosser sat at his desk and stewed for about ten minutes.

What the hell was Patriotism Over Politics? Jamaica was rampant with renegade political groups, but I have never heard of this one. They couldn't possibly know anything about my Highway 2000 activities, and I'm sure they don't have any pictures that could incriminate me. Either it's a prank or the naïve SOBs don't know who they're messing with.

He went back to work, but the phone call continued to gnaw at him.

But what if these jerk-wads really do have something? The disgrace would be horrid. It would ruin my family. I'd never recover.

He was dysfunctional, so he went to lunch but still couldn't get the call out of his mind.

If I've misjudged the danger and they really can incriminate me, I could go to prison. I'd lose everything. And if Hamilton or Coke were somehow implicated, jail wouldn't be the worst of my problems. I could actually end up a dead man.

Rosser returned to his office. He called several people without letting on why he was inquiring and asked them if they had ever heard of Patriotism Over Politics. No one had. Then a different thought hit.

My greedy associates may be trying to get me out of the picture so they have one less person to split profits with. If that's the case, I'm not going to let them get away with it. I've been told that the best defense is a good offense. I'll threaten to cut a deal and go public with what I know if I have to, and they'll be afraid to call my bluff. They've got as much or more to lose than I do. I'm not going to be anyone's sacrificial lamb. Whoever fucks with this bull is going to get the horn.

Rosser looked on Google for POP. *Nuthin'.* Each time a call came in during the afternoon, he casually asked the caller if he had ever heard of POP. The responses were 100% negative.

Who is this POP? What kind of dirt have they dug up? It can't possibly be anything.

Rosser went home and had a fitful night's sleep.

The following day Rosser got a plain 8x10 manila envelope in the mail. No return address. Postmark – St. Ann. *That's the same post office Hamilton uses.* He opened it. There was a picture of him taking the rolled up envelope out of the cannon at Shaw Park Gardens. There was a four-sentence note. "This picture is only the tip of the iceberg. Others are worse. The clock is ticking. Your days are numbered." The note was unsigned. Rosser saw red, and his gut tightened. *Dutty Bowcyat* **(dirty cocksucker)**! He picked up the phone and dialed Hamilton Sr. *If Neville is trying to pull something, I have to stop him – NOW.*

"Rosser, a good morning to you," a cheerful Hamilton answered.

"Do you have a problem with the way I'm handling company business?" Rosser asked.

"No. Have I led you to believe I do? If so, I apologize."

"Have you ever heard of Patriotism Over Politics?"

"Can't say that I have. Why do you ask?"

"I'd rather not say," Rosser said. "I will say this, however. If for some reason I'm ever designated like Grey to be a sacrificial lamb because I'm considered expendable or incompetent, I'll make sure I don't go down alone. Am I being clear? And make sure Bedward understands that as well."

"Calm down, and tell me what you're talking about," Neville Hamilton said.

"As if you don't already know," Rosser said but then told Hamilton about the POP call and about the picture he had gotten in the mail. "Just remember what I said, No one buggers mi batty hole **(butt-fucks me)** and gets away with it. Understand?" Rosser hung up.

Hamilton called Merle Dunster immediately.

"We may have a problem with Rosser. He's scared, and he's acting unstable."

Hamilton then repeated his conversation with Rosser. Dunster was unaware that his calls were being monitored by his partner Dudus Coke as well as an unaffiliated third party. Coke was not pleased by this latest turn of events and was equally puzzled as to just who or what POP was. Coke called Dr. Devon Bedward, the Minister of State of Water and Housing, gave him a heads-up in case Rosser threatened him and reminded him of the severe consequences of being the weak link in the organization. The anonymous eavesdropper also reported to his superior what he had heard.

Within a few days, Betsy received a phone call from Dr. Devon Bedward.

Betsy answered her phone, and Dr. Bedward identified himself. He politely reminded her that they had met previously.

"Of course, I remember you, Dr. Bedward," Betsy said.

A Jamaican Conspiracy

"I have been negligent in not getting to know you as well as I did your predecessor," Dr. Bedward began, "but unfortunately my duties keep me both very busy and in Kingston most of the time. I hope we can correct matters in the near future by having lunch together. I have heard so many compliments on you that I feel I need to get to know you better. I'm calling you today because I felt I needed to inform you that a fledgling renegade group entitled Patriots Over Politics is libeling the PNP. This group sometimes calls itself the POP. As you know, Jamaican politics can be very vicious, especially during an election year. I would not want unwarranted innuendos to reach the bank and taint the business relationship we have tried to foster with your fine institution."

"So the POP is libeling the PNP," Betsy said. "What type of libel are they spreading?"

"I would rather not say," Bedward replied. "I would not like to plant the seeds of any more distrust. I take it from your question that they have not sent any misleading information or pictures to the bank."

"None that I'm aware of," Betsy said. "Why don't you stop them?"

"We would like nothing better, but as of yet, we have not been able to identify the principals of this nefarious movement. If any misinformation reaches your ears, please feel free to call me, and I will gladly set the story straight. We value the relationship we have with our bank very highly."

"Of course, Dr. Bedward. Thank you for calling," Betsy said in an even, businesslike tone and hung up.

After she hung up, Betsy could barely contain herself. Will's plan had worked! They were starting to be able to trace the leak in the bank to people higher than Letha and Dr. Rosser. She desperately wanted to share her phone call with Will but knew it would be risky to do so on this phone. Things were working too well to risk screwing it up now just because she was impatient. There was no one she could confide in, not even Henry, since she and Will were the only people in Jamaica who were supposed to know about their plot to identify Letha's accomplices. Or so they thought.

Now the 64 thousand dollar question became, what should they do next?

```
K&J RASPHODY DRIVE

REFRESHEMENT      GO-GO
                  GIRL
                  NIGHTLY

SNACK             ALLNIGHT
                  SERVICE
       BEER
       GARDEN
```

CHAPTER 48

Betsy said nothing to Henry on the way home that afternoon. She felt guilty about their decision to keep POP confidential, but she knew Will was right. It was the prudent thing to do. For the time being this matter had to be kept just between the two of them. Poking their noses into the possibly unscrupulous affairs of powerful, ruthless people could lead to tragic repercussions.

When she arrived at Sundance, Betsy took Will into his office, closed the door, and excitedly told him about the phone call from Bedward.

"So you got a call from the honorable Devon Bedward?" Will asked. "One of the movers and shakers of the PNP nationwide is calling about POP, a name which popped into my head out of thin air."

"And also, don't forget, he's the minister in charge of the Highway 2000 project," Betsy said.

"Who is somehow in league with Dr. Rosser," Will said. "You gotta wonder about the big picture."

"This whole conspiracy may be more extensive than we thought it was."

"What I wouldn't give to have a better overview of their agenda."

"One thing I'm sure of is somehow it will all lead back to KSAC," Betsy said.

"Which means that Dudus Coke and Neville Hamilton are probably pulling the strings and the rest of the conspirators are the marionettes."

"I'm getting scared we may already be in water over our heads," Betsy said. "What next, O devious one?"

"We've been there before and didn't drown," Will said. "And to answer your question, damned if I know. I admitted to you upfront I was flying by the seat of my pants, and where we would take things would depend on just who the players turned out to be. Well, now we're starting to get a feel for the whom, it's a little intimidating. At least no one knows I'm Mr. POP, CEO to janitor ... and if we value our scalps, we better damned well keep it that way."

"Amen, my dear. And you were right about not trusting anyone, not even Henry and Rose. I don't want to get popped by the PNP over POP ... or have them get popped either. And don't forget, you better scrap the cell phone you've been using."

"Don't worry. I intend to," Will said. "Immediately. He sighed, "This is quickly turning into a double-rum day."

"Planning on celebrating or calming our nerves?"

"I'm not sure. Maybe some of both."

~ ~ ~

The chain of events triggered by Will's masquerade continued to get more bizarre. On Saturday morning, as he was reading *The Jamaican Gleaner* over breakfast, a headline jumped off the page at him. It was so startling he swallowed wrong and began to hack and clear his throat.

"Something wrong, dear?" Betsy asked as he sought to get his breath.

"This headline made my juice go down the wrong way," Will gasped. "Listen to this."

POP Links Deaths To Highway 2000

"How can the POP link anything to anything?" Betsy gasped. "It doesn't exist."

"I sure thought it was an inspiration resulting from my fertile imagination," Will said. "Hell, I just made up the acronym because it sounded catchy."

"Maybe you're in the wrong business," Betsy said.

He then read Betsy the letter-to-the-editor. It attributed both Jerry Smith's and John David Grey's deaths to their threat of being whistle-blowers about KSAC's probable underworld connections. The writer demanded a thorough reinvestigation of both deaths, letting the chips fall where they may, the political fallout be damned. The letter was signed by Patriotism Over Politicians.

"This ain't my writing," Will said.

"Well, you know I sure as hell didn't write it either," Betsy said. "I certainly would have cleared matters with you first."

"Same here."

So who wrote it?" they both said simultaneously.

"While I was still debating my next course of action..." Will said.

"Someone has booted the ball up to the next step for us," Betsy said.

"Who? And why?" Will said. "What's their motivation? Surely it's not your helpful buddy, Buried

Blade. He wouldn't know to use that acronym?"

"There's a leak in this boat somewhere," Betsy said. "And this time it's not Leaking Letha. I haven't uttered one word at the bank or around Ochi."

"And I haven't said one word around the staff ... or the Davises."

"I guess you're not the only geek who knows how to operate high-tech equipment. Somebody is eavesdropping somewhere. I feel violated," Betsy said. "Has the hunter become the hunted? I'm starting to get paranoid as hell."

"Rosser's phone must be the one which is bugged," Will exclaimed. "Mama Mia!"

"Is that a new patois phrase I've never heard?"

"No, that's colloquial Italian for we-may-be-in-deep-shit," Will said.

The next day a follow-up letter from the POP appeared in *The Gleaner*. This one said Highway 2000 was only the latest Jamaican government program where graft was wide spread. It insinuated that Dr. Devon Bedward was only the most recent of a long list of lax bureaucrats guilty of shoddy controls and aggressive sloppy accounting. The author recommended conducting an accountability investigation of not only Highway 2000 but Operation Pride as well. This letter was again signed Patriots Over Politics.

"This is getting freaky. Do you think these letters are originating with Seaga and the Jamaica Labour Party?" Will asked.

"Edward Seaga has never been shy about taking credit for his activities in the past and hasn't felt the need to hide behind shell organizations. Besides that, how could the JLP know about something you simply made up out of thin air unless they're tapping Rosser's phones?" Betsy asked.

Neither Will nor Betsy had an answer.

Over the ensuing days, the POP accusations started a nationwide avalanche of sympathy letters from other reformists. Finally *The Gleaner* reluctantly began to run editorials on the topic, and never once did anyone ask just what Patriots Over Politics was and who was behind it.

~ ~ ~

Will and Betsy were not the only ones disturbed by the public issues the letters had raised. When Damien Rosser saw the letters in the paper, he went ballistic. He began to plot CYA techniques to employ if protecting himself became necessary. He pictured almost everyone and anyone in KSAC as the likely source. His paranoia created various agendas. Devon Bedward was equally upset. *We've got to identify the goddamned loose cannon and stop him at any cost.*

Neville Hamilton Sr. also read *The Gleaner* and cringed. Bedward called him demanding he find and stop the culprit immediately. He suggested starting with Rosser. Rosser called with similar demands. Hamilton politely ignored both of them thinking the matter would blow over in a few days. He was wrong. In the ensuing days, it only got worse.

Hamilton also heard from his son, Neville Jr.

"Have you seen *The Gleaner*, Dad? Merle Dunster just called me. He is freaking that any investigation will highlight his affiliation with Swingles and link him to KSAC and then to Queisha and finally John David Grey. He is petrified that no matter what, the notoriety is going to make him a political leper. He is also swears that if he goes down, he's going take us all with him. He says he will not go down alone or quietly. Dad, what are you going to do about all this? My political career will also go up in smoke if I'm drawn into any type of PNP scandal," he whined.

A Jamaican Conspiracy

Hamilton Sr. assured his son he understood the ramifications and that he did not intend to let that happen. He had matters under control. He relayed the conversation to Dudus Coke.

Hamilton's report angered Coke more than he let on. On the surface, he maintained his usual unruffled and pragmatic appearance. After all, he was a businessman, and dilemmas were part of everyday business. His solutions, more often than not, were straightforward. If someone lit a fire, you put it out. If the person lighting the fire became an impediment, you simply made him vanish and then made sure the body was never found. Problem solved. Move on to new business. No one was indispensible. He evaluated the current crisis. It was time to send a clear message to his associates in case the heat continued. If Dunster felt inclined to cut a deal in exchange for immunity, it was time to end their partnership. Besides, he occasionally needed to make an example of someone. That was how you maintained your aura and reputation to stay in firm control. He was confident the remaining members of his inner group at KSAC would understand. You have a problem – you nip it in the bud.

~ ~ ~

Merle Dunster was driving home when he heard a *PING!*, and his front right tire began to deflate rapidly. *Damn, a flat!* He fought to maintain control of the car as it pulled into the right lane, but it went partially off the road's shoulder anyway. The car bounced to a stop just before hitting a tree. A car several car lengths behind him whipped off on the shoulder to his left, and a man walked toward him while a second man remained in the car. At first he thought the man was a Good Samaritan until he saw the man pull a pistol from his pants. Dunster assessed his predicament and immediately grasped the danger. He bolted out of his car and began to run.

He remembered passing an open-air roadside rum-bar called the R & J Drive at the last bend. He headed back for it as fast as he could run. He glanced behind him. His pursuer stumbled slightly on some loose rocks but continued chasing him. Dunster gasped as he reached the rum-bar first. He inadvertently wiped his brow with his sleeve and saw blood. He then remembered bumping his head on the rear-view mirror. As he gasped for breath, he barely noticed a white 1996 Toyota Chaser parked next to the R & J Drive and paid little heed to the Jamaican driver who got out of it. He saw half a dozen men at the bar. Two others were playing dominoes. The out-of-shape, winded Dunster panted, "I need help."

The inebriated patrons of the rum-bar looked up and saw Dunster's pursuer, pistol in hand. The bartender reached up under the bar and produced a rusty machete. He came around the bar, advancing menacingly towards Dunster with the rummies stumbling along behind him. The assassin stopped, quickly assessed the situation, and thought better of continuing his pursuit. He had been told to be discreet, but that would be impossible now. He turned on his heel without a word, and disappeared into the dark. The men walked the bleeding Dunster back to the bar where the bartender tore off a paper towel for Dunster to mop his bloody brow. The stranger from the white Toyota Chaser continued quietly sipping his Red Stripe and never left his seat.

"Wh'appen, mon?" the bartender asked Dunster in patois.

"Axxident **(Accident)**," Dunster uttered, not knowing the condition of his car. "Flat tyre. Mi will change hit misef **(Flat tire. I'll change it myself)**."

"Who de fiesty bwoy **(angry man)** wi' de bucky **(gun)**?" one patron asked.

Dunster panicked. He didn't want to disclose the true nature of his problem to drunken locals. He thought fast.

"Him vex dada who tink mi gaan abed him dawta **(He's an upset father who thinks I seduced his daughter)**," Dunster said and laughed nervously.

The half-drunk men guffawed and elbowed each other knowingly.

"Yu wan mi to call de beast **(Should I call the cops)**?" the bartender asked.

"Na dat dog dead **(No, it's over)**. He wan be back, and mi shure wan evah be back at him house either **(He won't be back, and I'm sure never going to his house again)**," Dunster said laughingly. He then offered to buy all the men a round of rum-drinks to show his appreciation for their scaring the "angry father" away. They readily accepted his generous offer. The man from the white Toyota Chaser sat at the bar silently sipping his Red Stripe, continuing to discreetly observe the scene but not joining in.

When he was pretty sure his assailant had left for good, Dunster risked a walk back to his car. The other car appeared to be gone. He changed the tire while his assailant quietly waited in the shadow of a tree. As Dunster was bent over to put the jack and lug wrench back in the trunk, the man silently slipped up behind him. Dunster heard something in the dark and turned. A flashlight blinded him. The last thing he would remember was a knife slashing his gut. He involuntarily grabbed his stomach, and the knife slashed him a second time, this time slitting his throat. He gurgled and collapsed onto the rough shoulder of the highway. The killer signaled his companion with his flashlight. The driver brought a professional body bag. Dunster was quickly zipped into it and roughly thrown into the trunk.

"I'll drive. You follow. The Don doesn't want either

the body or the vehicle to be found." Dunster's car immediately cranked, and was drivable despite its bent fender.

After Dunster left R & J Drive, the taciturn man in the white Toyota Chaser continued to sit at the bar sipping his Red Stripe, disregarding the other patrons. He was the only person present who had not bought into Dunster's "angry father" fabrication. After finishing his beer, Buried Blade wished the bartender a pleasant evening, got into his white Toyota Chaser and hit the highway. He rode slowly by where Dunster had his accident. The car was gone. He assumed Dunster had been able to change the tire and drive it home.

While Buried Blade may not have been aware of Dunster's murder, the evening's events had provided him proof of growing tensions developing within KSAC since the don now considered Dunster a threat who required removal. Buried Blade was secretly satisfied and wondered what the next part of his assignment was going to be. He would report Dunster's close call to his superior. He anticipated future dealings with Dunster. He had no way of knowing Dunster had no future.

```
SEALARNCORAL
BEACH  ⮌
  ROOMS,
            CAMPING
  SOARKLING TRIP
      HURRICANE ALLAN
          CORAL REEF
  (WITH BEAUTIFUL FISH & CORAL)
```

CHAPTER 49

Even a hall-of-fame quarterback occasionally wishes he could turn back the clock and not call a certain play or not throw a badly executed pass. No matter how well he has played up to that point in the contest, that one mistake sometimes can cause his team the ball game. The Merle Dunster murder was just such a play for Dudus Coke.

By the morning following Dunster's demise, his wife reported him as a missing person. A nationwide manhunt began, but Merle Dunster was nowhere to be found. Almost overnight, Dunster went from being an obscure PNP political hack to being a household name. Instead of less scrutiny, Dudus Coke and the KSAC were now exposed to more scrutiny than ever. The police were inundated with false Merle Dunster sightings. Some people thought he was hiding in the hills. Some believed he had left Jamaica and was in London or possibly Cuba.

A Jamaican Conspiracy

Some speculated he had been killed by the jealous spouse of an anonymous lover. Editorials began to appear in the media. One reporter compared him to Ivanhoe, the flawed character corrupted by the system in the popular Jamaican movie, *The Harder They Fall*. An especially creative and enterprising individual even printed T-shirts saying "Where is MDMD?" (mad-dog Merle Dunster had been coined by a local comedian) on the front and "Merle must be there because he's not here" on the back. A small independent studio in Kingston produced a reggae song about Dunster. This forced Hopeton Boothe, at Coke's insistence, to use his influence to try to kill the song's distribution.

An ambitious fledging reporter for the daily tabloid, *The Jamaica Star*, hoping to advance his career hired a sneak thief to break into Dunster's home. The main item stolen was his computer. From the pilfered computer the unscrupulous reporter was soon able to partially piece together Dunster's relationship to Damien Rosser and KSAC, and even publish some of the more flagrant and embarrassing e-mails. When asked where he got the information, the reporter claimed the information came from an unnamed confidential source he had promised to protect. Coke had a posse member beat up the reporter, but the damage was done. The continued exposure set up another round of bickering between Bedward, Hamilton and Rosser. Each was sure one of the others was a greedy traitor with a private agenda. As an audit began on the Highway 2000 project, Coke spoke to each one privately and reminded them of the extreme consequences of incurring his wrath. Attorneys for WB Bank in Charlotte soon became nervous and began to pressure Betsy to keep them informed about the findings of the various investigations. Patriotism Over Politics conveniently disappeared from public view and was soon yesterday's gossip. After a *Gleaner* editorial planted the idea of a PNP cover-up, embattled PNP officials were forced to create a special panel to investigate the deaths of John David Grey and Jerry Smith. Their true motive was not exposing the truth but controlling future damage from the whole scandal.

A now frantic Damien Rosser increased his frequency of transferring funds out of Jamaica to an account he had set up on Grand Cayman. He secretly made plans to flee should it become necessary, and he wanted to make damned sure adequate funds would be available if he should be forced to bail. He was determined not to be a scapegoat or a posse homicide victim. His fears approached manic levels when he was called to testify by the commission investigating Highway 2000.

A week prior to the hearings the nervous Rosser received an anonymous phone call.

"Dr. Rosser," the caller said, "I will just call myself Buried Blade. I am going to be short and will not answer any questions. You are being set up behind the scenes at the upcoming hearing. One of your rivals has provided the committee with information and pictures tying you into Merle Dunster's disappearance and will cast suspicion on you in the John David Grey affair. Your indictment will certainly follow."

"What! Wait! They can't do that to me!" said Rosser before he could catch himself.

Buried Blade hung up.

Rosser was speechless. Then as he panicked he almost blacked out with fear. *John David! Why can't that SOB stay buried? I don't know what happened to him. Why would anyone think I did? I may be a lot of things, but I'm not his murderer ... and no one is going to make me into the scapegoat ... Is it Hamilton or Coke setting me up? ... Just to be safe, I better move even more money*

A Jamaican Conspiracy

to Grand Cayman ... And maybe it's time for me to vanish. ... I'll call Smith. ... . And what about my wife? ... Oh hell, with money I can find another wife if I have to ... And my daughter? ... She's been acting like a teenage ass lately anyway. ... I'm better off without either of them. Neither is worth dying or going to prison for. I'm sure they'll both find a way to get by if I'm not there.*

Step one completed. Buried Blade had accomplished his goal of freaking out Rosser. Now, to take Rosser's paranoia and ratchet it up even more. He had studied the route Rosser took to go home each evening and knew his normal travel times. He preselected a secluded place in the road with good visibility and waited for Rosser to pass. He decided to handle this matter himself, not delegate it as he sometimes did. Buried Blade had a 6mm Winchester bolt-action rifle with a mounted scope. His goal was not to kill Rosser, though that would have been an easy shot, but to just panic him into making rasher, more irrational decisions. If for some reason Buried Blade miscalculated and Rosser died by accident, well, it was Jah's will. About an hour before he expected Rosser to arrive, he set up in the woods on a place where the highway went up an incline. If other traffic happened to be on the road, he would simply wait until another day. If Rosser was the sole car – the probability – he would strike.

Despite his fears, Rosser was a desk-jockey creature of habit with a clock-punching mentality who never considered deviating from his usual route home. As he drove, Rosser was troubled, preoccupied and not observant. *What detail could I have possibly forgotten?* He thought of the large sum of money he had transferred to his account in Grand Cayman that very day. As he drove up the incline, he was jarred by the sound of a gunshot. The outside rearview mirror on the driver's side suddenly shattered. He jerked the car but managed to maintain control. *Someone's trying to kill me.* He heard a second shot which seemed to hit nothing. He floored the car and shot over the crest of the hill.

Perfect, Buried Blade thought. *I hit just what I was aiming at – the rearview mirror. That should give Rosser something new to hyperventilate about.*

Rosser raced home, all the while looking behind him. *No one is following me.* When he pulled into his driveway, he immediately closed the electronic wall gate behind him. He sat trembling until his heartbeat slowed to normal. He rolled down the window and looked at his shattered rear-view mirror. It was totally destroyed. *A few more inches to the right and that could have been my head.* He took a deep breath, composed himself the best he could, and walked into his home.

Damien Rosser was noticeably preoccupied and edgy at home all evening as he tried to decide just who wanted him dead. *It must be one of my partners.* He tried unsuccessfully to mask his fears and to act normal around his wife, Estelle, and his daughter. The words from Buried Blade's phone call kept ringing in his ears, and in his mind's eye, he kept seeing the rear-view mirror explode. Each time he imagined himself dead or wounded, he would shudder. Grand Cayman or some other island – any island -was sounding better and better. By morning he had made his decision. It was time to go. He would put into play the plan he had conceived months earlier. He called Smith. Screw testifying.

It took two additional days to finalize Rosser's financial matters. His nerves remained on end. He slept poorly and began to carry his pistol everywhere. His wife kept asking what was worrying him, but he was evasive. *There's a lot going on at work, dear.* He told Estelle he had a business meeting out of town and wouldn't return

A Jamaican Conspiracy

for a few days. He told his office he needed a few personal days to take care of some family business.

Rosser paid cash to charter a small aircraft and flew to Grenada. From Grenada he planned to fly to Grand Cayman. He wasn't sure where he'd go from there. He'd talk to Smith about it. Rosser wouldn't have felt so secure if he had known that his activities were not as secret as he thought. Dudus Coke had ordered the Shower Posse to maintain surveillance on all of KSAC's partners. From experience, Coke knew he should trust no one. The Posse put out the word on the street that an incentive consisting of either drugs or cash was being offered to anyone who reported suspicious activities to them. Plus, the don would be eternally grateful and remember who is friends were. Shower Posse members would also receive a bonus if Dudus received useful information. As always, there was an implied threat to those tempted to refuse the don's generosity. Rosser's flight to Grenada was dutifully reported. When Letha leaked bank records to Coke, he became convinced Rosser had been embezzling money from their joint business ventures. This was unforgivable. Rosser never got to Grand Cayman. His body was found on a sidewalk outside his two-story hotel in Grenada. Authorities assumed he either fell or committed suicide. The Jamaican Constabulary wrote up the incident as probable suicide after Rosser's wife told authorities that her husband had been acting strangely before his mysterious departure. She also told them he had not confided in her that he intended to take an international trip.

A local small-time thief working as a hotel bellboy stole Rosser's luggage before the police arrived and sold the contents. In his hotel room desk drawer, however, the investigators also found an almost completed note on hotel stationary addressed to Minister of State Dr. Devon Bedward.

> Dr. Bedward:
> I have chosen to leave Jamaica and seek new opportunities abroad. Please use your influence to make certain that my wife and daughter are not subjected to harassment or asset seizure by Jamaican authorities.
> If word reaches me from my associates that either of these things has occurred, I will send a copy of my computerized NCB banking records which will link you and the PNP to KSAC in an unfavorable light. I have placed duplicate copies of the above referenced records at strategic locations. Do we ...

The unfinished, unsigned note ended there. In the drawer in the bedside table authorities found a hotel scratch pad. On it was a list of "to do" items – wife, DB, bank, airport, rental agent, auto rental. Wife, bank and airport had been checked. Beside wife was scratched "g-mail." "Rental agent" and "car rental" had not been checked. Next to them was the notation "call." DB had a doodle of an arrow or spear beside it.

All items were copied for retention by Grenadian authorities and the originals were sent back to Detective Carl Berry at the Organised Unit of the Jamaican Constabulary Force.

> **NOTICE.**
> WE SELL THE FOLLOW-ING : -COW MILK, ORANGE JU, Eggs, Tea, EGG SANWISH BRAKEFAST etc.

CHAPTER 50

As he put Rosser's flash drive into his computer, Dudus Coke silently congratulated himself on his street smarts. *I wondered for a long time*, he thought, *if Damien wasn't just a silver-tongued, cheap crook. Never really cared for or trusted that guy. Just tolerated him. Don't have to worry 'bout that no more. He dead, dead, dead. And he's gonna stay dead, because I put his worthless ass away. He thought he could steal from me and get away with it. And he thought he could collect information he could use to blackmail me. Not in this lifetime, baby cakes. Some things I'll tolerate, but reaching in my pocket is not one of them. Reach in Dudus's pocket and you gonna find a mousetrap. Now I need to find out more about Bedward.*

The 65 page Excel document before him opened. It was filled with neat rows and columns of numbers and figures. At the top of two columns were names of various banks. Running along the side of the document were bribe money transfer dates and "to" and "from" account numbers. The more unfamiliar, unauthorized transactions he saw, the angrier he became. He momentarily debated with himself about downloading the document into his computer for blackmail, if needed, against Devon Bedward. He decided no. The risk was too great if this information fell into the wrong hands. He shuddered at the thought of the consequences of that. Thinking he had the only copy of the damning document, Coke pulled the flash drive out of his computer, and with no further hesitation, ground it under his heel. *Lickle more (Goodbye) mutha-fucker. You will never come back to haunt me or any of my associates,* he thought. *It's a shame that damned peon who works for the hotel showed up when he did, forcing Cudjoe to have to scram before he could thoroughly search Rosser's room for other damaging items, but I guess you can't control everything.*

~ ~ ~

In Kingston, Estelle Rosser was rereading her life-altering e-mail from her now deceased husband.

> *My dearest Estelle,*
> *Unexpected circumstances have forced me to reevaluate some of my life choices. I am not at liberty to discuss specifics. Let me just say, sometimes we must make difficult choices. To compensate you for disrupting your life, I have placed J$50 million in your RBC account. If you have any questions, please call our sympathetic banker, Warren Smith. If you handle these funds judiciously, they should provide for your basic needs in the years ahead (I remind you that the house and automobile are debt free and*

registered in your name).

Should they occur, I have instructed Dr. Devon Bedward to intervene as necessary to minimize embarrassing aggravations from local authorities. Do not hesitate to involve Dr. Bedward if it becomes necessary. You will find an attachment to this communication which will give you leverage with Dr. Bedward should he prove to be uncooperative. Copy it, put it in a safe place, and then erase both it and this message. If Dr. Bedward is not solicitous, as a last resort, send the file to the editor at The Gleaner.

Please do not attempt to contact me. I will be unable to respond. This will be our final communication. I wish you only the best. Tell our daughter that her father loves her.

Damien

Estelle angrily stared at the keyboard and never bothered to read the attachment. Her eyes misted, and she began to sob. She kept stabbing her keyboard over and over, as if by punishing it, she would also injure her recently departed, vanishing husband. As she pummeled the keyboard, she accidentally hit the forward key and accidentally transmitted the e-mail to her daughter's school headmistress. When she recovered her composure, she angrily deleted the file.

~ ~ ~

In Ocho Rios, Detective Carl Berry of the Organised Unit of the Jamaican Constabulary Force was studying the unfinished letter to Devon Bedward found in Damien Rosser's Grenada hotel room. Several things were going through his mind. *Did Rosser commit suicide or was he assassinated? If he was killed, why? What leverage did*

Rosser have on the Minister of State of the Ministry of Water and Housing? Nothing incriminating had been found in the hotel room. Did the killer take the evidence I need? And where's Rosser's computer? Where are the duplicate copies of the blackmail material he mentioned in the Bedward letter? Just what type and level of graft was Bedward engaged in? Were they co-conspirators or was Rosser a whistle-blower? These are some pretty big fish on this line, so I can't just go out and shoot from the hip with assumptions and suspicions I can't back up – not with VIP's of this magnitude. The consequences could be career threatening if I don't investigate thoroughly dotting every "i" and crossing every "t".

He then looked at the "to-do" list found on the scratch pad in the bedside table drawer. Some items had been checked; some had not. *The "DB" item had not been checked. I assume that DB means the Devon Bedward blackmail letter is not checked since it had not been finished and mailed. The "wife" item, however, was checked. Whatever it was, it must have been completed. Why was g-mail scratched next to it? Maybe that is where the duplicate copy went ... Of course e-mail to Estelle! I'll subpoena her computer records immediately.*

Detective Berry had little trouble building a case to obtain an order to seize Estelle Rosser's computer. Despite her erasure, the damaging e-mail was recovered. Berry's superiors made a decision to make the illegal money transfer list classified information while they quietly obtained RBC's original bank records to further their investigation into government corruption. Investigators noted that the e-mail had been forwarded and tried to recapture it, but by the time the shocked headmistress was approached by the Constabulary, she had already re-forwarded Rosser's e-mail once again to her friend, Jaevion Nelson at *The Gleaner*, to get his opinion.

```
NUTS      BOLTS
 MOTORCYCLE
    BICYCLE
   ASSORIES
```

CHAPTER 51

When Detroit singer songwriter Smokey Robinson wrote the lyrics *Like a snowball rolling down the side of a snow covered hill, it's growing*, Jamaica and the West Indies were the farthest thing from his mind, but snowballs can grow, even in the steamier climes ... maybe especially in the steamier climes ... especially when these snowballs are *feeling hot hot hot*.

When Jaevion Nelson at *The Gleaner* received the surprise e-mail from the head schoolmistress at Columbus Preparatory School, he couldn't believe his good fortune. *The Gleaner's* past investigations about PNP or JLP corruption too often had either fallen flat or had not had the far-reaching impact he had hoped due to public apathy. Even though a special panel had been named to investigate the deaths of John David Grey and Jerry Smith after *The Gleaner's* last exposé, no heads had rolled and the chances of that happening were remote. PNP spinmeisters had skillfully stonewalled and then quietly, but impatiently waited, for the public outcry to end, and for the public's attention to shift to some more current scandals or perils. On the surface life in Jamaica was once again irie. The recent scandalous snowballs seemingly hadn't grown but simply melted. Merle Dunster was still presumed to be missing, but as expected, interest and pressure began to subside; Damien Rosser had died under questionable circumstances, but it seemed unlikely that his death would be ruled as anything more than suicide brought on by his disgrace; Grey and Smith were ancient, all but forgotten history; but *now* the newspaper had a possible juicy trail going all the way to the second most powerful man in the Ministry of Water and Housing. Would this finally lead Nelson into the mega-story he had often dreamed of, a story so big it would simply refuse to be swallowed by either public apathy or naiveté? Could this possibly be Prime Minister Pettis' Watergate? Nelson sighed as he thought about maybe, just maybe, the story of the year had been miraculously dumped in his lap. He enthusiastically called a staff strategy meeting to discuss the newspaper's windfall of good fortune.

The Gleaner did attempt to initiate a new investigation, but almost immediately, the newspaper's attorneys cautioned Nelson about publishing any reports until he had airtight evidence. He was reminded that a libel suit could end his career. The almost forgotten nonexistent watchdog organization Patriots Over Politics was not to be constrained by such scruples and fears. After one phone call from Colonel Winter to a *Gleaner* employee with a Maroon heritage, Buried Blade surreptitiously obtained both *The Gleaner* files and Rosser's e-mail, and with no hesitation, stole *The Gleaner's* thunder with a crude copy-machine produced newsletter. The newsletter proudly announced on the first page, "We regard journalism as a contact contest." Since Buried Blade felt safe from having the report traced back to him, he felt he could make any accusations he desired. The POP Report (as it came to be called) would soon trigger an avalanche of catastrophic events – the avalanche Nelson had hoped to be able to take credit for. It not only exposed the existence of Rosser's computer file, forcing Nelson to surrender his copy to the constabulary, but revealed that money was clearly being pilfered from Operation Pride, the People's National Party's cornerstone low-cost housing project. Investigators concluded that the thefts appeared to have been discovered by Neville Hamilton Sr. who had decided to capitalize on the situation. With the help of his son, Neville Jr., the Parish Councillor for St. Ann Parish, Neville Sr. had apparently used his knowledge as leverage to get contracts for Highway 2000 awarded to the Kingston and St. Ann Corporation. Hamilton had then allegedly hired favored subcontractors who willingly gave him kickbacks from their inflated contracts. The author of the POP Report deduced that unnamed PNP bureaucrats had been complicit in the deaths of John David Grey and Jerry Smith. He reasoned that the men's deaths resulted from a combination of their inside knowledge of these events and their threat as whistle-blowers. The report deduced that even if People's National Party officials were not directly complicit in the deaths of the two men, they were guilty of a cover-up after the fact. The POP Report further claimed that Rosser's flash drive Excel file also clearly implicated both PNP VIP's Dr. Damien Rosser and Merle Dunster, leading the author to the conclusion that foul play had likely been involved in their disappearance and death. It also seemed logical to the author that Neville Hamilton Jr. was no unselfish public servant but as avaricious as his father. The report finally stated that ultimate blame should be clearly placed on Dr. Devon Bedward, the Minister of

State of the Ministry of Water and Housing and the man in charge of Operation Pride. After all, these crimes had happened on Bedward's watch. Clearly he was either a co-conspirator or a gross bureaucratic incompetent. Even if the authorities felt they lacked the ironclad case needed to prosecute, Bedward should be removed from office. In other words, where there was smoke, there was fire. Dudus Coke was relieved that he and Hopeton Boothe were spared except for some vague in-passing comments about the possible involvement of other corporate entities. The newsletter lit a bomb.

~ ~ ~

From the sidelines, Will and Betsy watched the scandal they had helped create. They first saw the POP Report when Henry Davis walked into Sundance carrying several copies.

"I picked this up off the counter at the L & M Grocery in Runaway Bay. I think you'll find it interesting," he said as he handed each of them a copy. "I saw it as well at D & O Hardware and Scott's Texaco at Columbus Plaza.

Before commenting, Will and Betsy read Buried Blade's newsletter.

"Who do you think wrote this? If any of this is true, there's going to be major repercussions very soon," Will said. "I wonder how widely disseminated this newsletter is."

"Rose's church group is already gossiping about it," Henry said. "She's gotten at least three calls this morning."

"Mind it I take this copy to the bank?" Betsy asked.

"Not at all," Henry said. "That's why I snagged multiple copies."

Just then the phone rang in the kitchen. Leva answered it.

"You don't mean it," she said. "They did what? I've got to get a copy of that."

"Sounds like ganja gab. If she's talking about what I think she is, I think you can say distribution is pretty good," Betsy concluded. "I'll let her have one of my extra copies."

"Well, well," Will commented. "My POP has struck again ... But who in the hell is it?"

"As the nursery rhyme says, 'Pop goes the weasel'," Betsy said.

"You mean pop is a weasel," Will said.

~ ~ ~

This was the beginning of days, and then weeks, of accusations and rebuttals and more accusations and more rebuttals. The scandal seemed to be the primary topic of conversation throughout the island. Warren Smith seemed surprisingly cautious and blasé when Betsy first showed him POP's accusations. Internally he was quaking. Public outcry did not subside but intensified. One faction even demanded Prime Minister P.J. Pettis' resignation. The prime minister pleaded ignorance but began to distance himself from Bedward. When the controversy refused to subside, he finally offered Dr. Bedward as a sacrificial lamb. Bedward capitulated, resigned, and took an extended vacation in Nigeria. From this safe distance, thinking he had nothing more to lose, Bedward tried to lay the blame on the missing Merle Dunster and the deceased Damien Rosser. Despite Bedward's resignation, the controversy still refused to die, and the JLP called for a vote of no confidence on Pettis. This forced an election to be scheduled.

A police investigative team examined bank records at NCB. In a plea deal, Warren Smith finally admitted that he was related to fugitive Ponzi scheme financier, David Smith, as well as Dr. Bedward's wife. Smith said he had been pressured to look the other way as millions of dollars were illegally transferred to Grand Cayman.

Warren Smith was immediately terminated by the bank. After he was arrested, charged, and awaiting trial, he was mysteriously knifed in the jail shower. The guards claimed they heard nothing. No one was arrested for the homicide. The same day he was arrested, Letha Wardlow disappeared into the hills. She gave the bank no notice and didn't even bother to clean out her desk. Authorities still did not have enough evidence to bring charges against anyone for the deaths of John David Grey and Jerry Smith, even though fingers pointed to the possibility that Smith's death had come from damaging knowledge about KSAC he had gained by being a Smith family member. The Kingston and St. Ann Corporation was banned from bidding on future government contracts.

Neville Hamilton Jr. soon tendered his own resignation as Parish Councillor of St. Ann Parish, purportedly to pursue new and exciting opportunities in the private sector. He was given a cushy job in the newly created position, Director of Entertainment at Swingles. In due time, the special election for Prime Minister was held. P.J. Pettis lost in a resounding defeat to a novice Jamaica Labour Party candidate, thus ending the People's National Party's long dominance of Jamaican politics. Surprisingly enough, Edward Seaga chose not to run, but chose instead to help pick JLP's candidate and advise him behind the scenes. The new administration announced Highway 2000 would be completed. A bipartisan task force would be named to study Operation Pride's feasibility and to determine the project's focus.

Betsy Black received a commendation from the bank; she was replaced by a team of government and bank internal auditors. Betsy and Will would soon be returning to the Keys. The board of directors of WB gave Betsy a very generous award of bank stock and stock options for her efforts in Jamaica.

Patriots Over Politics mysteriously vanished. Investigations were conducted to attempt to identify the organization's principals, but all efforts failed. Soon POP became yesterday's dead file and was only the occasional subject of idle speculation and rum-bar chatter, much like the fate of Merle Dunster. Will and Betsy laughed in private about POP, but never told a soul what they knew of the movement's origin. Betsy began to call POP "Power Over Punks" and called Will her "Mighty Power-Buster." This became an inside joke no one else understood.

"Look in the sky. Do I see a bird; do I see a plane; do I hear a bull-shitter? No, it's just Will Black - POWER BUSTER," teased Betsy.

"Yu jus red eye **(you're just envious)**," Will said jokingly, "but if you're good, I'll share my secret of why POP is successful in bringing down corrupt government officials."

"I'll bite," Betsy said. "What's the secret of Patriots Over Politics success?"

"The answer's simple," Will continued. "As a wise Jamaican once said, 'the higher the monkey climbs, the more him expose.'"

> **TOMBSTONESES**
> ROWENS
> BARBERING SALO
> -ON FOR THE BEST
> IN AFRO AND
> STYLE SCOND
> DOOR UPSTAIRS

CHAPTER 52

"Looks as if the Jamaican conspiracy is all but concluded," Will said.

"And a far reaching conspiracy this was. A bittersweet adventure. I'm excited to get back to the Keys, and I can't wait to see our daughter, Lexie," Betsy said, "but I'm sure going to miss this place. My main regret is that Lexie didn't get to visit while we were living here."

"She's sure about as far from Jamaica as you can get and deeply engaged in carving out her own life. Who ever dreamed the daughter of two people from the Gulf Coast L.A. would choose to live in the Pacific L.A?" Will said.

"Well, as they say in Jamaica, 'every hoe ha dem stick a bush' **(to each his own)**."

"And we never dreamed two people from Gulf Coast L.A. would be living in Jamaica either," Will said.

"Living here sure gives you a different perspective

385

A Jamaican Conspiracy

from just briefly visiting here as a tourist and hitting all the tourist traps," Betsy said.

"That's for certain. As a tourist all we met were bartenders and waitresses. Now, I think we know every swindler, embezzler, and confidence man in the West Indies," Will said. "And don't forget. We met a few duppies. I never told you, that's one of the reasons I married you, because you introduce me to such interesting people. You raucous sinful bankers are always stimulating and never dull."

" That's because all you stock-jockeys cornered all the world's halos," Betsy said.

About that time Henry Davis walked in the house.

"Coffee or tea?" Betsy asked.

"Either is a capital idea. I'll take whatever is brewed," Henry responded. "Do you have a departure date yet? Not that I'm trying to push you out the door. In fact Rose and I are sure going to miss you two."

"You and Rose will promise to visit us in Florida, won't you?"

"I talked the bank into letting me finish out this month on the payroll since the rent on Sundance was paid in advance," Betsy said.

"Just let us know when the rum-bar opens in the Keys," Henry said, "and we'll be there."

"Not only are Key's rum-bars world class, but sometimes it seems as if they never close. There's an old Keys proverb that says, 'it's always five o'clock somewhere.' When you do come up, we'll infect you with Keys Disease."

"Then it's settled," Henry said. "We wouldn't miss it for the world. I know I sound like a broken record, but it's going to be awfully dull without you folks around."

Betsy gave Henry a peck on the cheek.

"I heard from Colonel Winter," Henry said after he

sipped his coffee. "He very much wants to see you both again."

"Oh, yeah," Will said. "Any particular reason?"

"He didn't say. He probably just wants to say goodbye and wish you the best in your future endeavors," Henry said. "Got any plans for Saturday? I'll drive you to Accompong."

Will and Betsy agreed to go Saturday assuming it was convenient for Colonel Winter.

Leva came out on the porch.

"Mr. Davis, may I speak to you?"

"Of course, Mrs. Carter."

"Kingtoo and I would like to give a farewell pool party for Will and Betsy," Leva said. "If we do, would you and Ms. Rose join us? Chicken says he will bring his equipment so we can jam the night away."

"We would be honored, and we want to help anyway we can."

"Oh, Leva, now I understand why they call you Honey-pye," Betsy said as she stood up, "you shouldn't go to all that trouble."

"Oh yes, we should, and we are," Leva said mistily. "Kingtoo and I agree. We have never enjoyed working for anyone as much as you two. We're really going to miss you."

Betsy hugged Leva and said, "I'll only agree if we all pitch in on the preparation equally. Tonight *everybody* is a host and a guest as well."

Will agreed and rose to hug Leva. E.J. silently beamed from the kitchen.

"We're going to miss you too," Betsy said. "You're like family."

"Have you ever thought about buying a place in Jamaica?" Leva asked.

"If we could, we'd love to," Will said.

387

A Jamaican Conspiracy

"Well, if you ever do," Leva said. "Just let us know. No matter where we're working, we'll tender our notice and join you because you're one cool cucumba."

"Well, thank you," Betsy said.

"Do you remember I told you that when your veins began to flow green and yellow, you would get a Jamaican nickname? Well, that time has come. From now on your Jamaican nickname is Cool Cucumba."

"That's sweet, Honey-pye. I like that."

"And who am I?" Will asked.

Kingtoo broke in and said, "We decided your name is Phone-ear."

"Where in the world did you come up with that one?" Will asked.

"Because every time we see you, you got a phone or your headset stuck in your ear," Kingtoo said.

"I guess there's some truth to that," Will said. "Yes, I guess I do, Kingtoo."

Leva and Betsy hugged again. Will shook E.J.'s hand.

They could hear Leva singing joyful hymns for the rest of the morning.

~ ~ ~

Saturday morning they got an early start to Accompong. Henry got on Highway B3 headed for Brown's Town. The traffic was light, and the weather was perfect. Henry honked at a few familiar folks along the way, but didn't stop and offer anyone a ride. At Brown's Town he got on A1 headed for Jackson Town. Will and Betsy enjoyed the now familiar route. At Jackson Town, Henry changed highways once again to B6, and they were off to Appleton. After passing through Maggoty, they knew they were getting close to their destination since the unpaved road turned bumpier and dustier. Will and Betsy had tired of riding on the bouncy road by now and were glad to see the "Welcome to Accompong" sign. Henry

388

tooted his horn and grinned at Flashy as they passed by his tiny bar. Flashy and the men playing dominoes waved back. He noted the 1996 white Toyota Chaser with a cracked windshield parked next to the building.

Within minutes, Henry parked his van in front of the Colonel's humble home. It was a small simple shotgun concrete structure with a rusted tin roof. It certainly did not look like the dwelling of a man of his stature. The sparse flowerbeds featuring native plants had been weeded. A massive royal Poinciana dominated the sparse front yard. It was in full bloom as if it were trying to welcome them.

"We didn't get to see the Colonel's home on our last visit," Betsy commented.

"Not surprising, he normally doesn't meet strangers at his home," Henry said, "but you're not strangers anymore."

The door opened and the Colonel came out smiling. He gave each of them a warm hug. "Welcome home to Accompong," he said.

"And thanks for having us to your home," Will said.

"Consider it your home as well," the Colonel said as he led them to an old concrete table beneath the Poinciana's canopy. The table was round and chipped and had semi-circular concrete benches around it. The Colonel had placed a bottle of Wray and Nephew rum on the table before their arrival. Betsy recognized the small glasses on the table. They were the 5 oz. glasses Kraft Pimento Spread was sold in. Betsy smiled when she saw them. Her mother had used similar glasses for juice glasses when she was a child.

Without asking, the Colonel poured each of them a glass of the clear rum. He held his glass up in a toast and said, "To your future success and happiness. Respect."

They each took a sip, and said nothing. The Colonel

A Jamaican Conspiracy

had a pensive faraway look as he watched a crested quail-dove fly across the yard.

Betsy finally broke the silence and said, "What a gorgeous Royal Poinciana tree."

"Yes, they are timeless, much like the Maroon people," The Colonel replied, "and the friendships we Maroons cultivate."

He paused again before he continued.

"I hear you will soon be leaving us."

"Yes, my employer has said my Jamaican assignment is at an end," Betsy said. "They wish me to return to Florida."

"But we hope to return for visits," Will added.

"Florida's gain will be Jamaica's loss."

"Believe me when I say we are leaving a part of ourselves here," Betsy said.

"As I would expect. I want you to know that this is always your home," The Colonel said.

"Yes, Jamaica will always be a part of us," Will said.

"No, I mean Accompong," The Colonel said. "I now consider you to be Maroon, my blood relatives, my children. We Maroons take matters involving our own very seriously. If you or yours ever need assistance or support, the entire Maroon nation will always be there to support or defend you. This is not an idle statement by an old man and not an invitation we Maroons extend often or lightly. We use whatever resources we have at our disposal - and they are farther reaching than they appear - to defend our own even if it involves our having to make the ultimate sacrifice. Accompong is now your home. If you ever need me, my childhood friend and brother, Henry Davis, will be our liaison."

Henry nodded in agreement, his eyes sparkling. Will and Betsy sat there in stunned silence. They didn't know what to say. No one had ever offered unconditionally to die for them.

Finally Betsy rose and, with tears in her eyes, kissed the old chief on the cheek.

"Thank you, we proudly accept your kind offer. We pledge our allegiance to you as well," Betsy said sincerely. "We will never take advantage of your generosity and will never ask unreasonable things of you."

Will shook the old man's hand as the old man's eyes bored into his. "Thank you, sir, and as my wife said, if you or the Maroons ever need us, we will respond and do whatever we can."

"I know you will," said The Colonel. "After all, you're now Maroon. May Jah go with you and protect you."

They finished drinking their rum and rose to leave.

"I wish I could think of something to say other than thank you for everything," Betsy said.

"Sometimes things are best left unsaid," The Colonel said. "I know you both have the soul and warrior spirit of Cudjoe. That is enough."

As they drove away, The Colonel did not wave. He just stood silently, smiled, and then slowly walked back into his house.

Everyone in the van was silent until they got back on the paved road at Maggotty. Finally Henry broke the silence.

"You have made a very powerful ally for life. What Colonel Winter has done today is the ultimate sign of respect. I have never regretted being his adopted cousin or his friend. It has always been nice to know I have the Maroons to fall back on if it should become necessary. And you know since I am also an adopted Maroon in addition to being your close friend, you can call on me any time as well."

"We didn't need today to tell us that," Will said.

Henry broke the serious mood in the car.

A Jamaican Conspiracy

"Now, how do you make maroon from white?" he asked.

"And how's that?" Will asked.

"You just throw in some Blacks for color," Henry replied.

"That's sooo baaad," Will said. "I hope you didn't sprain a brain thinking of that one."

Henry just smiled and said, "It was a no-brainer and sooo true."

> **See**
> VOGLER'S
> FOR
> CHOICED
> LIQUORS
> &
> LIQUERS

CHAPTER 53

The mood at the Royal Bank of Commerce was one of quiet desperation. After all, having their bank president arrested was not a common occurrence. Letha's sudden and unexpected disappearance added another layer of doubt and confusion. Having regulators and auditors under foot kept most of the bank employees on edge. People silently wondered if they would soon be spotlighted for having failed to strictly adhere to banking policy and regulations in the performance of their own duties at the bank and if so, what the potential consequences would be. BB freaked out and spread paranoia that there would be massive layoffs and a reorganization coming soon. He forecast economic chaos because of the government's recent scandals and political instability. The icing on the cake was the fear of the unknown, since it was common knowledge that Betsy Black would soon be leaving them.

The mood at Sundance was also bitter sweet. The staff hated to see Will and Betsy return to America. They almost dreaded the end of each day since that put them one day closer to Will and Betsy's departure date. Will and Betsy had mixed emotions about leaving as well but knew their time had come. After all, this was always a temporary assignment, now complete. Lucy and Dexter even sensed things were not normal. On the other hand, Jamaicans love a party. For them even funerals were a time of revelry. Everyone was excited to have a party at Sundance, even if the occasion was a going-away party. Will and Betsy heard the staff whispering to each other and wondered what mischief might be afloat.

The farewell dinner party was planned for two nights before Will and Betsy were scheduled to depart. This was fine with the Blacks since this shindig would allow them to relax and enjoy the evening without being concerned about preparing to leave the day after. The last day could then be spent packing and putting their last minute affairs in order.

E.J. decided to hang paper luminaries over the swimming pool. He took brown paper grocery bags and spray-painted each into a green, yellow, and red rainbow. Next he cut cardboard to give each bag a stiff, level bottom. He then covered the cardboard with a thin layer of sand and strengthened the bags with bent coat hangers to make them rigid enough to hang. When he was satisfied, he added a short luminary candle to each bag. When E.J. tried to hang the string of luminaries he did not have enough line to span the pool so he improvised and made up the shortfall with bungee cords. When finished he was satisfied with his artistic accomplishment.

This would make the back yard festive for this special occasion. Lastly he set up the barbeque to grill fish and lobster and to jerk some chicken.

Leva planned a special meal of some of Will and Betsy's favorite Jamaican dishes. She planned callaloo, fried plantains, ackee and yams as well as peas and rice. For dessert she debated over whether to prepare gizzadas, shamshuku, or banana cake. She found herself unable to decide, so she cooked all three.

Finally the day of the party arrived. Henry brought Rose to Sundance during the latter part of the afternoon to bring the Solomon Gundy she had prepared as an hors d'oeuvre. Henry then begged off apologetically, saying he had agreed to help a friend by picking up a guest at the Montego Bay airport. E.J. set up a rum-bar out by the pool and filled an ice chest with Red Stripes. Mikey Mo brought over his DJ sound system and began to set it up. Leva cautioned him about not jamming too loudly since that morning a newly arrived guest from England had checked into the villa next door.

As she was bringing crockery out to the back yard, Betsy heard a voice from next door.

"Peter," the woman called out in an English accent. "Please come here."

"Yes, Miriam," the man answered. "Give me a moment."

"Peter," Betsy exclaimed. "Surely it can't be ... "

"The guests we upset when we first arrived at Sundance," Will said. "Please let it be anyone else."

"I still giggle when I think about the fiasco that night," Betsy said. "We'll sure be telling that story and getting laughs back in the Keys for years to come."

"Those Limey tenderfeet sure as hell didn't think it was too damned funny at the time it happened," Will said and looked at his watch. "Henry's not back. I wonder who was important enough to make him have to run all the way to the Mo Bay airport today of all days," Will commented, changing the subject. "Must really be a VIP or a really big tipper."

"You might say that. Sometimes things come up, and you just have to do what you have to do," Rose responded. "But don't worry Henry promised to make it back for your party, and he's always good to his word. He wouldn't miss this evening for any VIP."

Leva overheard her and seemed to smile knowingly at E.J..

At last, about dark, Henry returned from the airport. He honked as he approached the front gate. E.J. ran faster than usual to open it. He and Chicken had lit the luminaries by now, and they glowed warmly overhead. Kingtoo had donned special party clothes - a black t-shirt and tight black pants. Imprinted on the t-shirt was a portrait of Elvis in his dress army uniform. The caption next to the portrait said "GI Blues". Over the tucked-in t-shirt, Kingtoo wore a white nail-head, decorative chain embroidered jumpsuit concert belt which matched his white zipper boots.

E.J. opened the van's sliding door and extended his hand to help Henry's passenger disembark. Betsy wondered why he had brought his passenger back to the villa. There was a moment's hesitation, and a white hand grabbed E.J.'s hand. They saw a smiling, familiar face - Will and Betsy's daughter, Lexie.

"Surprise!" Henry, Rose, E.J., Leva, and Mikey Mo called out in unison. Lexie ran over and hugged both of her shocked parents who hugged her in return.

"I can't believe this," Betsy exclaimed beaming. "This is the best gift of all."

She then kissed Henry on the cheek, "You sly dog. Thank you; thank you, thank you."

"Is this VIP important enough to make Henry drive all the way to Montego Bay?" Rose asked.

"Yes, yes, and yes again," Betsy exclaimed. "I can't believe all of you knew about this and kept it a secret. This is one of the most fantastic days of my life. Did you know about this plot, Will?"

"You kidding? I'm just as surprised as you are. Maybe more so," Will said as he hugged his daughter again. "Now this is truly a party to remember." E.J. dropped Lexie's bags inside the front door, and the group moved quickly to the back yard. Everyone took turns hugging Lexie as they walked.

When Lexie bounded down the stairs to the pool patio, Lucy and Dexter saw her and lunged towards her, yapping at the top of their lungs. Gina and Samantha got caught up in the excitement and galloped behind them, barking as well.

At that moment, as the revelers clomped down the back steps, a frightened rat ran from under the house. It was pursued by a four-foot Jamaican boa snake, quickly darting out from under a shrub, sensing it had found a quick tasty meal. Gina and Samantha tore off after the snake, upsetting a miniature potted purple bougainvillea on a table by the pool, knocking Rose down. Kingtoo grabbed the long telescoping aluminum pole with the pool net and chased after the rat, the snake, and the frantic dogs.

"A yellow snake!" he yelled. "No problem, don't worry. They aren't poisonous! I'll get it!"

He galloped after it, reached out, and scooped the yellow snake up with the pool net. It wrapped its tail around the pole, causing E.J. to try to shake it off. On the third wild swing, he heaved the yellow snake over the fence. The long pool net tangled in the bungee cords holding the luminaries. The elastic stretched and then

A Jamaican Conspiracy

twanged like a bowstring. Both the bungee cords and rope they were tied to shot over the fence like an arrow taking the sparking, lighted luminaries with them. The overturned luminaries caught on fire in mid air, and, when they hit the ground next door at Villa Brawta, they exploded into fiery missiles on the back yard. Gina and Samantha were yelping madly and trying to climb the fence. They saw the writhing snake splash into the hot tub next door. This was immediately followed by a terrified female shriek.

"Peter! Peter!" Miriam howled, "they're bloody doing it again," and then began to hiccup as she gasped for air. "I told you we should go to that all-inclusive in St. Lucia, but oh no, you wanted to visit damned Jamaica again so you could see the real Caribbean and immerse yourself in the local culture. Is this fucking real enough for you?"

As they peered over the fence a pale, plump, bare-assed familiar-looking woman stumbled barefoot across the rocky yard choking the thrashing yellow snake with her left hand. Her face was flushed with rage. Her heavy size-D breasts swung like a pendulum as she cursed after each hop. She was swinging an opened upturned wine bottle like a club with her right hand, whacking the stunned yellow snake as wine poured onto her naked front. The terrified rat had somehow managed to climb onto her head and was clinging for its life to her bouncing ponytail. The completely out-of-control woman was totally unaware of its presence. She dodged burning luminaries as she scampered clumsily through the rocky lawn. She stepped on a limestone rock with every other step causing her to let out a string of curse words followed by an inadvertent simultaneous hiccup and fart.

"Oh, shit! Déjà vu," Will yowled breathlessly. "This can't be happening again."

The woman heard him, stopped long enough to hurl

the snake at Will. At that moment, the rat seized its opportunity to escape. The snake missed Will but hit a rum bottle on the bar, causing it to crash onto the pool deck. The frightened snake quickly recovered and disappeared into the dark.

Lexie stared transfixed and speechless.

"Now you know what a tropical disturbance is," Will said to Lexie, who had finally recovered and begun laughing so hard she could barely stand. "I bet you can't get entertainment like this is California."

"What a welcome, Dad!" Lexie said when she finally caught her breath. "Did you arrange this entertainment just for me?"

"Nothing's too good for our daughter. Welcome to Sundance," Will said and hugged Lexie again.

Leva ran up and told Betsy, "May I be excused for a few minutes so I can go next door and try to repair the damage? Would you mind if I invited them to dinner?"

"Do whatever you have to do," Betsy said. "Invite Miss Cora and her houseboy as well."

It took half an hour of persuasive pleading and convincing for Leva and Cora to settle Peter and Miriam down, but then they and their staff joined the Sundance celebration.

"I bet you could convince a vegan Rasta to eat pork chops," Will whispered to Leva.

As expected, there was plenty of food to feed the numerous guests. Will and Betsy enjoyed introducing Lexie to their Jamaican friends. Mikey Mo was soon in championship form, taking his jamming rhythmic DJ. patter to new levels. E.J. too was in his best Elvis form. Together the staff and Mikey Mo sang a touching reggae rendition of Carole King's massive hit song *You've Got A Friend*, in Will and Betsy's honor as Mikey Mo played Big Mountain's version on his sound system. Peter and

Miriam knew the words, so they joined in. Betsy had to wipe away a tear as Will gave her a hug. Betsy secretly recorded their performance with her cell phone, so she could share it with their friends back in the Keys. With the assistance of the houseboy from next door, Kingtoo made sure there was no shortage of liquid libations. Both bartenders managed to consume their share of rum while serving the other guests. The party ran into the late hours and was declared a complete success, a perfect send-off to America. Even Miriam agreed the affair was better than the costume party they would have gone to at the all-inclusive resort in St. Lucia.

EPILOGUE

"May I offer you a rum?' Colonel Ferron Winter said.

"Thanks, that sounds refreshing," Mikey Mo said.

"Did the Blacks catch their flight for America without incident?" the Colonel asked.

"No problem, but we had a bit of a situation at their farewell party," Mikey Mo said and explained the evening's events at Sundance.

"For a moment I thought you were going to say you had some rude uninvited guests," The Colonel said and laughed. "Kingtoo is definitely one of a kind. You're fortunate to have him as your friend."

"It certainly facilitated my unquestioned acceptance at Sundance and made it much easier for me to monitor Betsy Black and RBC's involvement with Highway 2000. That made my decision making at critical junctures more informed," Mikey Mo said.

"I hate to think of the consequences of some of the situations Mrs. Black was thrown into," he continued. "If we had not been in a position to intervene, she would probably be dead now. You showed insight when you realized how badly she needed our protection and put her under surveillance. And to think she never suspected that good old Chicken was anything more than the house Rasta jester and DJ. I'm also glad we had other qualified people for the task since she would have recognized me at some point. I never could have maintained my cover if I had been forced to intercede that day she and Mr. Davis had the ill-advised confrontation with John David Grey's road construction crew or that fateful day they cornered Grey at Dornock River Head," Mikey Mo continued.

He laughed nervously.

"Mrs. Black was definitely out of her element in more ways than one in dealing with the likes of Dudus Coke and Neville Hamilton," agreed The Colonel as he took a sip of rum. "I suspected that the first time I met her, and she showed me the carved skull with a bullet in the brain which had been planted in her briefcase after the Martha Brae assassination. Jerry Smith had to be eliminated since he was about to go public and expose Coke and Hamilton's highway program scam. Because of Letha Wardlow, Coke knew that Mrs. Black was in contact with Smith. He did not know what Smith had told or not told Mrs. Black, so he felt compelled to send a message to her as well. The Shower Posse has often used this symbol to intimidate and terrify its foes. When the glass skull appeared on her wall, I knew I had been correct, and I should definitely intervene if she had hopes to survive."

"How did Hamilton get her briefcase to plant the skull carving in?" Mikey Mo asked.

"Once again, Letha Wardlow," said The Colonel. "He had Letha steal it so he could examine the contents to see if the reason her predecessor had been displaced was because the bank was becoming suspicious. Originally, he merely wanted to see what was in it and planned to return it after a short time. He hoped she would think it was merely misplaced, but then he panicked over Smith affair. This was a convenient way to put the fear of God into her."

"But why would he send any message?" Mikey Mo asked. "Betsy was new at that point and had done him no damage. She probably didn't even know who he was yet."

"Another miscalculation on Dudus's part. He was paranoid when the bank suddenly dismissed Mrs. Black's predecessor, and then Letha's comments to Hamilton led Dudus to believe Betsy had learned more from Smith than she had. Dudus is sadistic and likes to get inside people's heads immediately, and he's good at it," The

Colonel said. "He rules equally through both intimidation and violence. Dudus was also sending a subtle symbolic message to any locals who might be tempted to either interfere or cooperate with her to distance themselves from both her and her mission."

"A message so subtle only you and Merle Dunster understood it," Mikey Mo said.

"Oh, I'm sure we weren't the only ones. I understand Warren Smith was rattled as well. Now, am I to assume no one followed the Blacks to the airport?" Colonel Winter continued.

Mikey Mo shook his head and said, "I assigned a man to trail behind Mr. Davis' van just in case. He reported no unwanted company. I think Don Coke has given up this war as a lost cause and moved on to new challenges."

"Mr. Davis was my secondary responsibility," Colonel Winter said. "I have owed him a debt of gratitude since we were children."

"Do you think Mr. Davis suspected that the man driving the Chaser had been sent by you?" Mikey Mo asked.

"Not at first," The Colonel replied. "He may have towards the end."

"Well, if he did," Mikey Mo said, "he certainly kept it close to the vest."

"Yes, he would. Mr. Davis is not always as open as he seems. He is not only my lifelong friend but a very intelligent person as well. Just as Mr. Davis is a lifelong ally, I am now honored to have the Blacks as allies as well, which is why I made a commitment to them - a commitment we Maroons will honor going forward. We will certainly need strong honest allies in the future. I am glad we were able to help her. Helping her accomplish her goals aided us in accomplishing our ends as well. I still fret somewhat about the Don. He is a wily and vindictive man who does not take defeat lightly. You would be wise to never forget that. He also has a long memory and vast resources at his disposal, but fortunately for us, he should be preoccupied for the foreseeable future with thinking of ways to maximize the profit opportunities available to him with the Jamaica Labour Party now being back in power," The Colonel said.

"I guess the game doesn't change, only the players and referees," said Mikey Mo.

"Unfortunately your observation is very accurate. You have done a great service for me and your people. As your chief, I commend you for everything you have done, Buried Blade, and I wish to thank you ahead of time for the good you will do for the Maroon nation in the future."

"Thank you. Your approval means more to me than I know how to express. We both know that's why we Maroons have survived for many centuries," Mikey Mo said. "We were and continue to be dedicated guerrilla war experts of unparalleled guile and ability. Our enemies make a mistake when they underestimate us, but I also had a personal incentive to get retribution after the police shamed me and beat me up for no other reason than being a Maroon."

"Yes, that incident was a clear and unforgivable violation of the Blood Treaty," said The Colonel, "but I know there was more to the affair than just the random beating of a helpless Maroon. It was a head-game. My agents in his organization tell me Hamilton Sr. gave the order to send dirty police who were on the Don's payroll to put you in your place. Hamilton Sr. had heard rumors you were being groomed for more important responsibilities in our community, and he wanted to intimidate you. He and his people must to be taught that this was mistake in judgment. I will revisit that point momentarily."

Mikey Mo sipped his rum and waited for The Colonel to continue. He knew from experience not to rush the old man.

"Your recent actions have avenged violations of the Blood Treaty in more ways than one. Now we must send a message to Coke through Hamilton that Maroons will not tolerate being publicly beaten and humiliated. This message will be the closing chapter in our successful campaign to remove Prime Minister Pettis and his unscrupulous lieutenants from power. I may not have been able to stop the Highway 2000 project from passing through and corrupting Maroon lands, but at least I was able neutralize Pettis' efforts to assimilate our people into the mainstream of Jamaican society by using Operation Pride to build in the cockpit country subsidized housing for non-Maroons. Hamilton and Coke encouraged this invasion of our nation solely so they could make millions as a major contractor to the projects, but they were not content to merely plant a virus in our nation. They were also so greedy they were willing to corrupt the entire Jamaican government in their quests for windfall profits. This is unforgivable. Our ancestors won our independence in 1739. Many died in this effort. We have successfully maintained that independence to this day. We will not lose it now by being soft or shortsighted. Our traditions are proud. We have an obligation to our children and our grand children."

"I agree with all my heart," Mikey Mo replied.

"I am an old man. I know I will not live forever. I also know times are changing, and that it will become increasingly difficult to insulate our people from the inevitable lures and lies from the outside world. We can no longer be complete isolationists who can bury our heads in the sand thinking the modern world will go away. Our young people will be especially vulnerable and susceptible. That is why I have permitted our people to have cell phones, computers, and Internet access, and also why I have permitted tourists to visit Accompong. The new super-highway is going to make us even more accessible to the world and will present new and even larger challenges for your generation than the ones my generation has had to face. I believe you are the man who can lead us into the future."

The Colonels paused again, his eyes boring into Mikey Mo's.

"I have one more duty for you as Buried Blade. I want you to make Neville Hamilton Sr. pay the ultimate sacrifice for his transgressions against you and the Maroon people. This will accomplish two things. It will also send a strong message to the Shower Posse that we are as fierce as our ancestors were. It will also prevent you from having to deal with Hamilton again in the future. He is an unprincipled man who will at some point try to test us and corrupt future initiatives in Jamaica. I guess you can't right all the wrongs of the world, and I guess in this imperfect world partial victories are all we are entitled to. I am glad Cudjoe is out of politics, but I regret he is being rewarded with the cushy job of program director at Swingles. But that is a battle for another day. When your assignment is successfully completed I will have the confidence to retire and anoint you, Buried Blade, as my successor as Colonel. I will then feel I can entrust you with the reins to lead our people into a proud future."

Mikey Mo nodded in agreement and said, "I will never make you regret your support."

"One last matter of business – put out the word that Letha Wardlow can safely come out of hiding. I know she is an easily manipulated woman who was merely a pawn in a game she does not understand. I have begun to circulate the word to let bygones be bygones."

The men shook hands, and Mikey Mo departed to fulfill his mission.

~ ~ ~

Will was drinking a cup of coffee and eating a piece of toast for breakfast as he looked out over their canal on Little Torch Key.

"This sure ain't one of Leva Carter's scrumptious breakfasts," he said.

"And I'm not Aunt Jemima or Leva Carter," Betsy said. "If you want a big, fattening breakfast go to the Cracked Egg or the Big Pine Restaurant."

"Yessum, I sho' will, Miss Betsy. Don't hit me wif' dat iron skillet again, Massa ma'am. I'm glad to be home again in some ways," Will smiled and said, "but lordy, I sho does miss Sundance."

"And Henry and Rose and Leva and Kingtoo and Mikey Mo," Betsy said, "I even kind of miss blowhard Bob Bogle Blackmon and devious Letha Wardlow. I think Henry and Rose may come to visit us later this year."

"Well, if you want to return to Jamaica, Warren Smith's job is available," Will said.

"Yes, it is," Betsy replied.

Will opened his computer and Googled *The Gleaner*.

"I can't get out of the habit of looking on line at *The Gleaner* every day," Will commented.

Moments later he exclaimed, "Betsy, you're not going to believe this. Today's *Gleaner* says both Neville Hamilton Sr. and Jr. have been found dead. It was an execution style killing. The Constabulary is saying they have no clues as to who the killer or killers might be."

"My guess it is probably some kind of fight between rival Jamaican posses. Yu lie wit dawg, yu rise wit fleas. I wonder if the Shower Posse was involved?" Betsy said. "Most likely bad guys killing badder guys."

"That brings to mind another of Henry's sayings,"

Will said. "Show me yu friends, I see who yu are."

"Another of Henry's sayings comes to mind," Betsy said. "Ebry day debble help teef; wan dyah Gad wi 'elp watchman."

"Meaning?"

"Every day the devil helps the thief; one day God will help the watchman," replied Betsy.

"Jamaicans sure have a way of hitting the nail right on the head," Will said. "I'm sure going to miss Henry's platitudes."

"So will I," Betsy said.

"I wonder if the constabulary will ever find the Hamiltons' killer?" Will said.

"Probably not," Betsy replied. "Jamaica is a mysterious and remote country that hides secrets well."

"Very well put, my dear," Will said. "We did learn a lot about people in Jamaica, didn't we."

"Yes, a hell of a lot, my dear. One hell of a lot."

"Would you do it all over again?"

"In a minute. Or should I make that a second."

❉ ❉ ❉

Thank you for reading. Please review this book. Reviews help others find Absolutely Amazing eBooks and inspire us to keep providing these marvelous tales. If you would like to be put on our email list to receive updates on new releases, contests, and promotions, please go to AbsolutelyAmazingEbooks.com and sign up.

About the Authors

David Beckwith is a three-generation native of Greenville, Mississippi, with a BBA and an MBA from Ole Miss. His parents owned an independent cash commodity trading firm which also cleared securities trades through Goodbody & Co. David spent 40 years in the securities business, the first half of his career with Bache & Co. and its successors, the second half with Morgan Stanley. He retired as a Senior Vice President with approximately $500 million in responsibilities. For 25 years he has served as an adjunct professor at five different universities.

His first book was a narrative nonfiction work published by the University of Alabama Press in 2009 entitled *A New Day In The Delta*. The Mississippi Institute of Arts and Letters chose it as the runner-up for nonfiction book of the year. The book is often compared to Pat Conroy's *The Water Is Wide*.

David's wife Nancy earned a doctorate in finance and was the largest commercial lender and underwriter for Florida National Bank/1st Union/Wachovia, a member of their President's Club, and a board member. Also she served as the provost of the Brookley Campus for the University of South Alabama.

David and Nancy started writing the Will and Betsy Black Adventure Series in 2010. The protagonists of this series are a married couple somewhat reminiscent of Nick and Nora Charles of *The Thin Man* Series or Jonathan and Jennifer Hart of *Hart To Hart*. Their unique hook was that like the books' protagonists the authors were also a happily married couple.

Moving to Key West, the Beckwiths were tapped to write a book review column for the Key West *Citizen*, which David continues to produce on a weekly basis.

ABSOLUTELY AMAZING eBOOKS

AbsolutelyAmazingEbooks.com
or AA-eBooks.com

Made in the USA
Lexington, KY
10 October 2017